NIM

NIMROD RISING

Steven Griffiths

Futura

A Futura Book

First published in Great Britain in 1989 by
Futura Publications, a Division of
Macdonald & Co (Publishers) Ltd
London & Sydney

ISBN 0 7088 4294 1

Typeset by Selectmove Limited
Reproduced, printed and bound in Great Britain by
BPCC Hazell Books Ltd
Member of BPCC Ltd
Aylesbury, Bucks, England

A Division of
Macdonald & Co (Publishers) Ltd
66–73 Shoe Lane
London EC4P 4AB
A member of Maxwell Pergamon Publishing Corporation plc

To Susan
for all your love and support

ONE

THE MAN WITH emerald green eyes stood aloof from the shoppers swarming in the maelstrom of Oxford Circus. Zippering his parka to the chin against the bitter winter wind, he squinted in the half-gloom over the madding sea of heads towards the distant Christmas lights of Selfridges, and decided this was close enough.

Bloody close. Maybe too close.

He waited near the edge of the pavement, his nerves raw and the bile rising in his throat. The nod came right on time, warning him. It meant the big saloon was gunned and waiting on Regent Street, ready to scream away northward. Slowly his blunt, sweating fingers closed around the object buried deep in his pocket. Silicon and printed circuits – it was slim and black, with touch-membrane keys, and to the casual eye it might have been a video controller.

Once more the green eyes scanned the length of London's busiest street. Like an artist he was awed by the size of his canvas. It was the last Saturday before Christmas, and the crowds of people formed a buzzing, pulsating, multiplying organism. It must be

7

the busiest day of the year. Holy Mother, it would be his masterpiece.

HOLY MARY, MOTHER OF GOD,
PRAY FOR US SINNERS,
NOW, AND AT THE HOUR OF OUR DEATH
AMEN.

It was set to be a cold Christmas, with iron-grey cloud and not a sign of snow. Outside Selfridges a Highland piper in full tartan was competing with a one-armed busker carving out tortured carols from a polished trumpet. An occasional jingle of coins and a 'God bless you', but both men were largely ignored.

Across the street unlicensed street vendors shouted their wares. 'Fiver yer perfumes – any one. Look 'ere, Yves St Laurent.' The pavement was glutted as knots of curious punters surrounded the piles of boxes and listened to offers of cheap scent in expensive packaging.

'All Left Bank stuff, my friends. Straight up, no rubbish.' Micky Dillon was well into his pantomime. 'Look, she'll have one – thank you, darlin'. Who's next?'

Crushing deadlock of the Christmas rush. Salaries paid early into bank accounts in time for the holiday. On that day it seemed the entire population of Greater London had converged on the West End in a desperate search for presents. Madness. Progress was painfully slow along the surrounding pavement, and pedestrians began to spill onto the road to battle against the blaring horns of red London buses and black cabs.

Constable Collins was out on foot patrol with Woman Constable Petry when he observed the obstruction and immediately he knew it was dangerous. Micky Dillon doing brisk trade – and the pavement blocked. It was only a matter of time before someone fell or was pushed in front of a vehicle. They would have to get chummy and his perfumes shifted quickly.

Micky Dillon was harvesting a crop of five-pound notes when the whistle came. The lookout was a young black kid who had been standing on a litter bin, shelling roast chestnuts. The kid whistled again and signalled two police officers approaching from the direction of Marble Arch. Micky cursed under his breath and began stashing his gear back into a cabin trunk, grabbing vainly at a sea of silly money.

'Hey, wait a minute! Where's mine?' came the jostling protests.

'That's all, folks. Closing down.'

But escape was impossible. Already they were bearing down on him, and by the time he had closed up the trunk and turned to heft it onto a makeshift trolley, Constable Collins had him by the collar.

'And a Merry Christmas to you,' muttered the policeman, not without humour.

'Do me a favour, plod. This is straight gear. Simple supply and demand.'

'Save it, Micky. Hawking without a licence and causing an obstruction. I'll throw in breach of the peace if you don't come quietly.'

'Leave it out, Mr Collins. Look, have a free sample for the wife, compliments of the management. You too, love.' Petry just grinned at the man's cheek.

'Your mistake was not legging it straight away, Micky,' said Collins.

'What and leave this lot?' He indicated the cabin trunk. 'Do you know how much this stuff is worth?'

'Yes. That's why I wouldn't dream of giving such muck to the wife. Now come on, let's go.'

WPC Petry was already talking into the microphone of her beat radio, requesting a transit van to take away the seized goods.

Micky Dillon felt pretty sick. To be nicked on a day when the punters were literally throwing their money at him was a crying shame. Diabolical luck, he told himself.

But he was wrong.

Micky Dillon's luck was better than he knew. So, too, was that of the punters who had hurried off in all the commotion in the mistaken belief that they, too, would be arrested. In that moment all their lives were saved.

In less then two minutes a third policeman, PC Shepherd, arrived on the scene.. He took Micky by the arm and escorted him off in the direction of a police transit parked round the corner in Lumley Street, leaving Collins and Petry to secure and hump the seized goods. Hands on hips, Collins glumly surveyed the pile of cardboard boxes, the battered cabin trunk, and the discarded packing material dumped in the shop doorway behind Dillon's pitch. Playing dustman was one side of the job he hated. With equal distaste the woman officer stepped forward to inspect the debris. Stooping to pull clear a wad of shredded packing, she noticed something hidden there – something quite incongruous. It was a Scots-plaid sports holdall with a heavy brass zipper.

'John,' she whispered, staring at it unblinkingly. 'I think we've got an s.o. here.'

Collins took one look at the bag and knew she was right.

'Don't use your radio. Just get everyone clear,' said the girl, reacting professionally in spite of her fear. 'Do it now!'

Collins turned quickly in an attempt to warn the passers-by above the clamour of the street. But he was dead before he could open his mouth.

When it came, the blast seemed to rip the very air apart. The shock-wave shattered every plateglass window within screaming distance, sending murderous shards in all directions. Silhouetted by an incandescent sheet of yellow flame, people fell to the ground while glass fragments rained down on their heads. Already the discarded boxes were on fire – and so were crumpled bodies nearby, soaked in burning perfume. The tortured screams of the wounded floated skyward with the rising pall of smoke. The bodies of the two police officers had been hurled like dolls into the road, forcing a black cab to swerve across the street and collide broadside against a doubledecker bus. The cabby now lay across the bonnet of his cab, his cap under the bus's front wheel.

The screams of those merely in shock added to the rising level of panic – a surging crowd unsure which way to run. Some were already retching at the sight of all the blood. A traffic warden had removed his overcoat, determined to render help but dazedly wondering which of the bodies to cover first – his white face damp with tears of frustration. Unnoticed in the confusion, two young men reached through the shattered glass of a fashion shop and helped themselves to leather jackets and blue jeans.

Inside the transit van PC Shepherd heard the report and felt its sides shake. In disbelief he leapt out onto the road, losing his helmet in his headlong dash back to the disaster area. Dear God in heaven! His sergeant hardly recognised the strangled voice on the radio. Nothing in Shepherd's training had prepared him for this.

A fleet of wailing ambulances was now approaching painfully slowly. What they found was chaos and utter carnage. A press of onlookers was jockeying for sight of the bloodbath, and only by mounting the pavement could the ambulances negotiate the jam of backed-up traffic stuck behind the mangled bus and the taxi. In the gathering darkness blue beacons flashed, ghoulishly animating the faces of the dead, and lending an extra madness to the writhing of the wounded.

Ashen-faced ambulancemen fought their way through, the glass on the pavement crunching under their feet. As one reached the epicentre of the blast he was appalled by the open-mouthed inertia of the ablebodied people looking on – unable or just unwilling to help. Then he noticed a fair-haired man, stripped down to an olive-green T-shirt, who was applying a makeshift dressing to a young girl whose arm had been severed at the elbow. With one hand he gripped

11

her upper arm tightly to close off the brachial artery, whilst with the other hand and his teeth he desperately tried to tie off a bloody piece of cloth at the site of the spurting wound. This man clearly knew the dangers; he knew how quickly blood loss and shock could kill the injured, and that infection from soiled dressings was the least of their problems. The ambulanceman thanked God that someone had the presence of mind to act in time. This was good, basic, efficient casualty medicine: seal off the pipes and keep the poor sods breathing.

Looking around as he quickly went to work in checking blackened bodies for any glimmer of life, the ambulanceman saw other evidence of the man's handiwork. He had used a leather belt and strips torn from his own outer shirt to lash plastic bags over a sucking chest wound and pinion the casualty's arm over his stoved-in chest, thereby saving the victim from drowning in the frothy blood he was coughing. He had clearly treated others too: some of the unconscious were lying face-down with heads tilted into the recovery position, to prevent fluid seepage from blocking their air passages. They at least had now some chance of survival.

'That's all right, mate,' said the senior ambulanceman arriving with trauma pads and heavy-duty sterile dressings, as his men followed up with stretchers. 'You've done your bit, thanks. We'll take it from here.'

The man in the T-shirt spoke rapidly, as if his mind was on auto-pilot: 'The two in the gutter are dead. No throat pulse at all. We need IVs and plasma – fast. Tell your men to watch out for glass and nail fragments. There may also be booby traps, so don't touch any wires you see.

'Jesus Christ. Look after this little one – she's hurt bad. Lost a couple of units. Shallow breathing, weak pulse. Unconscious but still hanging in, poor kid.'

As the ambulanceman took over control of the brachial pressure point, the man in the T-shirt gently stroked the girl's cheek, feeling for a break beneath the swelling.

'It's OK, I've got her.' Numb with shock the uniforms took over, and a slow wail of fire-engine sirens accompanied their work. Fortunately the injured would not bleed as quickly in the cold weather, but many were still under threat of death through shock and exposure.

'Are you a doctor, sir?' The voice belonged to a police sergeant. 'The medics say you've saved some lives here.'

The man in the T-shirt was crouching by a blackened and twisted litter-bin. He gazed intently at the scorch marks on the shop-fronts and at the charred remains of the burned-out cardboard boxes. It was cold now and he shivered.

'Sir, for the record, are you a doctor?'

'No, I'm not a medic,' the man murmured at last and massaged the back of his neck. 'Just seen a lot of this stuff before, that's all.' He forced a reassuring grin. 'Sergeant, do you think they could spare one of those blankets. I'm freezing my nuts off.'

'I'll see what I can do. Bet you could do with a drop of brandy, too. I'll check if they've got a St Bernard in the wagon.' The young officer turned to walk away.

From out of the freezing darkness came the paddle of helicopter rotors accompanied by the blinking red and green spots of navigation lights. The police observers looked down upon an army of black-coated officers that were cordoning the area. Neither had seen anything like it before.

They saw the scene of desolation, of twisted bundles under grey blankets and the black oily puddles. There were large milling crowds at either end of Oxford Street, which had been closed off between Marble Arch and Regent Street with orange luminous tape and metal stanchions. Outside broadcast units could be seen taking equipment from huge trucks parked at the bottom of Baker Street.

For the onlookers the sight of gay Christmas lighting on the streets merely underlined the tragedy of the event: the eerie desolation of a deserted Oxford Street just before rush hour, and the innocent lives that were scattered on the concrete.

After two hours Chief Inspector Kramer, the senior uniformed officer at the scene, ran over his notes knowing there would be brass hats all over him in the morning if he had forgotten anything. In the Met you only screw up once.

The emergency medical teams had been deployed and the dead and injured had now been ferried away. Cordons were positioned, traffic cleared (some by tow trucks) and order restored. Forensics, EOD and Anti-Terrorist Branch had all been notified, and the District Commander briefed by phone. The immediate response had been handled by Tactical Support Group in their roving transits. The command post was a burger-bar from which Kramer coordinated media briefings. The press wanted every last detail – but what they wanted most were two things: the perpetrator of the outrage and the name of the man in the olive green T-shirt.

Kramer made no comment in response to the first question, despite what he thought privately. When he made enquiries on the second question, he was told that no one had bothered to ask. The man was fair, about five-eleven, tanned and fit-looking, with no distinguishing marks. He had simply disappeared into the crowd, leaving behind the borrowed blanket. One minute standing there with a plastic cup of brandy – the next minute gone.

The sergeant had been the last to speak to him.

'Sorry about the little girl. I take it she wasn't yours.'

'No. Not mine.' A heavy sigh.

'They say one minute she was doing fine; next minute she just went. Bloody shame.'

After that the man said nothing. Just melted away.

14

The man's disappearance was bad news. His evidence could be important for the inquest and for the criminal investigation that would inevitably follow. Chief Inspector Kramer felt a slow-burning mix of rage and despair rise within him. Was it just the evidence he wanted? Or something else? It was difficult to tell, as he relived the horrors he had witnessed. The deaths of two of his own officers. Two kids planning their wedding in the spring. Two lives wasted for a headline. Dear God, let someone pay for that!

Pay for all of it.

TWO

THE PAYMENT HAD begun with a 'Red Jacket', and it fell to Halliday to see the debt paid in full.

Sitting at his desk on the fifth floor of Century House, the gleaming glass-tower headquarters of the Secret Intelligence Service, he could remember it clearly. It had been early January, just after the holidays: the first day of snow that winter.

'I'd like you to handle this one, Peter,' the Deputy Director-General had said at the conclusion of morning prayers when the other senior officers had dawdled from the room and the two of them were alone.

Sir Alistair was not quite himself on that day, distant and brooding throughout the meeting. Not until later did Halliday realise how the older man had lain in ambush for him. For that's what it was: an ambush. 'I feel the matter merits our most special attention; *your* most special attention,' he had said without looking up from his notes. The folder slid across the polished surface of the table and came to rest just inches from Halliday's curious fingers.

16

A Red Jacket – Director-General's special enquiry.

Halliday had picked it up with equal measures of trepidation and excitement, sensing the political advantage it represented to a man like himself: one poised on the brink of directorship. He glanced at the title sheet already knowing what he would see.

'The Oxford Street bomb.' He raised his eyebrows in that urbane manner for which he was already well known. 'Something of a hot potato, I understand.'

'Quite. Stick your head out the window and you can hear it from here: gnashing teeth at the Cabinet Office and Fleet Street baying for blood. PM's furious with the Special Branch goon squad.'

'And you expect me to take it?'

Sir Alistair had expected a touch of reticence. That was good, a man too eager to stick his neck out would have ulterior motives, but Halliday was exercising a healthy degree of caution.

'Don't worry, Peter, there's no question of any pressure from Whitehall. We're not the ones on trial, the Defence of the Realm is still the responsibility of MI5, and they're the buggers who'll carry the can for the Oxford Street mess.' Sir Alistair put down his fountain-pen and fished in his jacket pocket for a crumpled white handkerchief which he used to dab the ink from the side of his index finger. The ink he used was green, as was the privilege of Directors-General of MI6. 'This is my investigation. No outsiders. You'll answer directly to me.'

'If that's what you wish, sir, then I'll do my best.' Nice touch of modesty from Halliday.

'It is – and you'd better.' There was a trace of a scowl as his wiry eyebrows knitted together aggressively. 'Bloody thing's been twice round Whitehall before landing at the Foreign Office. I'm not altogether happy we should be handling it, but there we are. Somebody has to clean up after Five.' Sir Alistair

17

was enjoying his current stint in the DG's chair while the old man convalesced after a major bowel resection. And he never missed a chance to rubbish the sister service.

'You'll keep the team small, pull young Stephenson in – he's a good man – and indoctrinate nobody without my express permission. Is that clear?'

It was. Perfectly.

That was back in January, Halliday reflected at his desk, staring out at bare branches against a white sky over the murky Thames. Nearly a month after the incident; Christmas and New Year already celebrated and forgotten. He had received the file then with decidedly mixed feelings. What had changed in the interim?

This was now mid-February and the Red Jacket that had come to him almost empty, and had occupied the majority of his working days since then, was now over four inches deep, with three hundred enclosures. But he was no happier about his custody of the file. How could he be? Reading the new enclosures as they trickled in, day after day – the frustration had infected him more than anyone. In quiet moments, long after the tumult had died away, he was struck by the obscenity of the act. Death by remote control. From the pages of the folder their names appealed to him for justice like Scrooge's Christmas ghosts, and in some strange way he felt himself the caretaker of their memory. For him, the dead would not rest easily while their killers still walked the streets.

Now had come the subtle change of attitude. The meetings with Sir Alistair – back in his own office after the return to duty of the Director-General – were becoming more frequent, more certain of their ultimate, inescapable course of action. Halliday now realised what Sir Alistair had intended all along, right from the morning he first slid that folder across the table.

18

Perhaps it would have been wisest for him to push the folder right back across the same table. Too late now. With each new meeting, he had to watch himself.

'What does C make of it all?' Halliday had asked, that very morning, giving the Director-General his traditional designation and expecting the reassurance of the master's blessing. Sir Alistair had gone very quiet at first.

'Sir Alistair, C *is* aware of the findings of my report?'

'He is not.' Stated simply, as headmaster to pupil. 'Nor shall he be. I told you right from the off that this was my enquiry and was restricted.'

'But I thought the Director-General, after all . . .'

'I'm afraid the DG is not one who is prepared to stand up and be counted. He is not one of us.'

'Us?' Halliday did his utmost not to appear impertinent. 'And who are *we* . . . sir?

'The Old School. Cold Warriors. Ways and Means Act, and all that. The man doesn't belong amongst us. Twenty-two years at the Ministry of Defence – good God, the man's never run an agent in his life. We both know the Cabinet Office insinuated him into that chair so that he could tattle back to Whitehall.' It was an open secret around SIS headquarters that Sir Alistair's accession to the chair, on the death of the previous DG, had been blocked at the last moment by the Cabinet Secretary. It was the Cabinet Secretary's job to chair the Joint Intelligence Committee and to appoint the chief of each intelligence service. Though the exact reasons remained shrouded in secrecy, Sir Alistair knew he would never be numbered amongst the immortals whose portraits gazed down from the walls of C's office. Understandably, perhaps, Sir Alistair now harboured a bitter resentment against the virtual invalid who had deprived him of the ultimate accolade.

There was a part of Halliday which sensed the danger that attended their conspiracy, and urged him to steer clear before his own career was dragged into the abyss. But there were the ghosts, too, to be considered, and a powerful sense of outrage behind his relentless investigation – one of blind justice crying out for action.

Now was the time for that action.

Dispassionately he regarded the Red Jacket on the desk before him. He opened the file and re-read the damning evidence once more.

There had been an indecency about the speed of the initial investigation and its conclusions, but when the Prime Minister wants answers, everyone moves fast. That goes without saying.

The whole circus had been drawn in: Police Bomb Disposal Unit assisted by specially attached Ammunition Technical Officers drawn from the army's Explosive Ordnance Disposal (EOD) units. They had moved in at first light with an impressive array of equipment designed to isolate and identify fragments of the bomb. Fortunately someone had covered the scene with plastic sheets so that the overnight winds and rain had not obliterated vital evidence. The blinking and beeping hand-held detectors played their part, but in the end it came down to the human touch: brushes and tweezers and numbered plastic packets, and the infinite patience of professionals. When all the many fragments of metal, canvas, leather, glass and unidentified charcoal had been collected from the scene, the jigsaw puzzle was taken away to the Police Forensic Laboratories in Chepstow where the bomb was to be rebuilt. There was a quite understandable delay in completing the job, due to the fact that many of the pieces had to be surgically removed from the bodies of the victims – the living and the dead.

Over two thousand individual fragments were catalogued, including the heavy-duty brass zipper from the Scotch-plaid hold-all which had held the device. Harmless enough in the normal course of events, that zipper had penetrated the spleen of a 34-year-old mother of three who had subsequently bled to death. Each twisted piece of metal or fragment of glass told its own grisly story: one of cowardly and senseless murder.

The report which eventually landed on the Prime Minister's desk put the bomb at about twelve pounds of fragmentation materials packed around an explosive charge of just sixteen ounces of commercial dynamite. There was an extra degree of cold-bloodedness in the way the nails and ball-bearings had been packed on one side of the charge only, so as to achieve a concentrated arc of destruction shooting away from the shop doorway and into the crowd of shoppers. A full report of casualties and statements from surviving witnesses was included, but their evidence added nothing to that of the forensic investigators – apart from chilling first-hand accounts of the experience. No one had seen anything suspicious or anyone actually placing the hold-all in the shop doorway. That was hardly surprising really; it was the holiday rush and everyone had been too busy. No one was expecting to be blown to pieces for Christmas.

Two days later, when the Metropolitan Police Commissioner presented the findings of his investigations to a specially convened briefing in the Cabinet Office in Whitehall, he had no hard evidence of who the bombers were or why they had acted. That wasn't good enough, the Prime Minister let him know – not when the whole country was screaming for answers and Fleet Street editorials were telling them the culprit was so bloody obvious.

Only Halliday's department had remained deliberately noncommittal, and for very good reasons. The agent they had been running inside the General Staff of the Provos had actually supplied details in advance of the planned outrage. Not exact details, but

21

close enough. Sir Alistair's decision then had been to protect the identity of his agent by sitting on the information, reasoning that the planned telephone warning would give police time to clear the area. In the event no warning was given. Those involved in the suppression of this information then closed ranks, hoping to God that 'Lochinvar' would prove to be worth the sacrifice.

On the third day after the explosion, and with Christmas Eve only days away, the incident took on an extra dimension. Within the the space of an hour, two separate claims of responsibility were logged. The first came from a man with an Irish accent who telephoned Moss Side Police Station in Manchester; after giving the correct recognition code, he claimed a victory for the Provisional IRA.

That seemed to be it: what the Security Service was waiting for.

But then came the second telephone call, one which flashed through Whitehall like wildfire. It was received by the International Affairs Editor of the *Economist*. According to this claim, a blow had been struck against 'military, economic and cultural imperialism' by a group calling itself 'Al Sharif'.

It was that which split the case wide open – and Special Branch liaison had been forced to call in the spooks.

Halliday studied the file with care. With the same care an expert uses to assemble a bomb, knowing that one slip might mean his own demise.

He heaved a long sigh, terminated with a public schoolboy's curse. Maybe he had been too many years in Her Majesty's armed forces, and later the Intelligence Service; now he felt his country had finally bled him dry. As group head in charge of Middle East theatre he was constantly on call, answerable at a moment's notice to the DDG, who was in turn frequently turned out in the middle of the night to answer questions at the Foreign Office. If he had had any real sense he would have followed his two brothers into merchant banking, and been worth a fortune by now.

Bollocks!

He knew that the Red Jacket had come to him for a reason: not because he was the one man at Century House who had all the pieces of the Middle East puzzle, but because he was reliable, the DDG's man, and allegiance mattered more than anything in their line of business.

He flicked through the folios to remind himself of the events which had led up to this latest outrage. The bulky file was jammed with copies of documents supplied by his contacts within friendly agencies, the network of Western Intelligence: CIA, FBI, RCMP, ASIO. Here and there were the distinctive over-sized transcripts of diplomatic cipher traffic accompanied by the crest of GCHQ in Cheltenham. As in all such investigations the file represented hundreds of hours of painstaking effort. But what it really represented was a mandate to act. His bomb was assembled.

A knock on his door.

'Yes.'

The door opened and a thin man entered, carrying a blank cover which contained a secret loose-minute folder. Within the building such folders, their contents temporarily extracted from the main file, were always carried around with titles and serial numbers covered; no one was to know who was working on what, unless it directly concerned them.

'Six minutes late, Stephenson.'

The other man winced in a well-practised manner which gratified Halliday. Just one of the few advantages in having such a passive animal working as one's section head was being able to vent one's anger upon him.

Stephenson checked his watch, knowing he was early.

'Sorry, I thought you said . . .'

23

'Never mind that now. Let's have it.'

Stephenson placed the loose-minute folder, an extract from the Red Jacket, into the extended hand of his boss. He was keenly aware of the shortness of Halliday's fuse these past weeks, but was still as yet unaware of the true reason for it.

'The evidence, Stephenson?'

It was to be yet another review.

'The connection is quite clear,' explained Stephenson, while Halliday read the results of their newest and most promising line of enquiry. 'The trail leads back to the Colonel.'

' "Quite clear" you say.'

'Yes, sir. Via the customary conduits and middle-men.'

Halliday decided to play devil's advocate for a while.

'If I were to tell you this all looks far too circumstantial, how would you handle that criticism?' Even Stephenson knew that this question was one Halliday was already anticipating from the DDG. 'Take it a stage at a time, walk me through to the conclusions.'

'OK. Leaving aside the negotiations with the Sanussis for the moment. Bomb goes off in London. Immediate speculation in the newspapers that the IRA are at it again. No particular reason for that, but it's the obvious conclusion to jump to. Then this chap at the *Economist* get's the phone call. There's a copy of his statement in the file – I think it's folio six. Anyway, he says the voice was that of a young, well-educated Arab or Middle-Eastern male; says the English was very good but the throaty intonation on some of the words was a giveaway. One of the boys at "Five" – Arabic speaker – sussed this Al Sharif. It means "The Sword".'

'Yes, I know that. That's why they made me Head of Middle East Group.'

'Well, then they knew that Arab terrorists were probably involved and they copied it to us. The day you minuted the file to me I smelled a rat. Like I told you at the time, it was a fingerprint, an intellectual fingerprint.' Stephenson was uneasy about having his thoughts dissected thus, but he was ex-military and allowed rank any favour.

'Tell me again. What was this fingerprint?'

'The wording of the telephone call to the *Economist* included the phrase "military, economic and cultural imperialism". That set me searching. I had a vague recollection.'

'And?'

'It turned out to be a direct quote from a speech we had on file. It's one of the Nasserist slogans from the fifties, but the speech was one broadcast by Radio Tripoli. That's when I began to suspect Qadaffi's people were involved.'

'Don't you think we're overestimating Libya's importance in international terrorism. Everyone knows the Syrians are the most pernicious of the Arab states currently funding terror campaigns. I don't want this turning into a scapegoat exercise.'

'I agree, sir. Absolutely. But the evidence is unequivocal. If you'll allow me. . . . You see, even the name of the group is a fingerprint. We've never heard of this lot before. Nothing on file in Central Registry. In the end I did a wild-card scan on the database and the computer came up with an interesting entry: "*Al Sharif al Islam* – The Sword of Islam. Codename for Libyan nuclear weapons programme". If this was a commercial fraud, I would say the name was a holding company set up as a front to confound detection.'

'You mean a generic, like *Islamic Jihad* is in Lebanon,' said Halliday noncommittally.

'That's right, only this one is probably a front for Libyan Intelligence.'

'So what we have is the IRA and the Libyans squabbling over a bombing.'

'I don't think so.'

'Well, what do you think?'

'Personally the Libyan angle is more credible, especially now the Sanussis are here in London looking for Foreign Office support in their bid to get back into Tripoli. Qadaffi could just be warning us off from supporting his enemies.'

Halliday had been wary of indoctrinating Stephenson into the details of the negotiation underway at the Foreign Office, but he had needed a man on the ground, one to chase around those damn awful cous-cous kitchens where the Sanussi's supporters held their meetings.

'I have it on the best authority from Five that Azziz's mongrels can't work on British soil,' Halliday interrupted. 'Whilst normally I take anything they say with a huge pinch of salt, on this occasion I think they're probably right. Since we cleared out that bloody Libyan People's Bureau they don't have a base from which to operate. The few agents that remain are known to us, and we get photographs every time one of them so much as takes a leak. Are you suggesting there's some Libyan cell which has eluded the police and MI5?'

Stephenson allowed himself a brief smirk of triumph.

'No, nothing of the kind. I think it's more likely that the Provos were commissioned by Azziz to hit Oxford Street. Payment to be in weapons, training or arms. It's been some time since that boat-load of rifles and missile-launchers was picked up off the Irish coast, but the links between Tripoli and the "boyos" are still there.'

'I assume by that stupid grin on your face you have something to back this up.'

'Of course, sir. If you check folio fifteen in the file, you'll see a source report from one of our men in Turin. There's a photograph attached, too. Our man followed known Provisional arms dealers to a flat in the suburbs and, with the help of the Italian liaison, set up an observation post in the building opposite.

'When was this?'

'About the middle of November. They photographed everyone going in or out of the flat, and then one day – bingo!'

Halliday was looking at the photograph now. A good-looking Arab in his early forties, with hair cut short and brushed back and a strong jet-black moustache. The man had been caught leaving the flat, striding towards a gold-coloured Mercedes sports, and the angle confirmed that the photograph had indeed been taken from an overlooking building.

'Colonel Azziz,' breathed Halliday in grudging admiration. 'Well, well. And still dressing like some poor-man's Omar Sharif. Nice suit – wonder what Qadaffi's paying him?'

'Quite,' said Stephenson. 'So I ask myself why is Azziz meeting personally with top-level Provos, and I say to myself: I reckon he's calling in a favour or two. Lo and behold, barely a month later and there's blood all over the pavements.'

'So why the double claim, eh, George? If it was a commission, or a favour for the Libyans, why did they take the credit themselves?'

Stephenson shrugged his shoulders, unconcerned.

'Haven't the foggiest, sir. My theory just takes the known facts and applies the line of best fit to them. Unfortunately some facts lie outside the regression line. I've analysed the intercepted signals to Libyan People's Bureaux in Europe, and there has been an increase in traffic but no specific reference to acts of terrorism on British soil. They appear to have played this one very close to their chests; probably handled by Azziz's private office. What was in all the traffic was a renewed call to root out and liquidate dissidents abroad.'

'An obvious reference to our little talks.'

'I believe so. I also believe that from this point on the visitors are in danger of being washed out.

Even the Americans say that they're the most credible opposition to Qadaffi's regime there's ever been. The dissidents over here are saying that this time the Colonel is running scared.'

'Oh really, and what do you say?'

'I say that if Britain wants the option of access to Libyan oil and a measure of peace in the Middle East, then supporting a Sanussi takeover is the best way to achieve those goals. But I have my doubts as to whether anything can topple Qadaffi; he's too well entrenched. His control of the army makes his position unassailable. The Sanussis could die of old age waiting for Qadaffi to step down or die himself.'

Halliday closed the loose-minute folder and tossed it onto the desk beside the secret file. For a while he leaned upon his elbows, steepling his fingers in ruminative fashion.

'What do you make of this nuclear programme business?'

Stephenson shook his head gravely.

'I honestly don't know. The very mention of it gives me the willies. Could be psychological warfare; could just be coincidence, though I rather doubt it. Maybe he's decided to go for the big one. He's never disguised his ultimate aim of Israeli annihilation.'

'What do you see as our options, then?'

'That's a two-fold question is it not? As to the nuclear threat, that's the Sword of Damocles hanging over all our heads; but then the same threat has been with us these past forty years. The terrorist bombings and the Irish: that's different. That has more of a moral dimension. How far are we prepared to go to protect ourselves? We may know who the bombers are, where they live and how they did it. But what if nothing can be proved. How do we proceed when justice fails us?'

A strange stillness was in the room, as if all clocks had stopped whilst the fate of man was decided. Halliday felt a chill touch him, and he shivered.

'You saw the TV pictures? The utter carnage?'

'Yes. And I read the accounts of lives cut short. The *Sunday Times*'s Insight team, etcetera. All good people – innocent people.'

'The DDG saw those pictures, too. He likes Rugby metaphors; he said they'd scored a spectacular try. He says it's now our kick-off.' Halliday's eyes narrowed and he steeled himself. 'What do you think he meant by that?'

In a chilling flash Stephenson saw where the conversation was leading; where it had been leading from the moment he had walked through the door. Slowly, carefully, and under Halliday's guidance.

'I really couldn't say, sir. Do you have any orders or directives to issue?' Stephenson knew full well that Halliday was about to ask him to do something that could not be recorded on paper – one of those small matters that no one would care to take the credit for if it became public knowledge.

Across the desk, Halliday's eyes were fixed on the thin yellow pencil he had slipped into a bronze paperweight that also held a sharpener. The paperweight was cast in the shape of an antelope, and bore the inscription: *'With much appreciation and high regard. Natal Headquarters.'* Halliday twirled the pencil and as usual was reminded of his nine-month attachment to BOSS, the South African Bureau of State Security. He spoke without raising his eyes.

'I was wondering, have you seen your man recently?'

Stephenson watched the pencil turn, and the wooden skin curling out from the blade of the sharpener.

'Which man is that?' he answered, deliberately obtuse.

'Your legionnaire. What's his name?'

'Tyler.'

'That's the man. Is he still available?'

'That depends.'

Halliday glanced reproachfully at his section head. He was tiring of the feigned ignorance of his purpose.

'Depends on what?'

'The mission and the money. And whether he's in the mood. He's not exactly my legionnaire – or anybody else's for that matter.'

'I'm sure he wouldn't wish to lose our goodwill; you must remind him we could make his trips to the Continent quite difficult. Surely he knows holding a forged passport is a serious offence.'

'He doesn't rattle . . . sir.'

'Nevertheless, I think you should contact him with a view to doing business.'

'Business, what kind of business?'

'A little lesson for the Provo General Staff. *Pour encourager les autres,* as the Frogs say. Bold Lochinvar is come out of the west once more with good information.'

'With respect, sir, that's not our area.'

'It is if I say so, and I do. The enquiry has a wide brief and I shall interpret it as I deem fit. Is that clear?'

'Yes, sir.' What else could he say. There was no way he was going to offer his bloody resignation over it.

'Good. Tell me, is Tyler still running errands for the dagos?'

'Yes. For the Spanish and for the Dutch sometimes. He says both pay better than we do.'

Halliday ignored the jibe.

'Good. Yes, that will muddy the water a bit. We don't want him linked too easily with this department. Yes, I really think we should be doing a spot of business.'

Halliday withdrew the pencil and blew away a stray shaving. Holding it up to the light he admired the fineness of the point. Stephenson waited, but no further qualification came.

'Will that be all, sir?'

'For the moment. We'll speak further when I've confirmed a few matters with the DDG.'

The door closed and Halliday was left alone with the withered bloom of his own conscience.

THREE

THE MAN IN suite 806 had signed the register using the name Peter John Sinclair. He had added EXTRUDED PLASTICS LTD for good measure and LIVERPOOL in the home address section. He even carried a black attaché case – which anyone who gave him a second glance would assume contained nothing more sinister than sales reports.

There was also nothing particularly noteworthy in his dress or demeanour. A quite forgettable character, he blended smoothly with the other upper-strata professionals thronging the lobby of the Savoy, one of London's most prestigious and historic hotels. Indeed, he looked the type of businessman who would prize its unique opera and art-deco atmosphere over the hi-tech, modern alternatives provided by other London hostelries – Pavarotti in preference to Dire Straits. His hair was cut close, and slicked back with gell so that it glistened at the temples. The colour might have been black or brown – with gell it was difficult to tell. His charcoal-grey suit was double-breasted, and sober enough to emphasise the scarlet silk Gucci tie knotted tightly at his throat in a small Windsor. Across his left shoulder he carried a Burberry's raincoat, slung carelessly in the manner that Americans often affect; the familiar orange-plaid lining turned outward.

He was the kind of gentleman Mr Gomez preferred to deal with personally.

Mr Gomez, a senior concierge, beaming and resplendent in immaculate green and gold livery, had been in London hotels for twenty-eight years – since the day he first left Barcelona. But twenty-eight years of upper-class and Americanised English had not taught him much about the mysteries of British regional accents. Even if it had, it would have been highly unlikely he would have detected the slight hint of a soft County Kerry brogue behind the guest's businesslike requests. And what he could not detect then, he could not recall later; or report.

One pair of eyes saw all this, and missed nothing. A pair of fathomless, black eyes that served a soldier's brain.

From the soft velvet sofa that faced the mahogany-panelled desk Tyler had watched the man check in. Then, with a casual air, he had approached the desk and dawdled over the brochure advertising winter-weekend mini-breaks. He had stood not three feet from his target, separated from him only by the porky New York Jewish widow protesting loudly about the peeping-tom window-cleaners outside her room. 'Goddammit! I want those SOBs canned,' she had screamed. In all the commotion and the arm-waving that ensued as Gomez politely reassured the distraught woman, Tyler quickly noted the room number allocated on the registration card.

He could have got that number at any time, but Tyler had other reasons for being there in the lobby as the man checked in. More than just a simple ID, he needed to get a feel for the quality of the opposition before . . . before he made up his mind. He wanted to visualise the way it would go. To put flesh upon the bones of the photograph. To visualise his own success. If he could not see that far, then he would call it off. Stephenson could then keep his money – less operational expenses. He knew that Stephenson could use one of the South London operators instead, and had done often enough in the past; but he did not choose to this time. They were tearaways at heart, none too clever, break-a-leg-for-a-monkey gangsters whose screw-ups would be delivered in embarrassing pink folders to Century House to be written off. And Scotland Yard never missed a chance to slap their fingers. No, the department had wanted Tyler for the job, as always, because the department hated to be embarrassed. Tyler was the professional. He laid his own ground rules and they took care of the corpses. He had never missed, and success was the best form of advertising. That's why he was here watching the dark good-looker from EXTRUDED PLASTICS follow a fawning porter through the lobby towards the main lift.

The porter carried the man's folding luggage: the expensive kind of suit-holder that packs everything for a business trip. But the guest insisted on carrying the black Samsonite attaché case himself. The black eyes registered that, too.

Tyler consulted the coloured five-by-three which was Sellotaped inside his copy of *Time*, and checked again the face of the guest standing calmly before the lift doors in the elegant surroundings of the Savoy's famous lobby. Tyler paused a moment to enjoy the irony of it. For the photograph showed a young man in military greens crouched in the yellow dust between two grinning Arabs who cradled Kalashnikov rifles in their laps. They were flanked by a battered military truck from which dark-haired youths wearing green bandanas were cheering and making V-signs. Bright sunlight, which made the men squint, and the distinctive red and black checkered *Keffiyahs* at their throats, meant the photo was taken somewhere in the Middle-East – perhaps at one of the training camps in the Bekaa Valley.

Of course, the man looked different out of fatigues; and watching him smile at a pretty French girl as he entered the lift, you would never have connected him with the trained terrorist in that incongruous graduation picture; or link him to the Manchester airport bombing that took the legs off a British Airways stewardess.

Tyler had memorised the face well. In the picture the hair was longer, the jowls covered with a heavy stubble, but one learned to see through the changeable aspects of the target's appearance. Facial hair and colouring were the most obvious forms of disguise, and tints were readily available in any branch of Boots the chemist. No, it was the shape of the jaw and the small hawklike nose which confirmed the identification. Bodyweight was lower in the picture, and that figured: food in those camps was known to be rat-shit; the instructors trained them to live on anything they could get their hands on whilst holed up in enemy territory. Starving the poor bastards encouraged them to scavenge for themselves. Still there was no denying the broad back and tapered waist of a mesomorph beneath that sober grey suit. And the eyes still shone with the same dangerous fire Tyler had noted in the small dossier photo.

It was Terence Lynch, all right. And Tyler's gut was telling him this was a dangerous bastard.

At the eighth floor the lift whispered to a halt and Peter Sinclair, the businessman, was ushered along a plushly carpeted corridor to his suite. The art-deco-furnished sitting-room faced south across the floodlit Adelphi Gardens and over the river Thames towards the National Film Theatre with its flashing neon pylon standing bright against the ferocity of the winter wind scudding across the darkened surface of the river. Wearily he tipped the porter, extracting a note from an expensive calfskin wallet. Finally alone, he paused a moment to draw back further the heavy velvet curtain and peer into the crouching darkness. A sudden shiver ran through him as his thoughts came crowding in – as if the dark night held some half-remembered childish nightmare. He released the curtain and turned from the window.

It was a first-class room. Lynch knew this particular suite was often reserved by wealthy guests who enjoyed the view it afforded. That small fact was the whole reason for his being there – and the reason why his palms crawled with sweat now. The principal target, Doctor Ibrahim, had specifically requested it.

He locked the door. He was tired. What he really needed was a scalding hot shower to ease the nagging ache in his shoulders. He slipped on the safety chain and kicked off his shoes. Liverpool to London in three and a half hours was not bad going. Wisely, he had resisted the temptation to gun the Saab Turbo to the speeds he really enjoyed. Motorway patrols would remember a flash bastard pulled for 'doing a ton'; and no way could the car have stood up to a decent search. In short, such insanity would have compromised the operation. He was too seasoned for that. Brady would have half killed him.

That thought made him smile.

There was a film of sweat on his back brought on by a series of small anxieties along the journey. He could not help that. Brady's handiwork over Christmas had brought Special Branch out in force and he knew he was carrying enough in that case to put him away for life. Liverpool was crawling with 'filth' and, worse, there was an air of resentment within the Irish community. People there, as in the rest of the country, had been shocked by the bloody television pictures served up with their evening meals. Mouths, even Catholic mouths, would be flapping. Anyone with the slightest Provo connection would be under surveillance. Downing Street would have leaned heavily on the media, reflected Lynch, hoping for the ones with weak stomachs to turn 'supergrass'. That is why he had

had to lie low. That is why it had needed orders from the very top to get him out on this little shout. Anyone else he would have told to shove it. But you could not argue with the General Staff.

He stepped eagerly into the hot jet that issued from the elephant-head spigot and worked the perfumed shower gel into a thick lather. It smelled pleasantly of musk. In his mind he ran through his cover. It would not stand up to a thorough check, but it was good enough to get him away and clear in the morning. Single-night stopover, then on to Gatwick for the 9.50 Sabena flight to Brussels. That would get him clear of the Savoy by 07.00 without any raised eyebrows.

There was no way he could have refused the job. He knew that for sure. Still, as he reached for the shampoo he was wondering what Brady would have done in his place.

Tyler had returned to the velvet sofa. Sitting patiently, hawk-like, his fingers played absently with the nap on the arm-rest as he read his magazine. He watched the porter return to the front desk. A few moments of nonchalant eavesdropping, with his gaze fixed to the magazine's coverage of the Oxford Street bomb, were enough to tell him that suite 806 had no further requirements and did not wish to be disturbed. He listened with mild interest as the porter commented on the sloppiness of the floor waiter: the courtesy basket of fruit and Swiss chocolates normally left in a guest's room had been forgotten.

Tyler checked his watch. It was almost 8.35. It was time to go to work. Careful to remove the photograph, he folded the magazine into a waste-basket and descended the steps into the main body of the hotel.

As he walked he could feel every nerve ending in his body coming alive. His brain was now locked into its deadly routine; examining all the angles and percentages. He reasoned that Lynch would probably not move at all that evening. Safer to stay put, to order up room service and watch TV. Information said he was working alone on this so there would not be any visitors – unless his sexual appetites led him to call in a further service. That could be awkward. He would leave the clearing up to George if it came to that; George was good at explaining things to Scotland Yard. The chances were that Lynch would not move a muscle – not if he was the disciplined operator they assumed. A good operator would not take such chances. Tyler's brief said this character had to be bright-eyed and bushy-tailed in the morning for a flight to Valencia and a meet with some big noise in the Basque organisation, ETA. Arms negotiation, they said.

'Not this time, mate.'

At that time anyone in the hotel both civilised and conscious was sitting down to dinner. The back staircase would be deserted. Tyler strolled nonchalantly past the harp stand where the girl played nightly for blue-rinsed matrons with heavy jewellery and too much make-up. At the River Room he made a left turn and headed for the back corridor that led to the banqueting room; each was named after some character from Gilbert and Sullivan. Midway along the corridor was the rear staircase from which he could reach the upper floors undetected by the desk staff. They would be watching for suspicious characters: the cockier room burglars dressed like Raffles, or the expensive 'Toms' who accepted all major credit cards in return for sex. It was not worth going for the front stairs. Not with Gomez squatting out front, the lord of all he surveyed. Gomez would already have him tagged as an outsider.

Tyler had done his homework. He knew the location of each staircase, corridor and lift; and where each of them led to. Furthermore, he knew the security officer took his dinner between eight and nine; he was a creature of habit – retired RAF.

There was no one on the backstairs. Tyler made the eight floors easily, aware of the battle-twitch that was surging through his muscles. A few seconds to slow his thudding pulse, and he slipped out from the landing onto the corridor. He moved to the first corner to orientate himself against the floor plans he had studied; the Savoy was a maze of passages in which new staff could easily lose themselves. The guest floors consisted of four corridors set in a quadrangle, with a deep well in the centre that began at the fourth floor. Each floor had a room waiter's station, and on the eighth it was at the south-west corner. Tyler made straight for it. Inside, a slim young man in a waiter's DJ was poring over a magazine called *Bound to Serve*. His long white fingers traced the words in the letters column, totally engrossed. An expertly-aimed blow to the base of the skull from the heel of Tyler's left palm put the waiter out of the game.

Shift-change was midnight. There were no other staff on that floor. Tyler had a free hand.

Slowly, respectfully, he drew the pistol from his belt and screwed home the silencer. The gun was his own, a Beretta .22, the assassin's choice for concealability and accuracy, not the crap the department pressed upon him. All anyone would hear would be a stifled cough – if that.

Tyler peeled off his overcoat and scarf and adjusted the bow-tie at his throat. The tuxedo was rented, and a little tight across the chest, but otherwise a good fit. It took barely a moment to discover the cupboard where the floor waiter hid his loot. Tyler pulled out a small basket that appeared to be the kind the porter had mentioned. He would deliver it, personally.

Still no one on the floor. Tyler rapped softly on 806.

Lynch started suddenly. He was standing in the bedroom swathed in a thick white terry bathrobe, towelling dry his wet hair. Unsure, he stopped and listened. Instinctively his eyes strove to find his weapon; the colt automatic lay on the padded chair by the window hidden beneath his trousers. It was a big-calibre weapon, the .45 auto, a man-stopper; if it did not kill the man outright, it would sure as hell knock him down. Most fire-fights are over so quickly that a grounded man is as good as dead.

A second knock. A muffled voice.

'Hospitality pack, sir.'

Lynch's fingers closed around the heavy colt and he moved towards the door. The Samsonite attaché case lay open upon the bed. He cursed himself.

'That's OK. I already have one, thanks.'

Bastard, thought Tyler; he wasn't going to buy it! Now he could feel his insides turn over. Think quick or you've blown it.

'Very good, sir. Will there be anything else? Perhaps sir would like some company. There's a very discreet service I could arrange.'

'Just a minute,' the voice inside the room cut in. A pause, followed by the rattle and scrape of the safety chain. Tyler could feel the sting of his own sweat, and the second or so it took to open the door was stretched to an agonising eternity. Go now? Not yet – no not yet. A crack appeared and slowly widened. Four, five, six inches the door opened. Tantalising. Lynch was good, he knew that, but how bloodly good? Where was he standing now inside that dimly lit room? Should he break left or right? Then slowly a hand snaked around the door offering a pair of rain-spattered shoes.

'Have these cleaned and back by five in the morning.'

The shoes were in the left hand. Lynch directly behind the door. Tyler could guess what was clutched in the right hand, but Lynch had made a bad mistake. It would be his last. A sudden green light flashed on in Tyler's brain. He drove a piercing kick against the reinforced centre panel of the door, driving forward with all his weight. The side panels

40

would have shattered under such a blow but the centre panel was sturdy and swung inwards, in spite of Lynch's bodyweight, slamming the Irishman into an ornate table. Tyler came through the door like an express train, zeroing in on the flailing body of the target, who was winded and trapped in the wreckage of the table. Lynch was groping madly for the colt, mouthing obscenities, his index finger now bleeding and broken by the trigger-guard as the gun was smashed from his hand. With a curse on his lips he caught up the gun and turned to his unknown assailant.

But Tyler was already crouched, aimed and sighted. Lynch had barely time to register the features of his killer before he found himself staring into the hell of the Beretta's silenced muzzle. Two rapid shots punched into Lynch's forehead and right eye and he died. Instinctively Tyler dived through the second door, rolled and came up aiming, but the sitting-room was empty. He rushed out past the body and checked the bathroom and bedroom, peripheral vision straining for signs of movement. Also empty. He was taking no chances; he had been trained never to assume anything. Lynch could have had an accomplice waiting on the stairs as he checked in. Unlikely, but still possible.

He kicked the main door shut. The hinges, now loosened, gave a soft groan. Cautiously he approached the body and checked for a throat pulse. Blood was streaming down the face and out of the hole in the back of Lynch's head. It was seeping quietly into the expensive carpet. The bathrobe was red around the collar, too. He was dead, all right. Tyler's fingers trembled on the man's skin. Adrenalin.

After he had searched the body he searched the bedroom. What he found there made him swallow hard and forget about Lynch.

Stephenson had told him not to touch anything in the room; to leave all that to the technical people. That meant he must have known about, or at least expected, what Tyler found in the already opened Samsonite attaché case.

Set into the wall of the case was approximately sixteen pounds of Semtex plastic explosive. Sixteen pounds, Jesus Christ! Tyler knew that a single eight-ounce stick of the stuff detonated in a room that size would blow all the walls down. What did Lynch want with sixteen pounds? Built into a small recess was a radio detonator as back-up to the integrated-circuit-driven timing device. There were also anti-tampering measures: mercury tilt-switches and a light-sensitive cell that would tell the bomb that someone was trying to dismantle it. Tyler heaved a sigh of relief as he noted that the arming switch was not set.

It was the mother of all bombs.

FOUR

THE RAIN WAS still pissing down at two in the morning when Tyler finally got through being debriefed on the hit – if that is what you could call it. Tyler had other words for it: he felt they had been blowing smoke up his arse all along, and he did not like it one little bit. What kind of mug did they take him for anyway? The secrecy he did not mind; that was understandable, just part and parcel of what he called simply 'the job'. But if his neck was on the line he had a bloody right to know exactly what was going down.

One thing he was sure of: Stephenson had lied. Though at first the spook denied everything.

Stephenson's car was parked outside the Italian restaurant in Southampton Street, facing into the Strand and within sight of the hotel. When Tyler climbed inside he could smell the usual Old Spice, and he could see just how pleased with himself the man was. There was murder on Tyler's face, and the spook attempted a disarming shrug. But before he could say how really sorry he was about the bomb, a punch shot out of the darkness and crunched into his stomach, collapsing him coughing against the steering-wheel.

'What kind of game are you playing with me, George? One false move and my arse would've been hanging off Waterloo Bridge!'

Stephenson raised his arms in defence but did not fight back. Tyler knew he was not a fighter; he was a bloody desk man who was losing his nerve almost as fast as his hair. When he saw those piano-player's hands go meekly to cover the man's head, Tyler immediately hated himself for lashing out at the pathetic figure.

'Still carrying a sledgehammer in each hand, I see,' Stephenson gasped when he was once again sitting upright and the pain had subsided. 'Do you feel better for that?'

'Not much.'

'Look, if it's any consolation I really am sorry. I can see you're upset, but I swear I knew nothing about that case. I told you just what Halliday told me, that Lynch was about to make a buy in Spain. It was all about a ship-load of arms. This is something different – a bonus.'

'That's bollocks, George. If that's all there was to it, why not simply lift him at the airport – nick him at the immigration desk and away to an interview room? That's usual procedure, isn't it? Why did it have to be a hit, George? Why here? Who were the Provos after blowing up?' He fixed Stephenson with a rigid stare that demanded an answer. 'This was a "Brighton" job, wasn't it?'

Stephenson wet his lips and tried to answer but he had run out of lies and he knew Tyler was just too shrewd to wear any more of it.

'Official Secrets Act, I'm afraid,' he said in the end, dashing behind the only available defence.

'Piss on that!'

Once more Richard Tyler was reminded of his role: a soldier walking the dark shadows of a world without fame or glory. A man working for powerful masters, but a man kept outside the masters' gate. 'Do me a murder,' they might say, 'but ask me no secrets!'

But they knew their business. Tyler was forced to award full marks to his controller for house-keeping. The one saving grace in the screw-up was the way Stephenson had organised the clearing up afterwards. One phone-call from room 806, and Tyler had locked the door and taken the key with him to wait in the Italian restaurant across the Strand. A covert team from Special Branch was down there before he had finished his first cappucino. They sealed off the room, made the device safe and disposed of the body in a very short space of time. Later the body was collected in an ambulance, and the story propagated amongst the hotel staff was that one of the guests had suffered a minor coronary. Even the floor waiter was taken care of. He was summoned for a talk in the general manager's office in the presence of a Special Branch Inspector, and that was that: one week's holiday and instant amnesia.

As a finishing touch Special Services were called in to strip out the stained carpet and remove all forensic evidence of the hit. The night manager that evening barely noticed the pencilled note in his briefing book which stated that room 806 was struck off until further notice, pending redecoration.

'It was a fine, clean hit,' offered Stephenson lamely, knowing full well that the younger man cared little for such praise, but trying his best to salvage the situation. 'We like it when there are no complications. Was he good?'

'Huh?'

'Lynch,' said Stephenson, pursuing it with relish. 'Was he good? Tasty? Did he make you work for it?'

'Christ!' Tyler was feeling sick to his stomach. 'That's a question you don't get to ask. He's dead isn't he? Let's leave it at that.'

'If you like. No matter. Just thought you might want . . .'

45

'George,' said Tyler with measured disgust, 'as a shit you're a collector's item.'

Stephenson's face blanched and his thin fingers drummed the steering-wheel. As they sat in silence, the desk-man felt the dull pain of the punch sitting like lead in his gut. Sometimes, he reflected, it was difficult to know which of them was in control. Damn it! Sometimes, Tyler could be an out-and-out bastard.

Beyond the misted windows the rain puddles glowed with a green and red fairground of traffic-lights and neon signs. Stephenson wiped a glove across the windscreen to clear a patch of the condensation, and he watched the tourists wandering back along the Strand from the theatres to their hotel rooms; occasionally one would stop and forlornly hail a black cab that swished by in the rain without stopping. The night looked every bit as cold and miserable as Stephenson felt.

He re-examined his motives. Of course he had with-held the truth. That was the only way to keep control of his man. He knew, well enough, that a mercenary with the full story is a dangerous animal indeed, possessing the opportunity and the means to discredit an employer if he should burn himself out and decide to buy a comfortable retirement on cheque-book journalism. But he knew Tyler better than that; knew he could rely on the man absolutely. Christ, how many other people could he say that of? Who could he trust any more? Not even his wife. True, that slug in the gut had hurt like hell, but it was nothing compared to the blow his wife had just dealt him. She was coming back into his thoughts more and more, distracting his work, now that he was sure beyond doubt there was someone else. Another man. God, he needed someone to trust. He bit his lower lip. Tyler's last remark had echoed his own low feelings of self-worth.

'This is it, George,' said Tyler breaking through the other man's reverie. 'I've had it up to the ears with you clowns. I try not to mix up my clients and my patriotism, but this country's intelligence service is becoming the worst employer in the business. Hell, I can get better cooperation and working conditions from the Spanish for clearing out Basque terrorist cells. I don't need this.'

'You know I can't bring you all the way in, Tyler. We've been through this before. You're good at what you do, but you're not one of us.'

'That's true enough,' said Tyler reaching for the door handle. 'I still have a backbone, while you lot are just bloody jellyfish – and liars. I'll tell my banker to expect a draft within the week. Been nice knowing you . . .'

Only then did Stephenson break. His hand grabbed the other's shoulder and held him in his seat.

'No, wait. Please . . .' There was a hint of desperation in his voice. Tyler's hand relaxed upon the door lever and he turned back. Stephenson's mind was racing now; embarrassed by his outburst, he was choosing the words he would use. If Tyler quit on them now there would be hell to pay at Century House. But there was far more to it than that, and Stephenson knew he needed even the meagre comfort their strange antagonistic relationship afforded, to temper the isolation he felt among his own working peers.

'It's going to be big,' said Stephenson, his hands grabbing the air in emphasis. 'Probably the biggest job of your life. Worth a lot to a man like you. None of this bloody couriering and consulting – I'm talking about writing a piece of history. Tyler, this thing tonight was just for openers – a warm up after your lay-off. What's to come will astonish you.'

'Keep going,' said Tyler when Stephenson paused to gauge his reaction. 'You've got your audience.'

'There's this important source called Lochinvar who's been feeding through grade-one material

47

from Belfast. It was he who delivered Lynch to us with all the trimmings. ... You remember the Christmas thing? Well, after that, Halliday wanted the Provos to get their fingers burned. They were having it too much their own way, so you were brought in. But now there's a new twist developing.

'As soon as I knew about the bomb I started checking with the Savoy's GM. One of the board of directors is an old friend of our deputy – same lodge or something. He was prevailed upon to assist us in our enquiries, and that's where all your dope came from. I was asking exactly the same question as you: who do they want to assassinate?'

'What did you get?'

'In eight days time the Savoy will entertain a party of eleven senior officials of the National Front for the Salvation of Libya.'

'Come again. Libyans?'

'Just listen a moment. It's the result of multiple mergers between Libya's most powerful political dissidents and the heirs of the deposed Sanussi royal family. It's also the strongest opposition group Qadaffi has ever had to contend with. Reports say he's "concerned".'

Suddenly Tyler's memory made the connections.

'I've got it now. They're the ones who were bombed in Moss Side, Manchester.'

'Correct – and the ones who were fired upon with a machine-gun from the Libyan People's Bureau in St James's Square. That was back when the Libyan opposition spent most of its time squabbling amongst itself; they were divided and riddled with rival factions. Then SIS took a hand in assisting the groups to find common ground. When things started to look good, the NFSL got more particular about who they dealt with, and insisted on speaking to the Foreign Office as a first step towards possible recognition in the event of a successful takeover in

Tripoli. The Foreign Secretary is champing at the bit, but it's still not something his people wish generally known.'

'So who's booked into the Savoy?'

'The self-declared government . in exile. The leaders are currently in Sudan and Iraq, but they'll be arriving early for two days of rallies in Trafalgar Square to consolidate support amongst the expatriate Libyan community.'

'Jesus! It'll be worse than New Year's Eve. The Met are going to love that.'

'That's just too bad. We anticipate Libyan exiles shipping in from all over the EEC – thousands of the buggers. The Police Commissioner's been screaming all the way to the Home Office, but he's been told to back off and ensure the Libyans get their chance to start the new movement rolling.'

'It'll be chaos.'

'FO has been given solemn assurances to the contrary.'

'Ha bloody ha! And why is the Foreign Office so generously hosting the party, may I ask, regardless of the consequences for public order?'

'I'll give you one guess.'

'Because FO would like a good friend in North Africa, and because a good friend is generous with his oil and pays over the odds for high-priced British export goods for the snob value.'

'Not exactly how the FO would put it,' said Stephenson with irony, 'but about right.'

Tyler sat quiet for a while attempting to digest all.

'So Lynch came to London to leave a time-bomb that would decimate the Libyan opposition?' offered Tyler, assessing the full complexity of the situation.

'That's the way it's looking. Now do you see why I didn't want to say too much? I could get thirty years for what I've just told you.'

It was true. Stephenson had gone out on a limb – further than ever before – to satisfy his agent's demands, but he respected Tyler too much to warn him to keep his mouth shut.

'So what's this job you have for me? The one where I write history?

Stephenson knew he had said too much already.

'All I can say is: keep a low profile and disengage from any regular commitments. Perhaps let it be known that you're planning a holiday. Get yourself prepared for the most dangerous thing you'll ever do. Don't get involved in any other contracts – you're on a retainer from SIS as of now.'

'This is all bloody mysterious. What danger?'

'I'll contact you in one week's time, when the wise men have made a decision. I think you'll be pleased at how far we're prepared to go in sweetening the pot for this contract.' The intelligence man checked himself, temporarily embarrassed by the depth of his comprehensive disclosures. He looked sheepish. 'Oh, and if by chance I have a colleague with me when next we meet, for Christ's sake act dumb when I mention the operation. Behave like it's the first time you've heard of it.'

Don't worry, George. I'll spare your blushes.' Tyler was grinning wickedly.

'I mean it. Halliday will have my balls for this if he finds out.'

Tyler could see just how scared Stephenson was. Scared, but obviously very excited. Was this a time for caution, he wondered.

'Give me one reason why I should trust you again,' he said, 'since you've just got through admitting you lied to me.'

Now Stephenson grinned. He grinned because, in spite of the continual fencing and the occasional animosity, he knew his agent. 'No, no. I admitted nothing,' he said lightly. 'As for a reason, that's easy. Some people demand security and certainty in their

50

lives; they depend upon it like a flower needs rain. Fortunately for us, you are not one of them. You're one of life's Great Train Robbers. If you weren't doing these things for us, taking risks, you'd be doing them for yourself. Maybe you'd already be in Wormwood Scrubs doing a stretch. Admit it, Tyler: you get off on this kind of thing.'

A thin smile crossed Tyler's face as he pushed open the door and stepped into the cold and wet of the London night.

'Don't bet on that,' he murmured.

Tyler found his own car, a Mitsubishi jeep, parked off the Covent Garden Piazza, and he drove back to his Islington flat intent upon getting outside a half bottle of Pernod. All the while he was thinking about this mission they were planning to serve up hot. He was primarily wondering how to keep control. It did not do to let them get too comfortable or complacent about his services; and he took most things they told him with a hefty pinch of salt, knowing that desk-men like Stephenson will tell a lie for no good reason other than that they need the practice.

But this was one time he half hoped the man was not lying. For months now Tyler had been out of it, doing consultancy for arms deals behind the scenes in Amsterdam and Lisbon; spending long hours in first-class cabins enroute to Zurich where the contracts were signed in anonymous offices by men shy of publicity.

That had been his life since he had left the Legion: weeks and months of dullness interspersed with quick shots of adrenalin. Aeroplanes and business deals, with the pimp's percentage for a reward. Now and again a job he had been trained for: a burglary, an infiltration, and sometimes a killing. But not like before, when it was noble and he had been proud. Oh no, now the clean lines of war were blurred, and who could tell which cause his bullet ultimately served. Not a day passed that he did not pause at the glass case in his apartment and gaze with affection on the green beret with its bold winged dagger and remember the good times – the hard times. There was nothing easy about that life; it was as brutal as it was glorious. But then he had always known, in his own simple, vaguely masochistic way, that nothing of worth is easily won.

He had been a restless kid, out of place everywhere and believing in nothing until at eighteen he gained a commission into the Royal Marines. The instructors had seen his type a thousand times before and they knew all the tricks. They broke down the sullen, smart-mouthed youth and from the pieces they put together a Marine Commando with a sense of purpose and a pride in the green beret he had won. Even now Tyler thanked them for that, for it was then that he discovered the meaning of the soldier's life and decided he wanted no other. Back then they were all still young enough to believe in causes worth dying for. Not any more.

Through Arctic Warfare training in Norway and then on the streets of Belfast he learned to trust few but the men of his own troop – least of all the politicians who directed their lives, sending them out in bandit country with their hands tied by overbearing rules of engagement. That was not the war they had trained for. As a young lieutenant, Tyler heard the complaints of his men, their frustration at not being allowed to do the job. Month by month he listened like a stranger to the explanations he had to give his men of what it was all about, protecting civil liberties and opening up the no-go areas, and the hollowness of these slogans gradually crept up on him until he was tired of it all. And he grew tired of having to bury the men who learned too slowly.

The crunch came during one morning patrol, when his troop was passing through a Catholic housing estate. As always the women were at their gates in huddles of bare, folded arms, their faces made

52

ugly by the vehemence of their abuse. Children were screaming up and down on bikes, and tossing stones around, making everyone jumpy. Then one of the troop, a kid who was too tightly strung for Belfast, came across an IRA propaganda poster and really flipped. The poster depicted a Royal Marine stamping his boot on the face of a fallen child, and apparently enjoying doing so. It was the kind of low-brow stuff the Provos went in for on the working-class estates, and most of the troop were inured to it. But this young bootneck let it get to him, and he marched up and tore down the poster with a single swipe before anyone could stop him. There was an ear-splitting explosion, and when the smoke and brick dust cleared, his intestines were strung across the road like fairy lights and a cheer went up from the women at their gates.

It had been a small enough bomb by Provo standards, just a few ounces of p.e. initiated by a light-sensitive cell hidden behind the poster, and typical of the clever come-ons which sometimes caught out the inexperienced soldier. But for Tyler the delighted cheer that went up from those women as that kid lay bleeding to death was far more damaging, appalling him more than any outrage he had ever yet witnessed. And it was then that he knew he had no place there anymore.

Not long after that incident his time was up, and he headed south for Paris for three months of restless bar-fly activity in and around the Latin Quarter, where he made friends with anyone who would help him spend his Royal Marines gratuity. By then he knew exactly what he wanted to do.

On a cold March day he took the Metro out to the old fort at Château Vincennes. There was no great hype, just a simple sign on the wall: *'bureau d'Engagement – Légion Etrangère – Ouvert jour et nuit'*. And Tyler walked up the stone steps and into the tiny office that would lead him to another world.

Part of a thirty-man intake, he was inducted in the time-honoured fashion at the Quartier Vienot barracks in Aubagne. From there they were moved to the Quartier Lapassat at Castelnaudary, near Toulouse, and the start of a living nightmare that drove many to desert even before the fifteen-week basic training course was over.

For Richard Tyler it was another leap in the dark. Yet at only twenty-three years old he had already decided that life for him, if it was to be at all worth living, must consist of a series of leaps into the unknown. In the quiet solitude of the cold barracks he had convinced himself of this basic truth – the only way of explaining his willingness to exchange the comfort of the officers mess for the austerity and brutality of this privates' barracks. In basic training he lived close to the edge of loneliness, keeping himself to himself. Fatigue was his constant companion in an endless round of training that was dependably agonising and always the same: range practice, weapon stripping and cleaning, hill marching, close combat, guard duty, endless inspections, sometimes punishments, more marching, more shooting and more punishments.

The sergeants were either French or German and they reserved a special hatred for the few English Legionnaires. There were prescribed punishments set down for breaches of discipline such as poorly-maintained kit, insubordination or drunkenness, but these NCOs had their own methods of dealing with such offences, none of which were to be found in the procedure manuals. That's the way the Legion operated, and if you couldn't take it you had no business being there. A hard, unrelenting life, perhaps, but those who survive the training are reborn. For them the white kepi and the flaming grenade badge are the most sacred of symbols. Tyler was proud to have been one of them. The Legion, like some benevolent parent, watched him grow in response to the hardship, and sent him for parachute training where he won his place in the legendary 2ème Regiment Etrangère de Parachutistes — 2 REP to those who recognised the name. Those who did know the name knew also that, after the disbanding of its sister regiment 1 REP in April 1961, for the attempted putsch against General de Gaulle, 2 REP became the undisputed experts in Special Warfare and Counterinsurgency techniques.

For five years Tyler was trained in 'Special Forces' at their base on the island of Corsica. There were frequent joint exercises with the Americans and the other European special forces, and courses at Fort Bragg in the States, and at Bradbury Lines in Hereford.

For five years they trained and were sent out on covert opérations across the African continent and through the Middle East. In Chad and Zaire they made surgical strikes against rebel guerilla groups at the secret request of the local governments. In Lebanon they were there to extract intelligence agents and other French nationals captured by the warring factions. Some of them died far from home, but for Tyler this was the real life of a soldier — not the frustration of being a walking target for stone-throwing kids on the Falls Road.

When the five years were up, and the sand and smoke were sticking in the back of his throat, he became restless again and cut loose and tried to make it in civvy street, believing it was the next logical step. He planned to work in military exports to the African states, where third-world armies were still in need of weapons and training. Western governments needed to use private intermediaries to hide their political blushes. He had often discussed such schemes with others in their drunken reveries in the bars of Philippeville. But first they would need the capital, and for a group of Legionnaires trained in sabotage and assault tactics, there is one method of obtaining cash which is blindingly obvious. Somehow the French police had discovered the plan, and that is when George

Stephenson had stepped in to save his hide. Good old George, always there with another job too dirty for Her Majesty's Government to do for itself.

Now in the quiet of the Islington apartment Tyler was slumped on his bed, a half tumbler of Pernod within easy reach. The aniseed mixed with ice and water was beginning to deaden his tongue, but it still brought back memories of the blistering hot Corsican hills they had marched through, and the songs they had sung to combat fatigue. They had sung those same stirring songs later in the bars of Philippeville, with the earnest concentration of choirboys, and each swearing to God that Edith Piaf must have been an angel.

All gone now. Voices scattered to the four winds.

He was now ready for another big mission – needed it more than anything. He could feel himself getting softer as he waited for that big something to happen; could feel the thickening roll around his waist and he hated it more than anything. Worst of all he was drunk again.

The antique wall clock was striking three o'clock when he opened the door and went out into the cold night. He paused on the step to tuck a rolled towel inside the collar of his sweatshirt and nodded to the slim, thumb-nail moon overhead. It was still raining and he was tired and ready to sleep, but the fiery blue devil within would not allow that. That same urgent voice that had driven him on through the pain since the days on Dartmoor with the Royals now urged him to go for the burn, to blow away the extra flesh and open up the engine. Dressed in the old blue tracksuit and spurred by the rolling dig of the weighted rucksack, he set off across Highbury Fields at a regular stiff pace. And behind the fierce cry of his fiery blue devil, the marching songs of Legionnaires long dead rang clear and sweet in his head.

FIVE

BRADY RETURNED TO Belfast with blood on his hands. But there was to be no hero's welcome, no laurels for the conqueror – nothing. Just that ominous silence which the operations man learns to make his friend. In Andersontown they met above a betting shop to decide his fate.

Brady had made his way back via France and a direct flight to Eire. Before that he had lain low just outside London for three weeks, until the harbours and airports were quiet and the Special Branch had more or less given up hope of tracing him.

Now the dust would have settled in Oxford Street and the bloodstains would be no more – sluiced away by winter and rain. But no one could deny his victory. No, the sudden queues of school kids at the Catholic Youth Centres, all now clamouring to be gun-men, said everything.

A series of safe-houses had protected and harboured him without question. That was the way it was done: chains of secluded cottages and farmhouses radiating from the outskirts of the English capital like printed circuits, all maintained by IRA sympathisers and the proceeds of IRA extortion. He moved between them frequently, but only in darkness, keeping his head very low in the knowledge that inevitably his name would have come up on the Scotland Yard computer as one of only five men who could have been responsible. A glance at the newspapers was enough to tell him they had pulled out all the stops on this one. The Home Secretary was demanding a Provo's scalp to offer the nation for that Oxford Street bomb. And Brady's would do nicely!

So on New Year's Day, when immigration vigilance at the ports was diminished by staff holidays, he boarded the cross-Channel ferry for Boulogne, using a forged passport. A few days in Paris to take in the sights, then back to Shannon airport via Orly. A change of identity – this time a 46-year-old pig farmer from County Kerry. Wearing the heavy beard he had grown over the Christmas period, and with cheek cavities filled with latex rubber, his face looked as full as that on the passport photograph. He need not have worried: the desk official, looking rather fragile, checked only that the travel document had not expired. He had obviously seen the New Year in with a bang.

Brady passed through the Border control-point in company with a woman he had never seen before. In the back of the battered Ford Anglia, there were two children who sat holding hands the whole journey. He could have risked a night crossing on foot but that was a very risky business. Word was that the SAS were once more pulling Border surveillance with night-scopes, and he judged his chances to be better with the regular squaddies manning the check points in daylight.

Brigade Headquarters had arranged their cover – as a family, name of Slevin, going north to spend the New Year holiday with relatives. During the few words of conversation they mustered on the way, he learned that the woman sitting beside him was a war widow receiving an IRA pension. Her face was hard and her eyes bore the cast of one who has little reason left for smiling. The woman knew better than to ask him any questions.

There were no lights on when he arrived at the farmhouse, and from its shabby silhouette Brady at first assumed the place was derelict. For a moment he wondered if he had taken the wrong road in the dark. No, this was definitely the place, though his feelings about being there were mixed. He had been back in the North for over a whole month now, without a word. The sense of isolation had made him bitter. Now they wanted to see him urgently. Why?

It was a moonless night in South Armagh, and a persistent drizzle had turned the country tracks to quagmire. In the darkness he made out the shapes of two outbuildings: one could be an equipment store, the other looked more like an outside privy. There were flat fields extending for one or two miles on either side, affording little cover to British surveillance teams. It was a good choice for this meeting.

Brady finished his cigarette with a long sigh and flicked it into the mud, satisfied. From his position half a mile along the deserted track, he flashed the car headlights six times, picking out the steady fall of rain and startling a rabbit into the safety of the knee-high grass. A few seconds later his signal was answered. A single light went on in an upstairs room, briefly illuminating the pink curtains, then was switched off again. Brady flashed his lights twice further, and drove up to the five-bar gate in darkness.

A broad figure in an oilskin stepped out from behind the gate-post and approached the driver's door. There was a metallic tap on the window, and Brady wound down the pane, his eyes immediately aware of a short-barrelled machine-pistol. Quickly he flattened both hands against the steering-wheel. The weapon was pointing at his head.

'Out of the car!' In the darkness he could not make out the thick black brows, nor the distinctive balding head which merged with a pair of hulking shoulders. That did not matter: the voice was enough. He recognised the deep growl of MacStifoin, like a rusty saw drawn against old timbers, and he complied immediately. His shoes squelched in the mud – it was treacherous underfoot. Here as everywhere else, he mused darkly, a good reason for him to watch his step. He could smell the man's sweat now. MacStifoin was the bulldog, a man charged with the security of the chiefs; a ruthlessly efficient veteran not given to argument. Brady drew aside his parka, hitched up his sweater and took the .45 automatic from the waistband of his jeans, offering it butt first.

'Clear the fuck'n thing,' hissed MacStifoin, angered by Brady's lax weapon-handling. 'Who do ya tink you are? Jimmy Cagney?'

Cursing under his breath, Brady removed the magazine and cocked back the slide to clear the round in the breach. MacStifoin took the 'proved' weapon and clip, and stuffed them into the chest pocket of his oilskin. In the darkness a powerful hand grabbed Brady's shoulder and turned him around, throwing him against the driver's door.

'Now lets's see them pockets. This had better be all, Brady.'

Brady placed his hands on the car and spread his feet in the mud. One day, he promised himself, he would kill this ageing enforcer, and he would enjoy that very much. MacStifoin patted him down carefully for concealed weapons and microphones, deliberately probing his crotch. Brady felt the cold rain running down his neck and he seethed with rage.

When he was finished, the enforcer grabbed Brady's collar and spoke to the back of his neck.

'Listen, boy,' he croaked thickly, the stink of stale Guinness on his breath, 'don't ever hand me a loaded weapon again. If you do, I'll blow your bleed'n head off wit' it.'

Another time, another place, thought Brady; you'll keep, you fat shit. But, sensibly, all he said was: 'Anything you say' – a beat of the pulse – 'old man.'

MacStifoin was one of the old guard, fiercely loyal to the Chief of Staff and all the old ways. Their day would soon be over, mused Brady. It was time for them to step aside, like it or not. The time was coming for a push from men like himself – men with new ideas; men who still had the stomach for bloody all-out war.

'The door straight ahead,' said MacStifoin with a trace of a gloat. 'They're waiting for you.'

Brady approached the door slowly, with a tight feeling in his chest. MacStifoin watched him enter, and when the door was shut behind him turned to flash a torch signal to each of the observation posts that formed the five-hundred-metre cordon around the farmhouse.

Inside the house the old-fashioned kitchen smelled of warm, damp straw. In the light from the kitchen fireplace Brady saw five steaming overcoats draped over chair backs, drying before a crackling wood fire. Five men sat hunched over the kitchen table, their faces lit by the dance of flames in the grate. Brady guessed the tenant was upstairs with his family, minding his own business.

'Come warm yourself by the fire, Liam,' said Sean Gallagher. Gallagher was a lean six-footer in his mid-fifties with greased-back hair that was badly in need of a cut and eyebrows that grew wildly out past his face, lending the appearance of satanic horns. In spite of this he was the most affable character on the General Staff, and the man responsible for logistics – the Fixer. 'There's a drink for you on the table, man.' He indicated the bottle of Jameson's made golden by the light of the fire.

'Thanks,' Brady answered, heaving off his parka and pouring a stiff measure into a tumbler. He took his drink to the fireplace, pulled aside two chairs and turned to warm the backs of his legs.

Gallagher felt the uneasy silence and quickly poured whisky into the five other glasses.

'We'll all have a drink, will we? A toast, yes a toast.'

All eyes at the table turned to the Chief of Staff, who was sitting quietly at the head, stroking one earlobe. Brady could still not fathom the mood of the man. He was a close bastard, that one – gave nothing away till he was good and ready. The underlying tension climbed another gear.

'All right, it's a toast, then,' said the Chief of Staff raising his glass. 'To a free, united and socialist Ireland!'

The toast was echoed immediately, and the glasses drained and slammed back on the table. Brady did likewise, gaining courage from the burn of the whisky as it struck his stomach.

'Come sit with us, Liam. There's a lot to talk about.'

He obeyed the Chief's summons, knowing it was now time to reckon the accounts. Carefully he studied the heavy lids and piercing eyes, trying to gauge the extent of the man's displeasure. The wide, brutal jut of the jaw, the fleshy lips almost covered by a drooping moustache flecked with grey – this was not a man to take lightly. This was a man with a keen, military brain and an instinctive understanding of the utility of violence.

'I trust you had a safe trip back?'

'Safe enough,' said Brady.

'Good. Thing's have been a bit quiet since you returned. Not been home, have ya?'

'Not once. You ought to know that; you put me on ice – or was it protective isolation?'

For a moment the Chief said nothing. A stout log which had burned well, and was now glowing red, collapsed and tumbled forward in the grate, breaking the silence.

'You caused quite a stir in the newspapers, Liam. I was about to ask did you see the pictures, but, then, you were there. You had a ringside seat so you saw it all: the arms and the legs; the bits of punter all over the place. Not a pretty sight. And then – against orders – you called the police and told them it was us.'

'Why shouldn't we take the credit? What's the point otherwise? I only did my job.' Brady managed to keep his voice even, taking another pull on his drink and draining the glass.

'No, you did not!' The Chief's voice rose only slightly, but in one who did not need to shout the effect was just as dramatic. 'Once again, Brady, you did what *you* thought the job required. That's not good for discipline, is it?'

'My brief was to cause maximum damage; to take out the British Airways shop. I wiped it off the street-map – what more do you want?'

Brady walked over to the table and reached for the bottle, deliberately avoiding the man's glare of outrage, but the broad hand of the Chief grabbed the bottle first and held it firm.

'What *I* want is for you to follow orders, boy. Understand? And that means without question, or any personal interpretation. Shall we have to teach you obedience now, Liam?' There was a deadly pause as the Chief scowled at his man with silent venom. Someone cleared his throat nervously, but nobody spoke. Nobody ever spoke before the Chief was finished – and by God he had not finished with this renegade yet.

Brady swallowed in spite of himself, trying not to let the older man sense the fear that was pulling at his chest. This was his way, thought Brady: the Old Man liked to play with his victims before chopping them. The Chief's eyelids closed and reopened in a languid yet subtly menacing gaze that rooted Brady to the floor. This was it: the question he knew must come.

'And who told you to detonate the bomb without a warning?'

Brady's brain groped for a smart answer; then for any answer.

'It's a war, for Christ's sake!' he burst out in a tone that was both defiant and imploring. 'London's a war-zone; everybody knows that! You have to do more than destroy a few bricks and sticks to influence those bastards in Whitehall, or you're wasting your time. The lads on the street are hungry for a victory, something they can be proud of, instead of just sitting on their arses and playing Chinese Whispers.'

Brady was now on the attack – the only way he knew to defend himself. In his gut he knew that tongues had been wagging. His own supporters in Newry and Portadown were being watched, checked out; he knew that for sure. There had been talk of him forming a splinter-group, and whilst that would be nothing new, this time it was just bullshit. No, Brady had loftier ambitions. He wanted nothing less than the whole bloody show; and when that day came they'd see rivers of blood on the British mainland. Too bloody right they would.

'Who told you to detonate the bomb without a warning?' The question came a second time; the unrepentant child offered a second chance to seek clemency. It was all part of the humiliation the Chief had planned for him. Brady had to be broken to be of any use to the Movement. He was just too unpredictable; and, worse still, he was hungry.

Five pairs of eyes were fixed on Brady. He looked around at each man in turn, finding no support there. Eamon Lynch, the propaganda co-ordinator, gave him a sour look. Lynch was a thick-set blond-haired man in his forties with a handsome, ruddy complexion and a tracery of red capillaries on the end of his nose; for years he had run two underground newspapers, and he claimed to be in touch with grass-roots opinion. The look on his face showed his poor opinion of the carnage wrought on Oxford Street.

A sudden noise behind him caught Brady unawares and without thinking he reached for his waistband, where his sweating palm closed upon the ghost of his beloved automatic. It was a telling reaction. Over his shoulder he saw MacStifoin step into the kitchen and close the door, a bulky mass under the dripping oilskin. But he did not move into the circle of light from the fire, but stood with his back against the door, blocking the only exit. The three fingers that remained of his right hand – after his careless handling of a detonator some six years previous – were folded like raw sausages around the pistol grip of a weapon. The weapon hung down by his right hip, the barrel tip-tapping against the door jamb.

From the corner of his eye – he refused to turn around fully – Brady thought he recognised the jutting menace of a silenced Ingram model 10 SMG, but, unarmed and helpless as he was, it really did not matter what it was. He was dead meat.

This time it was sweat and not rain that moistened Brady's neck, trickling down his back. This was beginning to look like a court-martial. Behind the pounding in his head arose the bleak mental picture of a sack dumped in some Godforsaken ditch, its neck bound with rope. Suddenly instinct took over: self-preservation. Brady was a bare-fisted killer but even he stood no chance here, like this! He could take one, maybe two of them, break a neck, grab the bottle off the table, blind an eye or go for the jugular. But he knew that to have any chance at all he must take out MacStifoin, and turn the machine-gun on them. He estimated six paces to the door. His fingers trembled: six paces and certain copper-jacketed death: MacStifoin could empty the whole fucking clip into him before he got halfway.

So he used his head instead.

65

'All right! All right!' He raised his hands like a prisoner. 'Time out here. So maybe I was wrong. Jesus Christ, can't a soldier use his initiative. You can't fault the motive, any of you! I was using a soldier's initiative. In the words of that chink general, Sun Tzu – what's he say? "Kill one to terrorise ten thousand". Well, the Brits are scared now, all right! There has to be some blood for all that!'

Desperately he fought to rein back the hysteria that was mingled into his words. Keep cool, boy.

'True,' said Eamon Lynch gazing absently at his fingernails, 'but within reason.'

'And then only when sanctioned by the Council,' interrupted the Chief. 'We set ourselves limited, achievable goals. Indiscriminate slaughter is not the business of this Council.'

'There is the US dimension to consider,' added Eddie Kelly. 'We've noticed a definite drop in donations to Noraid from the Irish-American community. Our people are persuasive, but it's clear we're not the darlings of New York no more, Liam. Dammit! we need those five and ten dollar bills in the bar-room collection boxes. That's our life's blood.'

Then the Chief broke in again. 'We have rules, Liam, and we have penalties. Always remember we have penalties. The undisciplined soldier is of little use to us. And when someone gets too big for his boots we have to swat him down. For the good of the Cause.'

Brady's face remained impassive, though his heart beat fiercely and his stomach turned over. Still he feared for his life; feared his fate was that tied sack in a stinking ditch. And MacStifoin would enjoy that.

And then suddenly the Chief began to smile.

'Let this little chat be a warning, Liam. That's all. We don't wish to stifle all initiative, but we need to curb uncontrolled zeal. You understand what I'm saying?'

'Yes, sir,' Brady said softly, fully aware that his life had just been handed back to him. 'It won't happen again, sir. Just send me south for a couple of months. I need a rest – yes, that would do me the world of good. Be right as rain then. Let me sort myself out for a bit. I need time to get me head back together.'

To consolidate his influence was what he really intended. Never again would these bastards catch him flat-footed. He'd see them in hell first! He'd be back soon enough, and ready for them next time!

The Chief of Staff exchanged a knowing look with Eamon Lynch.

'I'd like to say yes, Liam, but that will not be possible. There's another bit of business in London that would benefit from your attention.'

So that was it. They intended to keep him operational and on the move, so he had no time for the conspiracies which were rumoured. Well, OK, there was plenty of time. He was still only thirty-one. He had years on these old birds, and he'd see them gutted yet.

He pulled a chair towards the table and sat with his back to MacStifoin, contemptuously.

'Aren't active service units entitled to a break any more? I'm still hot with the security forces.'

At this the Old Man pinched his chin ruminatively and smiled.

'Is the nerve going, then, Liam? Or maybe you have other business to attend to?' His voice was laced with irony. 'Would you like that second drink now?'

Brady accepted the drink and with it the poverty of choice in his current situation. The whisky was in part a small guarantee of his safety. He enjoyed once more the burn of the whisky, as only a reprieved man can. When he put the glass down again he was reassured to find that his fingers had almost stopped trembling.

'What's the job?' he asked, throwing back his head and kneading the muscles of his neck with his right hand.

'It's what you might call a favour for a friend – a friend who has been more than generous in the past. Perhaps you remember the name Azziz?'

'No, can't say I do.'

'You should. You've much to thank him for, and taking the credit for an operation he commissioned is no way to repay the debt. We promised Oxford Street was theirs, so we had to deny being responsible for that phone-call to preserve goodwill.' The Chief glanced sideways at Eddie Kelly.

'Fancy you forgetting your little bucket-and-spade holiday in the desert.' Kelly smiled thinly. 'Home from home with the wogs was how you described it, if memory serves. Colonel Azziz paid your room and board, Liam.'

'What does he want now? A wet fortnight on the Falls Road in return? He'd freeze his Arab bollocks off!'

He knew immediately that his remark was ill received. The Chief let his sudden anger subside, then continued in businesslike fashion.

'He wants a favour from you, to redress the balance.'

The significance of that remark took barely a second to sink in: suddenly he was valuable to them again.

'What kind of favour?'

'An intelligence favour. Some thought you didn't have the qualifications, Liam.' An air of levity to underline his control of the situation. 'But I do. You see, it's all very complicated for them. Their own people are being watched like hawks: they can't move a muscle without it being photographed and recorded in infra-red. They're inexperienced – students mostly, kids really, liable to lose their visas just on suspicion of anything naughty. Basically they're fuck-ups on two legs, and even their own people don't trust them to do anything more demanding than organise a demo. The Brits can spot an Arab at two hundred yards in London.'

'Why me?'

'I thought we had already established that your unquestioning loyalty is what's required. However, in the circumstances, I'll explain. They asked for one of our best men. That's Arabs for you – always want the designer label.'

Brady felt a tingle of excitement. He sniffed and rubbed his nose, smiling inwardly. Flynn, Anderson and Peters were all in the Maze prison; O'Hara had blown his own leg off with cordtex – stupid prick; and Phil Devlin had simply had enough. Now they had to admit he was their best operational man. Yes, here was the edge – a power he could use, when the time came. Yes, he was their best man and that was why the old guard feared him. That was what this pantomime was really about.

The Chief, who had chosen his words with care, knew that at a push Brady could refuse this mission without loss of status, having just finished a perilous stretch of active service. But equally he knew that if the man's vanity and ambition were aroused, he would not.

'I have the name of a civil servant, an MI6 man we think, who has been showing his nose around in Libyan dissident circles. A proper nuisance, he's been. Colonel Azziz wants to know what's going on. It has the stink of a British-sponsored coup. You know how the Brits love to play with us little people. Find out what you can and report back. It's important we keep Azziz sweet if we want him to continue playing sugar daddy. The MI6 man shouldn't be too much trouble for you. He's in his fifties; the sedentary lifestyle, you know.'

'A paper-shuffler,' snorted Brady with disdain for the files upon the table.

'Yes,' said the Chief, ignoring the inference, 'a paper-shuffler. Find him. Follow him. As I said, find out whatever you can. I need answers quickly, so don't piss around with him. Eamon, the photograph . . .'

Lynch took an eight-by-five black-and-white photograph from his inside breast pocket and pushed it across the table. Brady picked it up and looked at the old-looking face. It seemed older than mid-fifties, and the pampered kind that filled Brady with both aggression and contempt. Slowly he turned it over in his hand and read the typing on the back.

GEORGE ARTHUR STEPHENSON,
17, THE SPINNEY,
KINGSTON-UPON-THAMES.

God, how sickeningly suburban, he thought.
'It will be a pleasure.'

SIX

ABOVE THE RAGGED line of palm trees that bordered the barracks' east wall, the silver disc of the spring morning sun was rising – and with it the wailing cry of the muezzin in a distant minaret, calling the faithful of Tripoli to prayer. In an enclosed strip of sandy ground, outside the black tanned-goatskin tent of his forefathers, a lone figure knelt upon a rough hessian prayer-mat and adjusted the folds of his bleached cotton robe before settling back upon sandal-less heels. The air was still cool in spite of the bright sunlight that slanted across the compound, and he was happy to face his God in that beautiful dawn; barefoot, alone and without vanity.

His two Korean bodyguards had risen as soon as they saw the first faint light through the tent flap, and had come to join him in the small unpaved courtyard where he prayed; but he had dismissed them abruptly. They had withdrawn sulkily behind the brick pillars that enclosed the courtyard, where they now practised callisthenics in conspicuous fashion. He did not particularly like either of them, nor could he bring himself to fully trust them (they were, after all, foreigners) but he recognised in their confident cat-like movements the power and strength of martial-arts technicians, and their skill reassured him against threats from within the barrack walls as much as from without.

But such concerns were for other times. This moment was for his God.

Concentrating his spirit and cleansing his thoughts, he filled his lungs with life and bowed low to touch his forehead to the ground. The rising sun confirmed that he was facing eastward towards Mecca, the spiritual centre of Islam. All over the country Moslems were prostrating themselves in similar fashion before the power of God, and raising their voices in worship. But the voice that was known the world over for its hectoring power was now low and filled with awe.

> 'Praise to be God, the Lord of the worlds!
> The compassionate, the merciful!
> King of the day of judgement!
> Thee only do we worship,
> And to Thee do we cry for help.
> Guide Thou us on the straight path,
> The path of those to whom Thou hast been gracious—
> With whom Thou art not angry,
> And who go not astray.'

It was always the first prayer in his day: the words of the first sura of the Koran. Each day he would faithfully observe the five periods set aside for prayer in strict obedience to the dictates of the Moslem holy book. As usual, his first prayers were for strength and guidance, and sitting there in the still of the morning with the infinite blue sky opening before him he was aware of his mortality and the feebleness of man's aspirations. He had brought his long-enslaved people out of perpetual darkness into the light of freedom and independence, and for this blessing he felt grateful. Grateful, though also a little tired. The burden of leading a nation forward, with enemies all around, was hard to bear. He was no longer the strong young soldier of Allah he had once been.

But it was God's will – of that he was sure.

His keen brown eyes followed the languid movements of the palm fronds and his cheek muscles relaxed in the warmth of the sun that spilled across his face. It was a handsome face, with high cheekbones and a strong masculine jaw. The face of a Bedu: noblest of Arabs. But it was also a careworn face, the eyes edged with a tracery of creases from years of squinting in desert sun. The cheeks were now sunken, and under the softening jowl was a neck that was swelling with the ravages of frequent ill-health. Just as his country was spending its oil wealth, he too had counted himself a national resource to be spent on the advancement of his people. If it had not been for his faith, he mused, his well would have long been exhausted.

There, in the dawn of a new day, his spirit longed for a finger of guidance to point the way – to be absolutely sure. The journey to this point had been years in the making. It was a lonely path paved with danger and temptation at every turn, and he was reminded of far-gone times in the desert with his father's goats – the comfort of distant memories. He was lost in another desert now, stranded between two oases which were as far apart as any two geographical points could ever be. And if the journey's end seemed unattainable, how much more did the point of departure seem lost in time. Did he still fear to lose his way – after all these years?

As a boy he had known that fear all too well. Many were the times he had set out in search of distant water courses in the burning Sirte, only to find himself tricked by the shifting sands; lost and alone, and armed only with sling-shot and crook to defend his father's herd against the packs of wild dogs. Even the strongest man does not last long in the Sirte when his tongue swells with thirst, for the desert does not forgive the fool! 'Keep an eye for the sun,' his father had charged him, 'and one for your footprints.' Sound advice! Only by watching the position of the sun and looking back the way he had come, to check the straightness of his footmarks in the sand, could he calculate the trueness of his intended course. He could still see them now: those footprints, in their dotted line, of a frightened boy trekking resolutely towards a burning, rocky horizon . . . Just as now his mind's eye peered backward to verify the course he had chosen those many years ago.

Muammar al Qadaffi.

Almost like a latter-day prophet he had come from out of the Sirtica, the burning three-hundred-mile wasteland dividing the rival provinces of Cyrenaica in the east and Tripolitania in the west. It was a fortunate accident, indeed, that placed him here in this politically-neutral corner. An accident which made his later leadership acceptable to tribal prejudices on both sides.

He was born of the Bedu people and of the Qadadfa tribe, a group of the Arab al-Gharb, the Arabs· of the West, who had been driven off their lands in Cyrenaica by an alliance of stronger tribes, and into the harsh, unforgiving desert of the Sirtica. Theirs was a simple life, controlled by the moods of the shifting desert sand and the constant fear of drought.

Like all good parents, his herdsman father and gentle mother had wanted education for their son. They had used what little money they made from the occasional sale of livestock to send him to school in the town of Sirte. For a ten-year-old who had never been away from home for more than a night before, it was a lonely experience: rubbing shoulders with the rich sons of middle-class Arabs, who were always aware of the poorness of his clothes – and they did not let him forget it. To them he was an object of fun, 'that poor desert Bedu', hardly worth their time or friendship. Yet it was his father's will that he be educated, and duty was everything.

So he worked hard to make his family proud, and to elevate their name and standing within the tribe. Far from home and without money for lodgings, he slept most nights in the town mosque protected and comforted by the 'angels' in the intricate ceramic mosaics on the floor and walls; and only during holidays did he hike barefoot back to the family encampment and to the press of his mother's loving arms. It was during those dark, friendless and often tearful nights in the mosque that he first found the comfort of his God. His strength. And on the choking, dusty roads home he discovered the patience and commitment that would set him apart from his schoolfellows.

The family encampment moved ever further away in search of water and grazing, and each time they moved he grew in strength and independence. By the time he was ready to enter secondary school the family had shifted far to the south, to Fezzan province, where he was enrolled in the Sebha Preparatory School, in preparation for eventual entrance to the university in Benghazi – his father's greatest dream for him.

But then 1956 came around, and with it the Suez crisis. It was Qadaffi's first experience of Western imperialism and foreign domination of the Arabs. There seemed something in the air at that time, something so exciting – like a trumpet call to his people to rise up against the West. He would listen eagerly to political debates amongst the other students about what Arabdom should do to realise its true position in the world. After all, hadn't Islam once been the dominant power in the world, producing the most brilliant minds of the time – generals, master-craftsmen, poets, astronomers, mathematicians and architects? A rich cultural heritage being slowly strangled by the West!

Now Suez was in all the newspapers – amid charges of aggression by Britain, France and Israel. So young men went east to enlist in Egypt's army and fight the imperialists and the Zionists. It was a time when impressionable young Arabs were consolidating their

75

political views; ideas that would endure for generations to come. And for the first time there was an obvious leader for the Arab world; a visionary willing to stand firm against exploitative and manipulating world powers: Colonel Gemal Abdul Nasser. Here was a man with clear, cohesive ideas for Arab socialism – and, like thousands of other young students, Qadaffi tuned his cheap transistor radio to Radio Cairo to hear those theories espoused on 'Voice of the Arabs'. Those ideas brought a new consciousness and sense of identity, but most of all the hope of a united Arab nation – a world power to be reckoned with instead of just a series of fiefs to be exploited in the East–West chess game.

Muammar Qadaffi became a convert to the Nasserist ideal and spent all his free time organising protest groups amongst his fellow students. They protested on a variety of issues, mainly against Britain and the USA, spilling onto the streets and whipping up their countrymen against the British and American military bases in Libya. Qadaffi's face became well known to the local police as he chanted his slogans and waved aloft a well-thumbed copy of Nasser's *Philosophy of the Revolution*.

They must have feared him, the authorities, those lackeys of the ruling administration, since they singled him out for special attention. The police labelled him a militant and had him expelled from school – as if that could stop the tidal wave that would topple a corrupt monarchy. Being singled out thus made him grow in stature in the eyes of other students. Increasingly he came to the conclusion that he had a special role to play in Nasser's grand strategy.

But his poor parents, with their naive and fearful belief in the implicit rightness of the prevailing social order, could not understand him or his ideas. Unable to bear the shame of their son's expulsion, the family moved north to Mizurata, second largest city in Tripolitania, where they begged him to complete his studies without further trouble. To no avail: he was developing a flair for organisation and motivation, based largely upon his undeniable charisma. This had to be used in the struggle for Libyan freedom – a gift from God to be used for his people.

He just kept on pushing. The students at Sebha formed a central committee holding secret meetings under his leadership. He was no longer the poor desert Bedu but an intelligent, passionate and erudite young Arab. The die was cast; his path chosen.

Having decided on the ultimate goal, a socialist revolution within Libya, the route was obvious. Civilian politics were rejected as ineffectual, given the stranglehold exercised by the Sanussi royal family over any form of organised opposition. If Qadaffi was to save his country, it must be through a military coup. The army was the only force capable of unseating the Sanussi.

At a secret meeting in 1963, Qadaffi's movement agreed on a covert infiltration of the junior officer cadre by their own members, reasoning that the better-educated, classless generation they represented would easily win support there. They were right. Qadaffi and two of his best men enrolled in the Military Academy in Benghazi, where they began sowing the seeds of discontent amongst other cadet officers. Recruits there were typically apolitical and unresponsive to new ideologies – after all, theirs was a simple life with many privileges and few cares – so it was only on the basis of a strongly-felt nationalist tendency that they were able to gather converts to the group which they called the Free Unionist Officers. Through personal appeals and the bonds of friendship, Qadaffi and his men were able to win ever more supporters until they became a substantial, though clandestine, force within the Academy.

The irony was that the army he sought to subvert also provided him with the means to accomplish his goal. It was they who despatched him to Sandhurst, the British Military College, to study advanced signals.

How they had laughed, Jalloud and he, when it was announced. By now his supporters had been posted to military outposts all over Libya. There were junior officers in all key areas working hard to recruit fresh minds who were tired of Western domination and the constant British and American military presence in their land. Then, in 1967, came the Six-Day War when the entire Egyptian air-force was destroyed on the ground by Israeli warplanes. Arab tempers burned, and Qadaffi's men fanned the flames with stories of how the West had conspired with Israel in the outrage. There was a rising groundswell of opinion that sought to depose the monarchy and throw out the Westerners from their bases in Libya.

Social unrest was also coming to Qadaffi's aid. The discovery of oil, heralded as an economic miracle and the salvation of all Libyans, had served only to deepen and entrench the corruption of the regime. For, predictably, Libya's wealth remained concentrated within a very small social group.

Conditions were right by the beginning of 1968, and careful plans were made amongst the Free Unionist Officers for the military overthrow of the hated regime. They had analysed the practicalities of seizing power down to the last detail. There were key targets to be neutralised: the police and the senior officer cadre within the army. There were also key facilities – the airports, border posts, public utilities and radio stations – which would need to be seized and controlled. Most of all, the radio stations, for if they controlled communications they could elicit support from the masses and diffuse attempts at organised resistance by the Sanussi family.

If the coup was to succeed, they would need to move when the King was away from his centre of support in Cyrenaica – his cultural homeland. Senior army commanders must all be within the country, and cabinet members all in the same place – so all the fish could be caught in the same net.

Qadaffi drew no distinction between the group's political aims and the duty of all Moslems to destroy the enemies of Islam. In a bare, borrowed hall outside Benghazi he told them all: 'We are not cringing dogs who plot treason for their own self-interest! Ours is a religious quest! Beginning with our own country, where we will build a new Islamic Socialist Republic, we will unite our Arab brothers, rid ourselves of the Great Satan in the West and ultimately destroy the Zionists in the east!' It was no less than what every red-blooded Arab longed for; and he, Muammar Qadaffi the poor desert Bedu, would give it to them.

The other prime movers in the organisation, all gifted tacticians and organisers, were Abdul Salam Jalloud, Mustafa Kharubi, Abu Bakr Yunis Jabir and Khuwaildi Hamidi; they would each occupy significant places in the new order. But first they must all risk death to make their dreams a reality.

The first coup attempt, set for 12 March 1969, was cancelled at the last moment. Conditions were perfect but many of the senior army officers targeted were attending a concert in Tripoli given by the famous Egyptian singer Un Kalthum. Not only was the concert televised, but the proceeds were to go to the Palestine Liberation Organisation. Qadaffi decided it was inappropriate to arrest the officers in full view of a national television audience, thereby warning other opposition targets not within his immediate grasp. Furthermore he did not wish to disrupt a charity benefit given for such a popular cause.

For a while their impetus seemed to be waning. The weeks slipped agonisingly by, as the conspirators ached for the word to move. It was a time of nerves and self-reproach; and a time to dig deep and find a greater strength through God.

Then the spur came when they needed it most. The eyes and ears of the King's intelligence service had got wind of the plot, and immediately overseas postings were arranged for Captain Qadaffi and his committee.

They were to be dispersed and scattered, thereby neutralising the threat. These foreign postings would take effect from 2 September. The great moment had been forced upon them, and the coup was set for the early hours of 1 September.

By that time King Idris had been out of the country for some months, supposedly taking a health cure in Greece and later in Turkey. Certainly he had known there were a number of plots being hatched against him, and his orderly departure had a certain finality about it. He had left the Crown Prince behind, but this was a weak man, whom the people called 'the man without a shadow'. When Qadaffi's men stormed the citadel of Sanussi power, it was in the knowledge that it was vacant.

They moved in the hours of darkness between the last day of August and the first day of September, meeting only token resistance and shedding little blood. All targets were quickly taken, and the Western military forces present in the country did nothing to stop them.

With the sound of automatic gunfire ringing out in celebration of their victory, Qadaffi went to the radio station in Benghazi. It was a night he would remember for a very long time: the realisation of a dream that had begun with the small, battered transistor radio tuned to 'Voice of the Arabs'.

At 7.30 am he spoke to the Libyan people for the first time. It took virtually no time to write his script, for he knew exactly what he wanted to say. In a sense he had been writing that speech since the day he was expelled from the school in Sebha.

Thus was proclaimed the creation of the Libyan Arab Republic whose motto would be that of Nasser's Egypt: '*Freedom, socialism and unity*'. The country would be run by a seven-member Revolutionary Command Council drawn from the members of the Free Unionist Officers. But in his heart Qadaffi knew it was his own destiny to be the guiding spirit of the revolution, for he was the dreamer of great dreams.

Some twenty years had intervened. Years of alliances and rivalries, of friendship and treachery. And still the Arab world was no closer to unification. Israel still endured, like a stake driven into the heart of the Arab lands. The Libyan Revolution had stalled from lack of new directions in which to spread. Qadaffi had cast about him looking for fledgling political groups who needed his support, had worked his will through fanatical groups of freedom fighters and urban guerrillas, yet still he could not create that all-consuming Islamic tide of rage that would sweep through the Middle East and destroy the enemy, Israel.

This had been his path.

Now there was only one option – but it also raised a question which returned time and time again to torment him: should Islam let loose that most fearful and devastating of all weapons to work the will of Allah? Well, he already knew that his atomic programme was a vital safeguard against Israel's own bomb; but could he finally unsheath the Sword of Islam? Did he have the strength? If he now failed to meet the challenge, would future generations revile his name?

'God give me strength,' he prayed, 'to do what must be done.'

Captain Kim noticed the President rise from his prayers and turn towards the courtyard entrance. Immediately he motioned to Captain Park and the two of them fell in three paces behind. The Libyan held his shoulders back as if trying to ease some nagging muscular pain between his scapulae. Kim was quick to notice any change in his principal's physical condition, as he was charged with the man's security within the grounds of the Azizyah barracks. He would have offered his skilled fingers to ease the condition, but he knew Qadaffi disapproved of such remedies. Though Kim was educated in acupressure, the oriental art of healing through the application of pressure at strategic body points, the President had previously refused the benefits of such heathen magic. Qadaffi did not, however, refuse the expertise of North Korean pilots in flying his MiGs, thought Kim bitterly, or the employment of South Korean workers in his oil-fields. For this was a pragmatist in the truest sense; and one whose death would go unmourned by many within Libya as well as outside.

Libya was, for the proud Korean, an uncivilised country full of dirty, uncivilised people who had the undeserved good fortune to be born on top of fantastic reserves of natural wealth. How he despised them all. But only nine months more before his contract was up; then he could go home to the gentle wife and small children he had not seen in over two years. If he served well, and if Qadaffi was kept alive for those two years, Kim could return to his own country a rich man and fulfil his dream of opening his own gymnasium. That was the dream which made it possible to stomach the obvious contempt of the man Qadaffi.

The two Koreans escorted the Libyan up to the ornamental garden of the new Presidential villa, where a steward was laying the table in the open air for breakfast. As Qadaffi sat down, Kim and Park moved discreetly to a smaller table some twenty feet away. Kim watched the steward's long, slender hands moving over the table; he was a bird-like man of middle years with a quick smile and a nervous manner. The President sipped from a glass of water and opened the folded copy of the *Jana* newspaper, keen to read at least something of the world news before his guest arrived.

Captain Park poured fresh orange juice for his colleague from a glass pitcher, but Kim was still intent on watching the steward. Who was this man anyway? He had never seen him before – and why were his hands shaking so? He watched as the steward picked up a covered basket used to contain unleavened bread . . . then as he quickly pulled back the cloth and snatched from it a revolver with an enormous barrel. Now there was the terror of confrontation in the steward's eyes, as he stood before his President. He dropped the basket to bring both hands together on the trembling gun, and as it hit the ground Qadaffi looked up. In that instant Kim jumped to his feet and cleared his ankle holster, bringing his weapon to bear on the assailant's sand-coloured forehead.

In that same moment, when his life hung in the balance, Qadaffi stood up, completely without fear – thereby obscuring Kim's aim. He suddenly fetched the back of his hand hard across the steward's face, in the way he always punished insolence, spinning him off the patio and onto the lawn. The thin man rolled over once – then was struck in the forehead by two rounds of hollow-point from Kim's pistol. His head exploded.

Suddenly a siren was blaring, and officials and soldiers ran towards the villa from all directions. Carefully, Captain Kim knelt and removed the pistol from the steward's fingers, weighing it appreciatively in his hand. He flicked open the cylinder and inspected the ammunition, noticing how the soft lead nose of each round had been scored and then dipped in some dark-staining liquid poison. Within a few moments there was a tight cordon of soldiers and advisers standing round the villa's perimeter, all gazing at Qadaffi as he stood watching Kim's inspection.

'Magnum 44, Mr President,' said Kim without looking up. 'Not the professional's choice, but still effective. I don't understand why he didn't shoot when he had the chance. Why did he hesitate?'

Qadaffi straightened his robe, calm and assured.

'Because he was another small man, unequal to the task. If they desire power and greatness, why do these traitors send only fleas to bite me? Qadaffi does not die so easily. Give me the pistol.'

Kim snapped the cylinder closed and handed over the weapon. Qadaffi felt its weight and smiled in appreciation. 'An impressive piece. I will keep it to ward off wild dogs,' he said, laying it on the table. 'Now, back to your posts, everyone – and send for another steward! I would finish my breakfast in peace.'

Immediately the throng dispersed, and two orderlies removed the body to the guardroom, to await the arrival of the People's Militia.

Ten minutes later, the Prime Minister arrived in a state of some agitation: Major Abdul Salaam Jalloud, Qadaffi's right hand, and the RCC member responsible for Internal Order.

'*Salaam alaikum*, brother Colonel! Are you well?'

'*Alaikum a'salaam*. Thanks to God, I am well, and still alive.'

'These people grow more desperate each day.'

'Indeed. It is time we crushed this opposition before it gains more strength. You will take personal charge of the investigation.' Qadaffi pointed to the dark stain on the lawn. 'I want public hangings for those involved, do you understand?'

'Perfectly, Brother Colonel. But let me sweeten this bitter pill with good news from London.'

Qadaffi pulled a handful of dates from a wooden bowl, and popped one into his mouth.

'London? By Great God, let it be news of that traitor Ibrahim!'

Jalloud allowed himself a small smirk of triumph. 'Indeed it is. You will remember that Azziz had a plan to bomb his hotel in London, but it failed miserably.' Triumphantly Jalloud turned the knife against his rival, Colonel Azziz. 'Since the Bureau of External Security had failed to send him forth to eternity, I decided to take a hand in the matter. Of course, all external operations should really be cleared through Azziz, but in this case . . .'

'Never mind that now. Go on,' the President enthused.

Jalloud smiled graciously. 'I placed a bomb of my own. A walking bomb.'

'What do you mean?'

'I found an agent willing to embrace martyrdom, and I sent him off to the rally in Trafalgar Square with a dozen hand-grenades attached to his belt. I had instructed him to make his way through the crowd to the front of the platform, and to wait for the arrival of Dr Ibrahim and his committee. When Ibrahim moved forward to the microphone, that was to be the moment.'

Barely able to conceal his excitement, Qadaffi grabbed the other man's sleeve, examining him with burning eyes.

'Your face is full of triumph, Jalloud. Tell me, when will this happen?'

'But, Colonel,' Jalloud stammered, his arm turning numb under the President's powerful grip. 'That is why I am here. It happened only minutes ago. Ibrahim is dead!'

On another continent, at that very moment, members of Qadaffi's most dangerous opposition group lay dead in the wreckage of a make-shift platform. The platform had stood in Trafalgar Square, a world-renowned haven of free-speech. But these men had dared to speak out against the Mad Dog of Tripoli.

'Dear God!' said the British Home Secretary, when he visited the scene, only a few hundred yards from his Whitehall office. 'Is there no limit to the man's arrogance!'

SEVEN

A LIGHT SNOW was dusting the runway as the British Airways 747 touched down at Dulles International Airport. Sir Alistair Cornwell stepped from the flight cabin, followed by his armed personal escort, and was met at the exit finger by a senior Company officer who pumped his hand warmly.

'Welcome to Washington, Mr Deputy Director. If you'd just step this way . . .'

The CIA man flashed a pass as he escorted the two guests through diplomatic channels, through a VIP lounge festooned with silk flowers, down to ground level in a private elevator, and out to a waiting Oldsmobile stretched limousine.

'This way please, Mr Deputy Director.' The escort broke open the left rear door. Sir Alistair gave a courteous incline of his head, and heaved his 62-year-old bulk into the seat immediately behind the driver – the position of honour. Protocol demanded that the British security escort take the jump seat, thus deferring his claim to the front passenger seat – the key security position in the vehicle – to his American counterpart. He listened with interest as the American instructed the driver on taking a little-used route out of the airport.

By the time they hit the beltway the snow had stopped, and pale sunshine had begun to paint the bare tree-line as they crossed the Potomac and sped towards Langley.

Sir Alistair had always enjoyed his visits to Virginia; Langley's hospitality was legend within the offices of Century House. But this visit was no social call – far from it. What he was about to suggest to the Director of the CIA could easily explode back in their faces. As for himself, it did not much matter either way. Sir Alistair was due to retire in four months, after a career spanning forty years in army and foreign intelligence, so he had nothing to lose. A pension would be nice, of course, but with a substantial private income from the family porcelain business it was hardly a crucial factor in his decision to proceed with this plan. At very worst he would be compelled to retire early 'in the public interest'. But if the plan succeeded, it would be his personal legacy to a world increasingly under threat of anarchy.

'How is London, Mr Deputy-Director?' the Company man inquired genially. 'I was there myself last year, and looked up some friends from the old days in Korea. Exciting city, London.'

'I'm afraid we don't see too many of your country-men over there just recently. I understand the popular view over here is that London is again no longer safe for Americans.'

The Company man could not quite put his finger on what irked him in that remark. He let his gaze drift out across the white-powdered verges. His voice was matter-of-fact when he spoke.

'Terrible news about that mess in Trafalgar Square, Mr Deputy-Director – so soon after the bomb on Oxford Street.'

Thereafter the journey continued in silence.

It was technically Sir Alistair's annual courtesy call on the Company: a chance to discuss topics of mutual concern, and co-operation over shared resources; an opportunity for them to appraise one another first-hand of future operations likely to affect the other chap's sphere of influence. Goodwill between the two sides was essential, not merely because of the NATO alliance or the 'Special Relationship' between their two governments, but because theirs had always been a symbiotic relationship wherein ideas were pooled and surplus funds re-routed to mutual benefit. The British Secret Intelligence Service (MI6 to those who still cared to use the name) was one of the oldest intelligence organisations in the world, with a wealth of knowledge, experience and influence that far outstripped its financial resources. The CIA director's budget was massive by comparison to the 'Secret Vote' granted to his British counterpart by Parliament, so he was always willing to sponsor a good idea.

The Oldsmobile swooped into view of CIA headquarters, pausing momentarily at the security barrier for ID verification, and then drew up at the broad steps of the main entrance. A follow car – which had tagged along at a distance of a hundred yards all the way from the airport, in order to check for prying eyes and cameras – broke off and returned to its underground car-lot, satisfied that the arrival had not been anticipated by any hostiles working in and around Washington.

Inspite of the cold, William Kelly was waiting by the front steps to greet his guest. It was a nice touch.

'Good morning, Alistair,' the Director beamed, eyes dancing behind thick-lensed spectacles. 'Great to see you again.' There was no discourtesy in Kelly's omission of Sir Alistair's title. They had known each other from way back when, and between two old friends such formalities were unnecessary. The intelligence community still thrived on relationships such as theirs, many of which were established during World War II.

'I do believe you've shed a pound or two,' said Sir Alistair benignly.

'Ha! Get outa here! That's what I love about you Brits – always such charming liars.'

With a chorus of polite laughter from the greeting party, they stepped inside and past the huge wall-mounted crest of the Central Intelligence Agency. A retinue of aides and staffers followed discreetly at Kelly's elbow; some were introduced, others merely hovered.

Kelly led the way into a large, window-less conference room containing a table with space enough to seat twenty people comfortably.

In the centre of the mirror-polished rosewood table stood a vase of winter flowers and grasses arranged in a most elegant and pleasing way. Kelly's love of *ikebana* and all things oriental was well know within the Company. What was not at all widely known was the story of how Kelly, the young deputy station chief in Tokyo in the early years of the CIA, had been forced to chose between his career and a certain Japanese girl with the most exquisitely beautiful face. The Company could turn a blind eye to an officer enjoying a temporary passionate fling, but it would have to yank his security clearance if he chose to marry a recent enemy. No one trusted the Japanese in those days.

Sir Alistair, who had heard the story years ago whilst occupying the next bar-stool in a Berlin nightclub, was warmed now by the continuing sentiment of his old friend. William Kelly was an excellent intelligence officer, but he certainly was not the bloodless, hard-assed shark he would have his section chiefs believe.

The meeting commenced with Kelly sitting at the head of the table, directly beneath a portrait of the President flanked by US flags – the Stars and

Stripes. Most of the staffers had retired from the group, leaving Deputy Director Fox and Senior Assistant Directors Burke and Johnson sitting on Kelly's left, and Sir Alistair on his right. Johnson, a powerfully built Bostonian and the first black man to reach directorate rank, was sharp as a razor: his planning abilities had earned him the nickname 'the ebony quarterback'. Burke was a journeyman agent who had plodded his way to high rank largely through covering his ass when blame was looking for a partner. Deputy Director Fox had been co-opted into the Company by Kelly, on his own appointment, because of his connections with academia; he had also been a contemporary and rival of Bob O'Neil, the Secretary of State, when both had worked at Infotel Computers.

The American side opened the meeting, with Johnson laying out their latest shopping-list of required assets. An agent in this trade delegation or that 'friendly society' . . . could Sir Alistair help? It was one way of Britain repaying the debt of intelligence supplied during the Falklands War, and for the hefty grant the US paid annually towards the running of GCHQ in Cheltenham. In intelligence circles defence cuts can be very embarrassing.

Sir Alistair made a mental note of three key areas where MI6 had already placed people, and he began to plot how best to use them as bargaining counters. He wondered which of the three was the important one, remembering similar situations in the past where they had hidden a crucial requirement inside a pack of jokers. It was their way of not tipping their hand too heavily; the implication being that Soviet penetration of British Intelligence was for them still a major source of worry. Sir Alistair inwardly cursed the names of past traitors; crosses the Service would have to bear for a long time to come.

He assured them that the British would be pleased to help in the appropriate areas. Sir Alistair would advise the Company when the handling

90

details were finalised. Naturally, since lives were at stake and trust had already been established, it would not be appropriate to replace these agents' controllers. That was Cornwell's polite way of indicating he would not give up control of such useful assets but would, of course, feed through any relevant intelligence gleaned.

Johnson bristled at the use of the word 'relevant'. The damn 'limey' was talking about pre-digesting Company intelligence.

Kelly spotted his subordinate's annoyance at once, and silenced him with a reproving glance shot over the top of his thick-lensed spectacles before he could voice any protest. There would be adequate time to twist the agreement to their advantage during the subsequent ironing-out of the details.

Cornwell drummed his fingers all through the discussion on perceived Soviet policy. Burke, the most experienced Kremlin-watcher in the Company, produced twenty-inch blown-up photographs of startling resolution and quality which showed troop and missile movements throughout the Ukraine; also two nuclear carriers under construction in the Kola peninsula. Since their pull-out from Afghanistan the Soviets had been able to release extra funding for their own Star Wars campaign, and now they were going for it – hell for leather. Furthermore, the antagonism of other Islamic states towards Russia had lessened noticeably as a result of the pull-out. That was bad news; it made them less receptive to Western advances and, God knows, there was enough bad feeling going around already, with hostages still going missing daily. Hell, any loss of influence was bad, for it had long been agreed by both intelligence services that in the Third World the key to winning the Cold War lay in the control of sea-lanes and client states.

Sir Alistair, for his part, was able to add encouraging indications of growing anti-Moscow feeling in Eastern Europe, which might dissuade the Russians from further repressive action against Poland. It was sad to report also that in Europe the Russians were winning the propaganda war, with unilateralism once more becoming a major trend. America could not afford to be seen warmongering, he cautioned, if she wished to preserve the Western Alliance.

Kelly remembered how, barely an hour ago, Burke had been speculating bitterly that perhaps it was time to cut loose from Western Europe and let them stew in their own shit. Burke, a Texan born and bred, was accustomed to speaking his mind in colourful ways. He was also a patriot and hated to think of Europeans biting the hand that continued to feed them.

After two hours of talk the meeting broke for lunch in the hospitality suite. When it resumed at two-fifteen, a new face was present at the table for the next topic: Low Intensity Operations, the new buzz-word for an area previously labelled simply 'International Terrorism'. On this subject Sir Alistair was quietly confident of being more qualified, in a very practical sense, than anyone else in the room. During first the Malayan Emergency and then later against the Mau-Mau in Kenya he had acted in an intelligence capacity, living for long periods in hostile terrain where a white face could buy you a night visit and a bloody and painful end. For the women it could be far worse.

He massaged his right knee under the tables; it still contained fragments of a CT fragmentation bomb that had exploded near him on a jungle path, and in damp weather such as now the rheumatism was bloody agonising.

The 'Young Turk' who had joined the meeting was introduced as Donald Tripp, ex-Harvard Professor of International Relations. At thirty-seven years of age, he was regarded as something of a flier. Keen and aggressively competitive in all matters, he had twice walked off with the Headquarters Racketball Trophy. Tripp had a Clark Kent jaw-line and shoulders to match; his suits – unlike those of his colleagues, who favoured a generous cut – tended to the French style. The gossip about him was that the man's thirst for power and influence was matched only by his ruthless pursuit of beautiful women on the Washington party circuit.

'Don here has been putting together a few thoughts in preparation for a paper we'll be publishing around our government departments on a restricted basis.'

Tripp thanked his boss for the introduction, savouring the compliment of their undivided attention. He knew how to handle an audience – back in the Harvard days the co-eds had hung on his every word; politics was a powerful aphrodisiac. He stood and waited till they were all listening, then began to speak, punctuating his words with aggressive hand gestures.

'Deputy-Director Cornwell, may I first say that whilst we fully sympathise with your position vis-à-vis the Irish Question, my paper is essentially concerned with issues that involve a more global impact. My paper does not, therefore, include reference to the PIRA, INLA, UVF or other Irish Separatists.'

Cornwell observed the younger man's studious avoidance of the word 'terrorist' in connection with matters Irish. He reminded himself of a short note for file which had been copied to him in 1984 regarding the visit of then-President Reagan to his family home in Southern Ireland. A certain Republican informer had one night whispered into his handler's ear that an American gentleman, sounding to him not unlike J.R. Ewing, had promised a substantial amount of money in return for an incident-free Presidential visit. In the absence of any corroborative intelligence, the DG had ordered that the loose minute be stamped DORMANT and filed in Central Registry. Cornwell, on the other hand, had been amongst those who thought there might be a grain of truth in the allegation of a CIA payment, and he eagerly awaited the day it could be proved. What concessions might he then buy?

'That's understood.' Sir Alistair motioned for Tripp to continue. 'Though I think you'll find, if you check your notes, that the UVF is a Unionist not a Separatist group.'

'Thank you for your attention to detail,' said Tripp with an edge to his voice; his academic ego had been slightly bruised before his colleagues. 'If I might continue . . .'

Honour satisfied, Sir Alistair relaxed and listened.

'Over the past few years the Palestinian struggle for a homeland has assumed a position of lessening importance on the world stage. The number of incidents directly attributable to the PLO and to its many splinter groups has fallen to only a fraction of the activity recorded between 1968 and 1982. Nor are these incidents as publicity-worthy as those of what could be referred to in terrorist circles as "the good old days". I am referring back, of course, to incidents such as the multiple sky-jackings to Dawson's field, Syria in 1968, the Munich Olympic slayings in 1972, and even the OPEC conference in Vienna in 1975 when Carlos kidnapped a group of Arab oil ministers.

'I don't wish to speculate at this time that the PLO is a spent force – a casual reading of any daily newspaper reminds us of the continued unrest in the occupied territories of the West Bank. The Palestinian uprising is, in spite of Israeli punitive action, still a going concern. But in the sense of already having played all their cards, and possessing no nuclear ace-in-the-hole, the Palestinians would appear to have –'

'Shot their wad!' interrupted Burke with characteristic bluntness. Nobody laughed.

94

Tripp continued, without acknowledging the remark.

'It is in a more general sense that the Middle East represents a threat to the West. Fundamentalism is a rising tide. Forget national boundaries. Islam is the uniting influence in that theatre, and our people detect fundamentalism as the sexy new drug amongst young Arabs – with America and the West portrayed as the source of all evils, from Coca-Cola to pornography. Even now they're playing kick-the-dog with US hostages in Beirut.

'What is perhaps more worrying, and for the Arabs more attractive, is that whilst the Palestinians promise their fighters real estate on the West Bank, the mad mullahs are guaranteeing their guys prime beach-front acreage in the Moslem heaven. In short, we're experiencing the revival of a momentum not unlike that of the Holy Crusades, and I for one see this as a threat far more immediate than any Soviet one. It's a trip-wire to a nuclear holocaust.'

A slickly edited slide show supported Tripp's analysis: atrocities wrought by Moslem groups in Lebanon, Israel, West Germany and France. Prudently he had excluded an excellent batch of pictures, culled from *Newsweek*, of the explosion on Oxford Street.

And then the sequence of slides changed to a close-up of Colonel Muammar al Qadaffi – de facto President of Libya.

'Check it out: public enemy numero uno,' said Tripp pointing accusingly at the screen, and reminding them all of some tacky prosecution lawyer.

Sir Alistair was already beginning to tire of this vaudeville presentation. Any such performance would have been quietly shown the side door, back at Century House. Under the present DG's captaincy the elegant understatement, the well-turned phrase had long held sway; and such an environment was

95

calculated to weed out the cowboys at an early stage in their careers.

Kelly read the Britisher's irritation and was amused by it, had counted on it. He had requested Tripp to deliver his paper for the sole purpose of shoving a weed up Cornwell's ass. They were old friends but he could not forget the 'told-you-so-old-man' jibes when 'Laramie' had been snatched in Leningrad. The arrest of that American businessman had proved conclusively that there was indeed a leak in the US Embassy in Moscow, and the show trial that followed had been one of the factors which conspired to scotch any hope of an East–West summit in Geneva that year.

'Thank you, Don,' said Kelly waving him to his seat. 'I'm sure I speak for all of us when I say it makes a change to hear an erstwhile academic perform with such lively and stimulating advocacy.'

Cornwell's pencil was tracing a carefully drawn sketch of a blimp.

'The next point for consideration is what we do about this – if I may borrow an expression from dear ol' Ronnie Reagan – this "loony tune". We all know the kind of barbaric lunacy he's capable of, and that more than ever he wants to unite the Arabs under his own leadership. That's been the main theme of his foreign policy all the way down the line – wouldn't you agree, Alistair?'

'Indeed. Since coming to power in that coup in '69 he's thought of little else. Offers of state mergers have been a regular feature of his administration: first it was Egypt and Sudan in 1969, then Tunisia in '73, Syria and Morocco; in 1981 it was Chad. But always it leads to disputes and the inevitable rift. Libya must be the most frequently married and divorced state in Africa.'

'Yes, and who can blame those other guys for suspecting Qadaffi's motives?' added Fox, determined to include his contribution. 'Take the planned

96

merger between Libya and Egypt in '73. Sadat starts to have second thoughts, so Qadaffi launches a "cultural revolution" aimed at bending Egyptian public opinion. Next thing anybody knows, there's a convoy of vehicles with forty thousand Libyans and a hefty sprinkling of intelligence and political operatives heading for Cairo to encourage the merger process. If that so-called "Green March" had ever reached its destination, there would surely have been a military repulsive action. As you know, they turned back and the episode ended in acute embarrassment for Qadaffi. Now they're at daggers drawn.'

'OK, so Qadaffi changes partners,' said the 'ebony quarterback'. 'But what ought to concern us more is his intentions towards the West and towards Israel. We know he wouldn't risk an all-out war against either – he's just too weak for conventional warfare, and he knows it. So what does he do? He hits out with terrorist action at points of weakness – soft targets. He funds and points Fundamentalist groups in the West, filling their ears with preaching about the evils of the Great Satan. It's one reason for his close association with Iran, while most other Arab nations favour Iraq.'

Kelly observed the exchanges of opinion, nodding gravely, but he noticed that Sir Alistair was fingering his briefcase absently; the Britisher would soon lay his cards on the table. Meanwhile the atmosphere was changing subtly from that of cool policy discussion to one of anti-Moslem paranoia.

'I wonder,' Kelly inquired, 'whether Alistair would like to give us a résumé of the findings of the inquiry into the Trafalgar Square outrage.'

Sir Alistair took a slim pink folder from his case and donned his famous half-moon spectacles.

'Where are we now? Yes, here it is. The rally was a two-day affair attended by some eight thousand people who came to hear a variety of Libyan exiles and opposition-party members speak. The platform on which committee members were seated had been constructed from wooden planks on a steel scaffolding, with open front and sides, thus providing little or no protection from the blast.

'The crowd seems to have been in an almost constant state of political euphoria, and had pushed forward to the very front of the platform. Uniformed police ringed the square, ready to intervene in case of disturbances, whilst a number of Special Branch officers mingled with the crowd in routine surveillance duties. Significantly SB did not report spotting any of the usual known Libyan intelligence operatives in the area, as is customary on such occasions. They are students mostly, who keep Tripoli appraised of the activities and whereabouts of subversives and opponents of the regime.

'On the morning of the second day, Dr Ibrahim was to give his key-note speech calling for a mass return to Libyan and the storming of Azizyah Barracks. As you all know, he was prevented from speaking at all by a young Arab standing in the front row of the audience, who exploded a number of grenades hidden on his person, killing himself in the process. The immediate blast radius was approximately thirty-five feet, and significant damage was inflicted on the crowd. All the committee members sitting in the first row on the platform were hit by fragments – forensics estimate there were probably ten or twelve grenades in all. Dr Ibrahim died instantly, and several other senior party members died within minutes of the explosion. It was bloody carnage. As might be expected, the resulting chaos within the square did much to impede the efforts of ambulancemen and doctors. It was fortunate indeed that a newly qualified squad of St John Ambulance Volunteers were in attendance, or else the number of secondary mortalities could have been much greater.'

Kelly was reminded of the horrific news photographs of bodies covered with red blankets lined up in the square. Sacrifices to the cause of democracy and free speech. He swallowed hard.

'What was the final body-count, Alistair?'

'Twenty-eight killed outright; a further nineteen died of their injuries – and more amputations than the London hospitals have performed in decades.

'We had been holding covert meetings with Dr Ibrahim aimed at assisting his party to win back popular support in Libya, prior to forming a government-in-exile that could provide a viable alternative to Qadaffi. We believe that there is a growing fund of discontent that is frustrated by the lack of a realistic alternative. Most notably, the army continues to wallow in a low state of morale at its failure to win a single significant conflict in the past twenty years. The bloody nose delivered by Chad, with the help of France, in 1984 and again in 1987 are cases in point. It now seems apparent that Qadaffi's agents discovered the link to our people, and decided to blow out the candle before the flame grew too bright.'

Then came the inevitable question.

'Excuse me for asking, but why didn't your people prevent the rally in view of the obvious dangers to the leading speakers?'

That was the question Sir Alistair knew they would all want to ask, but only Kelly was senior enough to get away with it. Take your medicine, Sir Alistair.

'We tried several times to stop it. We told them that an open-air rally was too visible an event. They responded with the kind of Third World chip-on-the-shoulder suspicions we're used to in these situations. Even accuse us of attempting to slow down their march towards democracy for our own purposes. They insisted they needed to create a popular crusade through such public meetings; it had to be something visible and democratic. To them the accompanying dangers were just facts of life. Quite brave of them in a

99

naive sort of way, I suppose. We would either help them or hinder them, but they would remember – either way. Imagine the Foreign Office reaction to possibly antagonising a future ally, so Whitehall was content to let them take their own risks. But we expected nothing on that scale.'

It was no more nor less than the Americans had expected to hear.

'The National Front for the Salvation of Libya is the only credible alternative. A number of its leading members once held cabinet rank in Qadaffi's revolutionary government, before the purges began and they fled the country. The remaining political groups are either too weak or are acting under the control of Egypt or Syria. These various factions are very prone to bickering and in-fighting; none, it seems, is willing to share power with the others. In short, gentlemen, it is unlikely that Qadaffi will be removed by any internally organised action.'

There was a brief silence as this last pronouncement sank in. Each man separately began to mentally project the likely scenarios of conflict in the Middle East with Qadaffi, the so-called 'unguided missile of Africa', remaining in power for the foreseeable future.

Sir Alistair was satisfied he had now created the correct climate for consideration of his option. But to make doubly sure he produced a transcript of the Tripoli Radio broadcast which had caused so much concern at Century House.

'I believe this document is pertinent to the issue.'

Kelly read the transcript. Normally he did not see such speeches; they were digested for him by one of the army of media reviewers in one of the Washington out-stations. When he came to the highlighted sentences, he stroked his heavy jowls thoughtfully and passed the sheets to his deputy.

Fox read the text aloud for the others:

'. . . Now are the enemies of Islam made known. Now does He deliver his fiery sword so that His people may destroy the infidel. Lo, they do plot and do evil and know not that justice is near . . .'

All attention now focused upon Sir Alistair. What was the significance of this threat?

The mood in the room was deadly serious.

'Would you now read another passage for me?' Sir Alistair enquired of the Deputy Director.

'Sure, if it's relevant.'

'Oh yes, I think it is. And I think you may recognise the book.'

A slim volume was opened at the relevant page, and pushed across the table. Fox picked it up and began to read the highlighted words.

'What seems to us particularly despicable is the conspiracy which has developed between the North Atlantic alliance and the Warsaw Pact. For many years now their governments have conspired to deprive the Arab Bloc of the means to use nuclear fuel, since they greatly fear we might wish to develop nuclear weapons of our own. Agents of the West and of the Zionists have destroyed our research facilities at every opportunity, as if they alone had the right to decide who is competent and who is not.

'What they fear is what many Arabs believe: that not until we have learned to wield God's flaming sword will Islam regain its rightful place in the world.'

Fox slowly closed the book and laid it on the table. The Americans waited for their boss to speak first, but the stunned silence continued for a further twenty seconds.

'Alistair, you know about the earth tremor in the south of Libya two days ago.'

'Yes, I do.'

'Those two extracts are only circumstantial evidence, but taken in conjunction with the tremor . . .'

'I agree. Of course there's no way of knowing for sure at this moment,' said Sir Alistair leaning closer to Kelly and meeting his gaze, 'but we tend to believe that earth tremor resulted from a small atomic underground test, probably no larger than the Hiroshima bomb.'

'But still large enough to destroy Tel Aviv,' Fox added ominously.

Kelly thought for a moment. 'Leaving aside the fact that he probably doesn't have a suitable delivery vehicle . . .'

'Oh, come off it, Bill,' interrupted Cornwell. 'We both know he's been pushing and cajoling every Third World nation in sight for a medium-range missile system. The Chinese keep refusing him their "East Wind" 3As, but he's getting very cosy with the Brazilians – and, God knows, his money must look good to them. We don't have eyes in the backs of our heads, Bill. Somehow, some way he's bound to get hold of one. And not just any old system; he's going to want state-of-the-art stuff with all that green-screen magic.'

Kelly waved a placating hand, aware that the old Britisher was perhaps becoming more excited than was good for men of his years. 'If you'd just let me finish, Alistair. I was about to say that owning don't necessarily mean using. But in these matters possession is nine-tenths of the threat. Qadaffi's is the wrong finger to have on the button. He's too unstable; just too unpredictable.'

There were nods of agreement from around the table. The psychological profiles built up at Langley clearly suggested that the Libyan leader regularly suffered from periods of deep depression interspersed with fits of aggression. Dr Hilary Wolfe, their chief psychiatric consultant, believed that Qadaffi's behaviour of recent years was entirely predictable. She characterised him as an emotionally retarded individual desperate for popular adulation, and willing to gamble anything in tit-for-tat retaliation against what he naively and paranoically perceived to be a thoroughly evil and vicious Western enemy. If Qadaffi was a child, she once remarked, he would be the kind to burst the ball if he could not be captain of the basket-ball team.

'A great shame your work with the NFSL had to end the way it did,' said Kelly gravely. 'A change of leadership in Tripoli would be most timely, it seems. What are we doing in Libya, Dave?'

The 'ebony quarterback' had little encouragement to offer.

'It's difficult to manoeuvre at this time. Most of the Americans who were based in Tripoli have since come home. We have no Embassy there, hence no definite base to work from. We have agents on the ground in deep cover but they are only information gatherers, providing details of military and economic developments. In fact, as you know, we have no covert action capability inside Libya since Pincher went over to their side.'

The very mention of Pincher's name was unwelcome at Langley. He had been a top covert operator in Vietnam and Angola, but when he got too greedy he left the Company to set up his own private security consultancy – a move he found extremely rewarding. In 1985 it was discovered that he was arranging arms deals for Libya in violation of Congressional Trade Restriction Agreements, and he fled to Tripoli before the FBI could nail his ass. There he had proved very useful to the Libyans in reorganising their intelligence service, and it was believed he set up for them a special counter-penetration wing based upon his knowledge of CIA tactics in Africa. Fortunately the Company was able to pull out most of their really important people before the Libyans could arrest and torture them.

'We've had to rely heavily on the Mossad in this theatre,' Johnson continued. 'Libya is one of their four major targets – along with Syria, Lebanon and the PLO. With the amount of US cash subsidising Israel's economy, they can hardly say no to any reasonable request from us.'

Kelly was not best pleased by this answer.

'Dammit we *must* have our own independent capability in Libya – traitors like Pincher notwithstanding. Get on it today. And I mean fast!'

'What sort of capability are you suggesting, Bill,' asked Sir Alistair probingly.

'We could start by finding and neutralising the installation that produced that earth tremor. Can you imagine Qadaffi holding the world to ransom with the threat of destruction of the State of Israel? I don't know whether the Soviets would come to his assistance if we aimed a preemptive nuclear strike. There are just too many "ifs" in this scenario.'

It was time for Sir Alistair to make known the main reason for his visit. The meeting thus far had provided a chance to sound out Kelly and his men before raising the crucial proposition.

'Bill, gentlemen, I would be grateful if you would now hear what I have to say. It's a matter which has exercised our people greatly over the past few weeks. In short we feel that we can no longer safely tolerate the threat which Qadaffi presents to ourselves and the Western democracies. He operates completely oblivious to all diplomatic and economic pressures, and with no regard for the lives of innocent civilians. His connections with various terrorist groups is not in doubt, and he makes no secret of his intention to destroy all the enemies of Islam, given the opportunity.

'Gentlemen, I know the constraints under which you yourselves now operate: the Presidential restrictions on covert action and the absolute ban on . . . other forms of action. Well, I have come here today with a proposal from the Director General of the Secret Intelligence Service that we remove Muammar Qadaffi from office by whatever means necessary.'

There was deep silence, then Kelly murmured, 'Go on please, Alistair.'

'We in the British service do not have orders forbidding assassination; they have not been thought necessary in the past. However, it is inconceivable that any of our politicians would agree to such an operation, because of the possible repercussions. That is why I have chosen to take personal reponsibility for initiating things. I am due to retire soon; my career is over and I cannot be hurt if matters are eventually made known.

'To come to the point, I have already begun preparations to put an operative into Libya to kill Qadaffi. You need say nothing – nor need you record anything that might incriminate yourselves.'

The CIA Director sat and stared at him. His brain was churning with questions, and though he could not fault the wisdom of the argument the conclusion was so potentially explosive.

'Why tell us, then? You must need something or you wouldn't have bothered to tell us,' said Kelly at last.

'That's true, and the reason is we don't have a logistical base in Tripoli from which to mount the operation. That's where you come in. Our own relationship with the Israeli secret service has been checkered, to say the least. But if this could be counted as a joint operation, then I'm sure they would provide that logistical support. I assure you, it will be made to look like an independent contract, paid for by Libyan exiles. I have taken great care to see that the operative will not be traced back to us. He is a freelance.'

Kelly was cornered: the decision his alone. He dared not tell the President, nor ask his subordinates what he should do. His men would comply with his decision, whichever way.

'I'm sorry, Alistair. Someone should nail that bastard, but you know I must say no.'

That evening Sir Alistair dismissed his escort and remained alone in his suite at the Washington Hotel. He was too jet-lagged to venture out to dinner. The muzak from the bedside entertainment centre, though soft and soothing, did nothing to assuage the concern he now felt. Had he misjudged the situation? he wondered over his drink. Had his last great coup evaporated into thin air? If so, to hell with the whole world, he thought, and he chugged back the last gulp of whisky and soda.

Then there came a soft, sharp rap on the door, like an urgent whisper in the dark. When he opened it his heart gave a small leap, though his only visible response was an indulgent smile.

Standing in the corridor, in a Burberry and plaid scarf, was his old friend William Kelly.

Sir Alistair put out a hand in greeting, drew him inside and closed the door again. Kelly walked straight over to the window and tugged at the curtain cord until the heavy drapes were completely closed and whatever it was he feared was blotted out. Then he turned slowly back to the room and began peeling off the overcoat and scarf. His face was deadly serious.

'We need to talk.'

EIGHT

THE BLOOD MADE Stephenson nauseous. But that was Tyler's style, the way he liked his steak; and it gratified Tyler to see the other man's discomfort.

A brief summons had been left on the answerphone saying merely: 'Simpson's in the Strand, 12.30, Wednesday.' Tyler had been mildly surprised at the extravagance of the venue, given the often tight-fisted attitude of British Intelligence. Simpson's was, after all, one of the classier eating establishments in town, and counted many politicians and socialites amongst its clientele – any regular reader of the London *Tatler* knew that. Stephenson stood him a beer at the bar before lunch, and it came served in a monogrammed silver tankard. A nice touch, thought Tyler – very British.

They were shown to their table in the corner by the captain in his immaculate black tails. The captain did Stephenson the courtesy of pretending to know him as a regular.

Whenever he ate at such places Tyler took some pleasure in contrasting the surrounding luxury with the times he had lived on whatever snakes and locusts he could catch and roast in the desert. On this occasion he spared his luncheon companion the details of those times. The man was already looking queasy.

A waiter in crisp white jacket and black bow-tie hovered discreetly and ladled out steamed broccoli, sauté potatoes and Hollandaise sauce. Stephenson thanked the waiter and looked down at the baked trout on his own plate, at the round mirthless eyes and weak open mouth.

'I don't know how you can eat meat that way. Puts me in mind of one of those awful first-form biology lessons.'

Tyler carved firmly into the rare fillet, splashing the red juices onto his vegetables, as if deliberately toying with him.

Stephenson studied the pale face of his own lunch and took a mouthful of lager. He had only ordered it in an effort to find common ground with his guest, but Tyler had asked for wine. Stephenson sensed the awkwardness between them, and knew he had to somehow make things right. Another mouthful of lager and he tried to ease the chill that was developing.

'Look here, I hope you don't harbour any ill-will after that business the other night.'

Tyler held up a restraining hand. His face was forgiving, philosophical even.

'How could I? What's a stray bomb between friends. This is an excellent lunch, old man.'

The civil servant sensed the sarcasm but chose to interpret this as a truce.

'The Department has an enlightened attitude toward entertainment – in certain circumstances.' Stephenson signalled the waiter to recharge Tyler's glass. Tyler watched the man pour the Beaujolais soundlessly, then picked it up, to savour the bouquet.

'Well, do you suppose the interest of the money you owe me for the last deal would cover this lunch? My bank has had no word of it yet.'

Stephenson looked genuinely surprised, and Tyler guessed the department holding the purse-strings had dropped him in it, leaving the man to explain things as best he could to his agent. What a circus!

'Look here, Tyler, there's absolutely nothing to worry about. Your fee is as safe as houses. It may take a few more days to get the warrant signed, that's all. Accounts have to be kept up to date, and even our department has auditors.'

Tyler glanced round the adjacent tables, at food filling faces and business being transacted: politicians with journalists, brokers with fund-managers — buyers and sellers, all of them. But one table was different: a lone diner sat poring over a tabloid newspaper, using only his fork to eat while he turned the pages with his free hand. Absently he took in the dining-room but avoided Tyler's eye.

'That's reassuring,' said Tyler turning to fix the civil servant's grey eyes. 'Who exactly do you want me to kill?'

The shock of the question caused Stephenson to suck in air, so he almost choked on a fish bone. With as much discretion as possible he coughed into his napkin and gulped a mouthful of lager to ease his throat.

'What is it with you, Tyler? Why do you have to turn these things into a fencing match? All right, let's cut the small-talk.' He crumpled his napkin and threw it on the table almost petulantly. There was more than a touch of defiance in the way he leaned across his plate. 'I can tell you only so much at this time, and the rest will have to wait until later. I've no wish to seem melodramatic, but I will outline the details and for security's sake you must stop me as soon as you hear something you do not feel you can comply with. If you decide against this contract you will receive the customary consultation fee plus expenses, and there will be no hard feelings. Is that understood?'

109

'Understood.'

'He is a very powerful and important individual always surrounded by efficient security – the best that money can buy. We're talking about SAS-standard bodyguard teams.'

'Keep going.' Tyler's heart was pumping hard against his chest.

'The operation will be based on the African Continent in decidedly hostile terrain, and with a minimum of logistical support on the ground. There are no diplomatic facilities for us to assist you in this mission. We have a trade presence there, but their hands are tied.'

It was all Tyler had hoped for and everything he had feared. He felt the prickle of sweat upon his back, a flutter in his stomach of excited butterflies in full flight. As each detail was fed to him he digested the implications. And Her Majesty's Government was willing to pay handsomely.

'Three hundred thousand,' said Stephenson slowly, as if counting the stacks of banknotes. 'Additional expenditure for equipment will have to be cleared through me first.'

'I presume we are talking nett of Inland Revenue,' said Tyler flippantly.

Both men smiled.

'Of course.'

It was indeed a sweet and tempting offer, and Tyler had a good idea of who the target was. If he was right it would be the most dangerous job of his life. It was as if he stood on the threshold waiting to take another leap into the unknown – possibly his last.

Stephenson looked around to ensure they were not overheard.

'Obviously you will have formed an opinion as to who we are talking about, but until I give you the name that's all it is – an opinion.' He was playing 'let's pretend' to cover his arse. 'This is your last opportunity to back out. You can get up from the table now and go back to the small-time jobs we throw your way, and continue to live a relatively safe and comfortable life. Or you can take this job – and with it everything a man like you desires from life.'

'Don't overplay your hand, mate,' Tyler sneered.

'Then what about it?'

Tyler cut another piece of steak and began to chew.

'I'm thinking.'

Stephenson sat quietly, and in the silence Tyler saw him exchange glances with the man reading the tabloid. It made him feel uncomfortable.

'I'm not sure whether I trust your promises. I don't risk my life for empty promises – I won't be fobbed off with a fucking OBE or anything. What I want is a never-work-again payday. It's got to be half a million.'

The die is cast, thought Tyler. If they buy that I'm in – if not, then stuff it!

With hardly a pause, Stephenson continued, 'In view of the importance of this business I am authorised to go as high as the figure you mention, but that must include all equipment. No additional expenses. I was hoping your patriotism would influence you. The Defence cuts affect all departments, you know.'

'Save that for the National Health workers, mate.'

'All right, so we have an agreement as to the fee.'

The civil servant reached into his left inside pocket with almost tantalising slowness and produced two brown envelopes. One of them had a sweaty thumb print on the back.

'Two choices here. One contains a cheque for initial consultation and expenses; the other contains a name. Choose the first and we'll knock it all on the head right now. If you choose the second, you accept our contract forthwith, and the constraints of the Official Secrets Act.'

Tyler could not help feeling amused by the pompous little show. Had Stephenson practised it in front of a mirror? Both envelopes were now angled towards him across the table.

He reached forward deliberately and took the second envelope, as they both knew he must. By now there was not much doubt as to whose name it contained, though Tyler would have to see it to assuage his residual disbelief. The enjoyment on Stephenson's careworn face was obvious. He had designed this piece of theatre as a consummatory act.

Now Tyler was committed.

He tore open the envelope and read the name handwritten on the single sheet of underlined paper: *Muammar Qadaffi*. It had been inscribed in green ink with an italic nib. After twenty seconds Tyler took a match from the book on the table and carefully incinerated the sheet, scrunching the charred remains into powder in the ashtray.

Stephenson, who like all good salesmen knew when to shut up, had watched Tyler's eyes flash at the sight of the name. He almost wanted him to voice some reaction – 'You're crazy!' or maybe even 'It can't be done' – but knew he never would. Tyler was, above all, a professional and this was the assassin's ultimate high: the ultimate contract. No way would he refuse it.

'All right, I'll do it,' said Tyler at last, his pulse moving back to base rate.

Stephenson beamed his approval, flushed with success. 'Thank you, Richard. I'm so glad. Now, if you'll pardon my presumption . . .' He raised a hand and an ever-responsive wine waiter lugged some champagne in an ice-bucket to the table.

The man lunching alone then folded his newspaper and began to settle his bill.

Tyler laughed in spite of himself. Stephenson really had no class at all, but he was every inch a winner.

They clinked glasses and drank – to success.

'Just one thing,' said Tyler, suddenly serious. 'Who was the joker at the table by the door? The one with the newspaper making eyes at us all through lunch.'

'It's nothing really, Richard. Just a precaution. HMG quite naturally feels this operation is extremely sensitive. So much so that had you declined the invitation, Inspector Woollard and his Special Branch colleagues in the lobby would have been on hand to escort you to a nice little place in the country. Just until the successful completion of the operation by our second-choice candidate.'

Cute, thought Tyler, very cute. Then he realised the reason for the champagne. That was the signal to those watching that they would not be required to do their duty.

'Let's hope you've thought of everything else,' he said and drained his glass.

When the echoing explosion of their Galil assault rifles had finally subsided, the soldiers jumped down from their jeep and moved in darkness through the scrub to where the two figures had fallen.

It was just off Highway 25, in a restricted Ministry of Defence area, and the intruders had no business there.

There was a strong wind blowing through the Negev Desert. There was always a strong wind in the early spring and the patrol had come to terms with the constant sound like the murmur of voices which it brought. Some said these were the voices of ghosts whose bleached bones lay buried there, but science told them it was only the rubbing together of countless grains of sand blown through the air in waves. Either way, the sound was unnerving to men whose job it was to watch and listen in the darkness.

The first soldier to reach the bodies removed his helmet and knelt, playing the beam of his torch over the ground. He was younger than the others, just eighteen and in his first year of conscription, the hair on his face no more than peach fuzz. His eyes were wide as he watched the blood flow from the big man's chest. It was this man who had raised his rifle when challenged, whilst the other one turned to run away. Now the runner was slumped face-down on the ground, dead as a stone. The big man wheezed and as he tore at the cloth around his throat, fighting to catch breath, a faint sucking sound, familiar to all soldiers, emerged from his chest.

Looking into a green-tinted world through their image-enhancing night-sights, the patrol had watched these two figures for almost an hour as they stole across the plain. Two men in Bedouin robes, with three mules – that did not make sense. The tribes knew this area to be off-limits – but, then, the nomads had never shown much respect for boundaries.

Suddenly the torch beam trained on the big man's face caught a glint of blond hair beneath his head-cloth.

'My God, this one is a European!' shouted the kneeling soldier, throwing aside his rifle. 'He's still alive. Quickly, bring a field dressing and some morphine.'

'Why brother?' grunted the second soldier. 'You know the rule: anyone caught in the inner zone must be shot on sight. Five minutes from now he'll be dead anyway.' Experience told him just how serious the wound was. 'What in hell is a European doing out here, anyway?'

It was not a question: more an indictment.

'We must keep him alive long enough to find that out. He's a foreign national.'

The second soldier cursed under his breath, but fetched a field dressing and tossed it over to his comrade. Of course, the young man was right – young men are always right. Then he returned to the jeep and took the walkie-talkie unit from its mounting. Less than a kilometre away, and just visible despite the dust, were the winking lights of the Facility. Inside the command post which had alerted them, the Security Coordinator was waiting for their report.

'Control desk, Echo One, over.'

'Go ahead, Echo One.'

'Illegals proved hostile. Infiltrators. Intercepted and neutralised. Please send medical team. Over.'

'Roger that, Echo One. Get back here immediately. Out.'

In his ground-level office the Coordinator of Security at Israel's Nuclear Weapons Research Facility began preparations to receive what was left of the infiltrators. Damn it! he brooded. It would mean another incident report, and another enquiry.

NINE

THE BRIEFING TYLER received came on a video cassette. It was passed to him on the London Underground by a middle-aged woman wearing a Hermès scarf and carrying a red leather shopping-bag.

He had amused himself for a while by trying to guess which of the stony-faced passengers would contact him, studying each in turn, though careful not to catch anyone's eye. The Arab tourists made him suspicious. Stephenson had warned him to be extremely careful, and to note anyone taking undue 'interest' in him. Clearly the spooks were not sure who might be monitoring their contacts, and some of their people had disappeared in the past – right off the streets. But Stephenson had assured him that Arab intelligence services preferred to buy the help of Europeans for field work, their own men being too easily visible to work effectively.

After the train had pulled into Leicester Square station, Tyler climbed the stairs marked NO EXIT, and was deftly passed the package by a woman coming down the steps towards him. She must have memorised his photograph, and did not even hesitate. She just shoved the manila envelope under his arm and hurried into the waiting train just as the doors were closing. He pushed the envelope into a sports hold-all, then made his way back towards Islington.

He noticed his palms were sweating slightly as he sank into his living-room sofa. The buff-coloured envelope stared back at him from the coffee table. His stomach felt tight – felt good. What was it the moment represented? A new beginning and another leap into the unknown. Dangerous, of course, but surely preferable to the half-life he had known these too many years. He could go for it – no reason not to.

Tyler had few ties or complications to bind him. For family there were parents he had not seen in three years, alienated from each other by divorce and from their sons by indifference, and a brother whose mental age condemned him to a nursing home for the rest of his days. Most of his real friends were dead or scattered across the battlefields of the world. That left only his professional contacts: a sordid assortment of characters who varied between the dangerous and the pathetic.

Shit. Who gave a damn, anyway? They were his cards, it was his hand, and he would have to play it. Who believed in happiness these days, anyway? In a greedy world what counted was being alive with at least six figures in a bank account.

In the quiet of his well-ordered world Tyler stared at the package, and suddenly it became a doorway. But a doorway to where? Outside the window a girl tottered past in high heels, laughing with her friends. Strange, he realised he had not heard a girl laugh like that in a very long time. He listened until the clacking of the heels died away. Inside that envelope was a man bound up and delivered – for death. That was the way they did it: like travel tour operators giving out some free giftpack. Expenses paid. Enjoy the trip. Got to shake that kind of shit, he warned himself. Introspection could really fuck your head up.

He fetched himself a beer from the fridge, took a long sip then tore the neck of the envelope.

Inside was a typewritten note, terse in its explanation: 'As promised, the details. Usual arrangement. Contact as per normal.' Another pull on his beer. At the bottom of the folded sheet was a capital letter 'S' by way of signature. He put down the beer can and tipped up the envelope. The video cassette fell into his hand: silent, shiny-black, label-less – no identifying marks. Tyler drew the curtains shut against the darkness outside, then locked the door and took the telephone off the hook. A symphony by Mahler was pouring from the hi-fi; he silenced it. He punched the *eject* button on the VCR, kicking out last week's middle-weight boxing bout, and fitted the new cassette. The jack plug of his headset gave a soft click as it connected with the socket.

Beer can in one hand and remote controller in the other, he pressed the *play* button and saw the screen fill with noise. The brightness from the screen sprayed the pale walls of the room. An interference line tracked down the tube as a gold plate appeared mid-frame; black letters announcing the legend ULTRA SECRET. At the bottom of the screen, for statistical purposes, more black lettering read COPY NUMBER 3 OF, but the final number was blanked out. Tyler snorted into his beer. Devious bastards.

The video film was a carefully edited, though essentially unimaginative, montage of newsreel and still photography taken from the international wire-service libraries and from SIS's own files. The spooks could always get the most difficult pictures – after all, they could get in anywhere they wanted to – but these showed nothing of the artistic composition or the spirit of those taken by professional photojournalists: the naked children blistered by napalm – that sort of thing.

It began with a touched-up version of a BBC documentary. Hardly top-secret stuff in itself,

118

just public-domain recent Libyan history. It was pretty safe garbage produced by some self-appointed Middle Eastern expert, with just the right amount of academic detachment and here and there the odd nugget of conscience, blaming Libyan nationalist fervour on years of Western exploitation in the ever fashionable reap-what-ye-sow-type subtext. Tyler recognised the voice-over from some TV programme, but could not identify it.

The pictures were on the whole good. There were long tracking shots of Azizyah Barracks, the military base in Tripoli where Qadaffi lived whilst in the capital. These had been rather obviously clipped and magnified by the Security Service laboratories to show as much detail as possible, but the resultant blurring was significant. Even computer-aided reconstruction could not provide much more surface detail.

The following segment showed scenes of the devastation wrought by the US air attacks on that base in April 1986 – stray dogs scavenging scraps amongst piles of rubble and burnt-out personnel carriers. There was the bombed-out shell of Qadaffi's own two-storey villa, in which his two sons had been wounded and his four-year-old adopted daughter killed. Tyler fast-forwarded over the hospital scene, cursing Stephenson for allowing them to include it. Which did they want: the man's head or sympathy for him?

There followed an interview with the Libyan President which was conducted through an interpreter, although Qadaffi spoke impeccable English; the President declared he had renounced that barbarian tongue. It showed a wild-eyed dangerous-looking man, who avoided the gaze of the British reporter or the lens of the camera. He was a religious man, he maintained, and an innocent victim of US aggression, though naturally he reserved the right to strike back mercilessly at the West, at his pleasure. Whenever angels looked the other way . . .

The quality of the film changed noticeably as an older interview was spliced in, one conducted by

119

Turkish Television soon after Qadaffi's rise to power. The colours were gaudier yet faded like those of a carpet exposed to strong sunlight, lending to the piece a downbeat feel. The film alternated between shots of the President's talking head and snips of the man's daily routine: time spent with the family, official visits and military inspections, volleyball and soccer games with the troops; Qadaffi visiting an experimental agricultural facility, grinning with pride from the driving seat of a locally manufactured tractor. It revealed the many moods of the man, and a fruit-salad fashion show of uniforms and medals.

As he watched, Tyler began to internalise the model; found he could spot the recurrent tics, like the way Qadaffi always carried his right shoulder slightly lower, his chin thrust high and forward. Like a homing missile, Tyler was acquiring his target.

The pictures had quite obviously been censored by Libyan media people in a clumsy attempt at PR. It was as if the Turkish cameras shooting upwards into the haughty, flaring nostrils were intent on profiling a saviour in the making. What bought such cooperation in a foreign broadcasting company, Tyler wondered.

He fast-forwarded again in frustration, creating a silent-screen comedy which Mack Sennet would have been proud of. Get to the meat, for Christ's sake. Just then the screen dissolved into captions, and he hit the normal *play* button.

The caption read PERSONAL SECURITY. Tyler put down his beer can and leaned forward with interest, elbows on knees, steepling his fingers. Slowly, like a long awaited sunrise, the face of Colonel Muammar al Qadaffi rose from the bottom of the screen until its olive-coloured majesty completely filled the frame – an official portrait. There was no mistaking that head: the springy coils of black hair and the broad, blunt jawline. The eyes carried that characteristic diamond-light glint of mania which commentators throughout the world had variously claimed as either religious or pathological in origin, depending on their own particular perspective.

'"Behold, the Tyrant's abhorr'ed head!"' breathed Tyler, suddenly excited and gripped by awakening dread. It was the only Shakespeare he could remember, but appropriate. His own part was, without doubt, to play the bloody role of Macduff, and in those brief seconds his eyelids were welded open by the power of that rough-hewn face and the leader's undeniable charisma. Yes, he could see that now, and it bore no resemblance to the mad-dog caricature of the Western press. What a joke they had made of him. Whistling in the dark, though. That face – it radiated energy like the rays from a gamma source. This was a man who had grasped hold of the lower branches and shaken the tree of history; one of those few touched by the hand of fate, and to whom is given the power to change the world. That really put the hook in Tyler.

A new voice spoke and he freed himself from the suspended moment with an involuntary shiver. It was a departmental voice which now took over the narrative; precise and characterless. Tyler imagined behind it an army of small, thin-lipped men in lab coats, drawing lots to decide who would provide the voice-over. He listened to the carefully chosen words.

'Ever since his seizure of power in the early hours of September 1969, President Muammar al Qadaffi has recognised the threat to his life from sources within as well as without his country. Indeed, it is said by those who have been in his confidence at one time or another, that he considers anyone born prior to the September revolution to be a potential threat to it because of their contamination with pre-revolutionary ideas.

'Despite official reports to the contrary, there is an active network of opposition groups, generally fragmented and dispirited, which have tried on numerous occasions to assassinate Qadaffi. These attacks have taken many different forms, the most spontaneous of which was a rather optimistic attempt to run down the President's limousine in its official motorcade on a desert road, and was made by a truck driver going in the opposite direction. Two motorcycle outriders were crushed to death in the incident, but the President was completely untouched. He is known to favour German or Italian cars – Libya owning a sizable interest in the Fiat car company – which are reinforced with over a ton of steel plate. The truck driver was never seen or heard of again.

'Other attempts have been far more serious and showed evidence of deliberate planning, if not entirely professional in their execution. Two such incidents, in May 1978 and October 1980, involved attempts by dissidents of the outlawed National Front for the Salvation of Libya (NFSL) to use firearms at close range in a public place. The first occurred whilst Qadaffi was arriving at the Russian Embassy in Tripoli as a dinner guest of the visiting Soviet Foreign Minister; when only the vigilance of a deadly accurate KGB killing group, who feared for the safety of their own man, saved the Libyan President. The second happened whilst he was opening an electro-generating plant outside Benghazi; when the Presidential Guard challenged two men acting suspiciously in a car park and were drawn into a fire-fight. The dissidents were said to be in possession of Italian-made machine-pistols, but they were no match for the President's crack troops. Later the bullet-riddled corpses were publically displayed in Tripoli's Green Square, the scene of many of Qadaffi's triumphs. Interestingly, although Benghazi is known to be a stronghold of elements still loyal to the old King, the incident was blamed upon "mongrel lackeys of the Western powers". A possible reason for this is Qadaffi's wish to preserve the illusion of peaceful unity within his country and to play down civilian discontent before the rest of the Arab world, thereby strengthening his claim to the mantle of senior Arab statesman – an honour unallotted since the death of President Nasser of Egypt.

'In 1984 Qadaffi's private helicopter was bombed . . .'

A black and white photograph was flashed onto the screen, showing the scorched black airframe of an executive transport helicopter. The landing gear was intact; it had been gutted on the ground. Ridges of foam from aviation fire-extinguishers were congealed onto the struts and cockpit frame. Tyler sucked in his breath sharply. This had never appeared in the Western press, nor had the covert operations grapevine given a whisper. Spooks only. Why?

'The bomb exploded minutes before the President was due to leave the compound of the Azizyah Barracks, killing the pilot and two groundcrew. It seems unlikely that this was due to poor timing; rather that a kind of warning shot across the bows was intended, perhaps originating from the Soviet Bloc. It will be remembered that in the previous autumn Qadaffi's virulent anti-communist rhetoric rang loud through the Arab world; and his denunciation of the occupation of Moslem Afghanistan by Soviet troops brought a frosty diplomatic response from Moscow. It is not inconceivable that the KGB made this their own highly eloquent warning against anti-Soviet politicking in the Middle East . . .'

About right, thought Tyler with a sardonic grin.

'Qadaffi now sees the major personal threat to himself as coming from foreign powers. Internal dissidents like the NFSL are containable, and represent no more than an irritation so long as he retains the support of the armed forces. Publicly he professes a lack of concern for his personal safety parallelled only by the Shi'ite truck bombers of Southern Lebanon. Privately, however, he is known to be far more worried, and his fears have frequently manifested themselves in paranoid outbursts and depressive moods which have induced actual physical illnesses. This is claimed as one reason for his periodic disappearances into the Sirte desert – the only place where he is said to feel truly safe.

'Since Qadaffi's rise to power, a succession of his personal bodyguards has come and gone. Lieutenant Hadad – dismissed for incompetence. Major al Wazir – imprisoned for negligence after the embarrassing incident at the Russian Embassy. Major Adam al Salam Rashid – fled the country; believed to be in the Sudan working with the leaders of the NFSL. Qadaffi is known to be particularly anxious for this lost man to return peacefully to Libya, or else he may face liquidation by a hit-team. Reports indicate that amongst Libyan army officers taking responsibility for the President's security is seen both as an honour and as a potential noose with which to hang oneself.

'Qadaffi's personal security is currently rated as extremely professional. He is usually protected by a screen of military personnel whenever he appears in public. Teams of plain-clothes officers form Close Protection Details to escort him within buildings and between vehicles. Transportation is usually by bullet-proof limousine with a breathtaking array of gee-whizz technology, or else by customised military helicopter whilst covering long distances. Doctors always accompany his entourage with a supply of blood and plasma for transfusion. This is largely as a result of techniques learned from the London-based International Risks Incorporated. IRI – the brain-child of Jeremy Fontainbleu, member of Lloyd's of London specialising in political risks – is a private security consultancy which boasts politicians, senior army and police officers as well as noted academics on its board of directors. Its advisers and instructors are almost exclusively troopers and NCOs head-hunted from 22 Special Air Service Regiment. For a time, during the currency of a CIA death threat, Qadaffi's bodyguard consisted entirely of ex-SAS officers and men. However, in 1984, after the debacle at the Libyan People's Bureau in London, their loyalty came into question and they were replaced once more by specially picked Moslem officers whose beliefs were more in line with the tenets of the President's own "Green Book".

'In 1985, Qadaffi hired CIA renegade James Earl Pincher. Pincher, a veteran of the CIA's Angola campaign, and sometime arms dealer, was recruited for his knowledge of the covert operations – usually referred to euphemistically as "wet jobs" – mounted by the Company. The CIA remains, in Qadaffi's mind at least, top of his threat list, in spite of much-publicised US Presidential orders forbidding "executive action". This association with Pincher did not last long; for six months later, whilst on a secret trip into Europe, Pincher disappeared – only to turn up a month later in Los Angeles, where he faced an indictment on twenty-three counts of espionage. He is now serving a sentence of twelve years in a Federal penitentiary.

'Second on Qadaffi's personal threat list is the seemingly superhuman Mossad. This threat is considered more imagined than real, exaggerating the relative importance of the Libyan leader in the Middle Eastern conflict, since he presents no immediate threat to the State of Israel unless he decides to use the atomic weapons he may have acquired, in which case Israel would, as always, strike swiftly.

'Today the primary responsibility for Presidential security is divided between the Presidential Guard of the Islamic Legion, which is an entirely separate branch of the armed forces, and a unit of oriental bodyguards . . .'

Tyler hit the *stop* button and pulled off the headset. He had heard enough for the moment. There were three hours of briefing on the tape: too much to assimilate in one sitting.

Christ, he would have to earn his money! Already there were some heavy numbers stacked against him. But the deal was undeniably good: the pot was sweet, and they had offered him a new identity and resettlement in a 'friendly' country, so he might even live long enough to spend what he had earned.

But it was no longer just the money; now it was something else. It was to do with the eyes, the face, the head of that man on the screen – waiting, brooding in the shadows of a fortress in North Africa. Bigger than life itself.

Liabilities? Tyler wondered how many copies of the cassette were in existence. How many people knew already? Too many, no doubt: British Security had been suspect for as long as anyone could remember. If penetrated by the Soviets, then why not also by the Arabs? Or why not a cosy exchange between the Soviets and their Arab clients? A whiff of possible treachery stung his nostrils. And if he entered Libya pre-announced, there would be only one end to the story: detention, torture and eventually – mercifully – death ... The ignominy of a televised public hanging Everything denied by all concerned, naturally.

Had not the money been good – so good he would never need to work again – maybe he would have told them where to shove it. But he was past that stage now: locked onto his target and launched; feeling more alive with danger than ever before.

From this moment he must banish all thought of failure. That was the first step in the journey towards success: think like a winner. Nor did he hate the face upon the screen. Rather he loved its rugged beauty, its awesome strength. A soldier loves strength. And somewhere in the infinite void Tyler's path had been chosen for him: his sole purpose, his own life, being dedicated to the death of another. A perfect balance: life for life.

There was a kind of beauty and peace in that knowledge, one that left no room for doubts or debate, fear or remorse.

Tyler slept soundly that night, knowing he would kill the Libyan.

TEN

AT 6 A.M. it was just getting light and Brady was waiting. He had parked the rented Ford Escort twenty metres from the house, where he could watch the front door. There were bare bushes and a short tarmac drive leading up to the five-bedroomed semi. No problem: a good view of anyone going in or out. At that time of morning The Spinney was deserted.

At 6.10 the milkman called and left one pint. A thin, attractive woman in a yellow dressing-gown opened the door to collect it, pausing in the morning chill just long enough to let the cat in. Upstairs a light came on in one window, and the diffused shape of a man in a white vest could be seen close behind the frosted glass – shaving. Brady put his gun inside the glove compartment and banged it shut.

At seven o'clock the newspaper boy arrived, folding a quality paper and forcing it through the letter-box. Behind the glass door a dark figure stooped and retrieved it from the hall carpet. Brady's pulse quickened; this was his man. He looked again at the photograph stuck to the dashboard with a blob of Blu-tack. The grey face it revealed was drawn and pointed like some Dickensian bookkeeper's. It was possible to believe nothing could escape the attention of such a man, yet in the watery eyes there was a look of dissipation – as of a man who was losing interest. Brady lost little time wondering why that should be; it was sufficient for him to know that his man might be the type to get careless, maybe even make mistakes. But, still, he reminded himself that Stephenson was a trained spook, and it would not be easy.

At 7.30 Stephenson left the house. Brady registered a positive ID as the man opened and closed the gate and came striding towards him along The Spinney, heading for the railway station. After a short interval Brady started the car's engine and followed at a distance. Good surveillance was an art, and he kept well back, avoiding any temptation to crowd in on his target. By now there was enough other traffic on the road to hide him, which was a plus.

At the railway station Brady parked in the commuters' car-park, bought a newspaper and stepped onto the platform with the London-bound commuters. He had come prepared and was wearing a dark-grey woollen overcoat, like scores of others waiting for the train. Quickly he looked around to locate Stephenson. He was standing almost at the far end of the platform. Was that *too* far if Stephenson decided to duck down the subway and out again? Should Brady move closer? No, watch it, boyo, this may be a paper-shuffler but he's bound to know the score. They don't let these fellows out of 'spy school' until they've learned how to wipe off a tail.

A moment later Stephenson turned and walked back along the platform slowly, as if taking in the scenery and the office girls, casually glancing at faces. Brady was now glad he had kept his beard; his photo must be one of those regularly circulated in MI5 and MI6. He raised his newspaper as Stephenson passed, and concentrated on the cricket scores in the latest

Australian test. Isn't that what these bloody English did on railway platforms?

Something was making the spook uncomfortable, though clearly he had not 'made' Brady's face.

As the train pulled in, Brady quickly bent down and tightened his shoelace until Stephenson had boarded, then he entered the adjacent carriage and continued reading his newspaper. The train jerked away slowly, gathered speed, and rolled on towards London while its bleary-eyed passengers sat in polite and vacant silence. Jesus, thought Brady darkly, just look at these zombies.

At Waterloo Station the flood gates opened and the echoing distortion of the tannoy woke those who had fallen asleep on the journey. Brady quickly fought his way clear of the carriage, ignoring protestations at his impoliteness. He had seen Stephenson's balding dome make a quick move for the door, and had to move fast himself if he was not to loose his target in the sea of office workers all surging towards the ticket barrier.

Having cleared the barrier, Stephenson came out into the station proper and darted suddenly into the gents. For a moment Brady was thrown into a panic. How many exits to the toilet? Was there another leading out directly into the street? He could not be sure: this was London, not South Armagh. Should he follow his man into the gents' toilet to make sure? If he did not, then Stephenson could take a back way out and leave him standing there like a mug.

He waited five long minutes, sure he had been wrong-footed, before the shiny head came bobbing back up the steps; this time the raincoat was folded over his left arm. Brady studied some concourse advertisements, using the glass case as a mirror to observe the man behind him. Another glance right and left, so nonchalantly, then the rabbit went down into the Underground. This time Brady followed immediately.

Stephenson rode the Underground to Embankment station then changed to the Circle Line and alighted at Westminster. The roads and pavements outside were now flooded with rush-hour traffic, allowing Brady to stay closer. The rabbit scooted across Whitehall, giving his daily sideways glance at the Houses of Parliament, and set out at a brisk pace across Westminster Bridge. As he followed, Brady watched the muddy, grey Thames crawl beneath. There was a cutting wind blowing across the water.

At the end of the bridge Stephenson made straight for the multistorey, glass tower building called Century House. That gave Brady all he needed to know. The information fed through to Belfast Brigade Headquarters had been accurate: this was one of SIS's people.

Had he been surveillance-aware? Brady wondered. Probably not. Just exercising routine security. But he had seemed mechanical and cursory in this attention to the details of field-craft; almost bored.

Brady took a cab back across the river and stopped off for breakfast in a Greek coffee shop, giving himself time to make some notes before his telephone calls. Quickly he jotted down the details of Stephenson's route in a black leather-bound Filofax. Train to Waterloo; tube to Embankment; then tube again to Westminster – not very imaginative. Brady knew that the security men had been warned to vary their routes to work, particularly those in high-risk employment, but Provisional operations revealed that only those on Irish soil took these precautions seriously. Stephenson would be no exception to that. Any deviation from his normal route would be an inconvenience, so he had settled for a few anti-surveillance drills on his way in. Brady snorted in derision: you could always rely on boredom to break down the opposition's vigilance.

When he had finished a breakfast of bacon, eggs and fried bread, Brady picked up the greasy phone and called a number in Kilburn. A middle-aged woman answered cheerily, quoting the name of her guesthouse. Yes, thought Brady, she was still there; and good as gold. Then he spoke the authorisation codes that would mobilise the Active Service Unit. The woman's response was pleasant: no need for further talk, she said; she would attend to everything. That meant contacting Shaunessy and O'Hagan; they would know to prepare a secure interrogation facility.

Stephenson passed an uneventful day. He lunched at the Royal Oak Tavern, just two streets away, then returned to his office to continue his latest budget reassessment. The last one had been politely thrown back at him by Halliday, with blue-pencilled comments about the size of the National Debt and the lack of flag days for Defence expenditure. Of course, Halliday's comments were more for the DG's benefit than Stephenson's own guidance. The effect of such niggardliness after the scope of the last two month's duties was numbing, to say the least.

If you can't take a joke, you should never have joined; it was a much-used saying in the service – and philosophical advice when faced with the frustrating, incomprehensible, contrary decisions one had to accept. Like the decision to refer Tyler's case upwards in the light of the Trafalgar Square business. Christ, the FO had been quick to distance themselves from that little lot! And at Century House the shutters were going up fast. Strangely enough there had been no further talk of Nimrod. Halliday had removed all papers which referred to the Libyan operation, and the fifth floor was now handling things. They supposedly had things well in hand, and he himself had become a victim of the 'need to know' principle. In the Service no one was told anything unless there was a definite operational need to know. This naturally placed severe limits on office small-talk; hence the conversational preoccupation of British career intelligence officers with cricket and sex.

132

Stephenson was only a section head, after all, and Nimrod was now being handled at Directorate level. Yes, it was a normal policy decision, but still he resented being frozen out, and the suggestion of mistrust. It was like a huge iron door clanging shut before his face – a further reminder that he was fifty-four years old without a mentor at Directorate level, and had therefore reached his professional ceiling.

Stephenson had joined the Secret Intelligence Service as a late entrant in 1964, after eight years in the Royal Navy. Those had been the best years of his life, the ones in HMS *Tamar,* Hong Kong, with only the odd typhoon or the occasional riot to spoil an otherwise unbroken sequence of junk trips, beach parties and mess nights. Practically every night there was a run ashore to the flashing neon jungle that hugged the Wanchai waterfront. They had been a rough and ready set of boys in those days, always rushing in where angels feared to tread. You could get drunk, laid, punched, have your laundry done, and your fortune told all in the same bar. A smile came to his lips as a series of half-remembered, naked bodies swam before his eyes. Vegas Pegg, that was her name, the one with the voice to drown out the *Jardine*'s noon-day gun. 'Ten dollar go topside! Ten dollar go topside! Come on, be nice. Buy one drink first, then go topside. Long time, short time, never mind. All same make very happy, yes?'

And so they had. Wise little bodies they had. Generous beyond words. But a lieutenant in Her Majesty's Navy also attends the right parties and meets nice girls on their summer vacations from English universities. He married one of them and made a home with her, but was unlucky enough to give her a nasty dose of clap. If memory served, that must have been caught from Baby, a Filipina whore who liked to play hostess to the US Seventh Fleet.

Divorce being out of the question, that left Joan with the moral leverage to do her worst. He found himself trapped, and riddled with guilt. No more runs ashore after that. It was quit the Royal Navy or else a life of unending misery. So he left the Navy for civilian life, armed with his knowledge of sea warfare and threats to the NATO alliance, a smattering of Mandarin and Russian, and a navigator's ticket.

Back in dear old England he took the Civil Service Selection Board and, God, they had put him through it. He had not had to work the old grey cells so hard since his days at Cambridge, where he had scraped through with a third in Modern History. He completed the board with a gentleman's pass and was recommended for a local government post. But there was only one job he was interested in: Foreign Intelligence. It was the thought of getting overseas again that attracted him.

When Foreign Intelligence interviewed him, they pointed out that the SIS was not, as popularly believed, a sort of masonic organisation for Cambridge alumni. Nevertheless they accepted him, for luckily the chairman of the interview panel was himself an old salt who had seen service in Hong Kong, and they spoke at length about mutual acquaintances and the odd bar on Kowloon side.

It took three months to complete his vetting and issue a formal offer of appointment. To his astonishment Joan was thrilled. Suddenly their sex life, a long grounded bird, took off again and soared to new heights.

Additionally Joan would enjoy the subterfuge at parties when she was asked what George did up in London.

'Something terribly stuffy, I'm sure,' she would answer with an airy wave of her gin and tonic, 'though he can't really talk about it, you understand. Defence of the Realm. It's a thankless task but *someone* has to do it.'

Thus she had made herself the centre of atten- tion at many a social gathering, with meaningful glances and knowing sighs: 'You don't know the half of it.' The truth was she did not know any of it, and that was the way George liked things. It was indeed the perfect job for a man who preferred to keep much of his life private and hidden from a voracious spouse. Her only real contact with the Service was the Christmas Ball, at which wives were paraded annually. Only stunningly trivial matters were discussed, and husbands slipped away to talk business.

Now he knew, with the last round of promotions, that his star was no longer in the ascendant. The promotion of a younger man over his head had been the final straw. A career notable only for its lack of mistakes or real risks had brought that little toad Bradshawe to the inside track, where the so-called 'flyers' are groomed for high office.

At five o'clock Stephenson cleared his desk and secured any sensitive material in his safe. His secretary secured the combination locks on the special filing cabinets and returned all class A files to Central Registry.

'Another day, another dollar.'

'Goodnight, Mr Stephenson.'

'Don't do anything I wouldn't do.'

'Chance would be a fine thing.'

Their little ritual.

Stephenson watched her slim bottom retreat along the corridor and finally disappear with the other nymphets into the elevator.

'A fine thing indeed,' he sighed.

As he left the great glass building he said good-evening to old Max, the MOD police officer on door duty, and stepped into the gloom. It was almost dark as he crossed Westminster Bridge, and the powerful hum of commuter traffic barely intruded on his thoughts. There was still one more meeting with Tyler, scheduled for tomorrow: matters to finalise before setting the man loose. Tyler was *his* agent, he told himself, and always would be. He was the best unattributable on their books, though a right bastard. The fact that they had kept him in spite of poaching from so-called allies was clearly due to Stephenson's own efforts. How quickly they forgot such things, he reflected with rancour.

The snatch team was waiting outside the church on Marlborough Crescent. Brady had picked the spot that morning, noticing a hundred-yard gap in the line of houses, and minimal street lighting at that point. Their car was facing away from the direction of approach, so they could use the rear-view mirrors without their faces being seen. Three young bucks, hard and dangerous, dressed in an assortment of donkey-jackets and combat smocks were waiting for Brady's order to pounce. They had each memorised the face in the photograph. They knew the target was a British spook, but no more.

Brady was standing at a bus-stop thirty yards beyond the car, with hands thrust deep into the pockets of his grey overcoat. His eyes gazed past the car to the turning into the Crescent – by a bare apple tree – where their man would appear. He stamped his feet against the cold, and prayed that Stephenson would not change his routine this evening.

They had stuck false number-plates on the front and rear of the vehicle in case anyone peeped out of their window into the otherwise deserted suburban street. It was a wise precaution, though in Brady's experience witnesses had a habit of being blind to such details. Fortunately it was so cold that there were no people hanging around the pavement.

Brady saw the shadow first, a long bobbing shape on the pavement by the apple tree, then came the click of metal-tipped heels. A moment later Stephenson turned the corner into view, his tall slim silhouette unmistakeable. Immediately Brady pulled on his leather gloves – the signal – and began to walk slowly towards the car, calculating his pace carefully. They met almost exactly at the car, Stephenson politely stepping aside to let the other man pass. A sideways glance alerted him to the danger, but it was too late. Brady turned on the ball of his foot and drove an upturned punch deep into the man's dorsal wall.

As Stephenson fell forward his left lung emptied, cutting off a half-strangled yelp of pain. His overcoat and jacket cushioned the blow a little, but it was aimed with such force and precision into the kidney region that the victim collapsed coughing to the concrete. Car doors flew open and they manhandled the crumpled body into the rear, pushing him down onto the floor. The engine roared into life. Brady swung himself easily into the front passenger seat but, before he could order the driver to go, he saw light spill from the opening door of the church vestry opposite. Framed in the doorway was the comfortable figure of an old priest. Instinctively Brady drew his pistol and aimed it at the man's face.

'Kill him, Liam!' the driver urged. 'Come on, man, for fuck's sake!'

The priest stepped forward to get a better view of the car, and Brady's eyes narrowed on the Catholic dog-collar . . . and on damnation.

'Say nothin', Father!' he hissed imploringly and kicked the driver into action. The car had travelled over a quarter of a mile before Brady let the driver switch on his headlights.

The old priest shivered in the cold for a minute, then he crossed himself and went back indoors.

ELEVEN

AT 5.15 THE SKY was growing dark. Joan Stephenson switched on the concealed strip-lighting in her kitchen, and then the two table-lamps in the sitting-room. She stopped for a moment to run an appreciative finger over the capice-shell lampshades, remembering a tiny shop on the beach front in Penang, and their first holiday together. The shades were so delicate that on the plane back to Hong Kong she had nursed them lovingly in her lap, afraid of damaging their fragile beauty. She sighed at the memory, and slowly began to lay the table for dinner.

There was a pie in the oven, carefully cross-hatched with her own shortcrust pastry. Assuming he arrived home at the customary time, it would be safe to begin steaming the vegetables now. It was her usual routine.

At 6.15 she checked her watch and pursed her lips in annoyance at his lateness. 'Oh, really!' Now she would have to reheat the meal and its impaired flavour would reflect upon her cooking. How thoughtless of him, after the time and effort she had lavished upon his favourite dish: best steak and lamb's kidney. She caught herself doing just what she had vowed not to. No, the meal might be spoiled but the evening would not be. It was to be a special evening, for his pleasure.

She took off her apron and examined her dress in the hall mirror. What she saw pleased her: stomach still flat enough for her to wear young clothes; and her face, though lined, still retained a youthful bloom that brought stares from other men. True, the men were older now, but they still stared, thank God. Satisfied, she patted her soft blonde hair and sat down in front of the muted television set, flicking the pages of a magazine.

As Channel Four News ended she realised he was over an hour late. Suddenly she was very angry. How thoughtless of him not to call if he was going to be quite so late! How thoughtless of him to spoil things for her when she had tried so hard. So be it. She slammed the steaming pie into the refrigerator.

After another hour she was confused, but continued watching television. Then, before she realised, it was almost ten o'clock – Horlicks time. Now she was worried. It was a cold, unfriendly night, not fit for a dog to be out in. It was no weather for gadding around, and her husband did not usually stop off in pubs on his way home. Finally, at midnight, with some reluctance she picked up the phone and called Halliday at home.

The man's weary voice announced his telephone number cautiously.

'Peter, it's Joan.'

'What's the matter? Why are you calling at this hour? You sound distressed.'

'It's George.'

'What do you mean? Christ, you haven't told him anything. I thought we agreed –'

'No, for Heaven's sake! Look, I didn't know who else to call. I'm beside myself. George didn't come home this evening.'

'Oh, I see.' Halliday's throat muscles relaxed and his voice recovered the calm, businesslike authority she recognised so well.

'I thought you might know if he was working late this evening. He didn't mention anything about it this morning. You haven't put him on some surveillance nonsense out of spite, have you?' Her voice was strident with anxiety.

He ignored the insinuation, which only their past intimacy made her bold enough to utter.

'As far as I'm aware, he left the office at the usual time. Just a minute . . .' He put down the leather-bound book he had been reading and listened for a moment to the stillness of the house, checking that his wife was still sleeping soundly upstairs. 'Look, shall I come over?'

'No, not now, please. Oh, Peter, where could he be? It's just not like him. You know what he's like; he never moves from his hearth. I'm really worried.'

'All right, calm down. Let's think this through. He didn' mention anything about meeting old friends, did he?'

'No, I would have remembered.'

'Not had any blazing rows this past week?'

'Just our usual – hardly spectacular.'

'Sounds just like George.'

'Don't be such a bastard,' she snapped, her conscience suddenly pricked. 'Haven't you done enough to him already?'

'You've hardly been the doting spouse,' he retaliated without thinking.

There was a cold silence before she found her tongue again. 'You really are a bastard, aren't you, Peter?'

'I suppose so,' he said grimly. 'That's what they pay me for. Look, it doesn't help matters if we quarrel.'

'I thought you'd know what to do. Aren't there procedures when a spy goes missing? Halliday was irritated by her assumption, though there was a grain of truth in what she said. True, he did have official responsibilities in such circumstances, but at this early stage it was better not to jump to conclusions – just stick to procedure.

'George is not a spy, my dear. He is a Grade Five administrative officer at the Foreign and Commonwealth Office. Try to remember that in case newspaper men ever come knocking at your door. Have you tried the local police station?'

'No, you don't think . . . an accident?'

'Perhaps, but not necessarily. They might have found him blind drunk and peeing in someone's flower-bed. There are hundreds of reasons why the police might come across him. No point in worrying too much at this stage. You give them a try, and I'll call the operations desk back at the office. There might just be something going on I haven't heard about.'

'I hope so. It's probably nothing, as you say.' She was trying to reassure herself.

'By the by,' he said, as if changing the subject, 'I don't like having to ask this, but is it possible there could be another woman – perhaps even another man?'

'I'll pretend I didn't hear that.' The very thought was too outrageous to consider. Not George.

Her anxiety was beginning to affect Halliday with doubts. 'Well, at least we can check one thing.'

'What's that?' she answered, still thinking about the possibility of George having a hidden life with another, possibly younger woman.

'Where does he keep his passport?'

'In the bureau along with the insurance policies and all the other bumph.'

'Would you go and see if it's there now?'

She put down the handset and went to check. In the interval he listened to the random ticking on the line. He could hear also the sound of rain gusting against his window-panes, and he asked himself why that fool Stephenson was not at home with the woman he himself suddenly longed to bed once more. What top-grade files had crossed the man's desk these past few months? Was it possible he was actually going rotten?

A click as the handset was lifted once more.

'Yes. Yes, it's still here.' Joan Stephenson was almost exultant with relief. 'I have it in my hand now. Do you want the number?'

'No, thank you,' said Halliday, both relieved and strangely disappointed. 'That's fine. We'll leave it for now. Don't forget to try the police station – and inform the enquiries desk if he turns up at home.'

Joan Stephenson was prickled by Halliday's cool attitude. He no longer seemed the man she had believed she was inviting into her arms and into her bed. Though a better lover, he was somehow less of a man than the one she had married – less feeling, less caring, less human. At that moment she just wished George would come home – would fling his arms around her and kiss her in his awkward way. Then they would laugh about the burnt offering in the refrigerator.

Instead she called the local police station and gave them a full description of her missing husband. The desk sergeant checked his lists of reported casualty admissions from traffic accidents, but found no one who matched the description.

The lights would be burning all night.

Halliday was now equally worried, but for different reasons. Anything that threatened his current operation was a source of concern. He wanted no screw-ups that could be laid at his door – not with a major reorganisation in the offing and a vacant desk in Fifth Floor Directorate up for grabs. The

DDG was a powerful ally but a dangerous enemy, and any 'embarrassment' that found its way to the old man's office would not be forgiven. Christ, he had seen too many sent to the wall in the past. Once out of favour, never back in again – that's the way it went. The Northern Ireland desk and oblivion! Never had he dreamed that Stephenson could become so crucial to his career.

Halliday's first move was to alert the duty-controller at Six's operations room, with instructions to follow standard procedures for missing officers. Those same procedures – Director General's Standing Orders – dictated that he return to headquarters to make a physical check of all files booked out of Central Registry in Stephenson's name. The Duty Security Officer was called back in to produce the sealed envelope that contained the combinations to Stephenson's safe and each of his filing cabinets. Hardly relishing the tedious job ahead of him, Halliday plucked the magnetic red reminder strip from the safe door, and replaced it inverted so that it now read OPEN.

By 4 a.m. he had wearily located and checked off each file against the computer-printed list. None of the folios was missing, nor were there any unauthorised files present. The only surprises were a copy of *Military Modelling* and a back issue of *Penthouse* which looked as if it had done the rounds a bit. This successful search did nothing to remove his suspicions: with photocopiers and fax machines all over the building, to say nothing of miniature cameras, only a bloody fool would lift an original document. Still, procedures had to be observed.

The Duty Controller had by now circulated details and a facsimile picture of the missing man to all out-stations and to all ports of entry, for future checking by Special Branch. On Halliday's orders, surveillance section supervisors were called in at six o'clock to check the hundreds of photographs taken

143

daily of persons entering and leaving Sov-Bloc diplomatic premises. Stephenson's face was not amongst them. All available officers in the operations room then divided up and telephoned casualty departments in the Greater London area. No George. In Kingston-upon-Thames the night-shift officers were cruising the streets and checking the length of the river, intrigued by Special Branch's request for assistance. But nothing was found.

At 9 a.m. a technical team appeared at number 17, The Spinney in an unmarked green transit van with a large aerial. Joan Stephenson noted cynically that Halliday had not bothered to turn up himself. She was by now too tired and too shocked to protest when they asked for permission to search the house.

'What is it you expect to find?' she asked lamely as they trooped into her sitting-room laden with metal cases that rattled and an assortment of electrical leads and probes.

'Can't really say, madam,' replied a technician wearing what looked like a hearing-aid plugged into a vacuum cleaner. 'If you could just keep clear of the areas we're working on, we'll be finished that much quicker. Thank you.'

They found no evidence of treason: no irregularities in his financial dealings; no hint either of intended flight in his wife's back account during the past month. There was a holiday planned in the Canaries – but, then, British winters did that to people.

At noon the DDG, who had read the morning SITREP with dismay, his grey eyes narrowing with subdued rage, sent for Halliday. For answers.

Halliday eased himself gingerly into the straight-backed chair before the old man's desk, trying to fathom the degree of blame which might attach to himself should the sewage hit the air-conditioning.

'Missing for eighteen hours now, Peter. What do you have?' The old man continued writing, peering through half-moon spectacles with mottled brown frames.

'No hard evidence of intention, I'm afraid, Sir.'

'You do well to be afraid, sir,' the DDG cut in quickly, without looking up – quietly menacing like a Victorian parent disciplining his offspring. 'Give me the likeliest explanation, then. Damn it, I can't have my people disappearing like extras in some Star Trek episode!' He stopped writing for a second, pen poised, and peered over his glasses. That look was enough. It said more than the screams and ravings of other senior men.

Halliday gave a shrug of submission.

'I can paint it up in a verbose report, but it comes down to just two possibilities.'

'And they are?'

'Kidnapping or suicide.'

The old man stopped writing and threw his pen onto the blotter almost petulantly.

'You know the importance of the little business we've been discussing. Everything has been agreed with the other firms, and now we're all relying upon you, Peter. There's a lot riding on it – for all of us. Only a handful of people alive know what we are planning, and suddenly one of them vanishes. I'm concerned, Peter – so should you be. I say again, this is very, very important. Now I'm going to ask a question and I want the proper answer, do you understand?'

'Yes, sir.'

'Very well, then, here's the question. Should I, after all this planning and all we have risked, after going cap-in-hand to the Americans and asking for favours, should I now call off the operation?'

Halliday looked at the sagging jowls of the old man who wanted to go out fighting. Clearly he was afraid for himself; he feared – as they all did – the ignominy of oblivion. But he realised that the DDG knew Halliday himself inside out – his aspirations, his dreams – and he sensed that from now on it would be every man for himself.

'Absolutely not, sir.'

The old man smiled. 'Thank you, Peter. I knew I could rely on your judgement.'

TWELVE

STEPHENSON BLINKED AWAKE, with crusts on both eyelids and a pain throbbing in the pit of his stomach. As coherence returned he smelled, then saw, a small pool of vomit, like that of a baby, next to him on the pillow.

It was morning.

The next thing he saw was the pockmarked face of the man who had used the hypodermic on him. That face was now indelibly printed in his subconscious, along with those of the other heavies with whom he had struggled briefly in the back of the car – before his brain turned to jelly.

There were no hoods to disguise them.

It was this fact above all that scared him. They had snatched him right off the street, and now they were calmly smoking and chatting in that dingy room, making no attempt to hide their faces. Clearly they were not afraid of being identified, so obviously intended to kill him.

He watched the pockmarked face retreat, then came an Irish voice heavily coated with scorn: 'Hey, Liam, it's awake.'

He saw he was lying on a stripped-down single bed in a room scarcely one step up from a Salvation Army flop-house. Against one wall there was a square washbasin with an A4-sized mirror fixed above it. The porcelain that had once been white was now mottled brown and grey. From beyond the sash window his ears caught the scream of a train passing close by; a bitter wind shook the thin flowered curtains.

Slowly the fog began to clear from his brain. The three men were now watching him, closely. The one who had jabbed him with the hypodermic perched at the end of the bed; the other two sat astride straight-backed chairs, one of them swaying backwards and forwards on its rear legs. Stephenson's mind panicked: there was only one reason to kidnap an intelligence officer.

For God's sake get a grip, he urged himself, as his eyes darted left and right. Think clearly. Assess the possible escape routes. Don't give up hope . . . Who's in charge? Where are their weapons? The lessons of the combat survival instructors at Dartmouth swam in his head. All serving officers in the SIS had undergone an escape and evasion course. That was followed by training in resistance to interrogation, in which the pursuers, great hulking paratroopers, had run them to earth and dragged them off hooded and trussed like turkeys. He had come through the test successfully, but the experience had chilled him to the bone. The subsequent depression and the nightmares were a normal reaction, they had said – but *this* was for real now, and he was not prepared for the immobilising fear that clung in his gut.

Ninety per cent of survival is mental attitude, he had been told, but the words might be a foreign language for all their meaning now. He had a mental flashback to the tough, uncompromising face of the SAS major who had pronounced these survival maxims, using an overhead projector and felt-tipped pens.

But what were his real chances? Was there a hope of rescue?

It was already daylight, which meant Joan would have spent a long night tossing and turning, checking the bedside clock and listening for his key in the lock. She would be frantic by now, but she was a clever girl. She would certainly have called his office.

Suddenly another thought occurred to him: would Joan really even care if he did not come home? Wasn't this a golden opportunity for her? No, please God, she's my wife!

He struggled to control this irrational doubt – no matter how much she might despise him she would have made that vital phone-call. Yes, by now they would be looking for him. The whole machinery would kick into gear: retracing his movements yesterday; rousting agents and their informers. But how long before they found him?

The room was cold and depressing: a bare fifteen feet by ten, with mouldy wallpaper, damp and peeling at the skirting. On the floor was a fading and worn rough-pile brown carpet that in a dog would have been diagnosed as having mange. The flower-patterned curtains were half drawn back, revealing a large sash window largely obscured by old lace curtains the colour of nicotine. They stuck to the condensation on the pane. The bedroom door was heavy and old-fashioned, but had a shiny new brass mortice-lock. Apart from the bed, the only furniture was a small collapsible table with a brown wood-grain formica top and the two chairs occupied by his kidnappers.

They watched him sit up. He shivered, then pressed his back against the wall where the headboard should have been but felt only the cold kiss of damp wallpaper. They had taken away his shoes and socks and shirt, but had left him his trousers and vest. His feet looked absurdly big, and white with the cold.

'Have a good sleep, did you, George?'

For some reason he could not explain, he winced when the bearded man in the parka used his name, though the voice was civil enough. The two thugs wearing combat jackets watched him like Dobermans, the heavier one chewing gum like a young Marlon Brando. Stephenson rubbed at his back where the first blow had landed. It hurt like hell. Was that kidney damage? Was that why his insides felt like jelly? He was not sure whether he needed the toilet. Then there was the nausea, which kept coming in waves; but perhaps that was a result of the injection.

Go on, he told himself, don't antagonise the bastard – make some response.

'Where am I?' he managed with firmness. Yes, it was lame, he knew, but it was a start.

He received a grin from the man in the parka, and the green wolfish eyes devoured him.

'That's not important. But you should get one thing straight before we start. This location is not known to your own people, so no one will come to help you. Believe me, George, I wouldn't want you to hold out any false hopes. That would only make our job more difficult.'

'What job?' he quizzed.

'You're here until we've finished with you.' The man stood and walked to the window, a broad silhouette in the semi-dark of the room.

Stephenson looked down at his own skinny body and the clean, white vest. There was a small hole visible near the hem. He placed a selfconscious hand over it.

Before we start! That's what he had said. Stephenson's heart thumped.

'You are George Stephenson, intelligence officer with the British Secret Intelligence Service – isn't that right, George?' He had turned to face the bed.

Stephenson moistened his lips but said nothing.

'Isn't that right?' the man tried again. 'Well, no matter. We know who you are. You see, we have very good information, just like yourselves.'

'Who's "we"?' Stephenson said in a half croak.

'You know who we are, George. We're your worst nightmare: the Republican Army. Surely you knew that from the start?'

The gum-chewing thug began to bite on his finger-nails which were already down to the quick. His fingers were large and clumsy, like beef sausages. Stephenson judged both of the thugs to be under twenty, and they had the looks and tattoos of soccer hooligans.

'Maybe that's a bit of a backhanded compliment, was it? – you not being able to place my accent. Or were you just being cute? I've travelled about a bit, that's for sure – lost a touch of the old brogue here and there. You're in very privileged company, George. Your people have been after me for a wee while now, and here's you with me all to yourself.'

Stephenson frowned.

'Don't you recognise my face? Try eliminating the beard. Remind you of anyone? Try a side view,' he said, offering his profile. 'The soldiers know me well enough. Every birthday they send a card to my mother's place, saying "Enjoy the birthday – it could be your last". They'd just love to get me for those three soldiers I did last year, the bastards!'

Stephenson shook his head in bewilderment. The two men watching started to share a grin, but thought better of it.

The man's sudden irritation showed in a piercing stare. 'The name is Liam Brady, from South Armagh. Yes,' he continued, seeing a flicker of recognition in those watery grey eyes. 'Now you know me.'

It was true. Stephenson had seen that name on the circulation lists: known Provo gunmen. it was one of the names on the ten-most-wanted list during the 'black' alert following that Oxford Street mess. But it was three years since Stephenson had worked on an Irish case himself, and back then Brady was just another punk out to win a name for himself. What the hell did he want here on the mainland?

'You listening to me, George?'

Stephenson felt the man's irritation rising, and instinct told him to cooperate. He gave a quick conciliatory nod.

'As I was saying,' Brady continued, 'you'll be feeling a bit dry. That's the injection. Nothing to worry about there. I'll get you a cup of tea to wet your whistle.' His thick beard stretched with a grin.

'No, thank you,' said Stephenson defensively – then, seeing their sardonic smiles, he cursed himself for the nervousness his blurted answer had betrayed.

'I'll get you one anyway. Might as well be civilised about this. That's the way the English like things, isn't it?' A jerk of the head sent the quiet thug out of the room. Brando grinned and continued struggling with the nail on his little finger. He had split and peeled it across to where it disappeared into the soft quick. Stephenson watched, his face contorting in anticipation of the snap as the nail tore free in the man's teeth.

'You're very interesting to us, George. I hear you know what's what. You must know some interesting stories. Tell us some things we don't already know – things you'd like to get off your chest. We've got plenty of time.'

Their eyes were on him as Stephenson shrank shoeless and sock-less against the wall. He knew only too well the techniques used by the IRA Active Service Units. They fell broadly into the category 'unsophisticated', and relied largely on the manipulation of pain. But slowly they were incorporating aspects of 'psy-war' into their armoury. Their most recent concession to psychological technique was to deny the prisoner lavatory and washing facilities. It had been proved that the resulting foul-smelling wretch became de-humanised that much quicker, and hence more vulnerable and more prone to breakdown.

Silence gathered in the dismal room. Another train screamed past the window. There was a soft snap and Brando's body jerked in pain as the fingernail tore free and blood began to ooze. The young thug stared in fascination as a thin red line formed across his finger. Stephenson had flinched at the sudden movement, his hands immediately covering his face against a blow that did not come. He lowered his hands in shame.

The door opened and the second thug returned with a tray of steaming mugs of tea and placed it on the formica table.

'Here, drink this,' said Brady with cold fire in his eyes. 'And when you've finished it, then we'll start.'

At these words Stephenson almost broke into tears. He had been born with a most unfortunate combination of personality traits: a tendency towards neuroticism together with an over-active imagination. For him the torture had already begun.

He made the tea last a very long time. He sipped it slowly, watching the specks of undissolved powdered milk, the brown crack in the rim, wondering all the while how these three hostile animals would get to work on him. From nowhere Brando produced a large monkey-wrench and began tossing it in the air and catching it again. Once he dropped it, and it fell with a heavy clunk to the floor. Stephenson was not feeling at all brave sitting there on the bed in his vest with the little hole in it. His body seemed so vulnerable, almost fragile in contrast to that metal. How much pain could he take? Why should he have to take any of it? What did they want to know? What could he safely tell them? The most important thing he currently knew about was the Libyan business, the stuff about Tyler, but it could not be that. He would never tell them about that – no matter what they did. But why shouldn't he talk? It was only a bloody job after all, and they didn't pay him enough to cover this bloody kind of business! But no. No! They were going to kill him anyway. Talking would not save him.

All too soon the tea was gone and he stared in disbelief at the empty cup. Brady stood up and stretched, like a builder's navvy finishing his lunch-break and preparing to return to work. He heard a small moan escape the SIS man on the bed. Jesus, is this what they send against us, thought Brady. First he ordered the cups to be collected and removed, thereby prolonging the agony. Stephenson found himself staring at his feet once more as the Irishmen moved into his peripheral vision. His long, white toes were trembling now and he noticed, absurdly, that the yellow toenails needed cutting. Oh please, he prayed, if there is a God in heaven . . .

But it started, anyway.

A nod from Brady and the two combat-jackets picked up the prisoner like a rag-doll and slammed him against the wall, forcing the air out of his lungs. When he hit the floor, they picked him up and punched him in the face five, or was it six, times – until his nose broke and blood blossomed onto the vest with the little hole in it.

At first he screamed out loud, but by the time they finished with his face he had learned that it hurt more with his mouth open. They threw him back on the bed, whimpering and spitting blood and mucus between his laboured breaths. Brady came close to inspect the damage.

'Fair bit of swelling there, George. Looks like you've lost a couple of pegs, too. Not bad for a man of your age – all your own are they?' His voice was patronising, like that of a game-show host. He returned to his seat. 'I won't bother asking you again, yet,' he said inspecting his fingernails. 'Not because I don't think that hurt – I know it did – but because you'll tell me everything in good time. You see, these two earn their living on building sites; they've got hands like bricks. They make a little money on the bare-knuckle circuit, don't you, boyos? Unlicensed prize fights. They know their business. Your face looks terrible, George. The wife would hardly know you. But I reckon that first

154

lot came as a bit of a relief after all the anticipation – particularly for a man like you, George. You look like a worrier. Are you a betting man? Here's a bet. I bet you right now you're wondering how much of this you can take.'

There was a moan of rage from the bed which hardly sounded like the 'bastards' it was meant to be.

They beat him every half hour for the next four hours, concentrating on a different area each time, in rotation: face, stomach, back, feet. Brady called the tune. He knew how far they could go just before the man blacked out, and he was left to recover while the numbness wore off. Then they began again.

Stephenson endured the initial beatings by retreating into a semi-trance, where his mind stood outside the sickening pain. He was back in the arms of Baby, the loving whore with the short, golden limbs that parted and engulfed him. He crawled into a crevice inside his own head and clung to hope with more passion than he knew he possessed.

After four hours they took away the rest of his clothes. That was the end of the softening-up. Brady was ready to begin in earnest.

The curtains were closed now and a single, fly-stained sixty-watt bulb hung from the ceiling. Blood had congealed over Stephenson's face, and he wheezed occasionally. On Brady's orders they had removed the bed sheet and placed a plastic dust sheet under him.

The SIS man lay flat on the bed, his head lolling back, the skin taut against the point of his Adam's apple. The blood-red streaks of thinning hair were plastered across his head in hard points, giving him the appearance of a decorated participant in some barbaric tribal ritual. The room was still cold, so between the thickening welts and bruises his skin was raised in rough goose-flesh. His fingers and toes were faintly tinged with blue and his genitals had all but shrunk away. At first he had made a vague attempt to preserve his dignity by covering his

155

groin with his hands – the way he had earlier hidden the hole in his vest – even while they rained down blows on his face; but in the end the pain was so great that his only course was to relinquish personal ownership of that frail body. Now he could not even remember where he was. The only thing that existed for him was the awful regularity of the pain – that and the meagre warmth radiating from the lightbulb overhead.

Brady needed answers for the chiefs. They had sent *him* here to get them, even though he was 'hot', so it had to be something big. They had hinted that this spook knew something about the Libyan operation the British were planning; that maybe he even knew what had happened to Terence Lynch, who had disappeared off the face of the earth – left Liverpool in a Saab Turbo and was never seen again. Some people were even making unkind suggestions that Lynch was the 'supergrass' they had been trying to root out but Brady refused to believe this. Could the man he had shared a cell with in the Maze really have gone over to the British? No, it was just bullshit! He had gone through internment with Terence Lynch; they had talked and planned and fed off each other during the long months behind the wire. Lynch was a good man, a man with heart and guts. Brady would stake his life on Lynch not being a 'tout'.

For Brady this spook was now a chance to find the answers to all the questions.

He pulled his chair up to the bed and leaned close to the bloody face.

'George, can you hear me?' It was like the voice of a doctor.

A grunt in response.

'Say "Yes, Liam". Say it, George.'

Stephenson coughed; then more laboured breaths. 'Yes . . . Liam.' Another cough.

'George, you've been good – do you hear me? You've done well. They'd be proud of you, all of them.'

A faint grimace of a smile could not find the strength to break on the spy's lips, and it perished before birth.

'George, I'm going to let you talk now, because I really believe that you're ready. I didn't believe it before when you said so. I admit I'm a bit of a cynic sometimes. But now I see you're sincere, so I'm going to let you tell me everything.'

'Everything?' The voice was tinged with relief, as if finding peace after a bitter struggle. Brando, who had long since run out of fingernails, sat swathed in a blanket unable to believe the depth of intimacy here achieved between the man from across the water and his prisoner.

'Yes, everything,' said Brady, stroking the poor man's forehead. 'You've been very good. You know I don't want them to hurt you anymore. Poor, poor, George. I won't let them hurt you if you talk to me. That's fair, isn't it? You don't have a friend in the world, do you George? Only me. That's right, isn't it?'

There was real warmth in Brady's voice. It was a nourishing flame that beckoned to Stephenson from out of the cold. He wanted very much to let go and cling to the warmth. For long seconds he said nothing, then his eyes screwed up tight and his mouth opened as if in silent scream. The thugs exchanged looks of disbelief as a heart-rending cry of despair escaped from the mouth of the SIS section head. His face changed in that instant: no longer old, it was the face of the young boy who has fallen from the apple-tree and skinned his knee; the face of the lost child who on finding the comfort of his mother's arms breaks down and weeps with despair. Brady lifted him into a sitting position.

'I can't. You know that,' he muttered between sobs.

Brady sighed a deep theatrical sigh, as if at the futility of it all.

'What are we to do with you, George, eh? I thought you were a smart fella.'

'Don't let them . . . Please don't let them, Liam. Not any more, for God's sake.'

'I don't know whether I can do that for you, George.' Brady knew then he had gained that crucial relationship. His man had drawn on all his reserves and had reached the bottom of the barrel. He needed someone else to be responsible for him. He now clung to the irrational belief that Brady was his only safe protection from the pain of the two savage beasts he controlled. It was the classic hard and soft approach, and Stephenson knew about it better than most. But this was the first time he had been on the receiving end, and his logic and reason had long since committed suicide.

'Please, Liam.' He blinked away tears, looking imploringly into Brady's hooded green eyes. How strong he seemed then to Stephenson. This man would protect him from it all, if anyone could.

'Please!'

'All right, then. Tell me something about your work. Anything will do.'

Stephenson thought for a moment.

'The regular doorman – his name is Max.'

Sunshine radiated from Brady's face.

'That'll do for a start. There, that wasn't so bad. Good, good. Get this man a blanket.' Brady took the woollen blanket from Brando and placed it around Stephenson's shoulders. Childlike, the older man pulled the blanket around himself and bent close to the warmth of Brady's body. Brady, sitting on the edge of the bed, placed an arm around the heaving shoulders and hugged the desperate, pathetic figure to himself. Out of control now and totally confused, Stephenson opened his heart and cried like a baby.

A shiver went through Brando. He had never seen anything like it. A kind of emotional-rape victim was now rocking gently backwards and forwards in the arms of his assailant. If he was not seeing it with his own eyes he would never have believed it.

Brady was gently shushing his man now. He looked away from the bed towards the two younger men, and victory shone in his eyes like the glint of a straight-edged razor.

'It's going to be all right now, George. I promise you.'

THIRTEEN

RAIN WAS FALLING steadily, like tears for the dead, as Tyler swung the Mitsubishi Shogun jeep into Berkeley Square, parked it, and dived for the doorway that bore the copper name-plate of Springfield Exports. It was a pretty upmarket area, with the kind of rents that kept out the riff-raff, but it was the only place to get the kind of quality service he demanded. The ground floor of the building housed an automobile showroom specialising in expensive toys for the rich. Through the rain-flecked window he could see the clean curves and glitzy colours of the expensive beasts rotating under arc-lights: Mercedes, Ferrari and Porsche. He slapped the rain from his ski-jacket and made his way past the wall-mounted security camera, up a single flight of stairs and into the reception area. The pretty Sloane behind the desk looked up from her copy of the London *Tatler*. Immediately she recognised the dark good looks and the squareness of the shoulders, and she released the lock on the armoured glass door with a quick stab of her foot switch.

'Good morning, Mr Fleming,' she said, smiling. 'Nice to see you again.'

'You, too, Emma,' he returned pleasantly. 'Is he free?'

'Just a moment, I'll see.' She picked up the handset and punched three numbers. As she waited for a reply her eyes appraised him as if she was an art critic and he a piece of sculpture. Unabashed he folded his arms and turned to admire the fine prints upon the wall: Derby winners all, sleek and nut-brown; creatures built for speed, he reflected, just like young Emma. He stepped from each picture to the next, aware of the bright green eyes that followed him, and something inside of him was grateful for the attention.

'Are you going to share your little secret?' she said with a hint of spice in her polished voice.

Tyler turned and smiled. Was he so obviously a man with a secret?

'Oh, what secret is that?'

'Well, still waters run deep, they say' – she was suggestive now, playing with him the way beautiful girls were born to – 'but we'll start with that neat little trick of the healthy bronze colour you always keep, even in midwinter. What really pisses me off,' she continued in her Cheltenham girl's prefect voice, 'is that the evidence of my own fortnight in the Seychelles is gone within ten days of coming home. A full-length mirror can be an awfully depressing feature to a bedroom.' The long shapely legs and small firm breasts belied this last remark.

'In your case I find that hard to believe,' he said at last, and saw the selfconscious pleasure she took in the heavily solicited compliment. Her eyes dropped to the desk as her call was answered, and she announced his arrival. She replaced the handset.

'You're to go straight in.' Then seeing such an opportunity passing her, by she half blurted, 'Don't think I've forgotten about your secret – I'm not easily put off. Why don't you tell me about it some-time?'

'Yes, maybe dinner one night?' he murmured,

161

more from a desire to spare her feelings than out of conviction.

She scribbled something onto the back of a business card and offered it with what might have seemed an air of studied indifference – the way she had probably once sentenced first-formers to extra prep. As he took it he felt the smoothness of her cool fingers touch his hand. For a moment he regarded her, stirred to excitement and weighing the proposal. The girl was young, and her body held the promise of urgent love-making. Why not? he asked himself, but the reply was all too obvious: he did not need complications. There would be time enough for lovers when it was all over.

'Thanks,' he said taking the card. 'Yes, I'd like that. Sometime.' But as he put the card in his pocket they both knew there would probably be no phone-call. Suddenly she felt very foolish and brash, and her head dropped forward so that the red hair fell across her face. Without looking up from the papers on her desk she attempted to regain her equilibrium by dismissing him.

'You know which door. Please go in. He's waiting for you now.'

Hamid rose from his desk and came over to greet him with a warm vigorous handshake, then steered him towards the twin sofas that faced each other across a low table inlaid with ebony and mother-of-pearl.

'It's been some time now, John.' He beamed, offering a silver box that contained cigarettes wrapped in Wedgwood blue.

As usual Tyler declined.

'Oh yes, I always forget. You don't. Disgusting habit, it's true, but ...' Hamid took a cigarette for himself, shrugged theatrically and lit it with a gold lighter whose ping, as he opened it, said quite distinctly Du Pont. He inhaled deeply and the smoke he blew was delicately perfumed. 'The ladies prefer it,' he had once explained.

Hamid was the face, the spirit, the very essence of Springfield Exports. For some he was a mystery. No one knew for sure how much he or the company were worth, though those who attended the parties given at his Kensington place – ironically only a stone's throw from the burnt-out shell of the Iranian Embassy – could attest to both his lavish generosity and to the opulence of his lifestyle. To most of those who met him, Hamid was a displaced Iranian who sold quality cars to the oil-rich, affected that sort of Omar Sharif gambler-womaniser image favoured by his generation of Middle Eastern men, and bragged unceasingly of his sexual prowess.

But to those who knew him better, those originally introduced and vouched for by a reputable source, there was quite another persona – that inhabiting the lucrative world of power-brokering through the subterranean world of the illegal arms dealer. Hamid supplied high-quality experimental or black-listed weaponry of all kinds and, according to his own discreet claims, could deliver anywhere in the world. His company could supply or commission customised pieces of the exact precision and specification that is often demanded by clients willing to pay handsomely for a bespoke service and absolute anonymity. On occasion he had hinted that even the Iron Curtain was no bar to his activities; and this fact fuelled his paranoia that within the greasy covers of those black books thumbed through at airport immigration desks, his name was prominently featured with stars 'or whatever those silly people use'.

Hamid had moved westward twelve years previously, whilst still in his twenties. He came looking for sex with blonde women of immense proportions – he made no bones about that. Fortunately his family had been wealthy enough to give him the start he required whilst waiting for Hefner's beauties to find him. First a carpet import business in a run-down quarter of Paris, just as Persian and Afghan were becoming chic again; then a minor jewellery salon with a suggestion of champagne-class drugs supplied for the wild, all-night parties of the more determined social-climbers. It was his further good fortune – for which he duly thanked his God every night before sleeping – to have been in Europe when that bloody revolution broke back home and 'enemies of the people' were purged. His father, a minor treasury official in the Shah's government, had been arrested one night by Khomeini guards and was never seen again; Hamid, too, now feared the dark and often heard the feet of Iranian agents upon the stair.

Surprisingly, he spoke little of the remaining family in Tehran, or their continuing vulnerability to the passing mob and the fickleness of Shia indignation. He had blotted that out quite completely. The inherent contradiction in a man who could successfully run arms behind the Iron Curtain but did nothing to spirit his own beleaguered family out of Iran was not lost on Tyler, and he knew to measure Hamid's loyalty only in dollars. A sad reflection – still he could not help liking the man himself. The open, smiling face – and the predictable sexual posturing encapsulated by the onyx ram paperweight which graced his low table. Tumescent with ego.

The office was perfumed with sandalwood and richly decorated; a tribute the Iranian's success. The effect was calculated to impress and, although not in keeping with his own tastes, Tyler recognised the aggressive pursuit of class at any price and was excited by it. The pastel-coloured ceiling was finely edged with gilt roses, and the lemon walls hung with scenes depicting the life of Louis XIV. Here and there a marble obelisk or a Renaissance bronze was picked out by muted spot-lighting, conveying all the elegance of the more exclusive and expensive Left Bank art dealers whence they were purchased. The desk and

chairs located immediately beside the immense case-
ment window were delicate affairs of wine-coloured
wood with slender, curving legs; and on the desk top,
standing out against a confusion of leather and gold, a
single red rose drank demurely from a tall, slim vase.
Softness amongst strength.

Hamid clapped his hands in that warm, excited
way of his which gave the impression he lived only
to be of service to his clients.

'A long time indeed since we last saw you, John.
You'll take a drink, of course.' It was not in the
nature of a question, rather a declaration, for, like most
of his countrymen, Hamid's behaviour was ruled by a
strict observance of etiquette. Proper hospitality had
to be offered and received in order to demonstrate no
ill-will on either side. Tugging rakishly at his diamond-
studded cufflinks, he moved to the pedestal-mounted
globe on which the northern hemisphere rotated to
reveal a well-stocked cocktail rack.

'Whisky soda with ice, if I remember rightly.'
Hamid's dark eyebrows rose and his brown eyes
twinkled.

'Fine,' said Tyler, smiling inwardly at the caricature before him. The Iranian drew no distinction
between business and pleasure – all was seduction.

Hamid carried over two glasses, and insisted
on a toast to old friends before settling back in
his seat.

'So where have you been for so long?'

'On vacation,' Tyler replied briefly, folding one
leg across the other.

Hamid laughed loudly and generously to show
he had grasped the irony of the response.

'And now you are back at work, and have
come to see Hamid.' He placed both hands on his
chest as he spoke his own name, flashing two rows of
perfectly capped teeth. 'Well, if I can assist you in some
small way, I shall go home a happy man today. Come,
tell me what you wish.'

Placing his glass on the table, Tyler reached for the inside pocket of his jacket and produced a folded slip of paper, momentarily reminded of Stephenson's little charade during lunch at Simpson's.

Hamid made a show of taking out half-lensed gold reading glasses that were years too old for his face, before unfolding the paper. His expression was serious as he read; with lips closed tight, he moved his jaw as if gravely assessing the quality of a wine. Slowly, he began to nod his head. Suddenly he whipped off the spectacles.

'Yes, yes. I think, no problem. This is nice hardware. This is good hardware. A little difficult to come by, as you know, but by no means impossible.'

Tyler smiled his satisfaction. He knew the difficulties of which Hamid spoke – that some of the items on the list were only available from military establishments. But he also knew that official arms shipments went missing, and had done so many times in the past; end-user certificates could be forged or sold, and countries eager to meet their IMF loan repayments could turn a blind eye for the sake of increased exports. The Iranian would know how to proceed. Even now the oriental brain would be arranging 'windows' in his Filofax for lunch with the right people.

But he was nettled by something. A vague reservation was percolating to the surface. Hamid knew his business and was shuffling towards a suggestion. 'Still I feel I should also tell you, as you are a valued client and, I hope I may say, a personal friend, that there is better on the market.'

Tyler had expected such a comment, but he was not prepared to discuss the list.

'That rather depends upon the use to which the weapon will be put,' said Tyler concentrating on the ice melting in his glass.

'True, true. I don't argue with your choice of small arms. That is personal – like his choice of

166

automobiles or women it is an extension of a man's personality, as is the way he signs his name. But a surface-to-air missile is another matter. In this case the certainty of a kill is the only real consideration. Why not have the NATO "stinger"? I have a number which became orphans when the Russians pulled back from Afghanistan. Or even the good old "Grail" SAM–7? There are thousands of these floating around the Middle East. Why would anyone want a SACLOS-guided rocket when there are tried and tested heat-seekers around that even a child can handle? These are fire-and-forget killers – pull the trigger and boom: big black cloud in fucking sky and no more aeroplane. Why do you want "Javelin"?'

Immediately Hamid registered in the Englishman's face that he had said too much – asked too much.

But Hamid knew his weapons, their strengths, their weaknesses, and like all experts liked to demonstrate his knowledge. Fleming, as Hamid knew him, was supposed to be a soldier of fortune, a covert specialist, and yet he was asking for a weapon which required a high degree of operator skill; one that relied upon the accurate tracking of a target over a distance, prior to detonation of the warhead. It did not make sense; not when there were intelligent missiles available which used infra-red sensors to lock onto an aircraft's engine exhaust vent and hound it to death. Surely Fleming knew that?

It was as Tyler had suspected: Hamid's professional curiosity was aroused. No questions need be answered, not in their business – the money guaranteed that. And yet he needed to assuage the man's suspicion. Too many people knew already. So he used the vague and imprecise lie he had already prepared for this moment.

'What you say is true. I said the same myself. Nevertheless I have no choice. In this I am only a go-between. The weapons will be procured and

167

delivered to a third party, perhaps even to a fourth thereafter, for all I know. Covert aid to insurgents. They'll probably blow themselves up by mistakes. What do I care?'

Both men shared the joke like card-players measuring a bluff.

'If it is a question of the cost . . .' Hamid offered with palms outstretched, 'perhaps we could come to some arrangement.'

'It's not the bread. It must be a British missile, that's all.' Tyler's face said 'discussion over', and his tone mirrored this. 'Can you fill the prescription or not?'

Steady, boy, he told himself. Keep it matter-of-fact.

'You know I can, John. My only concern is to provide a professional service. My advice is thrown in gratis, but I see in this case it is not appropriate.' Hamid was choosing his words carefully, indicating that Tyler's story was the fiction he would accept if that's what was required.

Tyler silently cursed himself for allowing himself to be drawn into details, true or otherwise; lies might be broken down by a quick mind like Hamid's. It made the next part more difficult. Still it had to be mentioned; it was the sole reason for coming to the Iranian in the first place. *Transportation.*

'I would like the goods delivered for collection in Tripoli.' The Iranian, who was about to sip his drink, pause briefly before touching the glass to his lips. He took a long time swallowing and smacked his lips appreciatively as he considered this new twist.

'Is that Tripoli, Lebanon' – he raised his eyebrows meaningfully – 'or the other one?'

The bastard was enjoying himself.

'The other one,' said Tyler without emphasis. 'Is that a problem?'

Now it was the Iranian's turn to defend. 'Of course not,' he countered. Then, slumping backwards into the soft upholstery, he blew out his cheeks and inclined his head, clearly impressed by the task ahead. 'But you must know that they have that place sown up tighter than a virgin's drawers. The price will have to reflect that fact.'

Tyler agitated his glass, letting the remaining ice cool the golden liquid further, keeping his nerves cool also.

'That's understood,' he conceded. 'But I shouldn't think you'll have too much difficulty – not with the volume of imports entering Tripoli from Italy and West Germany. I hear Tripoli is no different from any other port – a portion of each cargo goes missing. There is smuggling, there are drugs, there is also a hot trade in American video movies – the ones not dreamed of by the Prophet. In a country spoiled by sudden wealth, money acquires a loud voice. Don't you agree?'

'You are well informed, John. It's true, my friend, palms will need to be greased to ensure a safe journey. However, with my Roman airfreight shipping connections I have little doubt the order can be filled.' Hamid was now at pains to assure this client of the professionalism of his service; it did not do to play word games for too long with a volume client. 'I presume,' he continued pleasantly, 'you are familiar with the handling of "Javelin". My own technical staff would be pleased to demonstrate certain refinements for you at no further cost.'

'Thank you, that won't be necessary. I'll only be arranging transhipment from Tripoli to the third party. My responsibility ends there. If they want to know how to shoot they can learn from the bloody manual, for all I care.'

'Spoken like a true businessman,' grinned Hamid, raising his glass in mock salute. 'There is hope for you yet.' He took a quick drink and added, almost as an afterthought, 'Maybe that is not just a joke.'

'Meaning?' asked Tyler, catching the shadow in his tone.

'Meaning I would like to expand this enterprise. There is always financial backing, but I need good people – people like you who understand the meaning of professionalism and also of discretion. Especially discretion, huh, John?'

Tyler shrugged, amused by the backhanded compliment.

'You don't need to hand me a lot of bullshit about what goes where, John. Believe me, there are no causes left for me. I no longer choose sides. I long since ceased to care which side does what to whom.'

Tyler held his gaze steadily. 'Fine, then you'll have no problem developing amnesia if anyone should make enquiries in the future. That includes Her Majesty's Government.'

'To borrow your own expression,' said Hamid with obvious pleasure, 'that is understood.'

The Iranian's manner left no doubt as to the clarity of his perceptions or his reliability. Tyler was satisfied.

'In three days I'll expect to have hands on the kit for inspection. I won't quibble over a few dollars. Is a draft from my bank in Geneva acceptable to you?'

'Absolutely.'

'The usual guarantees?'

'The gilt-edged service. My insurance policy covers all unforeseen circumstances: Interpol, customs, security agencies – theirs and ours. If the stuff is seized, there will be a replacement dispatch the same working day; this much I guarantee. With the lower self-risk price, I cease to be responsible the moment the goods are placed in transit. Business entails a number of risks, don't you agree?'

'Yes, but not for you, Hamid,' Tyler grinned. 'Gilt-edged sounds good to me. What about the paperwork?'

'All paperwork will be handled by me; no hassle with certificates – nothing.'

They shook hands and it was done.

Stephenson had already promised any weapons Tyler required, but it was the delivery to Libya that was crucial and SIS would not deliver. British Intelligence had insisted he make his own arrangements in that respect. They needed this contract to bear the fingerprint of a private job. Well, they were paying highly for the privilege of calling the shots, so what did he care? For his part, making his own arrangements was what came naturally. The first lessons he had learned at Calvi were: always pack you own 'chute, and never let another man carry your rucksack. Safer that way.

He walked out into Berkeley Square again to find the rain had stopped and the rolling grey sky had peacefully dissipated. He checked the jeep, fed the parking meter and walked out of the Square. There was ample time to get to the greasy-spoon Italian café just off Piccadilly, and he wanted to savour the coldness of British winter and thereby enhance the contrast that a return to the parched dust of the dark continent would bring.

Forty minutes later he was sitting behind the remains of a cappuccino, stirring the froth and chocolate powder in his cup and watching the door to the café. He could not understand it: Stephenson had not arrived. It was like the quiet explosion of a long-treasured myth. Never before had the polished forehead, the comfortably shabby looks of the Whitehall man failed to appear for an appointment at 'the café'. Like a fox hearing the distant blast of the hunting horn, Tyler grew wary in every nerve and sensed a danger he could not name.

Something was going wrong.

171

He paid for the coffee and returned to the jeep, his mind filled with a hundred questions. When he reached the vehicle, he dropped his keys beside the door and took a long look underneath as he bent to pick them up again. He was feeling jumpy, cautious. Then he took a good look around at the other people in the Square, also at the other cars, then climbed in and started the engine.

After five miles and two turns around Piccadilly Circus he looked in the rear-view mirror and saw they were still hanging on. A red and yellow Golf GTI, just two cars back, all tooled up with spoilers and whip aerial – and, a little further behind, a cream Ford transit van that looked like it had been repainted with household emulsion. Not very subtle.

On the second circuit of Piccadilly Circus he had secured a good look at the occupants of the GTI: two rough young buggers wearing combat-jackets, whose bulk filled the windscreen. And he thought he caught sight of a Motorola packset radio in the passenger's hand. At that moment he could not guess how many more of them might be in the transit van, but the sight of that radio convinced him they were not just yobs; they were a team. The only trouble was: whose team?

'All right, boys,' he murmured to himself, 'if you want to play . . .'

He timed his next move meticulously, slowing at the traffic-lights so that the line behind him had to stop, then suddenly throwing the gear-stick into third and racing across the busy intersection at the first show of red – almost smashing into a black Porsche which was getting away early on the cross sequence. That left the tail stranded, and gave him a good half-mile start towards Putney Bridge and south across the river. The traffic ahead was beginning to slow up, forcing him to weave across lanes. Even then it was not long before they were back in his mirror, the GTI roaring hard up behind.

From then it was flat out, needling seventy, nip and tuck and no stopping for road junctions. Tyler came out of Putney just ahead of them, up the long hill, and crossed the busy A3 roundabout into Wimbledon village. Luck was with him: there was the smallest gap in the traffic and he took it, but the first pursuer was not so fortunate. The GTI came hard on his heels but its driver misjudged the speed of a container lorry on the roundabout, and was rammed into a metal crash-barrier.

As the transit van came into the roundabout its passengers saw the huge metal monster blocking the road, and the Golf squashed between its head and the barrier. Brady hit the brakes hard, throwing Brando into the dashboard, and they stopped just feet away from the lorry. For a while there was shouting and confusion. The lorry driver had jumped down from his rig and was running clear. A second later the Golf exploded. Just one scream, then a roar and thick smokey-yellow flames.

'Stupid bastards!' cursed Brady. 'Too close! I bloody told them!'

There was no helping them now.

Brady backed up the transit, fighting against the ancient steering, then manoeuvred behind the dead lorry and took the roundabout against the traffic with horn blaring, scattering other vehicles and bouncing off the wing of a Jaguar saloon. At the Wimbledon exit he almost spun out of control, skidding wildly, finally picking up again in second gear and regaining traction. 'Come on, come on,' he urged himself. 'Just keep driving!'

He followed the road bordering Wimbledon Common, aware that the daylight was fading rapidly, then suddenly he recognised the jeep up ahead. It had been driven up onto a grass verge that led away towards a wooded area. Brady pulled onto the verge behind the jeep, and leapt out with automatic pistol at the ready. Even as he approached the jeep he knew it was empty; from the tracks on the rain-soaked grass it was obvious the driver had taken off into the trees in a hurry.

'Watch yourself,' warned Brady, taking out a pocket knife and slashing both front tyres on the jeep. 'This one's no girl-guide; he's bloody dangerous.'

Brando nodded his understanding, and they moved into the cover of the trees, where the tracks faded almost immediately. It was getting dark and Tyler had gone for solid ground that would leave no trace of his feet. Clearly he knew what he was doing.

Tyler knew what he was doing all right. He knew that if he could make it to the Common, they would never find him. The wood was just too thick and the light too poor. But even in daylight they would likely still not have found him, for he was just too clever in his field craft. Still, he felt naked without the Browning. And now he knew there were two pursuers.

For a long time he lay still in the bushes, catching his breath, his body covered by a carpet of dead leaves that were wet and warm. He could hear them thrashing around nearby, trying vainly to be silent in their movements: two urban hunters out of their element. At one point he heard footsteps come close to his face, and looking up he saw a man with a beard clutching a big automatic. But the man did not see him, and moved away again.

Tyler knew he would remember that face.

Eventually darkness fell completely and the footsteps receded. Soon after, he heard car doors slamming and an engine being started.

But still he did not move.

He lay there another hour, to be sure. And as he lay there, his black eyes staring up at the star-less sky, he brooded on the team which had followed him. One thing seemed obvious: someone had set him up – but who? And why?

Some time later he heard another engine start up, and headlights shone over by the road as the car drove away. It might have been his pursuers leaving; they might have faked their departure the first time, but he could not know for sure.

When he moved eventually, he headed in the opposite direction, further into the Common, and kept walking. Crossing open scrub he followed a set of familiar lights until he emerged from the darkness near a pub which bordered the Common. He went inside and ordered a double whisky, and as he drank the thought occurred to him that these people must know an awful lot about him. Either they had picked him up at Hamid's office, or they had picked him up at his scheduled meet with Stephenson – but in both cases that was too much of a coincidence. So what were his chances back in Islington? Not good, he suspected.

Pushing a hand into the pocket of his jacket, he pulled out a small bunch of leaves.

'Jesus Christ,' he breathed, 'what a mess.' He was about to stuff them back into his pocket when he noticed the small white card crumpled amongst them. Straightening it out he recognised the business card the redhaired Emma had given him. When he turned it over he saw what she had written on the back: *Anytime you're free*.

That brought a smile. The whisky had put a fire back in his belly and he was starting to feel better. He smiled at the card. A good place to spend the night. He ordered another drink before going to use the phone. The jeep could wait until morning.

FOURTEEN

On THE WEST side of Tripoli, about half a mile from the airport highway, Colonel Muammar Qadaffi's stronghold, the Azizyah Barracks, lay basking in the spring heat. It was the fortress from which he governed the Socialist People's Libyan Arab Jamahiriya, assisted by a heirarchy of Revolutionary Committees.

High overhead a single kite was turning wide, lazy circles, riding the thermals. On the ground Colonel Azziz, Chief of the Bureau of External Security, new-speak for Libyan Foreign Intelligence, watched the bird's motions, shielding his own hawk-like eyes against the glare. A small black speck, it appeared against the vast blueness of the cloudless sky. It was 10 a.m. and already the mercury was nudging twenty-four centigrade.

He stood in the compound of the President's new villa – within sight of the ruins of the old one destroyed by US bombs – awaiting the great man's pleasure. Instinctively he stooped to wipe the red dust from the toes of his Italian shoes, smoothing down his trousers and jacket as he straightened up. The suit was a pale cream two-piece by Balmain, and had arrived only two days ago from Paris, where they kept a record of his measurements. Such luxury items were hard to come by in Libya, and were taxed heavily to finance the development programmes of the People's Jamahiriya. But for an intelligence officer frequent 'liaison' trips to Europe allowed a certain standard of sartorial elegance, and he was pleased that rank still bestowed its privileges.

Azziz had come to discuss important matters, but was informed that the President was still at prayer. So now he waited patiently in the compound, watching the comings and goings of green-uniformed military personnel. Jeeps buzzed about between the white-washed barrack huts and administration blocks. A fat-faced sergeant inspected the gun barrels of two guards standing ramrod straight to attention. In the distance, he could hear the screams of a drill instructor rehearsing the ranks on the parade square.

As for all military men, the order and discipline of the scene, the beat of a distant marching band, gave him a warm glow – made him feel proud. Here the very heart of the nation beat, proud and secure in spite of the Americans – may Allah damn their bones and curse their seed!

His deep-set eyes studied the wall fortifications, sixteen feet high and topped with two-foot steel spikes and a tangle of electrified barbed wire, remembering that night when death rained down upon their heads, killing women, children and military alike. What a night of death and confusion it had been – and then the time for mourning. Even the Head of State's own family had been visited with death and injury. How Qadaffi had mourned and wept, inconsolable in his grief. But Azziz had seen him come through the horror, changed in subtle ways: more aloof from the Revolutionary Council members; more fatalistic and surer of his own destiny. The God of Islam had spared his servant to avenge the evil brought down upon his people.

Colonel Azziz checked his watch again and reached for his cigarette case. Before he could click it open the Head of State's equerry appeared from under a tent flap.

'The Colonel will see you now.'

Azziz walked to the entrance topped by a broad awning, and stepped inside. The tent was about the size of an average sitting-room, furnished modestly with bedouin carpets and skins.

The tent walls were a patchwork of coloured squares, and here and there, embroidered into the fabric with green thread, were favourite quotations from Qadaffi's 'Green Book'. Amongst the modern conveniences installed were four electric radiators to warm the chill Tripoli nights, two telephones, and a small refrigerator filled with soft drinks.

Seeing his leader seated at the glass-topped writing desk, Azziz smiled and bowed in greeting. Qadaffi came forward and embraced him warmly, then bade him sit with him in a densely cushioned area of the floor. A steward proceeded to serve them tea, which always came first in small glasses, then left to prepare bedouin coffee over a copper brazier. The tea was refreshing, but by no means as significant as the ritual of offering a guest coffee. By receiving coffee Azziz was reassured that he still enjoyed the leader's favour.

Until it appeared, Azziz made small talk, knowing it was bad manners to pursue business before this ritual. When all was prepared, Qadaffi filled two small cups from a simple brass pot, and they drank appreciatively.

When they had finished the customary toasts, Colonel Azziz reached for his case. Carefully he withdrew a sheaf of papers.

'What news do you bring, Azziz, that you would wish to interrupt my devotions? Have the Zionists killed more of your European mercenaries? Perhaps we need another means to get hold of those infra-red pictures.'

178

Colonel Azziz ignored the jibe, having always known it was lunacy to send any man to penetrate the Demona installation, no matter how experienced; but knowing equally that he could not refuse a direct order to arrange it. He still felt bitter about it. Nor had Qadaffi told him what use the photographs would be put to, but he was sure that Jalloud would be somehow involved.

He put on a sweet smile.

'Forgive me, Colonel, it was thoughtless of me to interrupt you, but it is a matter of grave importance.' He was ever conscious that, although promoted to Major General, Qadaffi still favoured being addressed as Colonel, a minor foible copied from his erstwhile ally, Colonel Nasser.

'Indeed? Can you tell me what is more important to a man than the worship of his God? Perhaps you yourself should spend more time reading the Koran, and let your deputies travel to Paris and Amsterdam instead.'

Azziz knew the Head of State was concerned over his subordinate's love of European fashions and values.

'You are right, Colonel, but sadly it is my duty that takes me to these infidel places, to pursue your enemies and punish their crimes. Have I not pursued them with my utmost vigour?'

Qadaffi nodded in affirmation. 'You speak truly, Azziz, my friend and loyal supporter. Truly it was you who sent that traitor Mahmoud to hell for his crimes against the people's Jamahiriya . . . .' Azziz relaxed and let his face crease into a modest smile.

'But it was Jalloud who settled my account with Ibrahim in London.'

A sudden barb – one to encourage competition?

'Jalloud should stick to Internal Security, Brother Colonel! He should leave external threats to me.'

179

'I agree, Azziz. Nevertheless, a satisfying conclusion. Did he not scatter this so-called opposition?'

'*Insh Allah*,' said Azziz politely, though not sharing his leader's optimism. 'If God wills. Let us hope so.'

An audience with the Head of State was always a nerve-racking affair. Those who did not learn the correct answers to suit the leader's moods did not last long in office.

'Come then, Azziz, tell me your news.'

'Colonel, I have news of a serious threat to your person from the Western powers.'

Qadaffi took the document offered by his grave-faced Chief of Intelligence, and began to read.

'Talk me through while I read, Colonel.'

'Certainly. I realise that threats are not new to you. We know the CIA have often considered action against your person, but have hitherto been prevented by their own laws which prohibit such clandestine operations. But our information states that this threat comes from London – from the infamous MI6 who are not bound by such constraints.'

'What else does your intelligence tell you?'

'That a small team of two or three are to come to Tripoli and assassinate the Head of State. The principal agent is a professional killer who has worked for the SIS before. His code-name is Nimrod. He is to be assisted by agents of another power, possibly France or Israel, who operate from a safe-house in one of our cities. That is all we know at present.'

Qadaffi read the report in the same way he would peruse an economic brief. He seemed unmoved by fear – on the contrary, Azziz thought he spotted the tail-end of a smirk on his leader's lips. A certain wry pleasure at the compliment of being seen by the world as such a dangerous enemy?

'Many times we have heard similar whispers from across the sea. It is good that the dogs still fear me,' spat the Libyan leader, closing his fist emphatically.

'You know my views, Azziz. The whole of Arabdom knows my philosophy. I shall not be swerved from my holy duty.'

'I understand. But for safety . . .'

'I suspect this is so much hot wind from a camel's arse. They have leaked this nonsense before.'

'Yes indeed, but . . .'

'They have attacked us at every turn, flouted our borders, stolen our oil for years, fomented insurrection – especially among my officers.'

That particular barb was aimed at Azziz himself. He felt Qadaffi's eyes searching for any sign of disloyalty in him. So, even now he was not completely trusted.

'Colonel, I have been in personal contact with the leadership of the Irish separatist movement. Their assistance has been invaluable in uncovering this cowardly plot – a just repayment for our gifts to them.'

'Gifts? What gifts? I ordered no more gifts for Europeans!'

A thread of saliva broke away from Qadaffi's mobile lips, and caught Azziz on the cheek. Measuring the President's sudden anger, he made no move to wipe it away. Quickly he began to explain.

'They lack weapons with which to fight their urban guerilla war, Colonel. Your policy has always been one of assisting those who struggle against occupation by imperialist and colonialist powers. All was agreed beforehand. I beg you to recollect our discussions on the matter.'

'I remember something.' Qadaffi said, touching a hand to his temple. 'Perhaps you are right. I have too much to consider to be concerned with each individual group. That is your job.'

Qadaffi stroked his forehead, closing his eyes briefly. His rage had faltered. That was happening more these days: his reactions were unpredictable, his responses often incoherent or inappropriate. A nervous twitch in his left cheek had become the signal which announced a sudden bout of disintegration, causing Cabinet members to withdraw and reschedule important decisions to a more auspicious time.

Azziz seized the advantage.

'I repeat, Colonel, the assistance of the Irish separatists has been invaluable. Their leader is an extremely gifted tactician but his leadership is being challenged, so I arranged an arms shipment to bolster his position. In return I had their people follow up a piece of information about a certain intelligence officer in London who was regularly meeting with Ibrahim's people there. Their operator took the unusual step of kidnapping and interrogating that intelligence officer.'

The President was intrigued.

'Are the Irish so careless of military reprisals that they would do this in the English capital?'

'This man is a dedicated fighter, one of their best. His act was imprudent for an underground agent on enemy soil, nevertheless the information it yielded was worth the risk.'

'What happened to the British Intelligence man?'

'He was killed, eventually.'

Qadaffi nodded thoughtfully. 'Then the British must assume you have discovered their plot.'

'Yes, Colonel.'

'Then the British will obviously stop this foolish nonsense. They will cancel this man's contract – this Nimrod. It would be lunacy to send him here when we anticipate his arrival. These Christians have long since lost the taste for martyrdom.

'Probably correct, Brother Colonel. However we cannot know for certain. For this reason I have set up a task-force of my best officers to investigate the threat. Unfortunately a name is all we have. There are no photographs available, though our people in France are checking records and details of ex-soldiers of the Foreign Legion, where this man once served.'

'A legionnaire,' breathed Qadaffi with grudging respect. 'They send a desert fighter against us.'

182

'Just so, Colonel. The assassins may even be here already. If so, they will go to ground and await a suitable opportunity . . .'

'To kill me.' The Libyan leader was totally calm as he spoke.

Azziz, as if embarrassed by the words, looked away uncomfortably.

'Colonel, we . . .'

'Scour the cities! Cover the desert! Find this legionnaire! With such a man in our hands we could humble the British Parliament. There would be a show trial to end all show trials! If we can link the Americans and the Zionists also with this plot, so much the better.'

'If I might respectfully point out to you, Colonel, we have the co-operation of the Irishman. He has seen the assassin and can identify him. The IRA set a trap in London but Nimrod escaped, killing two of their men. The Irishman will now avenge the blood of his comrades here in Tripoli.'

From the firing-range came the distant clatter and echo of gunfire. The President cocked an ear, then his hand crept under the cushion and touched something reassuring. As the sounds died away he again fixed his gaze upon Azziz.

'Do whatever you feel necessary. If you must set a thief to catch a thief, then do so.'

With that the Libyan leader stood up and walked back to his desk. The interview was over.

Azziz bowed and walked from the tent into the bright sunshine. High above the compound the kite was still circling patiently, as he walked to where the driver was waiting by the official BMW with his personalised plates, and got in without speaking. The driver recognised the silent rage that gripped his charge, and did not speak all the way back to Intelligence Headquarters.

FIFTEEN

TYLER STAYED AT the girl's flat in Clapham for two days, sleeping in her bed and enjoying the proximity of her young body. On the first day he recovered the jeep from Wimbledon and had the tyres replaced – they had done a good job on those. On the second day he went back into central London and wandered between the locations where he had arranged to meet Stephenson in the past. He checked all the fallback locations at the correct hourly intervals. Nothing.

Stephenson had disappeared, and now some team was on Tyler's case. What to do now?

Paranoia came crowding into his brain, and he did not know what to make of the silence. The contract might even have been cancelled. If there had been a leak, or if the press had got wind of the Libyan plan, the shutters would go up bloody pronto at Century House – as he knew from experience. If one of those bloody TV crews were now running a story, he might never hear from Stephenson again.

If there was no further contact, he advised himself, better to quit the country for a while. The advance payment he would keep, as had been agreed at the outset. Thirty per cent up front as a sign of good faith, and to pay for personal and incidental expenses. That was the way it was done in a world where the client-supplier relationship was not protected by recourse to the law. For its part, British Intelligence never got stung. They could even protect their investment with the threat of a cast-iron drugs frame-up that would put him away for years. He had seen that happen before – so better just to get away.

Anyway there was almost nothing to keep him in England during these dull, wet months. And no special lady – God he only wished there was. It was a place he no longer felt he belonged to and the promise of the African contract had temporarily lifted his spirits. The heat of the sun-bleached scrub was his element, not this cold, wet land.

Suddenly a few weeks on the Côte d'Azur looked good. Or maybe he would take a boat across to North Africa. Perhaps look up Chevalier, and lose himself in a bottle. Chevalier had quit the Legion in 1980 to start up a bar in Casablanca for hard-drinking foreigners, expatriates looking for a rendezvous in a land full of Arabs and dust. He had called it 'Kepi Blanc' after the sacred emblem of the French Foreign Legion, and it had proved a magnet for ex-legionnaires and soldiers of fortune alike, some looking for commissions, others just looking for a respectful audience for their war stories. Right now it all sounded pretty attractive to Tyler.

But there was still Daniel to consider, and he could not leave without making arrangements for his brother's future. It was this tug upon his conscience which pulled him back to earth. Perhaps it was too soon for him to make plans to move; if anything had changed or gone wrong they would surely make contact. They must know that he could hurt them badly if he was left out in the cold, and they would not risk that.

There was always one thought that haunted him: if he should die overseas, who would tell his brother? He thought of that tree-circled nursing home in the Kent countryside and of Daniel standing by the day-room window, gazing with hopeful eyes down the length of the gravel drive, waiting for a car that would never come.

Tyler now made his decision. If no reassurance was forthcoming from the contractor, he would clear out and arrange for his solicitor to take care of the nursing-home fees. But now he must move. They would have to contact him sooner or later, and there was only one place they could guarantee to do that. He pointed the Shogun northwards towards Islington.

Having given the outside of the building the once-over, he walked down the street and called his own number from a public call-box. It rang for a full minute unanswered. Out in the street an ice-cream van played its jingle, also unanswered – the children were still in school. Parked cars thronged the kerb. He checked them: they were all unoccupied.

This was about as safe as it was going to get, he told himself, so he walked quickly towards the front door and bounded up the four steps. Without looking round, he slipped his key into the lock of the heavy outer door and stepped inside.

It was a four-storey eighteenth-century town house with fine old masonry and ornate plaster ceilings, which had been converted into six flats in the Seventies. Tyler inhabited the top-floor flat, with a view out over Highbury Fields – a haven of restful green grass that had once been community pasture land.

At the flat door he listened carefully, then quietly fitted his key and went in.

To his relief there was no welcoming committee waiting.

When he saw a curtain move in the top-floor flat, the ice-cream seller unclipped a powerful

Motorola radio handset from the dashboard and reported to the operations controller that the sun had just gone in. The controller promptly telephoned up to the fifth floor to inform 'the Grey Ghost' that his man had been housed, and that a car had already been ordered together with a back-up facility.

Hurriedly, Tyler packed a canvas kit-bag with two changes of clothing, knowing that when the time came he must move fast and would not be returning for some time. From a locked drawer in the bedroom he took two passports – one British, the other Belgian – and a linen bag with a draw-string which contained the Browning wrapped in a lightly-oiled cleaning cloth. He removed the weapon, gave it a wipe, and put the bag away. All the papers and maps, and the video-cassette Stephenson had supplied, were now stuffed at the bottom of the kit-bag, whilst the combat knife and Browning 9mm were tucked just inside the neck – close to hand.

Tyler assessed the degree of his nervousness: the electric pulse that waited for some unknown threat to break, and which sat upon his back like a monkey. Why so nervous? The smaller Heckler and Koch P95 pistol was now hard and snug in its leather holster set at a cross-draw position on his left hip, reversed and canted forward for a fast break and clean draw. He had never liked the shoulder rig, considering it all show and no go. When it came to the crunch, the elasticated cross-straps would always give a little bit, taking the crispness out of the draw. The holster came with the weapon when tugged, and that was dangerous. The barrel could easily catch on the lip of the holster or, worse still, become tangled in the shoulder loop. Then you were dead.

He changed into jeans and a sweater, with a red-and-blue patterned ski-jacket that was long enough to cover the belt holster. A small safety-deposit key was fished from a magnetic key-safe hidden amongst the cooling fins at the back of the refrigerator.

He might need some money and the second forged passport in a hurry.

Suddenly there came a shriek from the trimphone.

Startled by the noise, Tyler had almost cleared the holster before he recovered control of his instincts and moved over to the antique writing-desk and lifted the handset. He placed it against his ear, without speaking.

'Hello, Mr Tyler.' The voice was soft and calculatedly reassuring. 'I'm calling on behalf of George Stephenson. I think we need to talk rather urgently.'

'George who? I think you have a wrong number.'

'Very prudent, Mr Tyler. I wouldn't trust a phone-call like this either, but in this case neither one of us has any choice so you'll just have to trust me. I'm a colleague of Stephenson's. I understand you were due to meet him two days ago.'

'And supposing I was . . .'

'Didn't show, did he?'

'Keep talking.'

'No, not over the phone; not like this. For your own safety we need to talk urgently. There's been a slight change of plan. Some complications. Nothing to worry about. You're safe for the moment. Our people are keeping an eye on your place, but don't go out. I'd better come round and put you in the picture.'

Tyler recognised the understatement implicit in the oh-so-pukka public-school accent, and he multiplied up the seriousness accordingly. Spooks with gun teams on the street – now he knew his life really was in danger.

'What do you mean, don't go out? Where's Stephenson? Why didn't he call?'

'Do I call round or do I not?' continued the voice, steam-rollering across these questions. He had said enough to put the hook in. Why should Tyler

188

not go out? Safe for the moment? He needed more information. Needed to know what was going on.

'OK,' he breathed finally, 'but be prepared to identify yourself. What do I call you? Give me a name.'

'Call me Charles. Don't move until I get there, say in thirty minutes. Don't answer the phone, either.'

The armoured green Jaguar pulled into Highbury Place and finding itself conspicuous amongst the Escorts, Golfs and Citroëns, it cruised on a hundred yards past its destination before purring to a rest. The council road-sweeper glanced up from his brush as a tall distinguished-looking gent with a full head of neatly combed silver-grey hair, and wearing a navy-blue woollen overcoat that suggested Savile Row, stepped from the rear door, adjusted his leather gloves and walked across the street. Halliday ignored the gaze of the council worker and continued along the broad pavement that bordered Highbury Fields, until he reached the parked ice-cream van where he stopped to buy a choc-ice. Casually the vendor indicated the dark blue door, and reassured his superior that the flat was not under hostile surveillance and that no one had gone in or out since Tyler had returned.

Halliday climbed the three steps to the door and rang the bell for the top-floor flat, nodding approval as he registered that Tyler had removed the name card from the indicator beside the bell-push.

'Yes?' quizzed the metallic voice from within.

'Charles.'

A click and a buzz, and Halliday pushed his way through the door and stepped into the hallway. The ice-cream man, a heavy-set individual with a typically cheerful ice-cream seller's face, checked the weapon clipped beneath the dashboard of his vehicle. When deployed in this support role, he had been authorised to draw a piece of kit with a high rate of firing: the Heckler and Koch MP5K. He ran an appreciative hand over its lethal blackness and settled down to wait. Forbes, seated by the window in Costa's, a greasy-spoon joint less than thirty metres from the blue door, carried the same weapon secreted in a special harness beneath his raincoat. It gave him a measure of reassurance after the warning that a Provo kill-team might be in the area. He raised a hand to obscure his mouth and ear piece. The miniature microphone hidden by the knot of his Guards tie picked up that response and transmitted it to the ice-cream seller. Yes, he had clear sight of the door and the sash windows to the front of the house.

Both men settled themselves down to wait. They were used to waiting; it was their job.

At the top of the stairs Halliday knocked on the open door and stepped inside.

'Close it.' The voice came from some distance inside the flat.

Halliday obeyed and dropped the catch on the Yale with a loud click.

'Now come inside slowly, with your hands on your head.'

Cautiously Halliday complied.

'Come now, Tyler, let's not make this any more uncomfortable than necessary.' Halliday was an old hand at such games, and he knew Tyler had every right to feel nervous; spiteful even.

Halliday stepped into the sitting-room. Here, then, was the man his department believed was the best in the business. He looked the man over as a matador would a bull, or as a biologist eyes a specimen, checking the silhouette, the aggressive set of the limbs, the wide-jutting shoulders. He was pleased with what he saw – the signs immediately pronounced this a predator. *Our* predator.

Tyler's eyes remained two mirthless black points that speared him, warning him to do only what

190

he was told. The dark gaping mouth of the automatic pistol folded inside the square knuckles confirmed this threat. Here was death on two legs.

'OK, Charlie, turn around and place your hands on the desk.' Halliday moved slowly, assuming the familiar frisk position, and Tyler came behind him and kicked his legs apart.

'Come on, Charlie. You know the procedure.'

The scrape on his ankle hurt and Halliday chewed back an obscenity; it was part of the game, for this was the mercenary's own ground and Halliday had to understand that. Expertly Tyler's left hand reached round, unbuttoned the overcoat and patted him down. Instantly he found the wallet, removed it, and read the name on the neatly folded driving license.

'You cocky bastard,' spat Halliday: 'Are you going to rob me, too?'

'Not this time. Just checking.' Tyler frowned at the driving license. 'Mmmm, not a bad address. Either this year's pay round was particularly generous or you're a gentleman of private means. Peter John Halliday, it says here. Not Charles.'

'Of course not. If you check the second compartment you'll find my identification card.'

Tyler pulled a laminated card from its hiding place. It was laced with illuminated ink-scrolls and impressive phrases that would not look out of place at the front of a British passport.

Halliday's face now bore the discomfited look of a man forced to remove his trousers in Piccadilly Circus.

'I presume you don't usually walk around with this on you?'

'Not usually. It identifies me as an officer of the Crown. That's what you wanted, was it not?'

'It'll do for the moment. Don't worry, I won't tell anyone I've seen it.' The mercenary grinned, not without irony. Tyler let the gun drift down to

191

his side, and stepped over to the window where he peered out though the lace curtain. His movements were relaxed, though he never quite turned his back, always keeping Halliday in view. The man with the immaculate grey hair retrieved his wallet from the desk top, where it had been carelessly tossed, and placed it in his breast pocket, then he turned down his collar and tugged at the fingers of his gloves, peeling them off.

The mercenary had had his fun, and now his nerves had returned, Halliday needed to resume control.

'I see you've noticed the ice-cream van.'

Tyler allowed a wry grin to show. 'It's too close. They usually park nearer Highbury Corner, where the kids pass on their way to the bus-stop or tube station. It's yours, I presume.'

'Just a safety precaution.'

The grin disappeared as quickly as it had appeared. 'Oh, really? Your safety or mine?'

'Both. You needn't worry about us. We intend to protect our investment.'

'Who do I need to worry about?'

There was an unmistakeable venom behind Tyler's words which told the man from the fifth floor that he would need to arrange some patching up to the professional relationship between this man and the department.

'Do you think I could have a small gargle of that excellent whisky?' He indicated the twelve-year-old malt that glowed in a crystal decanter on the cherrywood sideboard. 'What we're paying you for this job will more than cover any entertainment expenses.' Slow things down, he had told himself.

With a shrug of his broad shoulders, Tyler holstered the pistol and poured the man a drink. He was now convinced as much by this man's arrogance, as by the laminated card, of his genuine affiliation with the British Intelligence community. He shucked off his jacket and settled himself into a well-upholstered armchair with a glass of fresh pineapple juice.

Halliday sat down opposite and regarded Tyler across the plate-glass coffee table. He grimaced at the sight of the fruit juice.

'Planning to leave, were you?' Halliday gestured towards the bulging canvas bag that had been tossed next to the armchair. 'A little premature maybe, before you know the facts?'

'And just what are the facts?' Tyler snarled. 'Look, I don't want to spoil your fun or anything, but unless you tell me what's going on, right now, then I'm gone – and so is your money. When I arrange to meet someone, I expect them there. If they're not, what am I supposed to think? Is the mission compromised? Am I about to be nicked by my own side?'

Halliday was nodding placatingly. 'Of course you were anxious. We understand that. That's why I'm here. I came over as soon as I heard you'd returned. But there were other matters. You weren't the only one he was due to meet.'

It was his use of past tense that provided the clue.

'So what's happened? Where is he?'

Halliday placed his glass on the coffee table with a soft clink. Then, as if suddenly lost in thought, he drew his right palm down his cheek and stroked the point of his chin. Where to begin?

'George Stephenson has disappeared.' It seemed like as good a starting point as any.

'Disappeared? You mean he's defected?'

'No. We're quite sure he hasn't done that. You must know yourself how reliable he is. His loyalty is beyond question.'

'If you don't know where he is, then how can you know for sure? Our friend George knows the details of my mission. He also knows just about everything about my life in Britain, and a good deal about my haunts when I'm overseas.'

'Now, wait a minute, Tyler, before you go jumping to conclusions. Exactly when did you last see him?'

Tyler thought for a second. 'A week ago. Thursday. So?'

'Stephenson was abducted three days ago.' The words came out matter-of-fact, small white words on a black background. 'Everything he was working on has been temporarily frozen, pending investigation and a decision on whether to proceed. Everything, that is, except your mission.'

'Why not that?'

'It's just too important. It can't be stopped for anything.'

Tyler weighed that pronouncement, then switched his line of questioning.

'All right. So who took him? They've already had him for three days now. Was it Tripoli?'

Then began the evasion and equivocations: the Intelligence trademark.

'It's by no means as simple as that.' Halliday was even now unsure how much he ought to tell this mercenary. How much was enough to keep him sweet? 'By the slimmest of chances a Catholic priest saw them take him – from a street near his home. He was walking back from the local train station. The priest was fairly old, but his eyes and ears were good enough to provide us with some descriptions and an accent. There was a car full of them: Provisionals.'

'Jesus Christ. God help the poor bastard.'

'Yes, quite.'

'What do *they* want with Stephenson? He's dead meat, you know that?' Tyler's question was rhetorical, for he knew there were many reasons why the IRA might want a well-placed Intelligence man – not the least of which was revenge. And if they had wanted the man who gave the order that extinguished the life of Sean Lynch at the Savoy Hotel, then the trigger man himself would be doubly valuable to them.

194

'Well now, there's the sixty-four thousand dollar question. We don't really know the answer –'

'What the fuck is the tax-payer paying you people for, then?'

The man from Whitehall did not even flinch. Tyler would not have lasted long at SIS, he told himself smugly; not with such a display of emotionalism and insubordination. It was very 'other ranks'.

'I was about to say that we've managed to identify the operations officer involved. The priest gave the police a positive ID, from surveillance blow-ups of a wanted terrorist called Liam Francis Brady.'

'Doesn't have a beard, does he?'

'At the moment, yes. Why?'

'He and his boys came looking for me two days ago. Trailed me round London pretty closely, then I took them for a little drive. They were pretty careless and two of them got burned to a crisp. I gave the other two the slip.'

'Then you were very lucky. Brady is rated by our people as one of their most determined killers. Have you ever heard of "The Five Fingers?"'

Tyler grimaced. 'Five men who broke out of the Maze Prison two years back and started a minor power struggle within the ranks.'

'That's them.'

Tyler placed his elbows on his knees and leaned on his fists, mentally tracing out random connections of facts. The Irish were an audacious bunch at the best of times, but this made no sense as yet.

But then one connection locked, and recognition flashed in his dark unforgiving eyes.

'Brady. Liam Brady. That was the name always hovering around the edges of the story, never holding still quite long enough to be implicated. It was him.'

Confusion was evident on the face of the man from SIS. What was it that Tyler knew?

'Come on, explain.'

'The arms dealing and the connections with the Basques which Stephenson put me onto. There was one man I was to be extra careful to find: careful because he was an important face in the organisation, but also careful because he was about the most dangerous gunman ever to come out of South Armagh. Didn't you know all this? Hell, you are his boss aren't you? I was to kill him on sight, if I ever got the chance. That's what Stephenson said.'

'We know exactly what Stephenson was doing, down to the last full stop.' Halliday bridled at the implication of incompetence. 'Everything had to be properly sanctioned. What he may have told you is quite different. How he handles his agents is a matter for his own judgement, and the opinions he expresses are entirely his own. So, where did Brady come into the picture?'

'The Savoy business. There was an outside chance he might be in on the same operation, waiting to meet Lynch somewhere in London.'

'Ah yes,' said Halliday at the mention of Lynch's name. 'There had been a rumour that Brady was along on that job. I didn't think it likely myself, not after the Oxford Street thing. I assumed the Provos would have him safely tucked away.'

His words yanked Tyler from his thoughts. 'Oxford Street? What about it?'

'The bomb fragments. We found his fingerprints on them. Pretty careless, really. He must know that intense heat affects materials in different ways; that salts in the sweat from a hand leave traces that harden when heated. It took a while, but with computer-enhanced graphic imagery we were able to get a match.'

Tyler came to the obvious conclusion. 'So you think he left the prints deliberately? Is he so eager for the blame?'

'No, just the credit, old man – just the credit.' Halliday took a cellophane packet from his wallet

196

and spread the contents out on the coffee table before him, like a tarot reader. They were photographs. A faint suggestion of a smile played around his lips, like a child playing with a secret.

'What's this?'

'It was pretty gloomy, and there were a lot of shadows and distracting heat sources, but the Special Branch Technical Team can do marvellous things with infra-red film. Look at these,' he said, spreading the prints carefully. 'They were taken at the scene of the blast. Look there, you can just see the two dead police officers. Not a pretty sight, is it? And here are the ambulancemen – and here's a chap tending to the injured. See how his arms come out dark and bluish because of the cold. Rather too cold to be performing topless, wasn't it, Tyler?'

Tyler's expression remained impassive. The blood-stained face in the photograph was unmistakably his own.

'I can understand why a man in your line of business would prefer to remain anonymous, Tyler, but the security forces leave no stone unturned when investigating this type of outrage. Nearly two thousand people had to be accounted for in that investigation. Special Branch wanted to pull you in for questioning – thought you might be some kind of pervert who got a kick out of causing this kind of carnage and then wallowing in the blood and guts afterwards. It was our department who gave you a clean bill of health; a coded reference on the file and you were never contacted.'

Tyler's eyes flicked over the pictures of death. His throat was tight.

'If Liam Brady did the business at Oxford Street, why haven't you lifted him yet?'

'We don't know exactly where he is.' Halliday shrugged. 'But we have it from military intelligence in Belfast that he'd been back over there around the New Year. Apparently he turned up at a number of gatherings as guest of honour – just a brief appearance to boost Provo morale. Anyway he's not there now, so we presume he's been reactivated.'

'Busy lad,' murmured Tyler. 'So that's goodbye George, is it?'

'Rather looks that way, but there's something else.'

'It gets worse?'

'Just listen a moment. It's not a Provo tactic, kidnapping our people on our own doorstep. They prefer to suss out our deep-penetration agents and pull their wings off like butterflies. After they get all the information they can, there's a bullet in the neck. We're lucky if we find a body to bury afterwards. So they must have a special reason for wanting Stephenson, and that can only involve your mission.'

The two men's eyes locked, as the buyer checked the seller for signs of fear, or anxiety.

'To cut a long story short, it's our feeling that Stephenson's abduction was commissioned by Libyan Intelligence – just like that bloody bomb. He had been meeting covertly with Libyan dissidents for a number of months, and Qadaffi's men employ their own low-level agents to monitor such dissidents abroad, using students and other Arab nationals. They must have been pretty desperate to learn what was going on, to pull this stunt. When Stephenson spills his guts – as he inevitably will – then they'll come looking for you.'

'Too late, mate. It's started already!'

'We'll be covering you from now on.'

Tyler reacted with anger. 'Just hold on here! A moment ago you said this mission was too important to cancel. Now you're telling me the opposition are going to know I'm on my way. Do you somehow expect me to beam into Qadaffi's tent like in *Star Trek*, waste the man, then beam out again?'

No matter how Halliday tried to sugar-coat the situation, it still had that bitter taste of poison.

Nevertheless it was still his job to get this man to see the contract through.

'We must assume that Stephenson has told them whatever he knows about everything he knows about.'

Tyler might have laughed at such guarded Intelligence jargon except for the gravity of the situation.

'Fortunately,' continued Halliday, 'you asked for – and were allowed – a completely free hand. That means there were no dates or places to give away.'

Tyler leaned back in the armchair, acutely aware of his sudden power over them; it was a curious and all-consuming pleasure. They were commissioning an artist, consulting an oracle of death, and he was master of all their fates.

'The link between Libya and the IRA is an old chestnut,' said Tyler, 'but this suggests a *new* relationship between them . . .' Tyler waved a hand as if searching for words.

'A relationship of almost indecent intimacy? Yes, I know.'

'Libyan Intelligence's dirty work being carried out on British soil by the micks? That's a big favour. Clearly somebody owes somebody a big drink.'

'Yes, but it really needn't concern us.'

'It's your concern, not mine,' Tyler corrected. 'I haven't agreed to continue with this contract – compromised as it now is.'

'Oh, for God's sake, man. So Tripoli learns of a suspected plot against their leader. So what? For a start, the source isn't exactly one hundred per cent reliable, is it? Intelligence officers distrust all information unless independently corroborated. And Qadaffi has feared a CIA hit for more years now than anyone can remember; there's a new rumour every time the oil price rises. He already thinks we're out to get him. It's a bloody whispering gallery.'

'The knee-jerk reaction will be enough: the ports will be locked tighter than a gnat's chuff. And those Libyan gaols are rough, they say, especially for those with a fair skin.'

They were now swapping moves like squash players, with Tyler occupying centre court and the spook running to field his shots. But Halliday was a man of experience, one used to getting his own way. He studied his empty glass, rotating it, inspecting its quality and the way the light from the window danced in ice-blue patches across its surface. His grey eyes narrowed.

'Yes, well, no one denied there were risks. That much hasn't changed. That's what the business is all about: the right man with the right skills, willing to take those risks. There are any number of knuckle-draggers out there who can shoot a man's face off in a back-street. Word had it that you had something more, but I'm beginning to have my doubts.'

'Spare me the psy-war, Halliday.'

'The way I see it, you can't afford to pull out now, for a number of reasons.'

'Spell them out.'

Halliday set the glass down firmly before him and began counting on the digits of his left hand. Tyler noticed the slender white fingers and manicured fingernails and was reminded of a Chinese money-lender he had patronised once in Corsica.

'First, Stephenson has been with them for more than seventy-two hours. The best SAS men can be broken down by experienced interrogators in well below that time, so we must presume he has spilled his guts. Therefore we assume Brady knows about you, and will communicate that information to Tripoli – and there will now be a price on your head. You know how that's arranged: Arab students, other freelance agents, perhaps even some of your old colleagues from the Legion. Then there's Brady himself, a cool bastard. He kills whatever he's aimed at. You'd be the next on his

200

list, especially since he's already on your case. A matter of professional pride to see which of you is best, maybe.

'Second, your financial situation is not exactly robust. I have statements on my desk that don't add up to the kind of lifestyle you like to lead. Then there's the medical bills for your brother Daniel. That place in Maidstone charges like a hotel, doesn't it? Still it's a very nice location.'

Did this arrogant spook from Whitehall sense the naked rage filling Tyler's mind at the mention of his brother's name? He must have registered something, for he slipped quickly on to his next point.

'Third, despite what you pretend, I suspect that you do care something about George Stephenson. You must know how they'll make him suffer – not just a little either. Between men such as yourselves there's often animosity, but there's also something else – a grudging respect.'

'Perhaps,' said Tyler. 'But George was your pawn. Your responsibility.'

A pang of conscience within the adulterer's brain seized upon the moment, and for a second his reasoning faltered.

'Come now, Tyler, it's no one's fault. Let's just remember that it's Brady that took him. Brady is in your way from now on – no matter which way you turn. You were there when his bomb went off: Merry Christmas from Belfast. Can you ignore that? You've either got to see this job through, or run from Brady for the rest of your days.'

Tyler rose from the chair and began to pace the room. It was not much of a choice for anyone, and a lesser man might have based his decision on fear; but he was both more and less of a man because he was a soldier. His head was filled with the rhythm of boots on sand. It was a strange music that lured him into the fatal dance. Like a tribal warrior, his was the dance of the hunter, and these were steps preordained by centuries of repetition.

'There's one more thing,' said Halliday, almost managing to make it appear a genuine after-thought. 'Stephenson must have told Brady about your role in the Savoy killing. He won't like that. Brady and Lynch were from the same housing estate off the Falls Road. They went through internment together – two of the hardest cases ever to go through the Maze prison.'

Halliday's voice trailed off when he realised the legionnaire was staring hard at him, a stray muscle in his jaw twitching rapidly.

'You want Brady pretty badly, don't you? That's what this little pep-talk is all about. The truth is, he scares you people to death because he won't play by your rules. Not the done thing to make one of your people disappear right off one of your own middle-class suburban streets. It's supposed to happen to the natives overseas, in their bombed-out apartment blocks in Beirut or Cambodia. Not here, never here. A man like Brady gets the old anal sphincter twitching up at Century House, doesn't he?'

The reason for his anger was none too clear to himself. Perhaps he saw in Brady a reflection of himself in different circumstances – another in the same mould. Whereas Halliday was too smug by half with his summaries, investigations and appraisals.

'Look, you don't have to be so damn rude about everything. We're prepared to up the ante for Brady's scalp.' A touch of the absurd.

'Just shut up and listen, spook.'

Halliday's brow was now damp, and instinctively he clutched the arm of the couch whilst the mercenary's tirade continued.

'The job has to be done, so I'll do it. Not because of anything you've just said – let's get that straight – but because *I* choose to take it on.'

There had never been the slightest doubt in the mind of the man from Whitehall that Tyler would take the job; but Halliday had needed to stoke a fire underneath him, and tap a vein of emotion that would launch him forth. Taking this job was the mercenary's only way of slapping their smug faces. And, more than this, he needed the fix. Tyler was only as good as his last job, and through living constantly with danger, facing real gut-wrenching fear, he must reconquer himself each time or never work again. And Tyler would always push that little bit further.

'I'll take them all on: the Libyans and the Provos. But the price is now one million sterling, take it or leave it.'

Halliday silently thanked the gods he had already gained the DD's approval to offer a seven-figure number if necessary (such approval granted in the form of a brief nod, after sight of a piece of paper he would never subsequently acknowledge having seen).

'A figure had previously been agreed between yourself and Stephenson. However, since circumstances have changed somewhat, I will, exceptionally, agree to that new figure.' The gloves came out as Halliday continued. 'We will watch your back as far as possible here in the UK. The police and the Security Service will be looking for Brady, and that should impede his progress, if nothing else. If you're ready, we aim to get you out of the country and safely into our consulate in Frankfurt within the next twenty-four hours. That'll be your jumping-off point, after you pick up the paperwork in Bonn.'

A snort from Tyler.

'When you get to Tripoli we'll have to call upon friends who have a capability in that theatre.'

'What are they? Actors or soldiers?'

Halliday did not rise to the bait.

'When you get to Tripoli, go to the Hotel Poseidon. It's a middle-of-the-range businessman's hotel, very quiet. Wait there to be contacted. Your man will hand you the other part of this five-dinar note.'

Halliday produced the right half of a Libyan banknote from his wallet and let it drop onto the glass table. It had been torn so as to leave an uneven edge.

'Bit melodramatic,' Tyler sneered.

Halliday allowed himself a smile.

'Bloody right. I saw it on a TV show years ago and thought it was rather neat. This is the first chance I've had to use it.' So, he did have a sense of humour, after all. 'And now, Mr Tyler, I think I must bid you good-day. It's unlikely I'll see you again . . . until you return, so I'll wish you the best of success.'

A hand was offered – and ignored.

'Just one more thing,' said Tyler, as the man with the immaculate tailoring stood to leave.

'What's that?'

'I want your office number in case of any further emergencies.'

Reluctantly a number was scratched on a telephone pad. Tyler wondered whether it was real, and decided he had no way of knowing – until the next time he needed it.

'I urge you to take Qadaffi at the earliest opportunity,' said Halliday, pausing at the door. 'And get Brady, too, if you can. We all had a soft spot for George Stephenson.'

He closed the door quietly, taking the truth with him, and was gone.

SIXTEEN

T HE SUMMONS CAME the very next morning. These
    boys did not hang around.

All the previous night Tyler had lain awake,
brooding about Liam Brady and how their lives
were now inextricably linked, and perhaps their deaths
too. The half-glimpsed bearded face haunted him. It
kept returning in that bitter twilight between sleep
and wakefulness, pursuing him like guilt itself across
the mist of a darkened field, and somewhere in the
distance the weeping ghost of a little girl. It worried
him more than he cared to admit; but even as a kid
he had always refused to be cowed by his fears, turning and confronting them with almost self-destructive
determination. Was that why he was set on this lunatic
job, when commonsense and all shades of reason cried
out that it was just too risky? Well, it was also juicy
enough, with the promise of a cool million in sterling
– or a short ride to hell. And if Brady did not get him,
then Qadaffi's men probably would . . .

They sent a car to take him to Gatwick, and
a minder too. That was funny: a minder for
Tyler. The guy smoked continuously, and he had

Special Branch written all over him. He warned Tyler in advance to keep his head well down on the journey; they had learned there were now four teams active in north London. The micks wanted him badly.

Before leaving, Tyler called his lawyer, telling her he was going abroad for the foreseeable future, and that she was to sell everything and transfer the proceeds to Zurich. In the event of his death, she was to use the contents of his numbered account to set up a trust in Daniel's name, with herself as trustee. A certified copy of his will was already in the post.

'Are you ready now, sir?' asked the SB man when he put down the phone. 'You have a plane to catch.'

'I'm ready,' Tyler answered, feeling a surge of relief as last-minute doubts gave way to total commitment. 'Let's get going.'

He picked up his bag and walked quickly out to the waiting car.

At eight o'clock that same evening the lounge bar of the Dog and Fox was tight with weekend sailors and their women: fisherman's sweaters grabbing a last snort to keep out the cold wind blowing off the south coast, before committing their boats to the evening tide.

It was a small upmarket bar a couple of streets removed from the Littlehampton seafront: a haven for the boating fraternity done up in red velvet and brass fittings. Over the high fireplace a glass case contained the strings and spars of a model tea clipper, and from the walls framed reproductions of antique navigation charts looked down upon the revellers.

He came through the smoked-glass swing doors feeling stiff after the long drive down from London. He felt uncomfortable, too. These south-coast ports were unfamiliar, the roads alien and populated with arseholes driving machines too fast for their small brains. But he had found the place – through the town centre and opposite the Nautical Book Shop, as they had directed. Now, by God, he had a thirst on him!

Carelessly, he elbowed his way up to the bar. The young barmaid offered a smile and asked for his order. He examined the labels with obvious disappointment and ordered Budweiser – the pub did not sell real beer.

'American shit!' he muttered in disgust and slammed down his money. The girl took it without a word, regarding him sulkily. Next time he came up to the bar she would look straight through him.

Brady turned to face the room and drank deeply from the glass, peering through the cigarette smoke that hung in a dense cloud. A crowd of a young back-slappers was celebrating a noisy birthday; pastel shirts, white socks, and deck shoes with ropes round the tops. A tanned blonde with her hair pulled into a top-knot, and with good breasts under her loose pink T-shirt, eyed him with interest. That look would have been enough, he told himself, had he not been working.

Then he saw them: two of them sitting hunched over pint glasses at a corner table, like refugees from a working men's club. He saw the ready smile of Eddie Kelly and the dark square-shaved head of MacStifoin. Kelly had spotted him and raised one bushy grey eyebrow: a summons to the table. Brady pressed through the birthday group, seizing the advantage of the situation to squeeze close to the blonde as he passed, rubbing against the back of her jeans. But by the time he sat down, he had already put her young body out of his mind.

'You've come then, have you?' Kelly was his usual bluff self, gripping Brady by the forearm and giving him a hearty slap which, had he been packing his Colt in the usual position, would have damn near broken his ribs. Brady resented this underhand check. MacStifoin sitting there slab-like and unsmiling made him doubly nervous.

'Satisfied? If you'd asked, I would've told you it wasn't there. Shall we go to the men's lavatory and do a full check?'

'No, no, that won't be necessary, Liam. Relax, boy! Tell us what you've got.'

Brady scratched his beard, thoughtfully. 'I bring many a tale for you, Kelly. Much to be concerned about: perhaps more than you're wantin' to hear. I'm thinkin' none of us can relax now – not after this.'

Kelly sipped his drink, carefully. 'Oh, really? Your man got away and now we've two corpses to fly home to their mothers – that's the only tale I've heard so far. I hope you have something better to offer, because this business is starting to get very messy. As field commander, they were your responsibility.'

'They screwed up!' Brady retaliated defensively. 'I was that far away.' He snapped his fingers. 'I could have taken Tyler softly softly if not for those two. I bloody told them not to crowd him out! You know how it is in this game, Kelly: no second chances, and we bury our mistakes.'

'We'll have to wait and see. There'll be a General Headquarters enquiry, and you can state your case then. In the meantime, what's this stuff about a mole among us?'

Christ! An enquiry. They were out for him at every turn – the bastards. Better tread carefully.

'Lochinvar?' asked Brady, tantalisingly; it was his ace in the hole. 'All in good time. I'd like to ask a question of me own first' – his eyes flicked over MacStifoin with obvious distaste – 'like what's this caveman doing here with you, eh?' They were barely an arm's length apart, Brady sneering down the big man's throat. 'Sure you're far from the kennel tonight, Three-Fingers.'

MacStifoin winced at the insult, his brow furrowed with hatred. So, he thought, Brady could not forget his little lesson; now he's pushing it.

Perversely, Kelly let them measure each other. MacStifoin was still the toughest, the hardest man on the staff; the kind of animal they encouraged – up to a point. 'Three-Fingers' – sweet Jesus few men would dare say that to his face. He had choked men with his bare hands for it, carved others with a straight razor. Nobody called him names and got away with it.

'Now, let's not be calling names tonight, Liam,' said MacStifoin breaking the eye-contact to diffuse the situation. 'Three lads far from home, and all.' Slowly, he opened his great paws and laid them flat upon the table, the finger stumps and scar tissue in full view. In that moment Brady knew just how tight Eddie Kelly was holding the leash. What Brady was into now gave him all the leverage he would need for what was to follow.

Far from home they were, indeed, and Brady had expected they would send a man of Kelly's rank. The situation demanded it: it was a ticking bomb, this news of a threat to their Middle-East arms connection – one which could not be managed from across the water. There was also the revelation of Lochinvar and all the many implications: just the rumour of a highly-placed deep-penetration agent could tear their current organisation apart. It needed the diplomatic touch of Eddie Kelly's capable hands to steer the rudder to the best advantage of the Cause. Brady had made his personal assessment: assassination in Libya had no direct impact on him, but a British tout close to the General Staff meant his life was in danger every time he went operational. All the more reason for clearing out the dead-wood and starting afresh – and he would be happy to do the culling himself.

'Listen to me now, Liam,' Kelly's bonhomie vanished as he took control. 'MacStifoin is here because I want him here – that's all you need to know and I don't have to explain to the likes of you, now do I?'

Brady shrugged.

'Thank you. This isn't a social call, and we're not here for you and him to kiss and cuddle. I've been meeting Arabs all bleedin' day, more Arabs than I've ever seen. They say our presence is required somewhere hot.'

'*Our* presence?' Brady, with his winning hand, was pushing from all sides. Here was power and influence and he would no more lose control of it than turn his back on MacStifoin ever again. 'Seems like I'm the one with something to sell now, doesn't it, Eddie?'

'Right enough, boy. But I'm in charge, like it or not . . .' Conversation ceased abruptly as a fisherman's sweater weaved past them searching for a non-existent door in their corner. Brady pointed the way to the men's room, and the sweater weaved away again.

'Where do we go from here?' asked Brady.

'No arguments this time. A deal has already been made: they want your head.'

'What!'

'For debriefing.'

'Very bloody funny. What's this about somewhere hot?' A hint of suspicion now in his low voice. 'I'm not going to Libya. Last time was bad enough: I had the shits for weeks.'

'Azziz gets your head, I said. I'm taking you to him, myself. But not to Libya – even though he pressed for it. It's difficult for him to leave the country just now. It seems like a precarious time for all their people; they've put the block on all trips abroad. I told them under no circumstances would the General Staff sanction a visit to Tripoli. What I didn't tell them was our reasons.'

'Which are?'

'That soddin' CIA surveillance is too bloody good in Qadaffi's backyard. They'd be bound to find out one way or another, and publicise our connection again.'

'Thereby losing American sympathy and money?'

'Absolutely right. So we compromised on somewhere close enough for him, and quiet enough for us. I'm afraid you've no choice, boy.'

But Brady was not complaining. In spite of what he would have them believe, inside he was rejoicing.

'Seems I'd do well to make the best of it,' he said, toying idly with a beer mat. 'And the arrangements? You called me here for a sea departure, was it?'

'There's a boat in the marina: a motorised yacht that can take the Channel crossing smooth as silk. We leave tonight on the tide. The three of us.'

Quickly, Kelly outlined the plan. They would board the *Tarsalus*, head south-east across the Channel for the small French fishing port of Fécamp, a few miles east of Calais. It was a small harbour used mainly by weekend tourists and their boats, and immigration details were handled by the local harbour master who registered boats and their passengers. The captain of the *Tarsalus* would make sure they arrived there around three in the morning, after the harbour office was closed. As was the convention, he would register his passengers when the office re-opened later that morning; but he would register only himself and his two crew members. So none of them would be checked against Interpol or French Security stop-lists. Once outside the UK they could move relatively freely again.

A Tunisian driver would be there to meet them, one of an army of 'students' in the pay of Colonel Azziz. He would be waiting by the harbour wall. The car would be a metallic green BMW. They would stop for the rest of the night at a small, anonymous guesthouse, and enjoy a fast, comfortable drive south the next day.

'Just where is "south"?' Brady wanted to know.

'Malta,' said Kelly, his grey eyes beginning to dance at the thought. 'Our appointment is for ten o'clock, Thursday morning, at the Libyan Cultural Affairs Bureau in Valetta. I thing you'll like it: the best hotel on the island, overlooking the bay and with views of the old Fortress of St Elmo. Mercedes and driver provided – a touch of luxury, I'm thinking.'

'You must have impressed someone.'

'Nothing of the sort. These Arabs look after their friends. But Trafalgar Square should have taught you how they treat their enemies. They were pretty anxious that we accept the invitation after what I told them. If you listen carefully you can hear it on the evening breeze: the sound of little Arab arseholes all quivering in fear.'

Brady cracked a grin in spite of himself, avoiding the solicitous leer of MacStifoin, who had reason to want some shared moment between them. Kelly held up a hand as if to ward off false impressions.

'That's not the mad Colonel, you understand. They say he's a game old bird, scared of nothin' but pork sausages, that one. It's those hangers-on who'll suffer if ever he goes. There'd be public executions for all his cronies. That's why they want to get this bastard mercenary, what's his name?'

'Tyler – Richard Christian Tyler.' Strangely, Brady found he enjoyed pronouncing the man's name. He had thought of little else since the bleeding and broken George Stephenson had informed him of the ex-legionnaire's tidy little job on Terence Lynch at the Savoy Hotel. Damn Tyler's soul for that! Now Brady uttered his name the way a hunter speaks of the awesome beast he longs to kill.

'Where's your car now?' asked Kelly.

'Round the back here. And yours?'

'The same.' Kelly tugged back his great cuff and scrutinised the steel Rolex. 'We'll best be away now, and take both cars. There's a boat boy at the marina to look after the loose ends. Drink up, now. I said we'd be aboard by 9.15.'

They drained their glasses quickly, Kelly and MacStifoin. As the older man set his own back on the table he noticed that Brady, who had not touched his, was smiling inscrutably to himself.

'Tell me,' said Brady. 'I've done a bellyful of work these past months. What if I'd told you to piss off? What if I'd refused to go?'

Kelly pursed his thin lips, then set his craggy face in that familiar expression that seemed bereft of emotion yet all the more menacing because of it.

'I don't think we need talk about that, do you?' His eyes steered Brady to the wall of muscle standing between them. The meaning was lost on no one.

Brady grinned goodnaturedly. 'You know, that's just what I thought you'd say.'

Stepping out into the darkness of the pub's rear car-park, Brady was flushed with lethal excitement. Here he was, once again, on top of the situation – like in those hell-fire street battles on the Falls Road when his unit wasted two army patrols and a dog team, and he knew it was his night. A strong, rapid pulse throbbed in his neck, where the blood was on fire. That humiliating evening in the farmhouse in South Armagh was replaying over and over in his head: the evening he was sure he was finished.

'Given the sack,' he murmured as they walked between the rows of cars, but neither of them heard. A dirty, bloody sack. Naked before the General Staff, MacStifoin's piss-hole eyes always behind him, always watching. A stick to beat the unruly dog. He was going to Valetta all right, but in their eyes it was only under the threat of MacStifoin's presence.

He hated that.

There were no lights in the car-park, only a soft orange glow from sodium lights in the street fronting the Dog and Fox. Kelly fumbled for his keys, cursing the while till he got the driver's door open.

'Will I follow the two of you in mine?' asked Brady. They could not see one another's faces now.

'No, don't do that,' Kelly cut in, a little too quickly. The soft hairs on Brady's neck stood up. 'Tell you what,

MacStifoin can go with you. He knows the way. I'd hate for you to get lost.'

Every shade of meaning, he missed nothing – and knew how far they trusted him.

'All right, fine by me,' Brady said. 'We'll be right behind you.' MacStifoin followed him to his Granada without a word.

As if in warning, Kelly called after them. 'Don't you take all night.'

Twenty minutes later Kelly was sitting on his car bonnet at the entrance to the boatyard – boats on blocks all around him, faint and pale in the near darkness. He pulled deeply on a cigarette, feeling the burning smoke fill his lungs. Below him the *Tarsalus* creaked against the sheets, pulling seaward with the ebbing tide, and the captain looked with concern at the sky.

Kelly checked his watch again.

There was no sign of Brady's Granada. After the second set of traffic lights it had vanished from his mirror. He flicked the dwindling butt into a kerb-side puddle, cursed once more, and started his own engine. At that moment there was a squeal of tyres and the big Ford spun round the gateway and into the boatyard, the low exhaust silencer crunching over the bump in the road. The engine raced loudly then died. Brady broke open the driver's door and emerged carrying a canvas holdall in his left hand. He was breathing heavily.

'Where've you been?' demanded Kelly. 'Can't you follow a simple instruc–'

But his anger stalled as he looked into the resolute face of the man from South Armagh and noticed the dripping cut at the edge of his left eye. Kelly peared into the Granada, but he knew in his gut that Brady was completely alone.

'Where is he, Liam?' Kelly heard himself almost stammer in disbelief. 'MacStifoin – where the fuck is he?'

With slow disdain Brady threw back his head. Cold, black blood fell upon his cheek. For a long second

214

he stood there silent, with the overhead street-light picking out the flat, brutal forehead and broad, blunt nose.

Kelly's voice was hoarse with outrage, almost a graveyard whisper. 'A fucking animal is what you are, Brady. A fucking animal.'

'That's right, Eddie,' he said, seemingly unaffected. 'One less for breakfast, I think.'

SEVENTEEN

TRANSFIXED ON A barren moonscape, hovering in half-light, the bedouin of the Libyan desert shiver under their goat-hair mantles and await the dawn. The instant, they say, when a white thread may be distinguished from a black one, then they must rise up and pray. Before that time they wait in a grey wilderness of dreams, and all around is God-less night.

It was Friday: the Sabbath.

In the capital – a wilderness of another kind – dawn came late on that Friday, for the storm, which had threatened for a day and a night now, had still not broken and the sun was a stranger. In the mosques across Tripoli the loud-speakers wailed their call to prayer – a pale substitute for the full and rich sound of the old muezzins who no longer climbed the steps to their minarets, having embraced the benefits of oil wealth and the coming of modern-age hi-fidelity.

The more superstitious of the holy men looked heavenward in bleak dismay, as if sensing that the glowering, leaden clouds that churned in the eastern sky willed the face of God not to look down upon their devotions.

Darkness pervaded their prayers.

But, come darkness or storm, Friday morning prayers must proceed; the life-blood of the Islamic State. This single event was the culmination of the Moslem week, and the time for rededication of the self to the cause of the one true God and to his prophet Mohammed.

So it was on that black Friday that the leader of the People's Jamahiriayah chose to harness that power and superstition for an historic meeting. In extraordinary fashion he had called together the reconstituted Revolutionary Command council, along with the Lesser Cabinet, in the Green Chamber of Azizyah Barracks, to be briefed on the results of his recent meditations. A self-styled philosopher and theologian, Qadaffi had long since ceased to involve himself with the minutiae of day-to-day government, and he allowed such of the more able civil servants that passed his criteria of selfless commitment to Islam to take control of the less sensitive posts. Small degrees of power and influence had thus gradually devolved on the bureaucratic minds of the Arab middle classes, in order that Qadaffi might further devote himself to the future path of the Popular Revolution. His meditations took him more and more frequently back to the desert of his childhood, where distractions from his holy mission were mercifully few. There solutions to the most insoluble of problems were often made clear to him.

Neither did he fear to venture from the capital, the seat of his power, where there were always voices in the shadows and ears that listened to those vile tongues, for he was careful to retain his grip on all *real* power. What need he fear? His acolytes controlled the strategic areas of government which would guarantee his continued leadership. *Insh allah* – as Allah wills it, he had told himself. By force, if necessary.

In the Green Chamber the atmosphere was one

of expectant dread, made all the more oppressive by the almost choking humidity of the room. They all waited patiently. Qadaffi would be the last to arrive, as befitted his position. On one side of the table sat his senior power brokers: those 'brothers' who had belonged to the Free Officers' Union which had launched the revolution, and those whose families were closely linked to the al Qadadfa tribe. They included Prime Minister Jalloud and Colonel Azziz, the controller of the Intelligence network; then the Commander-in-Chief of the Armed Forces, and next to him one of Jalloud's pawns, the Head of the Libyan police force or Popular Militia. The lesser lights, the Secretaries for Justice, Petroleum, the Treasury and the Interior, the privileged but essentially powerless puppets, were careful to acknowledge the hawks in the Chamber politely, with restrained greetings to each cheek. That was their protocol – to do less was a slight they could ill afford, for at that table enemies were easily acquired.

Yet, regardless of their various affiliations and political orientations, every man in the Green Chamber sat essentially alone. For the members of the Council, seated around the oval table like numerals on a watch-face, the tension in that strip-lit room was as palpable as that agitating the eastern sky. A sudden flash of sheet lightning outside emphasised the unease felt by each man present.

The past two weeks in Tripoli had brought news of the death of Ibrahim the traitor. Around the government buildings huddled groups had taken to falling silent when any stranger walked by. There had been further talk of spies in the Cabinet – men in league with all manner of devils, from the Great Satan of the West to the agents of Khomeini in the east. It was fairly standard hysterical gossip from minds whose ancestors had once spun great lyrical poems. And when rumour had risen to its most insidious, the order was given, clear and direct:

'The President of The People's Jamahiriya, Brother Colonel Muammar al Qadaffi requests and demands the presence of all loyal members of the People's Revolutionary Command council and the People's Lesser Cabinet to discuss the further advancement of the Popular Revolution.'

That one word '*loyal*' had seared their eyes like the white-hot metal of the camel brander's iron. The sub-text was also clear: all who do not attend are to be considered traitors to the People's Revolution and may be arrested and dealt with accordingly. It was a simple tactic, and was not the first time it had been used. Omar al Meheisha, a co-conspirator with Qadaffi in the September Revolution, had received such a summons in 1976 after his vocal opposition to extravagant funding of overseas operations. Meheisha had been lucky: he had escaped, and fled the country for Tunisia, where he had founded the Libyan National League opposition group from other expatriate dissidents there. But others, smaller men, had been arrested and subjected to popular justice and summary execution.

Now, once more, Qadaffi was playing to frighten the rabbit from the long grass. Of course, the rabbits trembled. And for those who had secret connections with proscribed political parties, the green-edged summons was a nerve-racking affair. It left only two courses of action: attend and pray that the light of suspicion fall upon the next man; or cut and run, like Meheisha and many since him, for the safety of a regime antagonistic to the Libyan leader – of which there were many even in the Arab world. If the former was a dangerous course, designed only for the strong, then the latter was no less perilous, for the People's assassins under the control of Colonel Azziz ranged far and wide across all continents – and with the blessing of the diplomatic passport. A seven-man hit squad had failed to take Meheisha in Cairo only due to the intervention of the Egyptian security forces. But

Azziz was a patient man, and the running must stop sometime.

In silence they sat and waited, the eerie half-light from outside and the room's own strip lights illuminating a world suspended in time. A white-jacketed steward poured water whilst the member's chairs scraped the marble floor nervously, but no one drank, as if no man trusted the steadiness of his own hand. Exactly how many of them had reason to fear that meeting was difficult to judge, but in any event the neurotic in each man knew that innocence was but a relative term when exposed to the uniquely subjective judgement of Muammar al Qadaffi, the herd boy from the Sirte.

At 8.59 a.m. two chairs still remained empty: those of the Secretary for the Economy and the Secretary for Justice. Their name-plates on the table, forlorn as headstones, only served to underline their absence; and in many eyes they must have already ceased to exist.

At 9 a.m. precisely, a uniformed adjutant appeared at the door, pert and officious, gold braid tumbling from his epaulettes, and announced the entry of the President of the Socialist People's Libyan Arab Jamahiriyah: Colonel Muammar Qadaffi. Instantly the room stood as one man, adjusted its unworthy cuffs and held its breath. Then in he came like a conqueror, striding confidently, head low as if oblivious of them.

A small gasp broke from the mouth of the Education Secretary at the sight of the Colonel's full military uniform and slim black swagger-stick. Neither had been seen in years, and the significance of their reappearance was lost on no one. The psychological effect was unsettling and awe-inspiring, exactly as he had planned it.

Qadaffi strode the length of the room, the cleated heels of his riding boots echoing to the high ceiling of the doomed chamber, till he came to a halt at the head of the table. He removed his peaked cap, black gloves and dark glasses with tantalising slowness. Whilst the Cabinet succumbed to silence, he laid the black stick

220

upon the table, where it rolled over under its own weight, drawing their eyes. Finally he adjusted his black leather Sam Browne belt and cross-brace, until both lay perfectly straight again over the pale green tunic. Centre-stage now, he threw his weight forward, spreading both palms theatrically over the table like some fundamentalist preacher, and gazed with satisfaction around the polished wooden surface until his eyes fell inevitably, though without surprise, upon the empty places. It was a glance that seals men's fate.

'It appears two of our number will not be joining us,' he offered sardonically. There was no sound around the table. Not a murmur, not a comment from the politicians standing behind their briefing notes. 'No matter, we shall come to that in a moment. Please be seated, brothers.'

The request was accompanied, in the usual Qadaffi style, by a gently benign lowering of his outstretched arms, as if he was commanding the waves to recede and fully expected their obedience.

'First, let me thank you all brothers, for answering the summons. It is a rare pleasure for us all to be together in full session instead of in those tedious small working parties, I think you will agree.' Nervous assent from those at the lower end of the predatory chain. 'As you'll have already noticed, I am dressed as a soldier, and it pleases me to do so once more. Let me give notice that from this moment I dress to do God's work – as should we all.' At this his eyes widened visibly, fixing on the Council members and drawing vigorous agreement.

Satisfied, he continued, 'Well, I say to you now, the only man God embraces, the only kind of man worthy of His divine favour, is the man who is willing to kill for Him – and, if necessary, die for him also. This much I know.'

The familiar abrasive rhetoric flowed with a new vitality. This was what the fundamentalists there, the ones who preached Jihad, had been longing to hear. But the intelligentsia and career bureaucrats found in

221

his strident words even greater reason to fear for the future of the People's Jamahiriyah. They were few in number, the ones who wished for a less passionate leadership and a more pragmatic government, but their fears were shared by many other, more compliant individuals at that table.

The Education Secretary, a corpulent and spent academic who had relinquished the Economics chair at Al Fatah University in Tripoli some five years prior, at the invitation of the RCC, chewed thoughtfully on his heavy black moustache. Despite his leader's energetic ranting he managed to partially block him out and slip into his own private and endangered world. From his place he watched Qadaffi with a certain detachment: the sweeping arm movements, the fist that crushed the enemy. The Education .Secretary's head was full of questions, ones he shared only with his wife, for he had learned to trust no one else. Brother Colonel, can mere rhetoric save the economy? Does it build markets or regulate inflation? Do you believe enlightenment can follow after the dark night of repression? What were the young minds under his own care to inherit from the vast wealth now being squandered on a succession of sponsored causes and foreign adventures? It was now a vulgar and expensive costume drama, this one-time dream of a People's Government; and what was most frightening to him was that he, supposedly one of the country's most gifted economists, no longer cared. But he held his tongue, as always, clutching for the comfort of his official limousine, the privilege of the official pass, and the villa at Janzur. For his family's sake, he told himself – only for them. Poor payment for a dream betrayed.

And Ibrahim was dead . . .

Yet he was not alone in his misery. The evidence was there for anyone not blinded by the passions of zealotry. There were serious economic and social problems facing the country, and with the fall of their oil revenues all the five-year plans had been revised downward yet again. The on-off war with Chad in the south had gone badly, with the loss of military hardware and equipment valued in millions. Foreign policy was a bitter joke, for in spite of an unregulated budget of billions given in aid to friends abroad, Libya remained isolated, was treated with suspicion by East and West alike, and was shunned by even its closest Arab neighbours. All was madness, and the lunatics had indeed taken over the asylum. And still the state was supporting a mishmash of insurgents and revolutionaries all over the world, with funds more urgently needed at home to establish agricultural and irrigation programmes, while Libya badly needed a manufacturing industry to offset the crippling cost of its dependency upon consumer items imported from abroad. The vital question was how long could the oil last? Another forty years maximum. Then what? A return to the precarious desert existence of their fathers? A life of preying one tribe upon the other whilst Washington and Moscow played chess with their homeland?

It was ninety minutes later before the President finished his sermon. His figure had softened slightly, as a man does when he has drunk his fill and satisfied a raging thirst. For the first time that morning he took his seat, then he sipped a little water – a small and feeble gesture so that all might see his frailty, his underlying humanity shining through.

Now they were waiting for an explanation for two empty chairs. But it was not Qadaffi that rose to satisfy their curiosity. His political brain chose to let Jalloud reveal the news to the Chamber. Let them associate retribution with Jalloud and not himself. Qadaffi eased back in his chair and watched their faces, his own face granite-hard and impassive.

After a moment Jalloud stood up, and consulted the blue folder in which he carried the report of his counter-subversion section of the militia. This body, which was known and feared wherever men met in secret to exchange ideas, had been set up with the

223

guidance of seconded officers from the German Democratic Republic, and like East German intelligence itself was both ruthless and thorough. The findings of this particular investigation had given Jalloud immense satisfaction, for he had suspected for some time what the report purported to prove: new traitors within the Cabinet, and behind them the elusive hand of Ibrahim's opposition group. He cleared his throat and gave a nod towards the head of the table before proceeding.

'Two days ago, and in response to information received from a friendly source,' he began in the smoke-screening jargon of intelligence men the world over, 'my Internal Security department began raiding certain locations around Tripoli which are known to be popular amongst malcontents. As a result we arrested a number of civil servants and army officers known to have had contacts with a proscribed organisation outside the country.' A wry smile came to Jalloud's lips – every man present knew the name of the group to which he referred but even the utterance of that name had been expressly forbidden within the people's Jamahiriyah. 'Two personal computers were also seized, which had the necessary paraphernalia for a desk-top publishing facility and a virtual library of subversive propaganda urging the violent overthrow of the state. Poorly argued gibberish. These pathetic traitors and criminals lost no time in implicating their contacts and co-conspirators, some of whom have been duplicitous enough to gain high office in the Government of the Jamahiriyah.'

His voice stopped now and he allowed himself a slow glance around at his audience. The President – a co-conspirator in Jalloud's own drama – put out a languid hand to recover his dark glasses. Their mirrored surfaces, perched again above the high, imperious nose and the broad, brutal lips, now haunted the hearts of guilty and innocent alike.

Jalloud continued: 'Two of those men are the former

224

Secretary for Justice and the former Secretary for the Economy. You will note their absence.

A blind man would notice their absence, thought the Education Secretary, but he said nothing.

'They were to have been denounced by myself at this very meeting.' Here Jalloud poked the table with a square-cut finger-nail, holding his audience with an accusing gaze. 'However, they appear to have received a prior warning and this morning attempted to flee the country, boarding a light aircraft at a small airfield to the south of the city. We waited until they had taken off before forcing them down with the help of fighters of the People's Air Force.'

Jalloud completed his report with just one sentence that chilled the Education Secretary quite completely. 'The two traitors are now in custody, awaiting intensive interrogation.' He let the paper drop with a whisper to the table. 'I must now insist, brother members of the Chamber, that pending the completion of my investigations, there will be no attempts to leave this country without the written permission of the President's Office. All official visits abroad should be cancelled, and rescheduled through the Controller of the Libyan People's Bureaux here in Azizyah Barracks.'

The pretence of a policy discussion was soon dispensed with and, having sown the seeds of fear, the President dismissed all but the most senior members of the Green Chamber, who went into closed session to discuss the looming threat to internal security. When that too was over, most of them proceeded from the Green Chamber to their waiting limousines.

But they did not all leave. Jalloud and a selected group of military men waited behind in an anteroom, careful not to be noticed by Colonel Azziz as he departed, careful that Azziz did not detect his own exclusion from the group.

Thirty minutes later, they reconvened in secret with the President once more at the head of the table. Outside the Chamber door Captain Kim kept vigil, smoking Marlboros continuously. He watched as a naval officer approached from the far end of the eastern corridor, recognising the gold rings on his blue sleeves and the white-peaked cap styled unmistakably after the Soviet fashion. When the officer reached the door he was challenged in English by the squat, muscular Korean. The man produced a sheet of green-edged paper stamped with Qadaffi's personal seal and the signature of the principal Private Secretary to the President's Office. As Kim returned the paper, he observed in the officer's sharp, tanned features the arrogant assurance of one whose presence is expected. Kim searched him thoroughly before allowing him to enter, enjoying that one small act of retaliation for his scorn. No Arab enjoyed the humiliation of a body search, and with venom upon his lips the naval officer straightened his uniform and entered the Chamber with a whipcrack salute.

Five heads looked up from their identical folders, but it was the head of the Armed Forces who invited the latecomer to the table.

'Brother Colonel, this is the man I was telling you about, Rear-Admiral Sidi Omar al Mukhtar.'

The Colonel's face brightened. He put down the map he had been studying and came forward to shake the hand of the naval officer and embrace him warmly. 'I believe you have important news to bring your President.'

Sidi Omar al Mukhtar was proud to ally himself to the holy cause and when he made the most important announcement of his life there was an unmistakable tinge of excitement in his words.

'The operation is proceeding according to the plan worked out by the Joint Military Committee. Shortly before dawn this morning, a Foxtrot-class submarine of the People's Naval Forces put to sea, undetected by the NATO forces in the Mediterranean.'

A sudden fear seized the President.

'Undetected, you say? How can that be, when their satellite pictures are bound to reveal the sudden disappearance of one of our vessels from dock?'

Satisfaction radiated from the Rear-Admiral.

'The satellites will report no movement from our submarine dock because the Foxtrot-class vessel was immediately replaced in its berth by a ninety-metre mock-up – an empty, metal shell whose external surfaces will be kept at the correct temperature for a fish undergoing routine maintenance. Not even their infra-red cameras will know the difference.'

The six other men in the Green Chamber looked from one to the other now with a satisfaction they could barely contain. Hands clasped, the President offered up a silent prayer to his God . . . and a second later a roll of thunder shook the foundations of Azizyah Barracks. The promised rain at last came down in torrents, bringing release to the darkened sky. Qadaffi received the sign with thanks and stepped to the window.

'It is good news you have brought us,' he said, and then laughed. 'Ha! The best is yet to come, and truly we shall be avenged. Let the People's terror begin!'

EIGHTEEN

THE LIBYAN ARAB Airways jet made its final approach to Tripoli airport from the seaward side. From his window seat in first class, Tyler could see the black ribbon of the coastal highway against the vast red expanse of forbidding desert, and the small, dotted settlements of run-down farm shacks once owned and worked by Italian colonisers. Dark olive groves by the acre.

With uncharacteristic nervousness, he checked his cover; ran through the details of his new West German identity. He fingered the passport, checking the dates on the visa stamps in the way the Libyans would: to ensure no prior or planned visits to Israel or South Africa. On page ten of the FDR passport was the green eagle stamp of the Libyan People's Bureau in Bonn; a stamp from any other Bureau would be rejected immediately. It was a perfect forgery, with just a hint of a blur to the Arabic script – nothing too cute.

Despite the hours of preparation Tyler was still jumpy. That was a good way to feel, he told himself; it kept him honed. Alcohol had not passed his lips in three days. He was physically fit

228

and his mind razor-sharp, the way it would need to be when the awkward questions began. He knew that once he stepped off the plane he would be alone in bandit country – naked as a baby, with only Halliday's warnings and advice to sustain him, and the lap-top computer they had given him in Bonn for coded communications. It was sitting next to him on the seat and he was to use it only in an emergency.

For a fleeting moment he wished his Arabic was better than the few stock phrases he had picked up, but that was not important now. What was important was to live his German cover until he was contacted by Halliday's man. They had given him a passport, a name and an occupation: Karl Heinz Toll, electrical engineer. But it needed more than a written identity to create a durable cover; he must breathe life into the part. When his heels hit the tarmac, he would model himself on Teufel, a German corporal he had met pulling duty in Beirut with the UN peace-keeping force. The dead man's precise, disciplined mannerisms and rapid, humourless smile would help him create the new persona. Overtly he would be just another expatriate engineer greedy for the huge tax-free consultancy fees offered by the People's Jamahiriyah. It was a solid cover, for without such men modernisation would come painfully slowly to Libya.

There was further incentive for them to be glad to receive him: troop-carrying aircraft for the Libyan armed forces. Tyler smiled to himself in satisfaction. The grip in the overhead locker contained his real passport, but also a politely-worded invitation to call upon the Libyan Secretary for Defence Acquisitions at his office. The hook had been baited from a fictitious holding address in Zurich; the bait was twenty-five US Army surplus Hercules C130 troop transports – top-quality aircraft denied to Qadaffi by rigorous US export bans and close end-use monitoring.

Good insurance, he told himself. But if Liam Brady was already in Tripoli he was as good as dead.

The plane taxied to a standstill before the main arrivals building. As the doors slid open, a sudden blast of hot, humid air shot through the flight cabin. Tyler stepped onto the embarkation stairs, buttoning the jacket of his light-weight beige suit with a sudden sense of forboding. Taking in the apron at a glance, and seeing no obvious reception committee, he descended the steps carrying his precious leather grip. There was the unmistakable putrid stink of drains in the air, which was common to most airports in the Middle East.

In front of him the line of disembarking passengers made its way up a flight of steps a hundred metres distant, to enter the glass complex of the arrivals hall. On the apron Tyler's face was a mask of disinterest, though his trained eye missed not the smallest detail. Aside from the usual ground crew in oily coveralls, there were armed guards. Twelve khaki-clad security men, carrying the worst-maintained machine-pistols he had ever seen, were slouched in the shade of the motorised stairways. His soldier's brain registered disgust at two cracked wooden stocks he noticed, and the general griminess of all the other weapons. Shit, no wonder the Egyptians had whipped their arses back in '77, he snorted inwardly. Four days was all the Libyan army had lasted in that border war. And small wonder the bastards had turned to low-intensity operations thereafter. And with a vengeance!

Atop the arrivals building a plastic hoarding announced their arrival in the People's Jamahiriyah in large white Arabic script. In accordance with the President's own directive, no translation was provided on public signs and notices. Like everything else he saw, the hoarding too was covered with a thin film of yellow dust. Fortunately, Tyler could read enough Arabic to distinguish a public toilet from a post office,

230

but little more. Hopefully, their man on the ground could supply the rest.

Tyler followed the line of Europeans to the non-Arab immigration desk. Again, there were no signs to announce which desk was which: the clear division by race spoke for itself. A fat security guard redirected any strays with eloquent jerks of the head, his fat face resembling that of a sullen infant. The butt of his machine-pistol was propped idly against a jutting hip-bone, the way Hollywood cowboys would pose with their Winchesters.

Tyler scanned the shuffling line ahead of him. They were businessmen mostly, and a handful of Turkish guestworkers laughing among themselves over the plunder they had each brought back with them: oil workers with the portable hi-fis and other luxuries they would need in the isolation of their residential camps. Almost no one, it seemed, came to Libya for a holiday.

He joined the queue of passengers being scrutinised in desultory fashion by immigration and security police officers. They too, were dressed in tight-fitting khaki and highly polished leather shoes, but those who worked inside the air-conditioned building were obviously of higher status than their colleagues languishing outside the heat. Two men operated each desk, their movements predictably arrogant, their faces uniformally impassive. When his turn came, Tyler stepped level with the desk and handed his passport to the moustachioed official.

In the pregnant silence he slid his free hand into his trouser pocket. There was sweat upon his palm; he wiped it on the cotton fabric inside the pocket and waited. The official glanced through the passport details which had been translated into Arabic in accordance with immigration regulations. Then slowly he flicked through his well-thumbed blue book for any record of the passport. Tyler knew he had nothing to fear; the book contained only those names and passport numbers supplied by Interpol or the Libyan Intelligence community. His German passport was cleaner than kleenex. Satisfied of that, the Libyan's quick brown eyes looked him up and down. Involuntarily, Tyler stiffened. Some sixth sense told the immigration man that this European was a shade too fit-looking to be just an ordinary businessman. Too much the classic mesomorph, Tyler's full musculature was in stark contrast to the paunches of some of the foreign passengers or the worn-out frailty of others. Double chins and spreading backsides.

'You are English?' The soft tones were almost an accusation.

'*Wie, bitte?*' Tyler feigned bemusement in response.

'I said, you are English. You look like an English.'

Tyler managed a faint good-humoured smile.

'Excuse me, please. I am German. There is my passport.'

'Why do you smile?'

'It is a joke, is it not? We all look the same, we Europeans. *Ja?*'

The immigration man was not amused. 'What is your business in the People's Jamahiriyah?' he asked, his foot discreetly operating a black stud on the floor beneath his desk.

Tyler opened his grip and produced the letter with a flourish. Suck on that, he thought; a little respect is what's needed here, I think.

The immigration man's eyes widened, obviously impressed. He knew better than to impede or harrass the guest of a Cabinet official, and he had no wish to be transferred to some fly-blown border-crossing station. He had already had his fill of checking camel trains in and out of Sudan.

'Thank you, Mr Karl, everything seems to be in order.' The immigration man returned the passport and the letter. 'Perhaps I could have one of my colleagues contact the Secretary's office and arrange a courtesy car and chauffeur for you. It would be no trouble.'

'That is very kind of you, Inspector, but not necessary, thank you.' Tyler threw both documents into the grip and snapped it shut. At that moment, whilst his face was still square-on to the covert observation window, a motor-driven camera snapped off a dozen close-up shots. They would be included in the day's batch when it was collected later by the man from the Interior Ministry. Behind the glass of the darkened window, hooded eyes watched the powerful European stride purposefully towards the baggage reclaim area.

It took him a whole hour to clear customs, as they made a great show of checking for booze and drugs. Incredibly, they even checked the labels in his underpants. Tyler enjoyed the high farce of the event; it soothed and distracted his nerves. Humour in the face of danger was important to his psychological survival. No, it was vital, since all the while his subconscious had been whispering 'If they catch you, Tyler, they'll burn your eyes out with a cigarette, boy.'

Outside at last, he pushed his way through a throng of greeters and hailed one of the yellow municipal taxis that plied between the airport and Tripoli itself. It was a Fiat, newish, though heavy use and cavalier driving by the Tunisian driver had broken its will. The driver's gold teeth grinned at him out of an ebony-coloured face.

'Where you go, John? Where you go?'

'Poseiden Hotel, downtown.'

The driver seemed to approve the choice of hotel and took off at speed, weaving madly through a chicane of parked vehicles.

It was twenty-four kilometers into Tripoli along a new, chocolate-smooth highway flanked by flat scrub and the occasional cultivated patch. At frequent intervals they passed road-surfacing gangs, where oriental faces predominated. At length, the bare dust-blown road gave way to large square housing developments sitting apparently in the middle of nowhere. The driver attempted to explain their significance, but

Tyler remained confused as to whether they were new towns for the local population or camps for foreign oil-workers. Nor did he care much – he was altogether glad to have made it through the first line. But he knew he would never be safe whilst he remained in the country; he was too conspicuous. And he had not missed the darkened window, had not missed a faint movement behind the glass, and he realised his face was now on record – instantly recognisable by anyone who knew him.

He could smell the harbour long before the taxi pulled onto the Sharia Gemal Abdul Nasser, the main road skirting the bay. To the left, the old go-downs and wooden warehouses had been painted green in commemoration of the 1 September Revolution, and beyond lay a series of intersecting streets and squares. In these squares sat men of all ages drinking coffee in street cafés; and on one disused lot, where an office building had once stood, a group of off-duty soldiers in camouflage pattern were kicking a plastic football back and forth. On the right side of the road was the busy cargo-handling area, where container ships and rusty freighters disgorged food and luxury items from Italy, West Germany and Japan. Stevedores leaned against stacks of pallets, smoking endless cigarettes and rereading their newspapers.

The driver stopped before the Poseidon Hotel on the Sharia First of September and cheerfully carried Tyler's case into the foyer, where he spoke excitedly with the short, dumpy chief clerk. The hotel was situated on the east side of the city, not half a mile from the sea that would bring the equipment he would need – God and Hamid willing. This would be as good a place as any to wait for the next stage of the operation to begin.

The chief clerk's face was blemished by a strawberry-coloured birthmark that covered the left side of his face. He grinned broadly at the broad-shouldered westerner – surely here would be a substantial gratuity.

234

Such a man would deem it his obligation to reward any helpful and discreet service.

Tyler signed the hotel register and waited patiently while the clerk selected one of the brass keys from the peg-board behind his desk. It was then, as the clerk peered past him and into the Sharia First of September, that Tyler followed his gaze and spotted the tail car.

Jesus Christ! His brain raced. Perhaps Brady was here, after all!

A smart white Mercedes automatic was double-parked a few metres from the hotel entrance. For a moment Tyler wondered if he had seen that very car overtake his taxi on the airport highway, but he could not quite be sure. There were so many cars just like it all over Tripoli: high-status wheels for Government acolytes. The man in the driving seat, a Libyan, wore a thick bushy moustache and mirrored sunglasses; a second man, tall and slender and wearing a steel-grey safari suit and leather sandals, was leaning in at the driver's window, apparently chatting idly. The car was clearly obstructing the busy street, but the two seemed in no hurry to move. When he snatched another look, Tyler noticed the man in the safari suit glance into the hotel lobby.

'Police?' said Tyler.

'Who knows?' the clerk responded affably. 'More likely they are Revolutionary Committee. They watch all our visitors.'

Tyler wondered whether the man in Immigration had informed officialdom of his arrival, or whether this was a routine surveillance drill for foreigners. Either way there was nothing to do but keep calm and play out his role.

Leaving his passport with the desk clerk, he was escorted by the porter to a room that reeked of mothballs. The clerk would deal with any formalities, for the Immigration Department imposed a duty on hotel staff to inform them of all foreign visitors staying on their premises within three days of arrival. Without proper registration, leaving the country would become extremely difficult.

Weary from the flight – or was it merely relief after the adrenalin surge of his arrival? – he unpacked and had a wash. The water that gushed from the shower-head ran brown at first. Once it had cleared, he stepped inside, catching his breath in the icy flow. As he soaped down his aching muscles, he was seized by a feeling he had not experienced for a long time: an indescribable surge of naked excitement. It was danger that now brought him alive again after months in a long soporific trance. The Savoy contract had whet his appetite for the old days, but from now on he would be living with that deadly buzz twenty-four hours a day. Hell, why not. He towelled himself dry vigorously, grinning to himself all the while. 'OK, you bastards, come get me!'

As he lay down on the double bed, the clean cotton sheets felt good against his tingling skin.

In the lobby – directly below where Tyler was napping – the man in the steel-grey suit was leaning across the clerk's desk reading with interest the registration card of the electrical engineer from the Federal Democratic Republic of Germany. The clerk watched, bemused, as the security man pored over the card in hopes of finding something significant there. Experience had taught the clerk not to obstruct the men of this shadowy department; even the fact that he cooperated with them was to remain confidential, he had been warned. These were the guardians of the People's Revolution.

'Here are his papers, brother,' the clerk offered, bowing respectfully to the younger men and reflecting on how they were all young these days, the bully boys. 'Karl something – see if you can pronounce it.'

'You'll pronounce his name well enough when his filthy wallet opens. His damned skin may be white, but your kind does not distinguish between shades of money,' spat the security man turning the card over.

'I must know his plans. Where will he go tomorrow? What is the true purpose of his visit? Any meetings? These things we must know.'

'Please, brother, I do not know these things . . . but I shall find out. You can rely upon me, as always.'

The security man smiled. 'Good. The people thank you for your cooperation. You will telephone the usual number as soon as there is anything to report.'

The clerk watched him stride out into the sunshine and cross the street to the white Mercedes. After a brief exchange, the man wearing mirrored lenses spoke into the handset of the car radio. It was a warm, humid day, and he was more than ready to wind up the operation then and there. The German's story had checked out; the passport appeared sound and he had duly registered at the address entered on the airport entry card. No sense in wasting time. That would do for now. He hung up the handset.

Then something intangible changed the officer's mind: some sixth sense inherited from his bedouin ancestors, who could smell rain on the desert wind. He called the controller once again.

'I've changed my mind.' he said. 'Contact the External Affairs bureau. I think this is one they ought to know about.'

Tyler woke to the sound of a chamber maid banging a door somewhere down the corridor, and immediately the smell of old paint and mothballs reminded him where he was. It was dusk, and the mosquitoes were biting. The curtains were drawn and the hotel room was dim. He had been dreaming of Daniel, and felt reassured by the knowledge that his brother would be safe in the nurses' care until he returned – and in that of the lawyer if he did not.

The three hours of sleep had been beneficial, but it was time now to shake the drowsiness from his body. He climbed to his feet and stretched himself, then began to glide through his ritual exercises – a Chinese combat form picked up in a sweatshop gym in one of Bangkok's sleazier districts. He concentrated hard upon each movement. This weird half-dance with its primitive rhythm always had the same effect on him, in tapping and focusing some hidden spring within him. He enjoyed each sweeping movement, enjoyed what he saw in the tall mirror over the dressing table. When finished, he felt calm and alert, and he checked himself out with a series of muscle isolations, culminating in an abdominal lift that sucked his stomach half up to his lungs. Then he slapped his gut and enjoyed the fact that it did not move. The shape was there again, just like the old days, and he was pleased by that.

Dropping naked to the floor, he punched off fifty push-ups in dead-slow time, balancing his weight upon ten fingertips. Muscles straining, breathing controlled – he had learned this important daily ritual from a Vietnamese combat instructor in French special forces. It always reminded him of that stoney-faced bastard as he supervised their morning callisthenics after *appel*. He could still picture the little Vietnamese strutting back and forth in his white and red-trimmed instructor's vest.

Finger push-ups were important in the special forces regime; the exercise builds amazing strength in the arms and wrists. But its true value lies in the power it imparts to the fingers: the power to tear out the throat of a sentry; to gouge and thrust in empty-handed combat without fear of dislocation or sprain. 'Gimme two hundred in twenties,' the tiny Vietnamese would roar. 'You break fingers in fight, you fuck good as dead, and that guy gonna kill you. Do this one right, get steel finger.' Tyler enjoyed the messages his arms sent back when the muscles were tight with blood.

Quickly he showered, and dressed in open-necked shirt and blue trousers. It was time to look around before the daylight failed completely. He needed to get a feel of the terrain, but before going out to reconnoitre, he carried the lap-top computer downstairs and checked it into the clerk's safe. It was still his only secure link with Halliday in London, and he did not feel like chancing it to the light fingers of room service.

It was early evening when he stepped out into the streets, and crowds still thronged the neon-lit thoroughfares. Most shops seemed to be doing brisk trade, except for the few hi-fi and photographic stores, which displayed sun-bleached posters advertising Japanese goods they could no longer obtain after the trade embargoes. The British Overseas Trade Board had produced a leaflet for business travellers to Libya, and this Tyler had read routinely during his preflight orientation. It explained how things were done in Tripoli: that most businesses worked split-shift, enjoying a siesta in the heat of midday then working on later. This pamphlet included useful details on how he could go about releasing the equipment Hamid had shipped to a bonded warehouse on the fringes of Tripoli airport.

There was a relaxed atmosphere among the small groups who promenaded or simply idled in cafés and restaurants. He was relieved to find more than just the mere handful of other white faces he had expected to see wandering the streets; that made him feel just slightly less conspicuous. With guidebook in hand he moved further away from the hotel, glancing around casually to take in the human scenery, knowing that somewhere close by Revolutionary Security would be watching his movements in the way they monitored all visiting foreigners.

There were old men dressed in long, flowing jellabas and head-cloths; business types in shiny, Italian suits; and young men in jeans, loud shirts and sports shoes. It was this latter type he was most wary of: the unsophisticated kids who had been fed on fundamentalism and liked to intimidate the foreigners. These were the foot-soldiers of the Revolutionary Committees, and Tyler had heard of their tricks. Often they would invite unwary visitors to drink coffee in a pavement café in order to trick them into criticising the Government before a concealed microphone. The visitor would then be arrested and forced to hear his incriminating words played back to him. He would then be accused of spying or subversion, and either expelled or sent for trial. In at least one case the unfortunate victim had agreed to spy for Libyan Intelligence rather than face one of their prisons.

But Tyler's more immediate concern was to survive the traffic. Crossing the streets, he found, was particularly dangerous. Cars weaved between lanes, cutting each other up, whilst the drivers banged fiercely on their horns whenever pedestrians attempted to use the zebra crossings.

At the southern end of Sharia First of September he found the huge, ornate edifice known as the People's Palace, a sprawling construction with exotic gardens – the former home of the Sanussi royal family. It was down this street that the screaming masses had marched on that September day back in 1969, spurred on by the promises of a gauche young army lieutenant; the promises of a more just society. Now the Palace had been turned into a national museum so the common people could witness the opulence enjoyed by the former tyrant. The northern end of the street terminated in a wide open space known as the Green Square.

Flanked by government buildings, residential blocks and street cafés, and facing the busy harbour on its open side, Green Square had been conceived of by Qadaffi as a public forum in the tradition of the Soviet's Red Square: a platform from which to stage-manage public debate, and to hear spontaneous demonstrations of support for himself as he spoke from a balcony overlooking the square. It was here that the Revolutionary Committees came to chant their vilifications of the Great Satan in the west and the Small Satan to the north.

Tyler took coffee at an outside table on the edge of Green Square and examined the public buildings opposite, where Qadaffi's balcony was draped with old bunting of green and yellow. From some of the smaller balconies hung banners painted with anti-American slogans in both Arabic and English. Outwardly here was a nation united in its opposition to the West and all its iniquities, but he knew this was far from the total truth, for most of the country's inhabitants had greater affinity to their own tribal groups than to any single national identity. They were bedouin and Berbers first, Arabs second, and Libyans a poor third. He watched knots of off-duty soldiers shamble around the square, joking and backslapping as young men do the world over; some even making eyes at girls safely escorted by their brothers or fathers and chastely covered from chin to ankle.

Suddenly there was a blur to his right, and a slim figure in tight black jeans and a red silk blouse was beside him. The figure leaned theatrically across the table, cigarette in hand, and asked him in Arabic for a light. It could have been Marlene Dietrich herself but for the dark hair. The light was not perfect at the pavement café, but Tyler knew instantly that the smooth skin, painted pink lips and permed hair did not belong to a woman. He was used to such blatant sights in Soho or Times Square, but here in Moslem Libya the impact was arresting. From behind a tangle of beads and feathers the man smiled with sickening sweetness and his eye flashed suggestively as he drew a blue tongue across the front of a perfect set of pearl-white teeth.

'What do you want?' muttered Tyler under his breath.

'Go back to the hotel immediately,' hissed the apparition, barely moving his mouth, as if fearful of lip-readers. 'Someone is looking for you. It is not safe here.'

At first Tyler did not react, feigning incomprehension.

'The man has half of a five-dinar banknote, and he is looking for the other half. Go now!' With that the slender figure jumped back in outrage, as if Tyler

241

had threatened him with violence; then he mouthed an obscenity and minced away quickly with his head thrown back.

It was a good act: the message had been passed quickly and smoothly. Mention of the five-dinar note clinched it.

It was just after nine o'clock when he reached the Hotel Poseiden, resigned to the selection of pasta dishes on its restaurant menu. He checked with the desk clerk and was told there were no messages for him.

Dinner was passable but he did not eat much of it. He kept brooding on the male prostitute's warning about his safety outside. He wondered whether a net was already closing around him, even as he sat here playing the German engineer from Frankfurt-am-Main. If trouble came he was ill-prepared – not even armed yet. Unable to find a European newspaper to read after dinner, he sat in the window of the hotel's coffee shop drinking strong black coffee and looking around him to check the neon-lit street. From where he sat he could see the flickering TV screen in the resident's lounge and, through a lace-curtained glass panel, the front desk and lobby.

'Is this seat free?'

Tyler looked up from the soccer highlights which had just begun. The man was tall – taller than himself by a couple of inches – and he was tanned and well groomed in a typically Mediterranean fashion, with an archetypal Roman nose and slightly hollow cheeks. His hair was beginning to recede on a forehead that was deeply lined, and his whole appearance spoke of self-assurance. He wore an open-necked shirt, and a medallion, and the sleeves of his cream-coloured sports jacket were rolled back in the kind of poseur fashion which Tyler particularly despised.

'*Wie, bitte?*'

'Is this seat free? I would like to sit down.' The man held Tyler's gaze, firmly, indicating that he was not just another tourist looking for idle chat about the weather.

'*Ja, bitte.* Help yourself. I myself am now going.'

The man laid a hand upon Tyler's wrist to prevent him from rising from the table. Tyler looked at the hand, then back at the man's eyes, trying to gauge how to react.

'We must leave immediately.'

'I'm sorry,' Tyler said, prizing his hand free and pushing clear of the table, 'is this some kind of joke?'

Reaching into his pocket, the stranger placed a piece of coloured paper on the table. It was the torn half of a five-dinar banknote. The tall man now looked agitated, and spoke in a rapid whisper.

'Look behind me now, Tyler. The fat clerk at the desk is on the telephone. He has been observing you since you arrived. Do I have to explain who he is calling, or will you come with me? There's no more time. Move now, or we are both dead.'

It was no occasion for caution, and Tyler realised he had no choice but to follow.

'OK, let's go.'

'Very good, Tyler. Stay smart and you might just stay alive.' The man's nerves were fraying at the edges. 'There are two men in a car outside – from the Revolutionary Committees. They will shoot if they suspect you are attempting to escape. I will leave now by the front entrance, and you take the side door. Go on round the block and wait outside the *bureau de change*. Don't talk to anyone – just wait for my car. And don't bother with your luggage; there's no time.'

'What about those two outside?'

'Leave them to me.'

They walked out to the lobby separately, and the tall men went out into the street.

Tyler was heading for the side entrance when he suddenly remembered the computer. It was still in safety deposit. Quickly he advanced to the desk, where the clerk was talking quietly into the phone.

'I need your help,' Tyler interrupted, pressing a hand on the phone's disconnect buttons.

The clerk's face registered disbelief and then fear. 'Please, sir. I make telephone . . .' he blurted feebly, trying to re-dial.

'Do it later. I need my machine now.'

'If you'll just wait a few minutes . . .'

Tyler seized the handset firmly and placed it on it's cradle.

The clerk withered under his menacing gaze. Turning, he quickly entered the combination on the safe behind him. Retrieving the slim grey case, he placed it on the desk.

'There you are, sir. All safe. No problem.'

Fifteen seconds later, Tyler was through the side entrance and out into the darkness of the alley. He glanced left and right, then pushed his way past four gaudy figures dressed rather like the one who had accosted him in Green Square. Jesus, they were everywhere!

'You buy Johnny Walker?' one called after him.

At the end of the alley Tyler turned left onto a narrow street hung with many shop signs, and proceeded quickly for another thirty metres until he spotted the illuminated window of the *bureau de change*. The street was almost deserted and he felt naked standing there under a sodium street-lamp, waiting for God knew what.

Suddenly, from the direction of Sharia First of September, came the sound of exploding metal. Just a small explosion, like a grenade going off. Then the sound of a gunning engine, and the glare of headlights swung in at the end of the street. Dazzled by the beam, for a second he could not discern the make of automobile. But when the vehicle braked sharply in front of him and a rear door swung open, he leapt inside. The car took off so rapidly that he was almost thrown back out into the street.

'Get down on the floor,' the driver yelled over his shoulder, swinging wildly through the narrow side streets. 'We're not clear yet. There may be others. I

244

took care of the white Mercedes out front, but there was another parked further up the street. Get under the blanket and lie still.'

Tyler complied, his heart beating fiercely, and wondering whether his computer had survived the tumble. Twice he almost retched at the stink of the floor and the bucking of the car as it weaved its way out of the maze of side streets and into the heavy flow of traffic roaring along the main thoroughfares.

It was many minutes before the tall man slowed the car to a respectable speed, and informed his battered passenger that they were now in the clear.

NINETEEN

WHEN THE CAR stopped, the driver got out and wrenched open the rear door. Tyler climbed out gingerly, and found himself standing in a parking bay outside an apartment block.

Block B was one of several facing a courtyard set back from the Sharia Al Fatah, a quiet road in the vicinity of the Al Fatah University. Adjacent to it were similar residential blocks populated by expatriate families from a dozen different countries. An old man, wearing a sort of uniform of peaked cap and white shirt with shoulder flashes, patrolled the grounds, nodding to residents but rarely challenging strangers. Like many such buildings in the Middle East, it had white concrete walls stained brown in places by the rusty drip of air-conditioners, and floors of pale blue ceramic littered with the ubiquitous dead cockroaches. Looking up, Tyler could see metal grilles fixed over many of the open windows, and behind them ceiling fans twirled lazily on apartment ceilings. The balconies were densely populated with a jungle of potted plants.

A blond-haired man came out of the elevator, jogging a crying toddler in his arms and making cooing noiser to appease the child. He spoke German to the child, but greeted Tyler's companion amiably with a phrase or two of Italian, then switched to English, the language common to European expatriates in Libya. From the casual intimacy Tyler guessed that they were neighbours.

Standing in that dark, narrow entrance, Tyler felt sudden concern as the man before him stepped into the elevator and punched the button for the sixth floor. Who exactly was this man? Not the usual Intelligence agent for sure. Far too brusque and aggressive. No, this cold fish had on him the unmistakable stamp of a military career. He wore his jacket slung over one shoulder, and above his dark forearms the sleeves of white shirt were rolled perfectly evenly, the way only a soldier used to inspections knows how.

The elevator shuddered up through six levels, and Tyler stood stiffly in the moist heat, always aware of the other man's cool gaze on him. At the sixth floor the stranger stepped out first, and Tyler followed cautiously. The front doors of two apartments faced each other across a small corridor. They turned to the left and, ignoring the lighted doorbell, the man knocked hard on the door of number 11. After a moment a woman's voice called out in Italian. The man answered, also in Italian, and a curt 'OK' was heard from inside. But the door was not opened up from within. Instead, the stranger produced his own key to operate the lock. Whoever these people were, their procedure was good and they were taking no chances.

After he swung the door open the stranger stood aside and indicated that Tyler should go in first. He stepped across the threshold cautiously, half expecting some kind of trap. The stranger stepped in behind him and immediately locked the door again.

'All right, friend, what's going on?' Tyler began, but a metallic grating somewhere to his right stole any further words from his throat. With ice in his stomach, he turned slowly. Staring fixedly from the kitchen doorway was the girl whose voice they must have heard. She was dark and beautiful, and she held an Uzi submachine-gun locked against her right hip. She had taken up a trained position, at an acute angle to the door, where she could see first before she was seen. Tyler was careful not to make any move.

Without a word, the man reached out and grabbed the computer from Tyler's hand, placing it on a wooden sideboard. Then he pushed Tyler roughly into the centre of the living-room.

It was the girl who did the talking. 'If you want to live, don't move until I say so.'

Tyler nodded, watching her face and trying not to look into the short, menacing barrel of the gun. He had heard those little bastards bark before.

The man darted forward and began to pat him down for concealed weapons. Tyler stood stock-still, hands away from his body, fingers outstretched. In the endless seconds he fought to keep thinking straight.

The weapon search completed, the man kicked Tyler's legs apart and proceeded to go through all his pockets. His wallet, passport and traveller's cheques were laid on the dining table, followed by comb, two ball-points and a handful of local coins.

'Satisfied?' said Tyler.

'Not yet,' said the girl mechanically. 'Take off all your clothes.'

Tyler bit back an obscenity. He did not need this humiliation and isolation shit. These people were supposed to be on his side – or were they?

'Just hold on . . .' he began to protest, but the girl stepped closer and her partner stepped aside to give her a clearer aim. Tyler saw her determination: the long brown fingers were white at the knuckles where she clutched the Uzi. In a flash he saw that the selector was set for automatic, and the span of her right hand was pressed against the release plate of the grip safety trigger. The exceptional stability of that little baby, together with its 128 rounds a minute, made it one of the most devastating close-quarter weapons ever invented; he had seen one cut a man in two at the waist. He began unfastening the buttons of his shirt.

'OK, whatever you say.'

'Until we are absolutely sure you are who you say you are, and are not concealing weapons or microphones, we'll keep to the precautions.' The girl sounded as clinical as a nurse treating a wound.

Under the ceiling lights Tyler stripped down to his shorts, handing each item of clothing over for inspection. The man felt carefully through the seams and creases, overlooking nothing. He soon found the five thousand dollars tucked inside the waistband of Tyler's trousers.

'The shorts, too.'

Tyler stepped out of his white boxers and kicked them towards the man. Then he stood upright, placing his hands on his hips, and almost contemptuously allowed the girl's eyes to take in his lean, hard muscles and deep chest. He knew he was in good shape and felt not the slightest embarrassment.

'Satisfied now?' he murmured with the trace of a smile. But the girl never turned a hair.

Tyler used the opportunity to study her. She was probably five feet eight, and about a hundred and twenty pounds. Her summer dress was a cotton-print number of white, green and red, secured across the collar-bone by a red draw-string. Nothing too revealing in view of Moslem sensibilities, still the effect of her pale caramel skin was not totally lost. Her hair was a lustrous black, scraped back and tied in a bunch behind, revealing high, wide cheekbones, small delicate ears, and a neck meant for kissing. She wore no make-up – and needed none with large eyes and long lashes like hers. Yet those eyes held a gaze so bereft of emotion that he was reminded of blue flame.

When the man took out a pen-line torch, Tyler's heart sank. God damn their efficiency! The silent stranger proceeded to make a meticulous check of Tyler's intimate body cavities, the way police might examine a drug-pusher. When he had finished he snapped off the torch and nodded to the girl. White rage was burning now in Tyler's breast; what he wouldn't do to this arrogant bastard. But he fought back his anger, promising repayment with interest at some later date.

The girl lowered her weapon.

'Very good. Now we may all behave as civilised people. We're sorry to have put you through this test, but if you have any experience of working under-cover in enemy territory, you'll understand. Please put on your clothes now.'

'Thank you, indeed,' said Tyler sarcastically. 'Now perhaps you can answer a few questions.' He reached for the pile of clothes on the dining-table.

'You may ask as many questions as you wish.' The girl took a seat at the table, removed the magazine from her weapon, and cleared the breach before laying it carefully by her elbow. She was thoroughly confident with it, Tyler noticed, needing neither the fold-away stock nor the sling to steady her aim. And someone had taught her room combat; that much was obvious from the way she had carved up the angles. Judging from the lithe contours of her body, somewhere in her past, he guessed, she had been a gymnast, maybe an aerobics instructor – or perhaps just an anorexic brat.

The girl crossed her legs and smoothed down her skirt. 'First let me tell you something you may not already know. You have been in Tripoli less than twelve hours, yet already Revolutionary Security are looking for you.'

'The young men who came after you at the Poseidon,' interrupted the man from behind him.

250

'They were a surveillance detail from Revolutionary Security. But they're just one of the gangs after you. The whole intelligence set-up is on your tail – Azziz has seen to that. All their cadres answer to Azziz, and he wants you very badly. The whole organisation's twitching, and they've been rousting foreigners for the past two days.'

'So they start a house-to-house search now,' Tyler ventured. 'How many people in Tripoli? Over a million? That still gives me some time.'

'Possibly true. Nevertheless, you're in danger every time you leave this apartment. We can't afford to lose you now—'

'Because if they get me,' Tyler interrupted, 'they get you too.'

'Precisely. Because you know our faces, you are a liability to us. I advise you not to go outside without one of us. We will help you as much as we can without compromising our own position here. But you will have to act quickly. Their intelligence is not as poor as the West might like to believe; nor are their people quite so stupid. We can provide automatic weapons, and we can get you information, but the rest is up to you.'

Tyler nodded thoughtfully.

'You may wish to take a shower after your dusty ride. There are two bathrooms: one at the end of the corridor and another off the master bedroom. There are four bedrooms, and yours is the first on the left. You will find clean towels and there are also spare clothes of an approximate fit in your room. Please do not enter the first room on the right unless one of us is with you. It has some sensitive communications equipment.'

'Do you two have names?' said Tyler. 'Or would that be compromising your position?'

The girl shifted uncomfortably. 'Yes, of course we do. This is Mario, and I am Sophia Tintorini. I hope we can get on together.'

But Tyler was not accepting anything, just yet. Climbing to his feet, he said, 'I'll take a shower now. Suddenly I feel very dirty.'

He walked off to the bedroom, leaving them staring at each other. They knew he was angry, but had expected it.

Tyler closed the bathroom door, lay down the towel and took a long shower to wash away the feel of the man's hand up his arse. Back in the Legion, where machismo was taken to its most brutal limits, men had had their faces carved off for less. But now was not the time to call a reckoning, for he needed these people to be his eyes and ears in this foreign land.

The clothes they had laid out for him, pale trousers and short-sleeved open-necked shirt, were a reasonable fit.

'Not bad,' said Mario when Tyler came back into the living-room. He was sprawled upon the sofa with his legs wide apart, and a sinewy bronzed arm draped along the sofa back. 'We are almost of a size, you and I.'

Tyler ignored the olive branch and took an easy chair opposite the sofa.

Mario sensed his animosity and forced a thin smile. 'You must excuse the rough handling,' he apologised. 'Just necessary precautions. You'll understand our concern. If our cover is blown, three years' work goes into the rubbish-bin – to say nothing of our lives.'

'I understand, all right.' It did make sense, but sounded a shade too glib coming from those thin lips.

'Now, you said you need answers. Fine. My real name is Yariv, but continue to call me Mario when others might hear.'

'So, you're Israeli. Well, that's a start. And the lady?'

'She, too. Her name is Sara – but always call

252

her Sophia. That is our cover: Mario and Sophia Tintorini. I am an engineering consultant working on petro-chemical projects over a range of areas. It gives me freedom of movement and access to Government officials.'

Just then the girl appeared from the kitchen bearing a tray with three glasses of beer. Her hair now hung free, floating about her face and gently framing it. She smiled warmly at Tyler, as if he was an old friend she had not seen for some time.

'The two of you are married?' Tyler asked, routinely.

The girl's eyes sparked in mirth. 'Sophia is, of course, Mario's devoted spouse,' she said, 'but that is just the cover.'

Yariv shifted uncomfortably, and Sara set the tray down on the low glass-topped table between them. Tyler noted the sway of her breasts as she bent over – a reflex reaction. Deliberately Sara chose the arm chair next to Tyler's, realising that to sit side-by-side with Yariv would imply a gulf between the pair of them and the Englishman. Her obvious talent was her binding influence; the generosity of spirit that binds and helps forge a team.

'Brew it yourself?' asked Tyler raising his glass.

'Of course not,' said Sara. 'This is Italian beer. Don't look so surprised. You can pick up most things around Tripoli. They do have this Moslem law, *sharia* – no alcohol, but the weaknesses of useful foreigners are tolerated provided they don't flaunt them in public.'

Sara was studying the Englishman's face with interest. It was not a handsome face like a movie-star's; no it was angular and masculine, with a straight, confident nose and deep, fathomless pools for eyes. But it was a face that radiated honesty when he let himself smile, and she had felt a strange pleasure when his eyes were fixed upon her body for a moment earlier. There was violence there, too. It would be no easy task

253

to control him. She had seen the murderous set of his jaw when Yariv had abused his nakedness. That could be a danger to their mission; it would need the greatest care.

First they must win his trust.

'Here's to success.' Sara raised her glass.

Tyler and Yariv reciprocated mechanically and without feeling. They all drank. For Tyler, the beer tasted good after the choking dust in the back of the car, and he realised just how badly he had needed it. He finished the glass at a single tilt and set down his glass. Yariv immediately followed suit and drew the back of one hand across his lips in satisfaction. Both men looked at each other, then at Sara. To Tyler's pleasure she, too, chugged the glass back in one, finishing with a broad grin. As she put down her glass, a loud burp escaped from her throat.

Suddenly, all three of them were laughing out loud. Yariv slapped his thigh and pointed weakly at Sara, who slapped away his hand. She blushed in embarrassment, though she was glad of the shared moment. The level of animosity between them had instantly dropped ten points. But there was still some there, just bubbling under the surface. They would need other such shared moments to built trust between them.

As the laughter died, Tyler began, 'I'm assuming you know why I'm here, and the identity of my target.' Both Israelis nodded. 'My brief told me that you two are assigned to assist in the execution of my mission. For this I'll need to know the extent of your resources and training. I don't work with amateurs.'

Immediately Yariv shot forward in his seat. It was a stupid crack, Tyler knew, but he was still testing them – watching their reactions. Maybe retaliating a little, too. Yariv was muttering now in Hebrew, full of threat and outraged self-importance.

The girl again showed a guiding hand in keeping things on an even keel.

'Come now, Mr Tyler. You are amongst professionals here – and friends,' Sara offered.

Tyler leaned back and muttered through gritted teeth, 'OK. Since we're friends, let's speak our minds and clear the air. No offence, Yogi, but if you ever put those hands on me again I'll smash your goddamn face.' His finger jabbed in Yariv's direction. 'Now, get this straight, this is *my* mission. That means I call the shots as best I see them. I've worked with your people before, and in my experience cooperation counts for nothing with the Israelis; they just do their own sweet thing, and the rest go fuck themselves. What have we got here anyway – Mossad hit team?'

'My name is Yariv,' the Israeli replied with quiet menace, nostrils flaring. 'Who we are apart from that is none of your business. Be grateful for our help. If not for us, you would now be in a cellar down-town begging for a chance to die. Unlike you, we did not come here for the money. We are here under orders – orders to help a foreign government in this half-arsed adventure. We're not crazy about mercenaries, and we are anything but amateurs!'

It was for Sara now to save the mission – to split up these sparring bucks. The unit's psychiatrist had alerted her at the final briefing. *'Beware of Yariv,'* he had told her. *'He is a loyal and formidable soldier, but he's as temperamental as a thoroughbred. Don't let him antagonise the English.'*

'Be calm, Yariv,' the girl spoke softly in her native tongue, but it was enough to ward off further confrontation. 'Go find Nineveh. Check that he is safe and come back later. Go.'

The tall Israeli visibly regained his composure. He was edgy, dangerously so, but he heeded the girl's words. Intrigued by her power over him, Tyler watched quietly as Yariv grabbed a set of keys and closed the door behind him.

'That's quite a trick you have there,' he said when he heard the elevator descend and the two of them were alone. 'Does it mean you're the one I deal with?'

'If you like. I'm for getting the job done.'

'And your friend, Tarzan the ape-man, what is he for?'

'The same. We're on the same side.'

'Yes, well that guy has a problem. I don't know what it is, but it isn't good.'

Sara gave a small shudder, as if the evening breeze suddenly bothered her. Absently she stood up and began to pace, rubbing her upper arm as if to dispel the chill.

'I'll get you another drink.'

Tyler followed her into the kitchen, where they sat down facing each other across a small table. This time Tyler refused the glass, and they sat with beer cans at their elbows. The girl was quiet for a time, as if not sure where to begin. Finally she took a pull on her beer, swallowed hard, and fixed her eyes on his.

'Mr Tyler, I know how important and how dangerous your mission is. I do not know the fine details, or the reasons for its timing. Please don't give me any details of the proposed operation unless you think it absolutely necessary. From a security viewpoint it's better not to know. Likewise, I'm not authorised to give you details of our set-up here in this country, but let me tell you only that we have extensively penetrated the armed forces and certain Government departments. Naturally, we have agents in all enemy countries to warn us of hostile activities, and Yariv and I control the Libyan network. But we are not with the Mossad; this is a military operation and our unit answers directly to the office of the Foreign Minister. Is that enough for you?'

Her demeanour was totally businesslike now. Gone was the soft charm of the hostess he had seen earlier. Tyler found reassurance in her determined manner. Perhaps Halliday had not thrown him to the lions alone after all.

'OK, I understand,' he conceded. 'How did you get involved in my business?'

'A favour for the Americans. We owe them. Do not flatter yourself that we would do the same for the British.'

'I know,' said Tyler short-circuiting her venom. 'We short-changed you on the Palestine Mandate after the war, and that's something we'll have to live with. Now, I guess it's State Department dollars that buy favours?'

She saw the shadow of distaste in his smile and shrugged. 'These are political realities. They are the givens in our world, Mr Tyler – the soldier's world. We work within the rules, lacking the power to change them. There is an exquisite agony in such a life, is there not?'

He raised his glass and swallowed, unsure of the tone of her reverie. What was it he sensed behind the calm assurance of this girl, who barely an hour ago had been ready to cut him in two? Perhaps it was a silhouette of the ghost that haunted him also.

'Perhaps you'd care to tell me about how you joined up?' He was reaching out – not sure what for.

'Perhaps I will.' Assurance returned to her bronzed features. 'But not tonight.'

There remained an uneasy atmosphere between them alone together in the apartment, which was only broken by Yariv's return nearly four hours later. He hurried in with a worried look, his hair out of place and breathing heavily as if he had been running, and he spoke rapidly to Sara in Hebrew.

The signs put Tyler on edge. 'What is it? What's wrong?' the Englishman demanded.

257

'Speak English, Yariv,' said Sara, taking Yariv's arm and propelling him to the sofa. 'Tell us again, in English.'

Yariv was clearly uncomfortable with the suggestion but he complied, his whole body tense.

'Nineveh wasn't there. Something's wrong. He's never missed before.'

'How long did you wait?' Sara demanded, clearly infected by the same anxiety that gripped her comrade.

Tyler was impatient. 'If this affects my mission you'd better explain quick,' he warned.

Yariv needed no encouragement. 'That skinny faggot who first contacted you, Tyler. He's one of my agents. His code-name is Nineveh. I arranged to meet him this evening, to check out any developments after we got you clear of Azziz's men at the Poseidon.'

'He didn't show?'

'We were to meet at a coffee house near the Green Square, but he wasn't there, so I didn't wait. He knows I won't wait if he misses the first meet. That's the procedure: no waiting at the principal location; but meet at the fall-back after two hours. So I then waited twenty minutes at the bus station. He didn't show there either.'

'You covered your trail back here, of course.'

'Why do you think I took so long?'

A silence fell as they each digested the consequences of Nineveh's non-appearance. The implications were not palatable.

'Clearly he didn't get clear of the Poseidon,' Yariv pronounced coldly. They looked ruefully at one another.

Tyler put his question quietly. 'Does Nineveh know the location of this apartment?'

'No,' Sara answered for him, irritated by this suggestion of operational incompetence. 'Nor does any other agent in the network. Don't worry, Mr English mercenary, you're safe – for the moment.'

Small bloody comfort, Tyler told himself bitterly. With every street corner alive to his presence, he did not rate his chances of making a clean hit, let alone living long enough afterwards to spend the money sitting in that numbered account.

Time was running out.

TWENTY

THE NEXT MORNING Tyler awoke early, knowing he had better get things moving – and keep them moving, to have any chance of success at all. There was no time to waste, now they were seriously on to him. And they were most certainly on to him after his hasty withdrawal from the Hotel Poseidon. The passport he had left with the head clerk would now be with the Revolutionary Security. They would circulate his photograph through the People's Militia, and he would need to keep his head well down on the street.

The clock was ticking, and he would be running from here on.

'Just how significant is Nineveh?' he had asked Yariv.

'Because of his sexual orientation he is a very important agent. He has many boyfriends, if you see what I mean. Some of them have been persuaded to give information.'

'Persuaded?'

'Come on, Tyler. You know how a honey-trap works.'

'Of course. But how was he recruited?'

'He was a low-life with a pretty face, whose only interest was the money. It began with drugs: I'd buy from him regularly, and he'd begin to open up, boasting of clients in high places. Homosexuals are a vain lot. Then I suggested how he could earn more money by selling information from his clients. He went for that; now I am his master. He knows that if he tries to double-cross me, I'll shop him to the Libyans and they'll tear him to pieces.'

'So he's definitely reliable?'

'One hundred percent. But if they have him . . .' The Israeli threw up his hands.

'What about his sources – any of them inside the barracks?'

'Yes, Nineveh's telephone number seems to have been shared around. The higher-grade sources I took over myself. Some have proved extremely cooperative, particularly so because they believe I am working for the Egyptians.'

'Very cute. What do they tell you about Qadaffi's movements and his security?'

'Naturally, he is heavily guarded inside the barracks. You weren't thinking of hitting him there?'

'Suicide isn't my game. No, I'll choose my own place, where he least expects it. The advantage in hunting a public figure is that he must constantly make public appearances.'

'Don't count on it, Tyler. Qadaffi is a bedouin, and underneath those fine uniforms is a man who loves the solitude of the desert.'

'Meaning?'

'Meaning that when the pressure is on, he always goes back to the desert. It is his strength.'

'Perhaps,' murmured Tyler thoughtfully, 'it may prove also to be his weakness. Now, about his security . . .'

'Whenever Qadaffi leaves the barracks he usually travels by convoy. Nine armoured Range

Rovers with run-flat tyres, bullet-proof windows and armoured petrol tanks. When he does go by car, there is no telling which vehicle he will ride in. The order is changed around to confuse ambush. Sometimes he sends the convoy out first, then leaves by helicopter some time later. Plans are changed at a moment's notice.'

Tyler listened with interest and a growing sense of admiration for the quality of the opposition. Obviously the Libyan investment in overseas security consultants had been money well spent. The bastards!

'It's nice – simple but effective. Makes an ambush into a crapshoot with the odds stacked against the attacker. What kind of fire-power do they have on board?'

Yariv allowed himself a sardonic grin. 'Let's just say heavy. All automatic weapons.'

'What about the personal bodyguard? What's this about Green Nuns?'

'Disbanded. It was more for show than effect. Qadaffi had a soft spot for them. He would turn up at political rallies surrounded by tall, attractive girl soldiers, looking like some pop singer with backing group. Perhaps it was the fantasy of a young Sirte goatherd. He loved it. But that's all changed now. If you want to get to the man, first you have to get through the Presidential bodyguard of the Islamic Legion, and then through those Koreans.'

As he finished speaking Yariv folded his arms and waited for the Englishman's response. Just then Sara came into the room. She was wearing loose-fitting bleached cotton trousers and a khaki shirt with epaulets, and her hair was tied back under a square of green silk. She smiled quickly and took a chair. For a moment her presence was distracting; the sun caught her face, reminding Tyler that this soldier was also a beautiful woman. He returned her smile.

Yariv's brow furrowed. 'Well? What's your play to be?'

His scowl made Tyler wonder: what was between these two – if anything?

'You'll know soon enough. Right now I need some information of my own. In one week Qadaffi will visit Brega. Is that correct?'

'Marsa al Brega? The oil and gas installation?' asked Sara.

'That's it.'

She leaned forward in her seat. 'Yes, now I remember something in the *Jamahiriya* newspaper a couple of months back. The new refinery came on stream last month, and the official opening takes place next week. Qadaffi is cutting the ribbon himself.'

'Even with a threat against his life?' said Tyler.

'He takes a very personal interest in petrochemicals, so he will go. But Brega is over eight hundred kilometres from here! It's sea to the north and desert to the south – all hostile terrain. An operation there would take time to set up. More time than you have.'

'Not the kind of hit I'm planning. There's no time for sophistication.' Tyler did not feel much like arguing. He turned quickly to Yariv who was already slipping on a jacket, preparing to go out. 'If that's the one way to pin the man down, then it has to be Brega. Get me everything you can.'

'You're mad!' shouted Yariv. 'I thought you said suicide was not your game?'

'I said get me everything you can: routes, timings, vehicles, units involved. There must be an operational order for a visit of this importance.'

'For sure,' said Yariv. 'The People's Militia in Brega will need to make preparations for the Presidential party, and the Jamahiriya Arab News Agency will want to cover it – to mention just two interested parties who'll need to see an operational order.'

'Then get one.' Tyler stabbed the air with a finger. 'That's always the first thing to be compromised in this kind of operation. They pass them round to every department, however slight their involvement, just out of bloody protocol.'

Clearly Yariv did not enjoy being sent upon errands, but he went off anyway, for there was also an urgent need for information from inside the barracks which might settle the question of Nineveh's fate. He was Yariv's agent, and only Yariv knew the real danger Nineveh represented.

When he was alone again with Sara, Tyler relaxed a few degrees. There was still much work to do, but he felt easier now in the girl's company, and sensed he could work with her. Perhaps, he would even like to get to know her better, if only they had more time. But there was just one week, so he forced his mind back to the operation.

The first priority was reconnaissance – but not with his present appearance.

He sent Sara out to the local chemist and she returned with black hair-tint and a creamy brown lotion which would further darken his skin. When the transformation was complete, the combination of darker complexion and his natural black eye colour meant Tyler could blend easily with the Arabs on the streets.

In the car-park they climbed into a Toyota LandCruiser and headed into downtown Tripoli. It was a big four-wheel-drive job – a car which was common in North Africa, for it could eat up any kind of road, including large stretches of desert.

Tyler drove cautiously in the unfamiliar environment, while Sara sat beside him indicating the roads and turnings to follow. It would have been easier if she had taken the wheel, for she could read the Arabic roadsigns, but that would have looked far too conspicuous: Arab men do not allow themselves to be driven by women.

Sara took him first to a department store in the city centre, to replace the clothes left behind at the Poseidon. She helped him choose between shades where normally he would not have cared to differentiate. His taste in clothes had always been practical and conservative, and his military peers had spurned stylish or flamboyant clothing as 'mincing kit' so he had adopted a standard military taste for blue blazers and charcoal-grey trousers. Still, he was gratified by her attention to detail and he enjoyed the way she leaned close when trying an item of clothing against him for size. She smelled of no perfume he had known before: a mixture of flowers and cornfields and sex – or was that just his imagination? He slipped off into another department as she paid for the clothes so that he could avoid direct contact with the sales staff.

When that was done, Sara insisted on showing him a sight no visitor to Tripoli should miss. Tyler followed her through a packed square until they emerged in a street market that was a riot of colour and sound.

'Don't worry. You're safe in a crowd,' she murmured, and then laughed. 'Just be sure to keep a tight hold on your wallet. These people can steal the very thoughts from your head.'

'What about the People's Militia?' he whispered.

'I said not to worry. Come and lose yourself in the crowd. Become one with it and be invisible. It's a long time since I did this.'

'You're crazy.'

The girl laughed. 'Maybe. Think of it as a safety valve. Come and watch me haggle with the merchants. Do this one thing with me, then I'll show you the things you wish to see.'

Tyler followed her in spite of his suspicions. All his training warned him never to relax.

They walked the busy pavements, avoiding bleating goats and braying donkeys, savouring the frenetic atmosphere and the mixture of aromas. They stopped at impossibly overloaded wooden stalls to buy Arab sweetmeats in small sticky packets, and they sampled barbecued snacks from small charcoal burners tended by wildly gesticulating vendors. The clamour of haggling merchants and customers in flowing cotton smocks and patterned caps blended appropriately with the myriad colours of goods on display: French cigarettes by the carton, mutton by the kilo, bolts of silk for the rich and cotton muslin for the poor. They sniffed a handful of fresh-roasted coffee beans before Sara beat the grey-faced, black-toothed old vendor down to an acceptable price.

And through it all he watched the light in her face intensify, as if she had stepped from her prison into some other normality. Under the circumstances, perhaps it was the bravest thing of all to do.

It was sweet and it was dangerous, but they enjoyed losing themselves in the clamour of the market. It was a small respite from the pressure building over their heads. And it was a pleasant fantasy that life could mean more than just their sad game of kill and counter-kill.

It was Tyler who broke the bubble.

'It's time. Let's go to the barracks while there's still enough light.'

They drove west towards the high-walled edifice of the Azizyah Barracks, and Tyler felt his pulse quickening the closer they came to his goal.

'Look, there it is,' said Sara, pointing into the distance.

Tyler shaded his eyes and saw the radio mast thrusting a hundred feet into the air. As they came closer, he could see the high stone walls and, outside, the hawkish silhouettes of anti-aircraft missiles also pointing skyward.

'We must stop here.'

'Why's that? We're still half a mile away.'

'Because there are prowling army patrols that stop and search vehicles which come too close. Believe me, this whole area is under constant surveillance.'

266

Tyler pulled the LandCruiser out of the sparse traffic and off the road, and parked it behind two trucks which were loaded down with camels from the market. One of the trucks had broken down, and the two young Arab drivers were arguing with their heads under the bonnet.

'Here use these,' said the girl, handing him a set of high-powered binoculars. 'See for yourself what you're up against. But be discreet.'

With the binoculars he could pick out the infra-red cameras mounted at intervals along the walls, and could even see them scanning the approach roads.

'Looks bloody solid. What's it like inside?'

'It's a fully operational military barracks – what do you expect?' She proceeded to describe the layout in detail. 'The base is six miles long and virtually attack-proof. Just beyond the main gate there are Russian tanks and armoured personnel-carriers. You can see the concrete blocks outside the main entrance; they're there to prevent the kind of suicide truck bombings which took place in Beirut in 1984. The story's the same for all the entrances, and the guards have automatic weapons and anti-tank rockets just in case the army turns against him.

'I expect you've heard about the bedouin tent and the camels tethered beside it. It's pitched between the Qadaffi home and the tennis courts, but he does not sleep there – that's just for the media – although he does conduct certain meetings there. He sleeps in an underground bunker near to the administration block. That's where he was when the Americans came calling.'

'And the house?'

'That was badly damaged by the bombing. It was a home for his wife and children, but not any more. They've moved to a new quarter, and the remains of the house have been turned into some sort of shrine – a reminder of the barbarism of the infidel.'

Tyler watched some trucks leave the barracks and grind their gears along the smooth asphalt road back into Tripoli, and then he slid the binoculars back into their case.

'Come on, I've seen enough.'

Sara gazed at him squarely, wondering what was passing through his head – and wondering how long they had before the edges began to fray and the Libyans unravelled their whole operation.

'Time really is against us, Tyler,' she said, her voice full of meaning.

'We'll see,' he said evenly, and looked at his watch. 'Right now there's something important I have to collect.'

They skirted Tripoli and headed out towards the airport cargo-handling area – an industrial complex where Tyler knew he would find the bonded warehouse mentioned by Hamid at their meeting. Along the way he attempted to fill in the cracks in his understanding by questioning the girl.

'So how long have you been here? You seem to know your way around.'

'Almost two and a half years now.'

'That's a long time undercover. Some people would go crazy.'

'The secret of survival is to be crazy before you arrive.'

Tyler flashed her a quick grin, sensing the opening he had been looking for. After all, you don't just ask someone straight out how they became a spy; but he was intrigued to know how she had come into this twilight world.

'I can see that before you trust you need first to understand,' she replied guardedly. 'If you want to understand me, then I must tell you.'

From the readiness of her answer Tyler sensed that she had been waiting to unburden herself, perhaps to cleanse her soul of deceit. As the LandCruiser hummed along the black asphalt, with open red scrub and rough grass on either side, she stared into the vanishing point of the horizon as if transfixed by a hypnotist's charm. She started to talk, and he did not interrupt.

'My name is Sara, my family name Gilan. My father was born in Hebron and married my mother in 1947 when she arrived as a refugee from a concentration camp in Poland. My father was a very brave man. During the revolt which established Israel he served in the Red Section of the Irgun under Menachem Begin. Then, when the fighting was over, he took my mother to live in a small village near the border with Egypt, believing it their duty to pioneer the territory for the State. It was a hard life and very dangerous, being constantly subject to border incursions. I was born in 1958, a welcome daughter after two sons, and my father died later that same year. He died fighting Egyptian soldiers who came across the border and destroyed our village. My two brothers were bayoneted – only six and eight years old. My mother and I escaped death by lying in a camouflaged dug-out which my father had constructed close to our home. Only twelve people survived out of the hundred and thirty who had lived there.

'We were then evacuated to Tel Aviv, where we lived with relatives of my father. They were very generous, but they say my mother was destroyed by her loss – that she lost interest in living. She was racked with guilt, and was still suffering chronic depressions caused by her years in Nazi camps. Her last words, written before ending her own life, were 'Will they never leave us alone?' I still have the note. I kept it because I never want to forget.

'I stayed with my relatives in Tel Aviv and took a job in a bank as soon as I was able to leave school. At seventeen I was drafted to do military service – in our country women must do two years. At that time I was assigned to the pay corps and I did not see active service. That was fine by me, because

269

gunfire scared the hell out of me; there were too many bad associations. When I returned after the two years, there was no longer much room in my relatives' house. I began dating one of the men from the bank. I was very young then and needed someone to belong to, so we were married very quickly.

'His name was David. He was a quiet, gentle man – very patient, and very kind to me. He had trained as a rabbi but at the last moment his faith faltered and he changed his mind. He had this exciting idea about raising a big family in one of the new West Bank settlements. He was convinced he could best do God's work by working and living together with the Palestinians. So we moved to Nablus, and David took a job in a small bank there. We had our child there, a son – we called him Ari – and for three years we were happy. So happy I cannot begin to tell you.

'David organised a friendship organisation with Palestinian moderates; it took two years to win their trust. There were plans to expand the organisation to neighbouring areas, but all that ended very suddenly. One night there was a raiding party. They came straight to *our* apartment block – they must have heard about this Jew who was organising peace meetings. They knew exactly where to . . .'

For a second she faltered, as the screams came flooding back; the flash and stutter of the Kalashnikov and the screams of fleeing children. Resolutely, she continued.

'They attacked only the homes of those involved in the peace movement: both Arab and Jew. They said it was to punish the traitors, and the Jews who had stolen their land. They called themselves Al Saiqua – the Thunderbolt – but their actions were not those of a wronged people returning injury for injury. They killed good people whose only wish was for a measure of peace in which to raise their children.

'There is no need to give details of their atrocities against us. The world is tired of such horror and I must confess I'm tired of it, too. It's enough to say that I lost a good husband and my beloved little boy.'

Tyler knew without looking that she was crying softly. There was a pause while she wiped her cheek, then she braced herself and continued.

'Somewhere in the noise and confusion I was attacked by one of the raiders. He pushed me to the ground and climbed on top of me. I managed to reach a steel knitting pin and I killed him with it – drove it up through his eye-socket into his brain. After that, they wanted to make me into some kind of heroine, but in the hospital I refused to see the reporters; to see anyone. Twice I tried to kill myself – well that had been good enough for my mother. But both times there was something there which held me back. I don't know, perhaps there is more of my father than my mother in me. Then I realised I had to cling to life with both hands, because I was the only one left to cherish the memory of two dead families. And, when I was at my lowest ebb a new family came to adopt me. When no one else offered me anything but pity, the unit offered me a sense of purpose. What they saw in me, lying hopeless in that hospital bed, I'll never know, but they stripped me down and rebuilt me. I mean they literally rebuilt me: mentally, physically and emotionally – everything. For this I owe them my life and, as for all of them, my first duty is to serve my country in any way I can. That is why I will help you.'

When she finished, Tyler kept his eyes fixed upon the road and did not speak for some time. Instead he watched the municipal taxis screaming ahead of him towards the airport, leapfrogging buses and trucks. He was unaccustomed to such honesty about personal feelings, having long since ceased to care about anyone else but his brother. But the intimacy of the moment had affected him – the girl had affected him – and suddenly he wanted to tell her something about himself.

'Thank you for telling me,' he said gravely. 'Now, I suppose its only fair that I tell you a little about myself.'

'That's your decision.'

'We're in this together, so I will.' Tyler was determined to be as honest as she had been. 'Once I was a career soldier: Royal Marines in Northern Ireland and later *Légion Etranger* – French Foreign Legion – in Chad and any other hellhole they chose to send us. But not any more.

'Now I'm a freelance. One of the men my Government calls upon infrequently to do a particularly nasty piece of work to which they would be embarrassed to admit in the event of a show-trial. To me this is just a way of life that pays the bills. I've tried one or two other things but they didn't work out.

'I may not have seen the same patriotic action as some of your people, but I think I can safely say I've occasionally done my bit. I was with the second parachute regiment in May 1978. We brought two and a half thousand European hostages out of Kolwesi in Zaire, who were being tortured and abused by the communist rebels. They were bloody animals, they were. That's where I got this.'

Tyler raised his left arm to reveal a pale patch of scar tissue underneath a hard, bulging bicep. Sara touched the scar gently with her outstretched fingers – like a lover. Then she caught herself.

'Better keep both hands on the wheel if we're to get there in one piece.'

'I'd never seen anything like it in my life,' he continued. The rebels were dragging women into the streets and just tearing the clothes off their backs. We passed the bodies of those who had fought back. The dust was black from the blood they had spilled. I tell you, I saw hardened troops weep with the tragedy of it. Legionnaires need no excuse for a fight; it's what they live for, anywhere, anytime, but that day we wrote

272

a new page in the Legion's history books. And I'm proud to say I was there.'

Sara listened to the story in silence, reliving him the hell that was Kolwezi on those fateful days in May 1978. But when he finally finished, she turned to him.

'And what do you have left of your previous life, Tyler?'

'Nothing much.' There was no self-pity in his reply, just a kind of bitter resignation.

Sara wondered what kind of private hell he would return to if he lived past this current mission.

'And no one . . . ?' she asked.

He thought for a while.

'There's my brother Daniel. We're all each other has.'

'Tell me about him,' she said, relieved but without admitting to herself the reason.

'He's in a nursing home in England. We're twins – identical. I was born first and became the athlete and soldier; he got tangled up in his unbilical cord and came out with brain-damage. Fate has this way of being both cruel and kind. It gave me everything. I don't know, should I feel lucky it was him and not me? Because I can't. Every time I look at him it's like looking in a mirror of what might have been.'

'Is that why you take such chances with your life,' she asked with a sudden flash of insight. 'Are you running from the mirror?'

He did not answer.

The bonded warehouse stood on the fringe of an industrial estate adjacent to the airport. Sara read the Arab signposts and guided them past a chequered barrier to the clearing office, a scruffy affair with a wooden counter and a bench seat for the customers.

Tyler approached the counter clutching the ownership document which Hamid had supplied.

273

The papers contained the appropriate air-freight, but the description appended was for personal effects belonging to his West German identity. The official examined the document carefully against a list of air-cargo receipts, stamped it with a green Government seal, and directed them to the collection point at the rear of a large warehouse.

Two men in leather aprons and brown vests brought over the crate and loaded it into the back of the Land Cruiser. It had almost the same dimensions as a coffin but the two burly men, one tall with bushy moustaches, the other fat and swarthy, lifted it easily. When it was loaded the fat man waved Tyler back inside, indicating that he must sign for receipt of goods. Hamid had said there would be palms to grease along the way and Tyler could tell that this was where the greasing would commence. It was worth every penny, he assured himself, if it got the gear into the country undetected, for he could not operate without it.

The warehouse was deserted as they were lead between aisles of stacked wooden pallets to the open space where stood a desk piled high with pads of yellow and pink invoices. The fat man took a seat at the desk, while the tall one leaned against an open crate with his hands dangling inside it. Suddenly Tyler began to feel uncomfortable.

The smiling fat man began to speak in a kind of English. 'In our country it is customary to render a tribute where good service is enjoyed.'

'That's understood,' said Tyler pulling a wad of notes from his wallet and watching the tall man's hands moving slowly insided the crate. 'There's a hundred dinars, that's almost 350 US dollars.' He tossed the money onto the desk and the fat man immediately scooped it up, his lips moving as he counted. The Libyan was chewing something that brought a thick yellow foam to his nicotine-stained teeth. When he had finished counting his face fell.

'What is this? An insult!' he said with menace.

274

'It is not enough. See the box is unbroken, we did not even take anything. That is indeed a special privilege.'

Tyler weighed the situation carefully. The Libyans did not realise the contents of the crate, or they would not be talking now; instead they would be negotiating a resale to the highest bidder. They were just getting greedy. And the tall man's fingers were probably resting on something that packed a mighty kick. Tyler had the Browning in his belt, but he knew he could not afford the attention it would bring if he revealed it. 'This was not mentioned by the shipping agent,' he said, continuing the negotiation. 'A hundred is fair.' His eyes checked the rear service area but there was no one else around.

Then Sara stepped forward and placed a hand upon his forearm. 'How much?' she asked wanting to avoid any trouble.

The fat man looked her up and down and scratched his groin. His eyes lingered over the jut of her breasts under the khaki shirt. 'Let us say five hundred dinars,' he said.

But Tyler wasn't buying. 'A couple of hundred is as good as it gets.'

Suddenly the fat man lost his smile, and his fist came down upon the desk with a bang. 'You do not have any choice, and I will not bargain. The price is now six hundred each.'

It did not look good and Tyler wasn't sure just how much they knew or how much they had guessed. Turning on his heel, he pulled Sara into a whispered confab.

'What do you think you're doing?' she hissed. 'Just give them the money. Do it now before you draw any more attention to that box.'

'It isn't that simple. I think they know too much, and they're pretty sure of themselves. My guess is that they fluoroscoped the crate but they don't have the connections to move the contents. They're just jacking up their end.'

'You're guessing, Tyler.'

'We can't take the chance.'

Her eyes darted back to the two Libyans, and she came to the same conclusion.

'Then do it quickly.'

Both knew what had to be done. Two slightly bent cargo-handlers who took a few coins for undeclared contraband was one thing, but this was quite another – two very greedy bastards who knew too much for their own good.

'OK,' said Tyler at last, feigning resignation and reaching into his wallet once more. 'Six hundred each, but . . .'

When he turned around he was facing a battered Kalashnikov which jutted from the stomach of the taller man.

'Don't move or my brother will shoot you in the head,' said the fat man, jumping up from the desk. The guttural command froze Tyler to the floor.

The tall Libyan held the weapon gingerly, and without confidence. Tyler guessed he was not used to handling such a weapon, and was more than a little afraid of it. That made Tyler afraid, too, for an automatic weapon is liable to go off at any time in the hands of an incompetent – with murderous consequences.

'OK, take it easy.'

'Take out all the money from your wallet and place it on the desk.'

Slowly, Tyler complied.

The fat one, who had been eyeing the girl, now came forward and pressed her against a pallet stack with his huge stomach. 'I think we play a little, eh, you and me?' His tall friend with the gun followed, still pointing the muzzle at Tyler's middle.

'Don't touch her,' Tyler warned. 'You have the money. Leave it at that.'

But the Libyans had other plans.

Sara kept her head, even with the man's sweat-stained bulk pinning her to the stack. But while his fingers were struggling with her button, she saw the man with the Kalashnikov straying closer to Tyler and knew what would happen. She saw Tyler make his move – saw him sweep the Kalashnikov sideways with a swift motion of his left hand, whilst the fingers of his right pierced deep into the Libyans' eyes. The man screamed with pain and let the rifle fall. Tyler caught it expertly and smashed the butt against the man's head with all his strength. The Libyan hit the ground hard and bleeding. He was already dead.

Tyler turned quickly to rescue Sara, but was too late to be of any use. Like the soldier she was, Sara had followed his lead with speed and aggression. The fat man now lay dead at her feet with her commando dagger in his throat. She had pushed the blade up into the man's brain.

Quickly, she retrieved it, wiping off the blood, and returned it to its pocket sheath.

Within minutes they were out of the warehouse.

TWENTY-ONE

CAPTAIN KIM STOOD in his hut, pulling on an old, grey sweatshirt with the arms ripped out, and thinking only of his regular training run around the barracks perimeter. It was the only relaxation he allowed himself from the endless vigilance required of his position as head of close protection to one of the most universally reviled political figures in the world. Now the tension was evident in the bunched muscles of his trapezius, and in spite of the heat he badly needed physical release. Qadaffi was safe enough in his bunker, lying naked under a single blanket in the darkened study, meditating.

But as he stepped out of the hut, Captain Park, his second in command, was waiting for him, wearing a face so bleak it made him stop dead.

'What is it, Park?'

The other man lowered his face to the ground.

'Excuse me, *sabum nim.*' His voice was softened by more than just the respect he bore Kim, and his eyes were moist. In his hand was an airmail envelope which bore a series of precise Korean characters. The broad edge had been slit and opened.

'What is it, little brother? You look as if you've come down with that cursed dysentery again.' Kim smiled in an attempt to cajole him into better mood. 'Curse this damn heat and their shitty food!'

Park returned a brief smile, but clearly his heart was heavy.

'*Sabum nim*, I have a letter from home. Bad news.'

'Bad news? Your grandfather? Did the illness take him?'

'No, *Sabum nim*. It is I who am sorry. Grandfather is well – may the gods preserve the old goat! No, I'm afraid the letter is . . . the letter is yours.'

'Mine! What does this mean? Immediately Park bowed and politely offered the letter in both hands. Confused, Kim took it without a word, turning it over and seeing that the letter was from his own dear wife. What could it mean? What bad news? He had received no letters at all in almost two months. Panic seized him now, and he almost tore the delicate blue paper in his haste to unfold it.

'So sorry that your private letter was opened, but it came by mistake to Kim Bok-man. The names were confused by the dark devils. He opened and read it in all innocence. Please do not be angry with him . . .'

Suddenly Park's feverish explanation came to a halt – now that the tragedy had registered. Kim's face was a mask of disbelief. The opened letter began shaking in his hands, then the tremor spread to his shoulders and a strangled cry broke from his lips. He covered his reddening face with both hands.

'No! Please not Jun-jae!' he cried. 'Oh, my little boy, my son, Jun-jae!' He repeated the boy's name like a soulful cry towards heaven.

'*Sabum nim!*' cried Park, grabbing his shoulder, hugging him in sympathy.

Kim was known as a hard man, but now his broad shoulders shook uncontrollably as he wept his heart out for his greatest treasure. Tenderly, Park took his arm and steered him back inside the hut, seating him at the table and pouring him some tea from a Chinese pot.

Park sat and waited quietly, aware of the other man's pain. It was horrific to see his friend and teacher, always so strong and resolute, now so devastated.

When some measure of composure had returned to him, Kim raised his head, sniffing away the tears.

'I should not be so selfish, for heaven has him now. Life's secrets are his already.'

'Do not fight it, *sabum nim*. There is no dishonour in grief.'

Kim looked at his friend gratefully for his understanding.

'Thank you, little brother, but I must keep control now. This is just a prelude to my grief. True grief will come later, in those solitary moments when I am reminded again of the life that is gone. A book, or perhaps a broken toy. Each time a bitter-sweet agony. It is those times I dread.'

'Once again, I am sorry.'

Kim gazed up at the whitewashed ceiling, then down at the table – trying to make his thoughts cohere.

'Did you read the letter, Park?' he said at last.

'Yes, and I feel ashamed. I could not help myself when Kim Bok-man told me. I wanted to tear out my eyes for reading of such sadness. I, too, have lost someone from pneumonia: my mother died of it last winter. Korean winters are hard, *sabum nim*.'

Kim just sat motionless, staring into space. 'Who would have thought it would take such a strong young boy?' He picked up the letter from the table once more, examining the characters. 'Two months ... My wife is beside herself. Two telegrams and three letters, with no reply from me!' There was hysteria in his voice and he smashed his hand down upon the table top, almost buckling the legs. 'Only by mistake did this one reach me!'

Park bowed his head nervously. 'We often thought they probably censored our mail.'

'How cruel, Park! How despicably cruel to keep me from my boy. The funeral was two months ago.'

'They knew you would be sure to go to it.'

'Yes, I would have gone to sprinkle blossoms upon his casket. But now he is in the earth and I cannot. I cannot. Nor can I ever forgive them. How I hate this place.'

'Will you go now, *sabum nim*? Will we both go?'

'I don't know,' Kim sighed heavily. 'I need time to gets things straight. To think what to do.'

'He sighed deeply, fighting back his sorrow and rage. Then he stood and walked to the locker which held his personal belongings. Carefully, he took from his wallet a photograph of his son Jun-jae laughing and playing. He kissed the picture tenderly in tearful farewell.

They arranged to catch the first available flight from Valetta – Brady and his two escorts from the People's Bureau. They would be landing in Tripoli only twenty-two hours later than the man Brady had come hunting.

At Valetta airport they were welcomed by the Libyan Arab Airways diplomatic liaison officer, who arranged for them to bypass immigration channels and ushered them to their seats in the first-class lounge without questions. The People's Bureau had told him to expect *two* foreigners – but that was before Brady had taken control.

Just before take-off Brady heard the French purser discreetly ask his Libyan escorts to surrender their weapons into the captain's safe-keeping, in accordance with international regulations, but both shrugged innocently and denied that they were carrying any. The purser was no fool but had no choice but to humour these diplomats, despite the obvious bulges in their jackets.

A big air-conditioned BMW was waiting for them in Tripoli, just beyond the VIP lounge where a junior official from the Bureau of External Security, who introduced himself as Mahmoud, shook Brady's hand firmly and welcomed him to Libya on behalf of Colonel Azziz. He steered Brady towards the car, instructing one of the escorts to ensure the baggage was fetched to Bureau headquarters in the follow-up car, and ordering the other escort to ride ahead of them in the standby Fiat as an extra precaution.

'Colonel Azziz is extremely busy at this moment, but has asked me to take you to him directly. Your flight was comfortable?' The official's manner was urbane and self-assured, as if he had spent time overseas on the embassy circuit.

A police motorcycle cut a hole in the traffic ahead, allowing the black BMW to get quickly clear of the free-for-all on the exit road. The three cars sped into Tripoli in close convoy, with the BMW's driver periodically unhooking his handset to radio in their current position.

There was not much to see on the way – occasional bright points of light in the near distance, and further out the dim flicker of a bedouin campfire glowing in the darkness – but it mattered little to Brady. Though his eyes stared fixedly through the window, his mind was elsewhere, savouring a sweet victory. He glanced at the gold watch on his left wrist, and saw it was 8.37. If Kelly had not yet untied himself from the straight-backed chair, then by now the chambermaid must surely have found him, bound and gagged in his underwear. It was undignified, yes, but necessary after that business with MacStifoin. Kelly had almost puked when they heaved the body over the side of the boat; then later he had sat silently below deck, his face like thunder, and Brady knew then that he would have to take further action. Killing the man would have been a bad move, he knew, for though he longed to smash the General Staff eventually, he still needed their political influence to work for him. MacStinfoin's death they could forgive – that had been a personal feud – but good old laughing Eddie 'Boy' Kelly was everyone's friend. No, let the old bugger live, he had decided; but there would be no place for him on this operation.

Brady laughed to himself. Christ, it was beautiful, all of it! The bowing and scraping and the VIP treatment from Azziz's scruffy specimens. Long on cash and short on taste, they were. In Valetta they had gone out and bought expensive Gucci luggage for his trip, and filled the bags with silk shirts and designer wear, believing he actually wore such gear. At the airport one of his escorts had even pressed a small box into his hand, which he opened in astonishment to reveal a solid-gold Rolex Oyster inside. Wads of US dollars were always in evidence – but you just can't buy class. Christ, Azziz had already thrown a shovelful of money in his direction! What would he pay for Tyler's dripping corpse?'

Priceless.

It was all a far cry from the misery and slog of his last little sojourn in Libya, he recalled, and he could not restrain a smirk of triumph; the comparison did not bear thinking about. It had been six years ago, almost to the month, that they had arrived by ferry in Tripoli – six of them, IRA delegates to Qadaffi's guerrilla warfare camp outside Benghazi, all puking their guts from the bumpy sea crossing and sweating like pigs. They had stayed for twenty-eight long weeks of gru-elling training and intensive political indoctrination, succumbing one by one to the inevitable dysentry which was rife in the spartan conditions of the camp. The weapons and explosives training were first-rate, he had to admit: all Soviet equipment and techniques. In the evenings guest lectures from such diverse organisations as the Shining Path – the legendary Peruvian revo-lutionary movement – and the Moroland Nationalist Army of the Philippines made for compelling listening. As in all such places, Neo-Marxism was the staple diet. But then there was the bull-shit to contend with: the interminable hours of translated speeches of Muammar Qadaffi pushing his much-vaunted alterna-tive to the NATO–SovBloc stand-off – his Third

Universal Theory. Not even the Arabs there could stand much of that stuff.

They had returned to Armagh wiser in many ways. Terry Lynch and himself – and the others who became known as the Desert Micks. Leaner, tougher fighters, more aware of the political power of horror, and its influence upon public consciousness. Once that lesson was learned, it was hard to go back to sniping at army patrols on the Falls Road.

As the welcome lights of Tripoli began to glow on the horizon, Brady was thinking of Terence Lynch. Stephenson had told him, eventually, exactly how Lynch was executed and hauled off like dogmeat. Not for him the drum and flute; not for him the black gloves and beret on a coffin lid. A soldier denied a soldier's burial. With a sudden shiver, Brady shook himself free of the past.

'You are cold?' asked Mahmoud amiably.

'Yes,' he responded quietly, without turning his head. 'Haven't you heard? I'm a killer.'

In the centre of Bin Ashur, a cosmopolitan district of Tripoli where the legacy of the Italian conquerors is evident in the elegance of its architecture, and where beleaguered East European diplomats fund their embassies on the proceeds of smuggled Scotch, there stands an anonymous sandstone building which is plain and unremarkable in every way except for the tall radio mast which reaches skyward from its roof, like a metal finger seeking to tap the power of God's wrath.

The modest size and aspect of the building, set apart from the expensive real estate of squares and boulevards, is out of all proportion to the real power and influence it wields within the People's Jamahiriyah; for here, as a brass plate states in finely etched green script, is the headquarters of the Bureau for External Security. An innocuous-sounding name for a department charged with the hunting out and liquidation of Qadaffi's enemies abroad, and responsible for every outrage committed in the Libyan leader's name. From this one building, seventy per cent of all staff in the Libyan People's bureaux overseas are controlled in a secret and undeclared war.

Colonel Azziz, a relentless pursuer of the People's enemies, was the Chief of the Bureau for External Security and de facto head of the four intelligence and security branches that fell within its aegis. He was still possessed of all the courage and tenacity of the career policemen he had been in the old King's police force and in the elite CYDEF, the Cyrenaican defence force which controlled the Sanussis' political enemies. But there was far more to him than this – there was the incisive and manipulative intelligence of a political leader, and it was this quality which had brought him to the attention of Muammar Qadaffi. Even then Qadaffi had possessed a keen nose for a potential political opponent, so was relieved when Azziz accepted an intelligence role which kept him free of the political arena.

Now in his mid-fifties, with a full head of silver-grey hair invariably dressed with perfumed oil, Azziz remained the suave, tough womaniser he had always enjoyed being. His movements remained as fluid, almost sensual, as they had been when a young man in Benghazi; and he knew that many of his junior officers longed to emulate his poise and charm, coupled with the sullen menace of a leopard. His eyes were still bright and clear, and though the brown lids now drooped into ever-deepening crow's feet, he felt sure that women enjoyed a little cragginess in men of his vintage. But the most intriguing physical aspect of Azziz was the pair of small green tattoos etched into the skin of his temples. These had become his signature, and the subject of much speculation whispered only between men who were sure of each other's loyalties.

No one was more aware of Azziz's real power and influence than Azziz himself. He knew the overt significance of having declined a Cabinet post: it was a declaration of his nursing no political ambitions, and that, by implication, he would be no threat to Qadaffi. Nevertheless his influence had grown in less tangible ways, for he was now a trusted adviser to the President and one of his closest confidants.

Or so he believed.

That evening, as he sat poring over task-force reports piled high on the calfskin blotter on his desk, such confident beliefs were ripe for shattering. And it needed just one phone-call from a well-placed agent in Azizyah's administrative building to put the cat squarely amongst the pigeons.

'Who calls at this hour, when all believers are at prayer?'

'By the life of the Prophet it is I, Zadmeh.'

It was an unwelcome interruption, doubly so whilst he was preparing to receive the rising young star of the Irish separatist movement. Nevertheless, when Ali Hassan Zadmeh requested an immediate confidential meeting, Azziz locked his safe, dismissed his driver and himself took his BWM down to the long stretch of beachfront road known as the Corniche.

He parked at some distance beyond the hotels, where the street-lamps were sparse and the shadows darkest. Zadmeh approached quickly and climbed into the passenger seat. One glance at his face in the pale light of the moon confirmed the seriousness of his mission.

Zadmeh was a middle-ranking civil servant with the Central Office of General Control at Azizyah Barracks, and in this capacity he came into daily contact with many sensitive documents prepared especially for the eyes of Qadaffi and his deputy Jalloud. It was said that not a single piece of paper reached the President except through him. This was no mere accident, for it was Azziz himself who years ago had recruited Zadmeh, the son of his own cousin, and steered him into this position for the express purpose of learning the things which Qadaffi chose not to tell him.

Zadmeh had proved reliable in the past, and he did not come running for nothing. From the way he was behaving now, Azziz sensed he had got hold of something explosive.

'Be quick, I have only a few minutes to spare.'

'Forgive me – by the Goodness of God you are well?'

'Thanks to His Goodness. Now speak out, boy.'

'You shall judge the importance of it, for I dare not.' Zadmeh gulped a quick breath and continued. 'Today I was in my office as usual, preparing the folders for the President's confidential boxes, when the security clerk ushered in a uniformed courier from naval head-quarters and said that the courier insisted on speaking to me personally. At first I was inclined to dismiss the impudent dog, but when I questioned him further his story intrigued me. He apologised for his interruption but said he had orders to place a briefcase personally into the hands of Rear-Admiral Sidi Omar al Mukhtari. When I told him the Rear-Admiral was not there, but was expected within the hour, he became very agitated for it seemed he had other important appointments to keep. I offered to act in his stead and, although at first reluctant, he eventually handed over the case, but not until I had roundly berated him for casting doubts upon my loyalty when the President himself relies upon my discretion. As soon as I was alone again, I examined the contents.'

Colonel Azziz allowed himself a thin smile.

'And what was in this case, Zadmeh, that it should arrive with a nursemaid bent upon circumventing the bureaucrats?'

'There were naval charts of the Mediterranean Sea, and other charts of land areas marked only with codenames I could not follow. Whoever compiled them was careful to exclude grid references, so as to confound the inquisitive. There was also an operational order describing something called PROJECT HOUN. I thought this strange because, although I keep a full list of every Government file which reaches the President, I have never heard of such a project.'

'Where are those documents now?'

'I delivered the case to the President's office, and I believe the Rear-Admiral claimed it at their meeting. I left no traces of my investigation, just as your people have taught me. There was not much time, and other people were working close by; the equerry and that damned yellow infidel bodyguard both watch me like hawks.'

'But still you copied the documents?'

'It would take too long to develop a photograph, so I took a chance and used the Xerox machine.'

'That was foolish. You know better than to risk discovery. If you had been caught, even I could not have saved you from the noose.'

Zadmeh patted the air soothingly, aware of his mistake.

'I am not concerned for myself, but you had to know of this.' He looked quickly around, making sure the Corniche was deserted, then unzipped the leather document wallet which was gripped under his arm. 'Details of a military operation. It's classified to the highest level. I can't think straight – the paper almost burns my fingers! Here.'

Azziz noted the man's fear and took the sheaf of papers.

'The charts came out dark.'

'No matter.' The Intelligence chief scanned each sheet rapidly and felt his ulcer begin to respond. 'Technical branch can rebuild the image with their computers. When they have finished it will look better than the original.'

He continued reading in stony silence, but when he came to the fourth sheet he could not restrain an oath.

'By the life of the Prophet!' He fixed Zadmeh with his leopard's glare, silver hair glowing ghostly white. 'You have read this?'

'It was my duty to inform you fully . . .'

Azziz gave a thoughtful nod as his brain clicked through a series of connections.

'Then from this moment consider yourself bound by the secrecy laws of the Jamahiriyah, and by the blood loyalty you owe to me. You understand?'

'Yes, Colonel, by Great God!'

'You do well to invoke His name. You are not a fool, and you know the consequences if our enemies learn of this operation. See that you do not break faith with me, for if you do, I will kill you with my own hands.'

Suddenly the young man's fears came frothing to the surface. 'You must prevent it, Colonel. You must stop this madness!'

'What, boy, do you dare to speak treason before me?' Azziz chastised him, covering his own position just in case this were a cunning plot to betray him as a conspirator to the jackals of Jalloud's Internal Order section. 'Enough – now go! I shall deal with the matter in my own way. You will carry on as if nothing had happened.'

'Yes, yes, you may depend upon me. I speak no treason, by merciful Allah!'

It was good that the spy still feared him; it reassured Azziz of his control over this valuable source. He softened a few degrees.

'You have done well, Zadmeh. I am pleased. Now you must return to your office, but keep me informed of every meeting attended by this Rear-Admiral al Mukhtar. I must know who else is involved.'

Zadmeh went quickly off into the night and sought the safety of the shadows.

When he was gone, Azziz turned and gazed out beyond the metal railings towards the darkened beach. He could hear the sea breaking against the shore, and he saw the pale glimmer of foam creep back and forth as the waves stole across the sand. He peered vainly into the distance, but saw only the dim flicker of white caps on the waves. It was there, alright. He did not need to see, but he could feel it, lurking in the cold blue depths. A hunter-killer.

Why now? he asked himself as he fired up the BMW and turned back towards Bin Ashur. The engine sounded good. He drove fast, aware of his imminent appointment with the foreigner, his mind racing in time with the powerful engine. Was the assassin not concern enough for him without this further intrigue? Of course, the papers could not be ignored, for he had recognised at first sight what Qadaffi intended to do. It was an operation Qadaffi had long dreamed of, but which Azziz had come to believe was merely an idle fancy. Now it was about to become a reality. May Allah bless the day he sent his spies into Azizyah!

It had begun with the LN 114 incident, he recalled bitterly. On 21 February 1973: the most infamous date in Libyan memory, and one the President could still not forget. In those razor-edged months that preceded the combined Arab forces' push against Israel, they were all still bleeding from the wounds of the Six Day War. The LN 114, a Boeing 727 of the Libyan Arab Airways, had been bound out of Benghazi for Cairo with a hundred and four passengers aboard. Who could tell what caused the navigational error which made the aircraft overshoot and stray into Israeli-occupied Sinai? It was a mistake the pilot would never repeat. Unwittingly, the aircraft had circled over Bir Gafgafa airfield, one of the Zionists' most sensitive military bases, bringing a swift reaction from the interdiction force of Israeli Phantoms. The jets made close passes attempting to force the airliner to land, but the pilot merely waved back from the cockpit, believing them to be Egyptian allies. When the LN 114 turned and headed back towards Cairo the Israeli jets shot it out of the sky.

Three bursts of air cannon had ripped into the fuselage, and it had crashed in a ball of flame killing everyone aboard. They knew this because the Egyptians were monitoring the incident and their version concurred with that given by the Israeli military inquiry.

Of course, there had been universal international condemnation for the act, but the Zionists were never punished for this slaughter of innocent Libyan civilians. Nor had the Egyptian airforce scrambled to their assistance, claiming that a sandstorm had prevented their take-off – a fact which had wounded Qadaffi deeply.

Two months later, whilst Libya and its Egyptian neighbour were still enjoying a close association intended to culminate in unification under one flag, Qadaffi had formed a brilliant plan to exact revenge upon Israel and to repay Egypt by implicating her as a conspirator. At this time the State of Israel was preparing to celebrate its twenty-fifth anniversary. For all Arabs this occasion uniquely symbolised their failure to dislodge the Zionists from the lands taken from the Palestinians, but only Qadaffi rose to the provocation. Libyan intelligence had learned that a group of wealthy American Jews had chartered the QE2 to take them from Southampton to Ashdod in order to take part in the anniversary celebrations. With breathtaking audacity Qadaffi ordered an Egyptian submarine then stationed in Tripoli harbour to put to sea, hunt down the QE2 and blow it out of the water.

Out in the stillness of the Mediterranean the submarine commander had hesitated over the order and sought confirmation from Cairo in a coded message. Beside himself with rage, President Sadat had recalled the submarine.

With hindsight Azziz now saw what Qadaffi refused to acknowledge, that such an operation would have jeopardised Sadat's preparations for the coming Yom Kippur war with Israel. At that time Sadat could ill afford such an adventure.

When he reached his office, Colonel Azziz put off the light and sat in the darkness smoking an American cigarette, his fingers twisting gold worry-beads busily.

It was obvious from the photocopied papers on his desk that the President was again set upon that desperate course. The target was once again to be the *QE2*, which had since served the British so well in the Falklands conflict. The passengers were Israelis and American and British Jews. They were prominent people in their community: tireless fund-raisers for the Zionist cause. And hosting the trip was the Israeli Minister for Tourism and a large party of officials. Only this time the weapon would be a Libyan vessel under Qadaffi's direct command; and success would be guaranteed, for the Foxtrots were now equipped with sea-launched Harpoon missiles.

As he assessed the consequences of this operation – one to which he had never been made privy – he was jerked from his reverie by the shrill electronic warble of the intercom.

'Colonel, your guest has arrived.'

'My guest?' His mind was elsewhere.

'Brady, the foreigner. He is with Mahmoud.'

'Excellent. Tell Mahmoud to bring him up immediately, and put the operations room on standby.'

Azziz closed the file and locked it away in his personal safe. In his diary he made a pencilled note to see the Education Secretary at the earliest opportunity. But for now there was the Irishman.

Mahmoud knocked and entered, followed by the dark, bearded figure of Liam Brady. The Irishman was wearing an open-necked shirt with the collar folded over the top of a light sports jacket, both tight across his broad chest. Swinging around in his swivel-chair Azziz took a moment to assess the man against the reports of his work. This, then, was the man who had controlled the bombing campaign in London with such deadly results; the man who had taken the fight into the very homes of the British Intelligence men. Strange, thought Azziz, that the blunt features and pugilist's brow gave no hint of a cunning brain or – if Belfast's fears were correct – the man's infernal lust for power.

'Welcome.' Azziz extended his hand and pumped Brady's in the way diplomats do to prepare the ground for negotiation. He indicated a chrome and leather chair and Brady took it, his eyes darting around the office and coming to rest on the rotating spindles of a portable tape-recorder. Azziz waved Mahmoud away, and the aide left the room with a small, graceful bow.

'A much anticipated pleasure, Mr Brady. Do you smoke?' began Azziz, taking out his pack of American cigarettes.

'Thanks, I will.'

Azziz lit their cigarettes with a gold Dunhill lighter, making a great show of snorting blue smoke from his nostrils.

'I have heard many impressive things about you, Mr Brady, and your work on our behalf has been extremely professional. Forgive me now if I proceed with what might seem undue haste, but, as you appreciate, the life of the President is at risk.'

'Let's not waste any time, then.' Brady took two audio cassettes from his breast pocket and tossed them on the desk.

Azziz looked at them curiously. 'What's this?'

'Those tapes were made during our interrogation of the British spy. His confession gives ample detail of the British plot to undermine your Government and replace it with this Nationalist Front organisation. It was only right at the end that he told us about the assassination plan.'

The Libyan frowned. 'Pardon a little healthy scepticism, Mr Brady. You're sure this is not one of those convoluted deception exercises?'

'Positive.'

'You see, I'd hate to have my men chasing all over Tripolitania for a man who doesn't exist. It could be very disruptive and would do my personal reputation much harm.'

'After what we put that Brit through ... No, he told us the truth – as far as he knew it. Besides, I've seen Tyler with my own two eyes. Believe me, he's real enough.'

Azziz took another pull on his cigarette and nodded his approval. Satisfied. He took the tapes between both hands and kissed them, giving thanks to God and secretly hoping he would find some Cabinet members implicated in the plot. That would enhance his status. The gold worry-beads still hung from the second and third fingers of his right hand.

'I can't tell you, Brady, how important this information will be in rooting out the traitors. We must smash their opposition to the Socialist People's Jamahiriyah once and for all. We might also administer a painful lesson to the British for once again fomenting discontent within this country. They worry so much about their image before the rest of the world, and this tape will hurt that image.'

'That's the general idea, Colonel.'

Azziz was warming to the Irishman, and his tactical sense, and that now showed in his voice. 'Happy the day that God delivered the spy Stephenson to us!'

Too bloody right, mused Brady. Without Stephenson they might never have learned of Nimrod. But there was still one unanswered question and Brady knew he had to ask it.

'Stephenson may have been the answer to your prayers, Colonel, but how did you get his name?'

The Intelligence chief tugged at his long grey eyebrow, playfully, amused by the question.

'It is important to you?'

'Just curious, Colonel. No disrespect, but I've worked against British Intelligence; they're the oldest in the business and they're just too good to be caught flat-footed by your people. You must have had first-division help.'

The barb stung.

'Curiosity can be very dangerous, Mr Brady. I seem to remember from my English teacher that a certain cat died of it. However, since you are man enough to ask, I shall be man enough to tell you. The East Germans provided the information; it was gleaned by one of their surveillance teams who routinely target the British on their own ground in London. Stephenson had become a regular visitor to those dissident hovels in the less fashionable parts of Kensington. Moscow Centre advised the East Germans to appraise me of Stephenson's clandestine interests, and that's where you came in. Does it bother you that you are also a pawn in Moscow's peevish game with the West?'

The Libyan smiled, the green tattoos hypnotically vivid against the bronze of his skin. It was a measured remark, one intended to probe Brady's loyalties, for Azziz had no particular love of communists and distrusted them as much as the God-cursed capitalists. They were all infidels to him.

'Frankly,' said Brady, 'I couldn't care less, as long as I get what I want from this.'

Azziz pulled on the cigarette and snorted blue smoke once more.

'Ah, Mr Brady. You have anticipated my next question – the fee for your services?'

'You don't hang around.'

'I cannot afford to.'

'No, I suppose not,' said Brady airily as he watched the tape-recorder roll – this would all be on record. 'Not with this bastard on the loose.'

The Libyan nodded his agreement.

Brady was glad his words were being recorded: that meant there would be no misunderstandings between them later. 'The fee will be in several stages, beginning with an immediate cash injection of six million US dollars to be controlled by myself without reference to Sinn Fein or the IRA General Staff,' he stated slowly.

Azziz fought back his surprise; his eyes narrowed. 'A large amount of money for a simple identification.

Your rates are very high for looking at Immigration photographs.'

'Let's understand each other. You're paying for what's been and what's to come. Help in the past and a similar arrangement for the future. I want to make that clear. I want a further assurance of support and political recognition for the New Irish People's Army as soon as it is constituted, and a pledge to sever all links with the old General Staff of the IRA.'

'You intend to take over control of the struggle for a free united Ireland?'

'That's right. It's a matter of political evolution: the dinosaurs have had their day. My soldiers are waiting to move, but we need funds and we need friends. Support us in Ireland, and you support your own autonomy and freedom from the superpowers.'

'You dare much, Brady.'

'I do indeed, Colonel. You will see the day come when I address the United Nations on behalf of my people, even as Yashir Arafat did on behalf of *his*. If I have to bomb my way into that chamber, then so be it.'

Colonel Azziz moved uncomfortably in his chair: such fervour in a non-Arab was rare. He marked the passion in that voice which Belfast now feared would shake its castle and bring down its walls. They were right to fear him, and his commitment, for such commitment had forced Brady to gamble everything upon this one chance in Tripoli, and he was clearly determined to launch his new movement out of the ashes of the old.

'You have given me much to think about,' said Azziz, nodding gravely and checking his watch. 'However, it is impossible to give a firm answer now. Colonel Qadaffi must be consulted; I am merely the instrument of his foreign policy. Do not worry, he will be most sympathetic to your aims and I will add my recommendations on your behalf. Does the delay disappoint you, Brady?'

'No, I can wait. If you'd agreed just like that,' he snapped his fingers, 'I would've suspected you

296

were only humouring some madman you saw before you.'

'Is it madness to dream of throwing off one's chains?' the Libyan enthused, grabbing Brady's hand and pressing it. 'Now come, it is time to earn your fee.'

The operations room was, in fact, four offices combined and converted to house the radio consoles, mapboards, telephones and computer hardware used by Azziz's hand-picked operational taskforce. The officers working there, in air-conditioned luxury under fluorescent strip-lighting, were men and women of unquestioned loyalty. They were the brightest stars culled from the ranks of young Libyans educated in the universities of Europe and America. It was they who directed the squads of Moslems set forth to destroy the 'stray dogs' abroad.

There were no introductions. Azziz gave little away of the other operations underway that night – a roller-blind had been drawn down over the huge wall-map, obscuring the mass of coloured pins concentrated around Northern Europe and the Middle East.

Brady was led over to a computer console where a young Libyan woman sat navigating the menu-screens of the Immigration records system. On instructions from Azziz, the girl retrieved a list of Caucasians who had entered Libya within the past five days. That would have to be the period of Nimrod's infiltration – Brady had seen the man with his own eyes in London the previous week.

Tripoli and Benghazi were the main entry points by air and sea, but there were also the land borders to consider. There were crossing points from Tunisia and Algeria to the west, from Niger to the south, and from Sudan in the south-east. The land border with Egypt had long been closed, and that with Chad was still a war-zone. These land borders were controlled by customs posts which regulated the influx of foreigners; cross-border movements of the nomadic tribes were monitored by the police in each administrative region and by the camel corps in the open desert. It was rare for Europeans to enter via the land borders; those who did so were usually tourists venturing into the Sahara in VW buses. In all cases, entry was strictly controlled by visa.

Land border immigration posts were currently on full alert for unauthorised infiltrators. They had reported no border crossings by Europeans in the past five days. If Nimrod was in Libya he had come in by air.

The girl noted the airport references and explored them one by one. Over 650 male Caucasians had arrived in those four days, but many were too old to qualify. She extracted for closer scrutiny those where the passport date-of-birth indicated the bearer was aged under forty. Images of all photographs taken in the previous month had been routinely transferred to computer video disc. There were 420 possibles, and she brought each image to the enhanced graphics screen for a visual check.

One by one, Brady had studied the illuminated and magnified colour images for ninety minutes before he came to a face which made him stop dead. His finger froze upon the 'enter' key and his teeth clenched.

'There's your man. There's Nimrod.'

'West German national,' said the girl, turning to Colonel Azziz and speaking in Arabic. 'Toll, Karl Heinz. Electrical Engineer. Thirty-two years old. Registered address Hotel Poseidon, Sharia First of September.'

Azziz turned to the ops room controller who was hovering attentively, waiting for direction.

'Get on to the Militia office at Green Square and have that whole block sealed.'

'Colonel,' the girl interrupted, 'there's an appended file to this image.' Her fingers were flying across the keyboard. 'Just as I thought, a reference to a report by Revolutionary Security. It's graded routine.'

'Then get it, at once!'

The report did not improve the Colonel's humour. Angrily he read how his men had been within only minutes of making an arrest, but had screwed up.

'May God strike them!' he cursed. He had ordered increased routine surveillance of in-bound aliens the moment the threat became known. Any alien behaving suspiciously was to be detained and questioned – not allowed to escape! The report told of a routine surveillance of the West German at his hotel – but one which had gone wrong. The foreigner had fled the location with the aid of a second European who drove off like a demon. The surveillance car had been blown up with a grenade – standard Soviet issue. One man was dead, the other had scrambled clear and escaped with cuts and burns.

'No arrests?'

'A possible accomplice previously seen talking with the West German. Interrogation still has him.'

'Then get a report, by God! I want more details,' Azziz thundered. 'Descriptions of the men and vehicles. Direction of flight. Anything. Get out and interview the hotel clerk again. I want the West German's belongings from his room. Then start by tearing the expatriate apartments to pieces. Someone must be hiding these men.'

A flurry of activity ensued. Phones came to life.

Back in the privacy of the Colonel's office, he turned to Brady once more.

'So, it is to be a hunting party, after all. I had hoped that with your help we could have caused this Nimrod to disappear quietly.'

'I'm ready to start when you are, Colonel,' said Brady resolutely. 'He can't stay hidden long in this country, and when he comes up for air I'll personally blow his fucking head off.'

'May Allah steady your hand, Brady. But I have a bad feeling about this Nimrod. He comes at a difficult time.'

The older man's face was lined with uncertainty; he was worried. That gave Brady his chance to get near him.

'We must work close now, and I can help you. If he's blown he'll try to go for a quick hit and get clear the instant he can. Give me a free hand and I'll give you his dripping corpse.'

'Our security is already tight enough,' said Azziz defiantly. 'And yet where the President's life is concerned . . . What will you need?'

'I must see the serials on the President's itinerary from now until the end of the month. Exclude nothing. Choosing a place and time to assassinate a president is a specialised skill. There are only so many possibilities which offer the right combination of access, opportunity and escape. Believe me, I know.' He tapped his gut. 'This never lets me down.'

When the list arrived, Brady took off his jacket and rolled up his skirtsleeves. He studied the list carefully, the way Nimrod would – with an eye for a clean shot and a quick getaway, or a chance to infiltrate explosives that could be initiated from a distance. For a moment he experienced a sense of envy at the magnitude of Nimrod's mission. In other circumstances he might have jumped at the contract himself. But right now the Libyan leader meant far more to him alive than the half million sterling Stephenson said they had offered Nimrod. The Libyan Intelligence chief had snorted his disgust when he heard how little had been offered for Qadaffi's life. He deemed it a great insult to his country; in his eyes Qadaffi's head was worth many millions.

In the end, when they had eliminated closed functions and others which would be cancelled in future, there was only one event which qualified; one event which had already gained sufficient publicity. Brega.

'That would be madness,' said Azziz. 'Brega will be cordoned and well protected during the opening ceremony. He couldn't possibly get close enough.'

'Lots of foreign workers there?'

'Of course, hundreds of them. Cubans, Canadians, British, Americans, Turks – you name it, they're there.'

'He'd blend in beautifully. Don't you see it's the only public appearance that the President *must* make, for national prestige. It's Nimrod's one guaranteed sight of him.'

'Do you have any idea how many men will be there, watching and guarding the President. He'll be fully prepared to fend off an attack from the army if necessary.'

'It's about the same number as were guarding the Brighton Grand Hotel when our people bombed the British Prime Minister. Things don't work that way: the number of guards is directly proportional to the number of chances for a screw-up. Particularly if there are different units in attendance who use different lines of communication and whose duties overlap. The security chain, like all chains, is only as strong as the weakest link.'

Azziz blew out his cheeks in resignation. 'All right, I take your point. After seeing the lines of communication between the Revolutionary Security, the People's Militia and Jamahiriyah Security at work, I cannot really argue.'

'Tell me, Colonel, who is directly responsible for the President's personal protection?'

'Captain Kim is chief of Protective Security.'

'Kim? A Chink?'

'A South Korean. His credentials are impressive: highly decorated in Vietnam, veteran of ROK special forces, unarmed combat instructor. Shoots like a machine, steady as a rock. There are ten of them altogether, but Kim is in charge. Qadaffi chose them himself: he currently favours the Roman idea of a foreign bodyguard whose only loyalty is to the hand that feeds it.'

Brady caught a whiff of disdain in that comment.

301

'There's some doubt about loyalties at the barracks?' he asked carefully. 'The threat from the Nationalist Front?'

'Do not concern yourself with our internal politics, Brady.' Azziz could feel the Irishman encroaching upon his territory. 'We are grateful for your help in identifying the Englishman, but we do not require you to perform Intelligence duties here.'

That was a broadside to Brady's gut, but he accepted it knowing he was dancing close to the line. Better back off, and save the Arab's face.

'Forgive me, Colonel. I meant nothing.'

'Already forgiven,' said Azziz, lying.

'Let me meet this man Kim.'

'I have arranged it for tomorrow. Colonel Qadaffi returns to Azizyah, and Kim will be with him. But remember, Brady, when you meet him, take care you do not upset him. He is slow to anger but he is a proud man and a little unpredictable.'

Brady promised he would make the right noises to appease the man's ego. It was all bullshit to him, anyway. What really mattered was baiting the trap to catch Nimrod. The rest was incidental.

'Whatever you say. Just let me review his procedures and test his men. I'll soon tell you how good your gooks are.'

All day he had watched the giant tankers slide by, leaving their irridescent trails in the water. He cursed those he suspected of washing out their empty tanks at sea, polluting it, and yet still he exchanged courtesies with their captains via ship-to-ship radio. Now with his vessel well clear of Cadiz, and the warmer waters of the Med in the offing, Bill Hammond, the Second Officer, knew the traffic would be heavy from here on. He would need to keep his wits about him in the Straits.

The liner was just a few short hours from Gibraltar, on a sea as smooth as glass – a welcome change from the chop of the Atlantic which had accompanied her these past two days since sailing from Southampton.

Not that a ship the length of three football pitches couldn't hold its own in a swell, thought Hammond, as he inspected weather and tidal reports on the teleprinter for the coming twenty-four hours. Thirteen decks high, a virtual red-white-and-blue floating city, the lady could ride easily through anything she was likely to encounter. But Hammond knew the importance which its charterer, the Israeli Government, placed upon this voyage – and its consequent importance to the Company – and he was glad of the calm seas and the Mediterranean's warm scented breezes to lull the high spirits of his passengers.

It had not been a particularly easy voyage. Nothing which involved the Israelis ever was. There had been trouble with the crew. They were none too happy about having their rooms routinely searched by heavy-handed Israeli security men; their sullen looks revealed that much. Searches in the catering areas were always sensitive; there was always the implication of dishonestly among the staff. But they would have liked it even less, Hammond reflected, had they known that Mossad had required the Company to provide a full vetting list of names, addresses and personal particulars for everyone from room-maid upwards.

The details had first been checked against Interpol's criminal indices at the Israeli Embassy in London, then against Mossad's own terrorist intelligence index in Tel Aviv. It was symptomatic of their thoroughness that, although they had apparently found no adverse traces, the security men had asked for the removal of four crew members to another ship- due to certain unexplained coincidences they preferred not to discuss. Clearly these men took no chances.

In the passenger areas security had now taken a back seat to more political business.

In the four main restaurants seven hundred of the world's richest Jews and their families were enjoying a

303

sumptuous meal washed down by literally cases of the ship's best champagne. The atmosphere was boisterous, with occasional spontaneous outbursts of singing in both Hebrew and Yiddish. The women's sparkling gowns were a dazzle to the eye, leaving no one in any doubt that diamonds were very definitely the order of the day.

They were happy: they were going home to Israel.

All through dinner, name cards were changing hands and old acquaintanceships being renewed. Here was a heady cocktail of political influence, including many Washington lobbyists on whom Israel had long been able to rely for support. There were newspaper owners, delegates from the New York Israeli Support Group, consultants from the Mount Sinai Hospital, investment bankers, company lawyers, television and movie producers, Wall Street warriors, diamond dealers, and two Hollywood actors. High above the aroma of French cuisine was the clear unmistakable odour of money – money which was being *given away*. It was a celebration of extravagance: a kind of 'Oscar' awards for the philanthropic gesture.

Periodically, a dapper TV personality would make his way between restaurants to announce over a microphone that so-and-so had just pledged a large donation. These amounts were invariably quoted in thousands, and followed by immediate spontaneous applause. Passengers even found themselves holding their breaths in anticipation of the next record-breaking figure committed. By now it was proving to be a very expensive trip for almost everyone aboard, but no one minded in the least. Not when the money was earmarked for development funds to be used in West Bank settlements. A good cause, they all agreed, since the more settlements they could plant in the occupied territories, the less chance there was of an independent Palestinian state ever taking hold there.

After dinner the Israeli Minister for Tourism adjourned, with his press secretary, to the Yacht Club

Bar at the stern of the ship, where he had agreed to give an interview to a stringer for *Newsweek*, a girl who had joined the ship at Cadiz. They took a window table which looked out over the rippling dark water.

'Such a truly beautiful sight will always warm the heart,' offered the Minister warmly, gazing over the head of the girl as she set her mini-recorder in motion on the table.

'What's that, Minister, the sight of bank-drafts in a champagne bucket?'

'Ah, a cynic,' he smiled disarmingly.

'A realist, maybe.'

'Then I shall not attempt to deceive you. Yes, this is a fund-raising venture. Events such as this help to secure and maintain ties between Israel and her friends.'

'Does that mean your country is currently concerned over adverse publicity and growing world opposition to repressive acts against the Palestinians?'

'Not unduly. And please do not put words in my mouth, my dear. The position, as we see it, has not changed significantly in the past forty years. We still retain a loyal following of friendly groups – if not governments.'

She didn't care much for his 'my dear'.

'How do you assess the current state of tension between Israel and the front-line Arab states? Some commentators are predicting another war. Just how great is the threat?'

The Minister's hands came up in mock surrender. 'Please, please. Let's remember the purpose of this interview. I thought you wished to cover the voyage not to get into matters of policy outside my portfolio . . .'

After that the interview continued in a more light-hearted tone, with only the occasional barb. The girl was clever; she probed hard without appearing to, but the Minister was a wily old bird, well-versed in political hedging, closing up tight just when she thought she had exposed a weak flank.

In the end it was the press secretary who rescued him, reminding him of his duties in the Grand Lounge. He made his apologies.

'Thank you for your time, Minister,' said the girl, not without irony.

In the Grand Lounge on the upper deck, seating was restricted to those passengers with particularly deep pockets. A select group of supporters were waiting to hear from the Minister: some at their tables on the main floor; others standing against the railing of the upper floor, facing out over the stage. Every available railing had been festooned with dozens of small Israeli flags.

When the Minister approached the raised platform at the head of the dance floor, the pulsing overhead disco lighting gave way to a single spotlight which fell dramatically upon the host of the gathering. The white cloth behind his head was embroidered with tall gold lettering which said SOUTHAMPTON – HAIFA. Suddenly the twelve-piece band struck up an intro – a single chorus of 'Hey, Big Spender' – followed by a drum-roll and a double thump on the bass drum.

'He never bought a drink all night,' heckled the cigar-chewing head of a television station loudly but goodnaturedly. His wife shushed him.

The Minister laughed louder than anyone.

'Ladies and Gentlemen,' he began, waving his arms like an orchestra conductor. 'Friends of Israel.' General applause interspersed with whoops and cheers. 'God forbid this should be my song!' His deadpan delivery doubled the laughter. 'No, it is you, good, generous people who are celebrated in the words of this tune – not I. You are the Big Spenders, my friends; and I thank God for your continuing generosity.' More applause. 'I thank everyone who has pledged money to strengthen our hand on the West Bank. I would also like to extend a personal thank-you to each one of you for joining me on this historic journey, this journey back to the land which was given to the Jewish people by the hand of God at the time of Abraham. Four more days and we are already in Haifa. A journey I myself made after the war in less happy circumstances.' It was a poignant memory, one he had vowed he would not dwell upon, so he bit back his emotions. 'Friends, I know this will be a pilgrimage you will remember for the rest of your lives. My heart is full. Thank you.'

This time the applause was thunderous: a standing ovation. For a moment the ageing and white-haired Israeli seemed lost in the surrounding noise and in his memories. Then one of his aides was at his side and whispering into his ear. With an effort his face brightened.

'But we are also here to enjoy! Ladies, prepare to have your beautiful gowns judged in our fund-raiser competition one hour from now.'

The band took its next cue from his words, and struck up with their tribute to Glenn Miller.

The Minister beamed at his wife. 'Now I believe it is time to dance.'

TWENTY-TWO

'I WISH I knew what's got into Yariv,' said Sarah worriedly. 'Since Nineveh disappeared, every time I try to talk to him he bites my head off. He's pretty hyper.'

'Yeah,' answered Tyler, not really listening. 'We need to get away from here soon. To higher ground.'

He was wrinkling his brow at the large-scale map spilling over the edges of the table. Wearing only cotton jeans, he towelled his hair dry with one hand whilst the other traced the flat contours between the coast of the Mediterranean and the northern Sahara.

'What was that?' Sara turned from the balcony door, where she had been admiring the distant hills as they changed from their early-morning blue to the familiar purple heat haze.

'High ground. We need some form of curtain.'

Sara came and stood at his shoulder. His finger drew a quick ellipse around the coastal area known locally as the Jefara.

'The area where we are now is too highly populated – agreed?'

'Agreed. Military installations and coastal radar defences, too, at these bases.' She indicated the locations with a trimmed but unvarnished fingernail. 'That whole coastline is alive with air-defence hardware – not that they could keep the US Sixth Fleet out if the Pentagon wanted in. There are wooded plateaux further out.'

'Has to be open ground,' he said, still regarding the map.

'Then it would have to be further inland – the Sirtica.'

Tyler gave her a look of uncertainty. 'And the curtain . . . ?'

'I know a place, maybe three hundred and fifty kilometres from here. Quite a journey. It's off the main road, a rather bumpy ride down dry wadis, but it's surrounded on three sides by steep rock formations, with about half a kilometre of clear ground between.'

'Sounds promising.'

'The land is owned by a Sulubbi.'

'What's that?'

'Not what,' she corrected. 'Who! The Sulubbi have been outsiders amongst the Bedu for hundreds of years. They are the outcasts, the lowest of the very low – tinkers. They have become a cunning and enterprising breed in order to survive amongst the so-called noble Bedu tribes. But this one has wealth; he now owns land. We must ask his permission. That is fair.'

'OK,' said Tyler, 'if you think that's safe.'

She shot him a quick reproving glance. 'It would be very unsafe to do otherwise. If we forget our manners, he will forget Bedu hospitality, and we need that. By tradition a Bedu will shelter and feed any guest for three nights, even an enemy. It is the way in the unforgiving desert.'

'Enemies, too? I thought they were pretty divided by tribal differences and blood feuds.'

'So they are, Tyler. But it brings honour on a man to display hospitality, even to an enemy. His name will grow because of it; just as his name will diminish if thieves trespass upon his land and steal his water without permission yet go unpunished.'

'Is that what we seem? Thieves and trespassers?'

'In this land we are.'

'Well, whatever we are, it's not safe here in Tripoli after what happened at the Poseidon – and I need that testing ground.'

'Then we must approach the Sulubbi.' She was adamant.

'Are you saying that if we go there without permission, this Sulubbi character would try to kill us?'

'He would undoubtedly kill you, not just try. The Sulubbi are the finest hunters and trackers in the desert. They know the secret paths across saltmarsh and sand sea; and most important they can smell water better than any camel. They've been used as guides for hundreds of years by the other feuding tribes; they are the original special forces of the desert. This man would readily kill you for violating his land – honour would require it.'

'Sounds like a good one to have on our side.'

'Yes, he'll be useful in many ways. 'He lives close to the lands of the Qadadfa tribe, and knows a lot about them.'

'I think I'd like to meet him, after all.'

When Yariv returned, his mood was as black as ever.

'What's up?' asked Sara, steering him to the table with a glass of tea.

My God, what's happening?' he blurted. 'It's confirmed that Nineveh is in their hands. He was bundled into the back of a car that same night. They think it was Azziz's people.'

'Stay calm, Yariv. Nineveh can't harm us.' She sounded comforting, but Yariv's eyes came back to Tyler, the cause of all his trouble.

'Dammit, man, why don't you get on with it? How long can you last now the Irishman's here?'

'Tell me,' Tyler put aside the map.

'He's here in Tripoli helping Azziz, and they have photographs of you. How will you get near Brega now, even if I do get you that operational order?'

The Englishman thought hard. 'That's my problem. As long as they don't find me, we're still all safe.'

'But for how long? They're already ransacking the expatriate blocks less than a kilometre from here. You mustn't be seen, in case the neighbours talk. Our intelligence set-up is too valuable to risk!'

'Don't worry, I'm leaving Tripoli today,' said Tyler. 'I need a testing ground for the hardware.'

Sara shot Yariv a reproving glance. What was wrong with him? Why did his fingers shake so?

Suddenly Yariv stood up, forcing his chair back against the wall with a crash. 'Sara, there's a military operation in the offing against Israel. One of my deep covers is currently risking his life to get classified documents out of Azizyah. I must get that information back to Tel Aviv.'

'Fine,' said Tyler, folding up the map. 'You do what you have to, but we're going now.'

'We?' The tall Israeli looked from one to the other.

Sara put a hand on his. 'I'm going, too. Tyler doesn't know the terrain and I have to take him to the Sulubbi camp. We'll be back here in a day or two.'

They assembled their gear in silence, aware of Yariv's brooding eyes. It was obvious he did not like what he had heard. His face and voice were both emotionless when Sara said goodbye.

'If that's what you've decided, I guess I'll have to watch your backs from this end.'

'Yes, do that,' she said softly. 'Watch out for Brady and get what you can on Qadaffi's visit to Brega.' Then she walked up and kissed him on the cheek.

He shot her a shy smile. 'Go then. Just take care of the Cruiser and bring it back in one piece.'

An hour later the LandCruiser was heading out of Tripoli, with the two crates stowed neatly in back between two twelve-gallon water drums. They drove south-east, passing through the towns of Bani Walid and Al Qadahiyah, where there was much light industry so the roads were good, then out into the bare desert that lay beyond. There were army jeeps on most desert roads, Tyler had learned from Yariv, but serious security and the manned checkpoints were concentrated around the vulnerable pipelines of the country's oil-rich central region. The only checks they had to fear would be from police-posts in the towns they passed through, but those were soon taken care of with Yariv's pass from the Oil Ministry: a stamped document allowing him free passage through all non-restricted areas.

Tyler's heart soared. God, it felt good to be free of the city, and out here with desert pressing in on both sides of the road. He felt safe here – perhaps even a part of it.

Casually, he looked across at Sara. 'You must know this country pretty well,' he said, his eyes moving between her face and the smooth black tarmac of the road ahead. 'Those formations you pointed out earlier weren't marked, so it seems you know more than the map.'

She smiled back. 'Maps are for roads – and even then they're usually out of date. Terrain has to be studied. All the best generals throughout history knew that.'

Was she teasing him?

'Oh, yes? Tell me about it!' he snorted, half-joking.

'All right, I will.' She folded her arms neatly beneath her breasts and hit him with the facts. 'Tripoli, for your information, sits on the eastern horn of a crescent-shaped escarpment approximately 400 kilometres in length and 150 kilometres deep at its broadest point. This area, the Jefara, is a shallow coastal plain formed by a subsided anticline of sedimentary rocks. Its surface is composed largely of quaternary aeolian sands, gravels, conglomerates and desert crust, and is underlain by a cocktail of Miocene and Triassic rock series, which in places are exposed to the surface. Shall I continue?'

'Don't stop now,' he muttered in bemusement. 'Sounds fascinating. Can't wait to hear the ending.' So let the girl have her fun.

Her face was softened by humour, made even more beautiful by laughter. And now her brown eyes danced.

'The topography of this small home-from-home is by no means uniform . . .'

'Lord, perish the thought!'

'. . . near the coast, and again in the centre and western portions, are extensive sand-dunes. But to the south . . .' she slowed down; the pearl of wisdom was nigh, 'to the south we note the existence of impressive and imposing fault scarps. This area is the junction of the Jefara and the rocky Jebal Nefusah range, and it is here that the original soaring cliff-like formations have been broken down by deep-cut wadis. Actually it is more like a series of jebels all split by the water that cut those wadis.'

'I presume there's a point to all this.'

'Be patient, Tyler. Education is a wonderful thing,' she chided. 'It is here that the uplands rise to two or three hundred metres above the desert floor; here that the rock structures I described along the Nefusah range will provide whatever shelter or cover you may require. Now, surrender, or I'll continue with the lava cones of the stony desert.'

313

Her smile of satisfaction was radiant. For a moment he was stirred by the sudden change in her; she could be so witty and warm if she chose to be. For a moment he wanted to kiss that full mouth. Had he not been struggling with the loose steering of the Toyota, he might have risked it.

'Well, are you impressed?' she asked, full of pride.

'Should I be?'

'Yes, you bastard. There, I too can swear like the English.'

Tyler's eyes widened in mock horror. '*Now* I'm impressed.' She growled displeasure and swung a hammer-blow that bounced off his right thigh, numbing the muscle. Caught unawares, his foot stabbed the accelerator and the Cruiser lurched, throwing the pair of them forward, then back into their seats.

'Jesus Christ,' he swore.

'Never heard of him!'

When Tyler had recovered full control of the steering-wheel, he turned to berate her as a crazy bitch, but she flashed him a slightly lopsided grin and his anger melted. He could see what was left of the little girl in her, as she sat there swathed in one of Yariv's khaki shirts. He began to laugh as he rubbed the aching muscle of his thigh.

'You, Sara, are dangerous.'

'For me, you too are dangerous,' she said, and immediately looked away towards the thinning scrub grasses by the roadside.

He did not quite know how to deal with that one, but it struck home – touched some private place where his softer emotions were held prisoner. But he let the moment go without even knowing why. Perhaps, he mused in the silence that followed, he had forgotten how to do otherwise.

The black-top continued southward, flanked still by red earth on both sides, and intermittent stretches of dark olive groves. Occasionally large white

314

Peugeot taxis would cruise past them, loaded with white-robed passengers heading for Tripoli. It seemed commonplace for whole families to use these vehicles in place of buses. Tyler felt his legs sticking damply to the imitation leather seat, and he envied the taxis their air-conditioner units. Even with the roof vent fully open, and with the windows rolled down as far as they dared in view of the constant ninety-kilometre-per-hour blast of dust that accompanied the in-rush of warm air, it was still oppressively warm and muggy in the Cruiser. After four hours, he could taste nothing but dust.

Soon afterwards they passed through a small town called al Qhaybat, where they stopped to refill the tank and take a cool drink. A handful of stone houses and wooden shacks huddled around a tatty petrol-station cum roadside café with the unlikely name of 'Mario's'; obviously a left-over from the pre-war Italian colonial era. At one of the tables in the shade of Mario's café, local men wearing ankle-length jalabas were smoking Marlboros and playing backgammon. Two half-starved mongrels ferreted around a pile of refuse, panting in the heat; but there was scarcely anyone else around, and no women to be seen. The locals watched without speaking as the two foreigners climbed out of the bright red four-wheel drive and approached one of the empty tables.

Automatically, Sara flicked at the flies that crawled lazily across the stained formica table top. She called for service and a teenage boy with peach-fuzz on his upper lip, and a white cap on the crown of his head, came and took their order. Like all such roadside stops, they sold a fizzy red sugary drink called 'bitter'. Tyler tried a glass of it but Sara grinned and ordered Pepsi.

'I suppose they don't see many European faces around here,' he said, sipping gingerly from his glass. The locals had abandoned their backgammon for the moment, and intently watched their movements without speaking. Sara looked around at them, knowing she was the cause, and grinned.

'Not this far south of the capital, nor this far west of the oil sites. The truck is something of a novelty, too. How's your drink?'

Tyler grinned. 'I've had worse.'

'Oh really?'

'Back in the Legion. There was this Belgian sergeant called Chanel. He encouraged us to make use of all manner of liquids so as to survive in an emergency.'

'Urine,' she said, quite unabashed. 'You mean urine. Why don't you say it. I've had that experience, but I still prefer Pepsi.'

Once again, Tyler laughed. 'You're a pretty remarkable woman, Sara.'

'Yes, I *am*. Even I know that now, though I didn't when they first took me from the hospital and gave me this new life to lead. I kept yearning to go back to the bank where my girlfriends worked – just to be ordinary. Isn't it strange what we sometimes become, in spite of what seems planned for us?'

When they had beaten down the price of the petrol, they returned to the LandCruiser and Sara insisted on doing a share of the driving. Normally women were not permitted to drive a car – another quirk of the Moslem law, the sharia – but now they were three hundred kilometres away from the main population centres. And Tyler's back and legs ached, so he did not argue with her.

A half-hour out of al Qhaybat, Sara swung off the road and began to follow the Wadi al Ihrdham, a poorly marked channel across an expanse of red-coloured stony desert that stretched to distant black rocks on the horizon. Once again Tyler was impressed by her local knowledge, and by the way she could follow a track which petered out in places, when covered by shifting dust, then reappeared again without warning. She seemed to follow her own internalised compass, and he remembered what she had told him about the tracking skills of the Sulubbi.

'How long have you been in Libya?' he asked her.

'Not long this time, but often enough in the past. This country represents the starting point for much of the murder and destruction that finds its way into Israel, so my unit keeps a close watch – a finger on its pulse. Between this country, Syria and Jordan we're kept pretty busy looking after the safety of our people. Even the Americans agree that Libya is *our* sphere of influence for intelligence operations. They have sources with the press and media, but they cannot operate here themselves. They say it's too dangerous for them.'

'They have a point,' said Tyler.

'It depends how much risk you feel is acceptable – how much a person will dare, to guarantee the safety of his homeland. The Americans prefer to work from diplomatic cover or else they prime businessmen and reporters to gather their information. That's the wrong way to conduct such matters. The businessmen are mostly concerned with money, or their own power and influence, so they cannot be relied upon. You need to put in independent people, with deep cover – people who don't need to rush off to meet some Embassy official every five minutes. So the Americans are content to let us risk our lives here, and are ready to accept an edited version of any information we produce. Our relationship works, however.'

'So you don't mind – risking your own life?'

'What kind of question is that? It's for my country. But then, I forgot, you're English.'

Tyler took his eyes from the road for a second but she was not smiling. He was goaded by the comment.

'I no longer consider myself as any nationality, so what the hell does that mean?'

Sara shook her head. 'Nothing. Forget it.'

317

Ahead of them the black rocks loomed taller now, and the pick-up followed a broad channel between two cliff-faces on which wind and sand had weathered the rock in bands like wood-grain. The track was much rougher now, and the sand thicker, so they were forced to tie handkerchiefs round their faces, and to put on dark glasses as protection against the flying dust.

At Century House, Havers, one of the junior desk officers (Middle East), had read the synopses of state broadcasting units with more than usual concern that day, and had called for a full translation of Colonel Qadaffi's extraordinary address on Tripoli Radio.

Part of Haver's job involved the routine monitoring of pro- and anti-British feeling in that theatre, and it was his responsibility to provide the Foreign Office with a constant brief on threats to British interests there. The job had originally been covered by a single officer, usually fairly junior in service and not necessarily very knowledgeable of Arabic or Arab affairs.

That was back in the old days after the war, and before oil became a cause for concern – before the PLO and its myriad splinter groups had become household names. Now there were three desk officers, each with an assistant, covering the Arab states, which were split into Allies, Hostiles and Non-aligned or Floaters. Now the Middle East was watched very closely: a wild card in the political pack.

Havers had managed to secure the job of junior to the Hostiles desk only after much judicious angling in the staff canteen. He knew that was the position to be in if he was to get himself noticed, for it lay within Peter Halliday's rapidly expanding empire. Halliday was in tight with the DDG and anyone who got squarely under Halliday's wing was bound to have a bright future. Havers reminded himself that George Stephenson's desk was now vacant – but not for long if he had his way.

As he checked the translation provided by BBC World Translation Services once more, he felt a twinge of excitement in his belly. This was pure gold! Just what Halliday would want to see.

He played back the tape as he read, absorbing the power of Qadaffi's oration.

'Arab workers, Arab students, masses of Arab peasants, valiant soldiers and officers of Arabdom, masses of teachers, engineers, doctors, technicians, cohorts of Arab womanhood . . .'

So far, the usual salutation. Havers made a casual note: Arab women had been promoted from 'masses' to 'cohorts'.

'. . . act now to punish the Great Satan of America and the evil Zionists who occupy the Arab homelands. Move against their embassies, companies and bases, and the nests of imperialist espionage. Neither let the subservient appeasers of Western Europe escape your retribution, for their connivance has sought to bring Arabs everywhere to their knees.

'Move, burn and destroy them with whatever weapon you find. They prey upon you and conspire to annihilate you from the earth. Shame, curse and disgrace be upon the agents of the Western conspiracy within the Arab homeland, who welcome NATO blockades and lend succour to stray dogs and traitors abroad. The wrath of God be upon those who lend aid to the devils who break Arab arms and legs. The wrath of God be upon the evil Zionists who commit murder at will on Arab soil. The wrath of God be upon the dogs of the mad terrorist Reagan . . .'

319

Havers could not help but blink when he read that one. How many years had Ronald Reagan already been out of office?

'... those who hold dubious meetings with them and offer them facilities, and even open to them the bedrooms of their wives ...'

Oh, for God's sake! Hardly very sophisticated stuff – but effective in inflaming Arab passions.

'The masses of these countries must now encircle the headquarters of those humiliated, treacherous, languid governments; also the embassies, companies and bases of the United States and Western Europe alliance, and kill every dog, civilian or military, without mercy, and ruthlessly pursue them.

'Long dark ages they have spent hoping to subdue our peoples and control our economic life-blood. They cannot! Our strength flows from God, not from oil. We will starve and die in rags before we kneel to the dogs of the unholy alliance. But we will die with guns in our hands, killing every last Zionist when the time is upon us.

'Long years have we felt the scorn of the nuclear powers. They have conspired to deny the United Arab armies the equality of those weapons, yet soon will they know the true power of Islam. The desert wind blows from another quarter now, threatening the roofs and walls of their houses. Let them look now to their faith, for we will send them forth to eternity .'

The voice broke off abruptly, followed by a muffled thud as if the microphone had been knocked over. Strange, thought Havers as he sucked his pen top with knitted brow. A translator's comment stated that it appeared the speaker had then lost momentary control and had given up on the rest of the speech. It had happened once before when Qadaffi was suffering from acute depression.

Quickly Havers drafted a note-for-file, drawing Halliday's attention to Qadaffi's current state of mind as he perceived it: tense, slightly hysterical, paranoid, aggressive – dangerous. It was nothing new, merely a change in intensity, but it would be prudent now to consider banning British defence engineering firms from conducting further business with Tripoli. As for the other thing . . . well, nobody in their right mind would take seriously his ravings about nuclear weapons. Yet the situation would have to be 'monitored closely'. SIS notes always ended that way: it was another way of saying 'Do nothing'.

The note was typed quickly, without revisions, and taken by hand to Halliday's office. The secretary received it and logged it in, but had to apologise that unfortunately Halliday was not in the office at the moment. Away on business.

Disappointed, Havers walked back to his desk on the second floor wondering what had taken Halliday away, and where he could be. It was naturally inconceivable that Halliday's loyal secretary, a spinster of advanced years, would dream of revealing anything – least of all that Halliday was currently sitting beside the pool of the Jerusalem Hilton, engaged in heated conversation with a burly major from Israeli military intelligence.

TWENTY-THREE

IT WAS ALREADY mid-afternoon when they came to the place where the Sulubbi were camped.

They had seen the tents from a distance of two miles across the flat plain, four black and two white, shimmering in the heat haze rising from the baked ground. Dust devils churned the sandy surface like miniature water-spouts. As the Cruiser came closer, Tyler was able to discern a rough stone well beside which more than a dozen camels were tethered, and off to the side a mixed flock of sheep and goats diligently searched out the last of the coarse grass and thorny flowering plants. Two Sulubbi women were drawing water at the well. As the truck approached, the noise of its engine disturbing the peace, they set down their leather buckets to watch its trail of dust weave its way into the encampment.

Tyler stepped gingerly from the vehicle, mindful of Sara's advice to seem polite and respectful towards their potential hosts. Now he became aware of perhaps a dozen other adults and a handful of children ranged in front of the tents, their bodies covered by the dark, flowing robes and head-dresses of the Bedu. The women stood to the rear, some of them concealed by indigo-dyed masks that contained only thin slits for their eyes; others bare-faced, with the blue tattooed crosses of the Sulubbi on their cheeks. To the front of the group were four young men, all tall and implacable-looking; and carrying curved daggers at their belts in deference to tradition, whilst in their hands they clutched Kalashnikov rifles, some of which were vintage models that had been repaired many times with layers of wound-about plastic tape.

Sara smiled reassuringly and stepped forward to the entrance of the largest tent. Tyler followed one step behind, attempting to avoid the ordure of camp dogs, and unsure of what to expect.

Immediately inside the open doorway, Sara stopped and bowed, touching her chest, mouth and forehead like an Arab in respectful greeting to their prospective host. Tyler followed and did likewise.

Seated in the centre of the tent, reclining in lordly fashion against a brightly-coloured camel saddle, was Rababah al Tayyih, the proud head of this extended family. He nodded sphinx-like, as if though some ancient nomadic sixth sense he had expected their arrival, and bad them sit upon the floor. Sara addressed him in fluent Arabic, wishing on him and his family the blessings of God, and for his herds plentiful water and good grazing.

'*Allah u' akhbar!*' he responded, and looked with interest at her companion. 'Welcome to my home. For the sake of your friend I think it better we speak English – or is it German?'

Tyler gave her an inquisitive look which she brushed aside.

'Speak English, al Tayyih. His Arabic would make you wince.' At that the Sulubbi clapped his hands in mirth, then called for refreshment. At this point his sons came into the tent and took their places at his side, each finding a cushion or saddle to lean against on the loose carpeted floor.

323

They sat and talked of inconsequentials while the Sulubbi's wife, a scrawny individual covered in a black robe, served them glasses of sweet tea whilst the more important beverage was being prepared – Bedu coffee.

One of the young women had fetched the necessary implements and laid them in front of Tayyih. There was a leather bag containing coffee beans, a skillet and stirrer linked by a fine silver chain, a copper roasting pan, and a wooden mortar and stone pestle.

Then the women withdrew to another area of the tent partitioned off by a curtain over which they peeped coyly.

'This is Tyler,' said Sara pointing. 'He has come a long way to visit you.'

The Sulubbi busied himself in poking the small fire and arranging the richly decorated and enamelled implements.

'I see,' he answered at last, digging into the leather bag and tossing a small handful of beans on to the roasting pan, his brow wrinkled in concentration. 'And is this your first time in a black tent, Tyler?'

'Yes.'

'Then allow me to explain this small ceremony. The first thing any civilised host must do for his guests is to personally make them some fresh coffee. If I seem distracted as we talk, then I ask your indulgence.' Here he picked up the skillet and prodded the beans, arranging them in a regular pattern. 'Coffee-making is a serious business and requires much attention. As you are my honoured guest, I shall educate you.' He arranged the roasting pan so that its four legs now stood astride the coffee hearth scooped out of the sand, in which a small fire burned, fuelled by dried camel dung. Almost immediately the beans began to hiss and darken, and gradually the tent was filled with a rich aroma.

Tyler lounged comfortably against a camel saddle, his head upon his hand. 'Thank you for receiving us, Tayyih,' he responded, fixing his host with those fathomless black eyes. 'I'll be most grateful for anything I might learn, from you. Forgive me, then, but do you own a radio transmitter?'

Suddenly Sara turned and glared at him.

'A strange question from a guest,' reflected the Sulubbi as he expertly flicked the dark brown beans into the wooden mortar and began to pound them rhythmically with the stone pestle.

'Forgive me, Tayyih, but it seemed that you were not surprised at our arrival. Why's that?'

Sara stopped him before he went further. 'Relax, Tyler. I've said nothing to al Tayyih or his family. It's the Sulubbi gift of knowledge.'

The Sulubbi smiled in genial good humour. 'It is true my people have the gift of prophecy,' he laughed. 'I had expected a visit from Sara, and I knew she would not be alone this time. How did I know? Now, that I can't tell. Perhaps the Jinns informed me.' His eyes were wide with irony, and a chubby finger touched his hooked nose.

'And who are these Jinns? Are they your neighbours?' Both Sara and the Sulubbi laughed out loud.

'The Jinns are not another tribe, Tyler.' She touched his arm to assuage any pique. 'They're the spirits of the desert. Their voices are heard in the desert winds. Some claim it is only the sound of sand-grains rubbing against each other in the dust storms, but the Bedu believe otherwise.'

When Tyler looked around, even the teenage boys were grinning sheepishly. He laughed, too, sharing the joke.

'I thought you were Sulubbi – not Bedu?'

'Those of mixed parentage may choose from either culture. But forget the Jinns. Even my blind old uncle could sense you are a man with a secret, and something preys upon your spirit. There is a danger surrounding you, is there not? You are a man with a mission, and I wonder is it good or bad. No matter, I'll not ask! You are introduced by Sara, whom my family loves dearly, so are welcome regardless of your intentions. Please, relax and tell me of the favour you require. But first the coffee.'

Sitting in the smoky atmosphere of the Sulubbi tent, with the vast open desert on all sides, and hundreds of kilometres from any town. Tyler was mesmerised by al Tayyih's words. Until that point he had felt he was carving out a path; now he knew he was merely following one – locked into his destiny. It was an eerie sensation for a man who professed no belief in the occult. And why was Sara received in this tent like a family member?

All watched in silence as al Tayyih transferred the ground beans from the mortar to a large copper pot which had already been brought back to the boil on another part of the fire. Subsequently, the water was brought back to the boil three times before the beverage was finally transferred to a copper-and-brass coffee pot with a swan's-neck spout and silver beadwork around its lid.

Porcelain cups, small as eggcups, were arranged upon an enamelled tray, and filled from the pot. After all this pomp and ceremony the coffee tasted delicious. Each time a cup was drained, their host replenished it. The rest of the family did not share in the ritual; their role merely to look on dutifully whilst al Tayyih entertained his honoured guests.

Once or twice Tyler caught sight of younger women peering over the curtain. They were gazing not at him, but at Sara: the beautiful, confident, young woman who dressed in trousers and participated with the men. In their eyes he sensed the distant longing of captive souls as they looked upon the face of freedom.

'And now let's hear your request,' said al Tayyih when he had drained his final cup. 'You must sleep here tonight, for the sun is already low in the sky.'

Tyler kept quiet as Sara proceeded. 'Once more we thank you for your generosity. We wish to go the place

326

of the Stone Curtain, and we need a safe place in which to prepare ourselves.'

Suddenly al Tayyih caught his breath and stretched out a hand. 'It is the Qadaffi you have come for, is it not?'

Tyler froze.

'You cannot deny it,' the Sulubbi continued, fixing him with his keen eyes. 'You have the face of the hunter – and you have come for him? Tell me the truth or you must leave my tent.'

A finger of ice touched Tyler's neck as the Sulubbi spoke. You can cling to professionalism for just so long before the time comes when you must take a chance. He decided to break all the rules and trust his instincts.

'Yes, I've come for him. What then?'

Al Tayyih nodded, assessing the Englishman with his eyes. At last an approving smile lit his face.

'Then I will help you. I remember the *Inglesi* during the war. They rescued us from the Italians.'

Tyler smiled at the old man, touched by the Sulubbi's fond memories of a time when Britain still had much to offer the world.

'Thank you, I am honoured by your trust. Sara has told me that the lands of the Qadadfa tribe lie close.'

'Indeed. We have quarrelled over stolen camels many times: they steal one camel – I steal one back. I can take you to a well they own in just one day's ride. They have built an open-air mosque there in which to pray.'

'Do you know where he goes when he comes from Tripoli?'

'He spends much time in the oasis town of Houn, quite close, but often goes much further into the dessert. I know from my sons, who take the herds great distances, that there is a military base three days' camel ride east of Houn – equipped with trucks and caterpillar vehicles. My sons have seen Qadaffi's helicopters in the sky – always two of them with small wings, like this.' He pulled back a rug and drew the shape in the sand.

'Hinds,' said Tyler under breath, recognising the outline of the Soviet gunship.

Al Tayyih leaned forward on his cushion. 'No one knows what is happening there, but my eldest son has seen rockets fired into the sky.'

'You didn't mention these rockets before?' Sara's brow wrinkled, her whole body alive to new threat.

'It was very recent – only last week. Rockets with tails as bright as the sun.'

'Please tell your son we need to know more about this base.'

'As you wish, Sara. Now I must give you a warning.'

'Yes?'

'Be careful when you reach the Stone Curtain; it is a place which attracts bandits. Only a month ago we killed two soldiers there – deserters. There are still many wandering around who have fled the war in the south. They still have their rifles, and prey upon any camps they find. It is not safe for our women. That is why my sons go armed into the desert. You must be very careful. Two of my sons will go with you, if you wish.'

'That's won't be necessary,' Tyler broke in quickly. 'But thank you.'

'Al Tayyih is, as usual, too generous,' corrected Sara, smoothing away any chance of offence. 'Thank you for your many gifts, and may Allah ever bless your line. We'll leave at first light.'

At midday a fitful calm descended upon the Azizyah Barracks, as civilian and soldier alike broke off from the morning's rigours to take a slow meal and rest away from the sun's heat. It was heat which only the lizards were willing to brave.

This was a special day, a day full of guarded tension. The President had ordered a higher state of readiness amongst the army units, and an increase in security for his person. That morning as he had walked to his gymnasium in the Azizyah grounds, he had stopped

328

to admire the uniforms of his Presidential Guard. Crimson berets, gold braid on olive tunics, and with gleaming bayonets fixed to the Kalashnikovs – they assured his safety.

The Presidential Guard was his own idea. Six hundred crack troops, all expatriate Arabs, all devout Moslems; each highly paid and owing allegiance only to the President himself. And each willing to give his life, if necessary – for Islam.

When Qadaffi's travelling circus moved around the country, opening factories, refineries or water reclamation installations, a small number always moved with him; but when he was in Tripoli, directing the nations affairs, he was attended in strength. It was a precaution inspired by intelligence reports of dissent within the officer cadre of the armed forces. Even now there were small groups of officers just waiting for the chance to topple him. Like jackals following the lion, they waited for a moment of weakness in which to make their move. Just let them try – his leopards would cut them down with swift and bloody ferocity.

Within sight of the President's two-storey villa, across the parade ground, stood the barrack blocks of the Presidential Guard – shoebox buildings with green wooden shutters thrown back from the windows; white stucco blocks shimmering in the noonday heat.

Upon the wooden verandah outside their block the men of number 2 platoon were scattered in postures of repose, their shirts unbuttoned, boot laces loosened. Theirs was standby duty, not on guard but training. All that morning they had trained with sandbags and bayonets, and then on to the assault course they had nicknamed 'the Line of Death'. It was a murderous regime of exercises: walls to climb over, pipes and tunnels to scramble through, burning structures to burst through with flames licking their limbs and singeing their beards. And then, when they were almost too weak to climb the ropes, there was hand-to-hand fighting and clouds of dust to swallow. That morning they were lucky, for the sun did not clear the thin cloud until they had broken to eat, so no one had collapsed from heat exhaustion. That would have earned the entire platoon extra fatigue duties.

At midday the officers and NCOs dismissed them and they dispersed to their respective messes. There they ate a light meal and gulped water like dying fish. Now, the awning over the verandah provided welcome shade from the ferocity of the sun, and it was here they came to unclip their belts and relax for the remainder of the rest period. Steel-tipped boots rasped upon the wooden flooring in idle frustration, but no one dared move from his spot lest another man steal his shade. Instead they huddled close enough to be irritated by the stink of each other's sweat.

One of the young soldiers, whose spot was uncomfortable and not worth guarding, took a thin mug and a stick and captured two scorpions that were sleeping in the dark space under the verandah. Within minutes a contest was arranged and money began to change hands.

From where he was sitting, Abdallah could see the two enemies tentatively probe each other's defences – then lock pincers and begin their dance of death. He sat back with apparent lack of interest whilst the other men urged on this or that fighter. The game he had in mind would be far more interesting – and more dangerous. Abdallah was an Egyptian by birth, and a man fanatically committed to the cause of uniting all Arabs in a Moslem Republic. It was for this reason that he had quit Cairo and come west to Tripoli when Anwar Sadat had sued for what he felt to be a dishonourable peace with the Jews. It was a hard life here in the Guard, each day harder than the last, but at least it was somewhere for a Arab to serve with pride.

He mopped the sweat from his brow using it to slick down his thick black hair. At only twenty-eight he had begun to notice the grey hairs multiplying. His joints were not now as supple as they had once been.

It was sad to feel his vitality being exhausted in wars that left the cause no nearer to realisation. Suddenly a movement caught his eye: a screen door opening in the old NCO block fifty yards away. Two orientals stepped out, carrying steaming bowls of rice and plates of meat and vegetables, which they placed carefully upon a dazzling white cotton sheet spread out on the ground. They turned to face each other, gave quick nods of their heads, then squatted down to eat. There were many orientals in the country these days, guest-workers mainly, but Abdallah immediately recognised the President's Korean bodyguards. Eventually he returned his thoughts to the sling which Youssef now wore to cradle his injured arm. Youssef had taken a bad fall, landing awkwardly, but it was the weight of the other man's body falling upon him that had brought the agonised cry from his friend.

The voices of the onlookers were raised now as the darker, redder scorpion strove to turn its enemy over on its back. Suddenly the cheering stopped, as a large shadow fell across the men seated around the makeshift arena and they turned to look up into the arrogant face of Sirhan the Palestinian, who had stopped to observe the cause of the excitement. In a flash the darker scorpion flipped the other over, arched its tail and struck with deadly accuracy. The young soldier who had initiated the contest looked down to see the loser writhing in poisoned agony – then a heavy boot came down upon the insects, squashing both completely.

'Hey! Why did you do that?' the young soldier protested, squinting upwards into the sun. There were gasps of disbelief from other soldiers sitting in the tight circle.

'It pleases me,' came the defiant reply. 'When I see an insect, I must crush it. Take care I do not crush you, too, little one.' The Palestinian lifted his boot and scraped the sticky carcases off against the wooden step. The young soldier turned away in disgust, but nobody spoke. Satisfied that none meant to challenge him, the Palestinian moved on to the far corner of the verandah. He stopped to pour some water from a cooler into his aluminium cup, then pushed another soldier aside into the dust so he could sit down to drink it.

Cautiously the men exchanged resentful looks. The bastard was just too damn strong. Abdallah looked across at his friend Youssef, sitting with legs crossed and his right hand resting protectively across the clean white bandage that restrained his left arm to ease the pain of the fractured collar-bone. Youssef was not a big man, and there had been no call for it. Abdallah had soldiered with the toughest, had seen small men come in first and big men cry like babies; he had seen hot-shots licked into shape or cracked by the system; he had seen the most resolute of lone wolves forced to change his tune, but he had never encountered a man more violent, malicious or needlessly brutal than Sirhan the Palestinian. The man was for ever spoiling for a fight, seeing insult in the most innocent of remarks; constantly out to assert himself in spite of his enormous size. And, by Allah's beard, the man was big: he estimated his bulk at 280 pounds, and his height at six feet seven. It was a matter of wonder amongst the platoon how such a giant could have emerged from the disease and starvation of a refugee camp in Jordan. One brave man had asked him once. 'I ate my brothers,' was the reply. Who could disbelieve it?

Never once had the bastard attempted to become a part of the platoon, preferring always to sit on the fringes, aloof and truculent though barely twenty-two years old. He could have been their champion, the defender of unit pride and honour, but instead he chose only himself. That very morning he had bested all comers in close-quarter combat, and there had been a sadistic grin on his bearded face as he fell upon Youssef with his entire bodyweight, crushing the breath from his body. OK, so you're the bull in this herd, thought Abdallah, but leave the rest of us in peace.

Soldiering was hard enough already with bastard NCOs and incompetent officers.

And then a sweet, sardonic smile broke across the Egyptian's handsome face, like poisoned honey.

The Palestinian lifted his peaked cap away from his eyes to see who had spoken. The gamblers, who had returned to their places in quiet resentment, were now all staring at Abdallah. Sirhan stared, too. This was the Egyptian with the clever tongue; a popular man, lean and tough – though not tough enough. He spoke again.

'See, see the great monkey, brothers.' Abdallah's face split in a broad grin, and the others began to laugh as he scratched at his armpits and bounced up and down.

Sirhan waited, poised to react. Who was the insult aimed at?

'Two of the bastards, look at them!' Abdallah pointed across at the NCO block. Loud guffaws erupted from the soldiers at the absurdity of the mime, but also at the puzzled look on the face of the Palestinian.

See, Youssef, how they sit like the chimpanzee.'

'Better to keep your voice down, brother.'

'Why?'

'You know why,' admonished Youssef pointing to his shoulder. 'Those two yellow men are killers. They'll cut you in two.' Youssef chopped the air with his good hand.

Abdallah stole a glance at the big Palestinian. Though he lounged against a wooden support, his mouth was set firm, and the bastard was obviously listening carefully.

'Don't make me laugh, Youssef. They are nothing more than children. I'm amazed they should hire such tiny people to protect our President.'

'A good desert wind would blow them away,' another man intervened. 'Maybe a snake will carry them off to its burrow.' The men sitting around them erupted in shouts of rebuke or agreement. Then, one soldier, one of the oldest in the platoon, leaned forward to point a finger at Abdallah.

'Bullshit. It's bullshit.' The harangue stopped as every man waited to hear what Kareem had to say. 'You fornicating fools. The Koreans are specialists: Special Forces trained by the Americans, but much more deadly. They fight for money, and they have no other loyalty.'

'And what of us, the Presidential Guard, what are we — mannequins dressed up in pretty uniforms to adorn his barracks?' Abdallah's face reddened with mock rage. 'They don't look much to me. Those lightweights could never take on our best men. What if Al Qadaffi is attacked by a mad Christian, or a man the size of Sirhan? What then? It would be laughable.' Abdallah looked around to grins of approval.

Kareem was annoyed now. 'Listen, I'm telling you, one of them is a Special Forces captain and fifth-degree black belt in Tae kwon-do. Their hands and feet talk fast. Size means nothing to them. If you think they are children, go play with them a while.'

Abdallah grimaced as if unimpressed and scratched the back of his neck.

'If I was the size of Sirhan, our own champion,' he said, 'I think I would go and play with those little yellow men. Arrogant bastards!'

At the mention of his name, the Palestinian sat upright and pushed the cap back on his head.

'Yes, arrogant little bastards,' agreed one young soldier. 'They won't touch our food — not clean enough for them.'

'They said that?'

All hands turned to look across the baked ground to where the two Koreans squatted beside the white sheet, their chop-sticks darting between delicate porcelain bowls. Their bare feet were spread wide in the dust for balance, their elastic limbs stretched in a comfortable squat that brought their shoulders between their knees. They were dressed in dark blue nylon tracksuits with white-striped trim. With ritual deference, the heavier of the two proffered a plate of green vegetables, which the other received with a quick nod of the head. Their gestures were humble yet imbued with a dignity that belied the simplicity of their surroundings – the heat of the day and the dust of the earth. The Koreans stopped momentarily to share a joke, covering their mouths to laugh, as young girls do.

Expert fighters?

'Even now they mock us,' said Abdallah stoking the fires of outrage. He could sense the deep competitive anger now stirring in the silent Palestinian.

You're a fool, Egyptian,' said Kareem dismissively. 'Say what you will, there's no Arab in the land to touch them. Be content our President's life is in their hands.'

The men could not quite believe their ears. This was a slight which could not go unchallenged.

Abdallah exploded into arm-waving fury. 'How dare you! Would you spit on the honour of all Arabs? Do you suggest these monkeys are better men than we? Bullshit! By Allah's beard, a man such as Sirhan here.'

'What about me?' Sirhan's voice interrupted like thunder. His powerful arms hung across his knees; his sleeves, as usual, were rolled up high so all could see the huge, hard biceps and forearms. This talk of the Korean's fighting prowess had pricked his vanity and he threw his chest out defiantly.

'No offence, brother,' said Abdallah. 'I was merely telling this fornicating infidel that those are not supermen, those Koreans. And certainly no better than us Arabs. Call me son of a whore, but seeing them there refusing our food – and then all their talk about how they can take on the best of our fighters. Does the pride of the Presidential Guard count for nothing?'

A defiant cheer broke from the mouths of the younger soldiers, who waved their fists aloft and started the soldier's Islamic chant.

Abdallah turned to Kareem once more. 'I tell you Sirhan could crush them with one hand.'

Heads nodded in agreement and faces turned expectantly towards Sirhan. After moments of silence he leaned back against the upright and snorted. 'They have a reputation, it's true, but such reputations are like promises to women. They are made to be broken. Their time will come.'

'Sirhan is big and fierce,' added Youssef. 'Who could resist him? He will save our honour.'

Before the Palestinian could reply, Kareem spoke again. 'Sirhan is formidable, I agree. But we are talking about the life of the President, don't you see? They are the best – understand? The best.'

This was the moment, and Abdallah struck with ferocity. 'Camel dung! You are full of dung. Always the same. I have a hundred dinars with which to prove you a liar! I say Sirhan could take either of them – or both if he chose to – and grind their bones to flour. Here – here's a bet!' Practised fingers flicked open a shirt pocket and pulled out a wad of folded banknotes. All eyes went to the money.

Immediately Kareem leapt to his feet, slid a hand into his hip pocket, and matched the bet in tens and twenties.

'There is money! One hundred is nothing to me.' He laughed without mirth. 'Talk is cheap, Egyptian. Such a bet is no bet at all. We both know there will be no fight, so your money is safe.'

Abdallah turned and looked expectantly towards the Palestinian. Sirhan was already searching his face for something he suspected but could not be sure of.

'What about it?' spoke Abdallah evenly. 'Will you not make a liar of this old man?'

Everyone present now knew the answer. It was a bet not of his making but one which seriously threatened Sirhan's standing. He looked from one man to the other, their hands thrusting money under each other's noses.

You're like women!' he roared, and spat theatrically into the dust. 'Just impotent spectators. You bet on scorpions, you bet on other men, but neither of you has what it takes to fill his own shorts. I spit upon both of you. Do you wish to see how a real Arab can fight? Then watch a Palestinian – not an Egyptian – not a Syrian. My people grow old waiting for the other Arab countries to help them recover their homeland. Only Palestinians will restore Arab pride.'

There was a shamed silence, for Sirhan had spoken what was already felt by many.

'But you will pay for the privilege, dogs.' Quickly Sirhan snatched the money from their hands, twisting their fingers to overcome momentary resistance.

'Hey, that's ours,' protested Abdallah.

'Shut up, Egyptian!' A heavy hand struck Abdallah a blow upon the cheekbone and sent him tumbling back into the wooden rail. When he dabbed at his swelling mouth he found it was bleeding. At that moment he hated the Palestinian more than he had ever hated anyone. Sirhan was poised for some retaliation that did not come. All Abdallah need do now was sit back and watch the fulfilment.

'Thank you for the money, Egyptian bastard. I go now to sort out a small matter, and when I am finished I'll return and kick your balls through your eye sockets.' The Palestinian turned his broad back and began striding towards the NCO block.

'How is your face, brother?' whispered Youssef.

'Better than your shoulder, by Allah's grace.' Abdallah smiled in spite of the swelling of his lip.

Kareem's gaze followed the progress of the giant Palestinian across the bright sunlight. 'That's done it,' he said with a smile.

'What did I say?' protested Abdallah with feigned innocence.

'Just enough, my brother,' laughed Youssef. 'Just enough to do the trick.'

337

'Sirhan is a proud man, and he has a bad temper,' observed Kareem. 'If he fulfils his promise, I fear you will not be blessed with grandchildren in your old age.'

Kim knew from the aggressive set of the big man's body that there would soon be trouble. He had been monitoring the jabberings of the Arab soldiers across their barracks, without appearing to. He had noticed the waving arms and the aggressive glares, and when the big man had stepped down the walk towards them he knew a challenge was about to be made. It had been the same in other places: Seoul, Saigon, Bangkok. Always the big men made the challenge: US Marines, airborne soldiers, boxers from Harlem. Kim continued eating, and when Park too noticed the Arab and put down his rice bowl, he ordered his colleague to do nothing.

The Palestinian halted directly in front of them, his great feet planted upon the white sheet, upsetting a porcelain teacup. Kim watched the tea soak into the cloth with a widening green stain, then he turned to look at the Arab. He put down his bowl. 'You are very clumsy, soldier. What is it you want?' He spoke patiently, as if to a child.

The Palestinian folded his arms as he towered above their squatting figures. Why didn't they stand?

'You two number-one fighters, very good?' said Sirhan shoving out a fist with the thumb extended. 'Yes?' He spoke pidgin English, knowing the Koreans knew no Arabic.

Kim examined him without blinking. This Arab was certainly strong; his chest was deep and powerful, and his forearms bore the tracery of thin scars from knife duels. When Kim did not respond, Park rose to his feet. This interruption was sheer bad manners, and Park knew it could not have come at a worse time, as Kim still wrestled with the shock of his wife's letter. Captain Kim was a man of disciplined restraint,

338

but this was not the time to push him.

'Jesus Christ, man,' he whined in the Brooklyn accent of his high-school days. 'You number-one asshole. Why don't you go play with the other A-rabs, fella? Before you get hurt.'

The Arab squared himself as Kim came to his feet, touching Park on the elbow. It was barely a touch, but Park deferred immediately and stepped backed with a quick bow of the head. Kim looked up into the dark, sweating face, unmoved by the fire he saw there. He was a full foot shorter than the Arab, but square-framed and thickly muscled. His tracksuit was zipped modestly up his throat, in contrast to Sirhan's open shirt that displayed the thick black mat of hair on his chest. The smell of the Arab's body affronted Kim's nostrils.

'This close to insubordination, soldier? Why your manner is bad?'

'Bad manner, you say,' Sirhan spat in the dust at Kim's feet. Park flinched in disbelief. 'I saw you spit upon the ground as you passed the regiment badge upon our block. This is an insult no soldier of the Presidential Guard can stand for. You insult our honour.'

Kim might have felt depressed by the regularity of such absurd claims, always in the name of honour. But instinctively he cleared his mind, so that his perceptions were now crystal clear. Emotion was a weakness which had been trained out of him by his master.

'You are mistaken, soldier. Go away now, and I forget all this happen.' Kim's broad, flat face was implacable, his eyes did not blink. The Palestinian searched for signs of nervousness, to bolster his own courage, but found none. He laughed, a little shrilly.

'I will break you, little man. Apologise now!'

Two chisel-like fingers jabbed towards Kim's face. Park gasped at the audacity of the insult. The hand had invaded Kim's dignity – his face.

Then Kim made his move, with the speed and

aggression of a big cat, as he seized the Arab's wrist. Pivoting his body, he dropped to one knee, turning hard to his left and simultaneously twisting the Arab's wrist-joint, so as to hurl him head over heels into the dust. There was a loud gasp from the verandah. The Palestinian landed hard, but Sirhan was an experienced fighter and he hit the ground rolling and flipped back into a crouch, shaken but still with thunder in his face. With a great booming roar he turned again, to see Kim advancing upon him with hands held high and extended, like some giant scorpion. Sirhan roared an oath and lunged forward, swinging his massive balled fists, knowing that if he could close in and grab the smaller man he could use his weight to crush him. Kim met the attack with expert timing, swaying to the left. A punch grazed his right shoulder as he swung a kick into the side of the Arab's leading leg, buckling it and shattering the knee joint. Immediately a scream of agony broke from the Arab's throat, but an eye-blink later it was cut short by a second blow, as Kim's body twisted once more, sending his heel high above his head in a blurr of an arc that struck his opponent's temple with deadly precision and knocked him again to the ground. A soft explosion of dust swirled madly in the air, then began to settle upon the body of the fallen Palestinian. Kim awaited for a further onslaught – primed to finish it now. But the big man did not move. He lay still with limbs spread, his left leg bent at an obscene angle.

Finally Kim lowered his arms and relaxed.

On the verandah the Arab faces presented a tableau of shock. Abdallah held his breath for a long moment, then let out a tuneless whistle. 'That God should make a creature with such speed . . .'

A second later and the world came crashing back to life. There were cries from the administration block, and a Libyan officer came running pellmell across the square. Other uniforms followed in rapid pursuit, hands gripping precariously perched caps. The men of Two Platoon raced over and formed an untidy semi-circle around the fallen Palestinian.

'What's the meaning of this, Captain Kim?' the officer demanded breathlessly.

Kim stared back at the officer, his crimson beret, gold braid and badges of rank. He was unimpressed.

'*No* meaning, Major,' he said bluntly but the irony was lost upon the officer. Without emotion Kim knelt down by the unconscious body and inspected its throat for a pulse. 'He will recover soon. Do not worry.' Then he turned back to the Libyan officer. 'Can you not control your men, Major?'

The officer bridled noticeably, then turned his rage upon his own men and prodded the nearest two with his stick, ordering them to summon a stretcher team. The other men were ordered back to their duties. Backed up by his two lieutenants, the Major turned again to Kim.

'Captain, you are to come with me. *Now.*' He struck the palm of his hand with his swagger-stick.

Kim did not like his manner any better than that of the Palestinian. This was indeed a barbarian country. He drew a deep breath, then turned his back on the officer and his crimson beret. Normally he would have complied immediately, out of good manners, but he was still registering insult and needed in some small way to assert himself amongst these barbarians.

'You go. I shall come soon,' he said at last. Moving slowly back to the white cotton sheet, he crouched as he had done before. Park fetched a clean cup and poured some tea for him.

The Libyan officer was more than agitated now. 'Captain Kim, you are to come with me or there will be trouble.' He was young, with a thin face and carefully trimmed moustache. The collar of his uniform was too large for his neck.

'Then you may wait, if you wish, Major,' said Kim,

taking the cup from Park's hands and bowing as
etiquette required.

The officer folded his hands behind his back and
waited, tapping the stick against his leg. Fuming.

Kim raised his cup and drank slowly with dignity.

TWENTY-FOUR

WHEN COLONEL AZZIZ'S black BMW cruised to a halt in the palm-lined forecourt of the administration block at Azizyah, the first thing he noticed was a knot of uniformed officers bustling out from the main entrance, in deep conversation. Immediately, his eyes narrowed to slits of suspicion as he recognised the thin features of the Prime Minister, Jalloud, at the head of the group. By the beard of the Prophet! he thought, a powerful group, indeed: Jalloud and the Joint Military High Command. He watched as the group boarded the three Chevrolet limousines drawn up in line, their drivers dutifully holding open the doors. Then the convoy swept out of the main barracks gate and turned west.

There had to be some very special reason for assembling the Military Chiefs of Staff at this time; one involving national security. Inevitably, Azziz's thoughts returned to the contents of the folder, for he had thought of little else during the previous night, and he wondered now if he had not underestimated the scale of the Houn project. One way or another, he was determined to find out more.

As Azziz stepped from the car into the bright afternoon sunlight, Liam Brady followed him without a word. He turned in a slow, contemplative circle, shading his eyes to take in the full extravagance of the panorama. Jesus Christ, he breathed in disbelief; it was all true! The tanks, the missiles, the sheer bloody size. There was a warm surge in his gut as he looked upon this impressive display of strength, and he realised now he had been right to align himself to the Libyan cause. Then his eye lighted upon the incongruous sight of Qadaffi's famous black tent pitched on a turfed area in the near distance, a she-camel standing contentedly beside it as her calf suckled. For a moment Brady felt light-headed: he could not quite believe he had come this far, to within arm's reach of the man himself.

'Your face says everything, Brady.' Azziz smiled at his wide-eyed reaction. 'Come, we must be brief, for I have an important appointment later.'

Inside the V-shaped administration block, Colonel Azziz demonstrated his power by stopping a uniformed major dead in his tracks with a snap of the fingers, and ordering the man to go fetch Captain Kim to the first-floor conference room. Brady followed along a narrow corridor, his head turning left and right as he took in the building's bare interior. They passed a communications room, where Azziz received enthusiastic salutes and telex machines clattered loudly in the background, and another, smaller room without windows where thick pungent clouds of cigarette smoke drifted and guards in green uniforms watched flickering banks of closed-circuit TV screens. Their footsteps echoed the bareness of the concrete walls as they climbed to the first floor.

The conference room also smelled of tobacco, and the delicate porcelain ashtrays were all filled to overflowing. Azziz wondered whether Jalloud and his men had been the ones to fill them. He walked to the windows and flung them open.

344

They sat down at the long walnut table and waited a full twenty minutes, beneath the wash of two ornate ceiling fans, before the door swung open and in walked Captain Kim. He greeted Azziz with a ninety-degree bow from the waist: the correct greeting for one of his rank.

Azziz glanced at his watch but made no comment. The hint was clear, and Kim could not fail to grasp it, but his smooth oriental features barely moved.

'Captain, I have a serious problem. Please sit down.'

Kim moved stiffly to the nearest empty chair, glancing quickly at the stranger then turning once more to the head of Intelligence.

'There are rumours circulating within the barracks, are there not?'

Kim smiled briefly, his brown irises almost disappearing in the creases around his eyes. 'Soldiers enjoy rumour. But they say that the opposition groups grow in strength; that the Education Minister may be the next summoned by Jalloud's inquisition group.'

Colonel Azziz was surprised to hear how widely that information had already spread, though he waved away the remark. 'All traitors within Government posts will eventually be hunted out, thanks to the efforts of brother Jalloud, but that does not concern me for the moment. Tell me, what have you heard about Nimrod? Has anyone discussed the name with you?'

'I know only of some threat, nothing of the details,' he lied. 'No one tells me the details.' Kim intimated his annoyance with security procedures, though careful to protect his secret. No one in the barracks realised his fluency in written and spoken Arabic, and it was best to keep it that way, for even Qadaffi and Jalloud spoke freely in front of him believing their conversation safe. 'Nimrod, what is that?' he feigned.

'Nimrod is the code-name for an assassin: a British agent sent here to kill the President.'

'Why would a British do that when their country trades so widely with Libya?'

'My information comes from a reliable source, so I need to know whether you can handle this threat.'

Kim thought for a moment, then nodded with the air of confidence which was expected. 'I will extend existing security coverage, of course, but I will need sight of your information before proceeding to harden the target.'

'All in good time,' said Azziz, unwilling to disclose the dearth of available information. 'First let me introduce Brady.' Azziz's wrist rotated elegantly, indicating the Irishman in the chair to his right. Kim's gaze fell squarely upon Brady, who was unsure of how to greet the powerful-looking Korean, so simply nodded. But Kim stood up and stiffly offered his hand, so Brady was forced to offer his own. As Brady took the Korean's hand, feeling the hard muscle at the heel of his palm, he knew something between them was wrong. Something that could never be right in a thousand years. So be it.

'Brady will be accorded full courtesy and cooperation whilst he is here, and you are to assist him in his review of security procedures. He has the equivalent rank of major within his own organisation, and you will observe that.'

'His organisation is . . . ?' queried Kim, determined to receive at least some explanation of this breach of protocol in an area over which he had been promised complete control and final say.

'Friendly, and dependant upon Libyan aid.'

'The Irish Republican Army is an independent force, Colonel,' cut in Brady, smiling, though clearly annoyed by the patronising introduction. The Irishman had already observed it was one of Azziz's fantasies – shared with his political master – that Libya sat at the centre of some great subversive empire.

'Pardon me, but no slight was intended.' Azziz was satisfied that he had reminded Brady of his place, but now poured oil upon the troubled waters with customary elegance. 'Let me assure you, we always appreciate the fraternal support of the IRA in matters which affect the security of the Jamahiriyah.'

'No problem, Colonel.' A tight jaw.

The Colonel returned to Kim.

'Brady has already provided invaluable assistance to us in our efforts to trace this Nimrod before he has time to strike. He may be of further help in matters of the President's personal security.'

'In the matter of the President's life, I do as my experience advises, Colonel. It is difficult for me to bear responsibility for the principal's safety if my procedures are to be influenced by an outsider.' Kim's face had not changed, but the tone of his voice was cooling by the second. Like all orientals Kim knew a word which would have better demonstrated his disdain for this foreigner, but in English 'outsider' would have to do.

'I think Major Brady will bring a certain freshness to our thinking. He can look at the situation from the killer's point of view.' The Intelligence chief smiled without humour, seeing in Brady's face that he did not care for that remark either. 'It's ironic, isn't it, that you and this Englishman should be exchanging roles – hunter and hunted?'

'And which is which, Colonel?' Kim put the question, but he did not miss the emotion that showed upon Brady's face and was gone. So, there was more between the Irishman and this Nimrod than he wished to disclose.

'Starting today, you demonstrate all security precautions for Major Brady. He will accompany you everywhere.'

'The President is aware of this?'

Azziz nodded. 'And he has approved. However, be as discreet as possible. The Brother Colonel

347

is understandably concerned about his public image. These are sensitive days. The last thing we wish is to create the impression that the subversives are winning.'

'Step up security without letting anyone see, you mean?'

'Just do it.' This time the Colonel in charge of the Bureau of External Security wanted no argument.

'As you wish, Colonel.'

A phone-call brought Captain Park hurrying to the Command Block with one of the Range Rovers. Brady and Kim climbed in and were swept away, past the busy parade grounds, down the long straight road to the training hangar.

After he had watched them go, Azziz walked quickly over to the bunker which served as Qadaffi's office. The scarlet-bereted guards of the Islamic Legion saluted and parted to allow him through, for they recognised the familiar tattooed face, and his name was marked upon the day's access list.

Qadaffi sat at his rosewood desk, relaxing in a purple sports shirt buttoned at the neck, and a dark-green jacket. As he rose in greeting, Azziz noted from the dark circles around the man's eyes and the muscular tic in his left cheek that he had clearly not slept the previous night. Such was often the case when policy changes were in the wind, or military action.

'Salaam alaikum,' said the President, embracing his Chief of Intelligence like a brother.

'Alaikum salaam,' responded Azziz politely. 'You are well, brother Colonel?'

'Thanks to God, I am well', he sighed. 'And you, my brother, how are you?'

'Troubled,' said Azziz as both men sat.

Immediately Qadaffi stiffened. 'Really? What troubles you?'

'Naturally, any threat to the life of my President gives cause for concern,' said Azziz, removing a report from

348

not guess whether it was fear or outrage which made his hand shake.

'I should have known better than to exclude you – your spies are too good. But you had enough to deal with already. The Houn project is a holy duty, and the burden is mine alone. As for Jalloud, he is my right hand. He was there when the Free Unionist Officers took their oath, so naturally I turned to him first. I see now that I was wrong not to inform you. This secrecy between brothers has spawned suspicion, and because of this you must now know everything.'

Qadaffi paused and drew a deep breath, his eyes seeming to fill with the strange, hard glitter that was his personal signature.

'Yes, our submarine will send the Zionists to the bottom of the sea, but that is unimportant: a mere adjustment to the balance of history and a debt repaid. The real target is the Zionist nuclear weapons facility in the Negev, and the instrument shall be our own cruise missile.'

Azziz gazed back in disbelief. 'The Demona Facility?'

'Yes.'

'That would explain the need for the infra-red photographs of that area. But the technology of sea-launched missiles?' he probed, knowing that Libya's atomic programme was barely a year old, and believing that bombing capability was all they possessed.

'Not sea-launched, brother – land-launched. The operational control base is already prepared at a secret launch-site in the Sirte desert. It is safe enough: the area has been closed and secured for twenty miles in all directions by the Bureau for Internal Security.'

'Jalloud's men.'

'Yes, Jalloud's men,' nodded Qadaffi, as he strode to the wall map beside his desk. His finger touched the orange expanse of the Sirtica and began to trace a dog-leg route. 'On my personal order the missile will fly north-east, passing low across the Benghazi headland. On clearing the coastline, it will drop down to almost wave height, thereby avoiding radar detection by the US Sixth Fleet, and then turn just south of due east. It will proceed undetected over the Mediterranean and will cross the Israeli border just inside the Gaza Strip. Another adjustment to its course, and the contour-mapping unit will take over, hugging the valleys and avoiding the hills until it reaches Demona in the barren flatness of the Negev. There its homing radar will easily recognise the unique signature of the nuclear facility's domed structure. A few seconds more and . . . no more Zionist nuclear programme.' His finger pressed on the map at the spot marking Demona and twisted hard, as if squashing an insect which had landed there. 'No more Zionist nuclear programme. It will be my gift to the Arab world. My legacy.' He turned towards Azziz, gauging his response. 'Perhaps you do not believe it could be so simple?'

The intelligence man checked himself, for he was still shocked to the core by Qadaffi's cool announcement. 'Forgive me, I had not expected so audacious a plan. But surely the Zionists will shoot it down as it crosses their coastline.'

'Impossible. Jalloud prepared a summary of the Israeli response options and has found that the major air defences were primed for interdiction at land borders with Syria, Jordan and Egypt. Radar and missile installations are thin on the ground between Gaza and Demona because it is already within occupied territory. This missile will strike their blind spot, and it will come by night. Their response would need to come within five minutes of crossing the coast, otherwise it is too late. Even if they scramble their jets in time, in darkness they will not sight it, and the radar will not see it flying low until it is too late.'

'Colonel, their facility is mainly underground. It will be a hardened site. Have you considered that fact?'

'Of course, but it will not withstand an atomic blast. The yield from the device will tear the top off.' His active hands demonstrated the destruction. 'There will be fires inside. Remember Chernobyl. Every nation states publically that their nuclear facilities are perfectly safe, even though they know that's untrue. At last I shall see my dream become a reality. Israel will wither away like a fallen fig.'

'I think I'm beginning to understand the significance of it all,' said Colonel Azziz. 'The objective is not merely destruction but the deadly contamination that will follow. The desert winds will spread nuclear fall-out over the population centres; and their agricultural programme will be decimated for the next twenty years or more. The State of Israel will be brought to its knees.'

'And in its weakness it can be absorbed by the United Arab forces on all sides,' said Qadaffi, bringing his cupped hands together like a boy catching a butterfly. 'I swear you were to have been informed within the week.'

'Really?' said Azziz.

'Truly. But there's not much time. All People's Bureaux are to be put on alert. And I want you to draft a personal warning message to all the Arab leaders, to be delivered twelve hours before our attack. Just say enough to preclude any accusations later of endangering their safety.'

'And if Israel should respond in kind, with nuclear bombs? What then, brother Colonel? What then?'

'Ha!' Qadaffi laughed out loud: 'Against whom will they respond? Everyone knows Libya possesses no nuclear weapons.'

For a long time Azziz sat in stunned silence, and even Qadaffi wondered if he had been right to speak so freely. In that silence Azziz's heart faltered on the brink of faith, but he saw with sudden clarity that it was worldly fears which troubled him.

'If the words of the blessed Koran are true' – his voice was tentative – 'that all rewards are indeed to be found in heaven, then we have nothing to fear.'

'That is the truth. And do you believe that Allah is the one God, and that Mohammed was his prophet?' asked

352

Qadaffi, offering his hand, and recalling the way he had recruited his followers amongst the young officers of the military academy in Benghazi those many years ago.

'I believe,' said Azziz taking the extended hand and feeding off its strength.

Qadaffi smiled contentedly. 'Then you will come with me to my native Sirtica, and be with me when the hour is upon us. Believe me, Azziz, it is close.'

'I see now, brother Colonel, why you do not fear the assassin's bullet.'

A slow shake of Qadaffi's head. 'No, I do not fear him – only that he might prevent me from doing my duty to God and to my people.'

'And the visit to Brega?' ventured the intelligence man.

Qadaffi considered: yes, it would be wise to make this concession, if only to bestow favour upon Azziz's judgement and consolidate the support he had won.

'The visit shall be cancelled. We will gather our friends and return, as Bedouin, to the land which contains the bones of our ancestors.'

Liam Brady was still feeling groggy from the journey, and from the debauched night of entertainment Libyan Intelligence had arranged for him in Valetta. The rhythm of the engine was soothing, and he paid little attention to the landscape outside the windows. They were now passing administration blocks, Nissen huts and barrack blocks. Transport trucks and jeeps buzzed along the road beside them. In the front seats of the vehicle the two Koreans conversed in their own tongue.

The Range Rover came at last to a large tarmac area with four aircraft hangars ranged at its edges. It pulled up in front of the first. The hangar was a huge fifty metres by fifty, topped by an external cover of corrugated iron. Inside its open-ended structure, six more Range Rovers were drawn up nose-to-tail in convoy formation – gold, red and metallic green – and a group of young Koreans in blue overalls stood around talking. As Kim and Brady climbed down, they stepped into line and bowed as one. Kim quickly dispensed with the formalities and steered Park inside, briefing him on the scheduled drills.

'Every morning the Presidential transport is checked thoroughly by my men for explosives and incendiary devices. They are also given a routine mechanical inspection. You can appreciate that any breakdown can prove very dangerous, and tempts opportunistic attacks.'

'Don't the Libyan mechanics see to that, anyway?' asked Brady.

'Of course. However we prefer to keep to our own standards. My men risk their own lives when they ride in these automobiles. Now please observe.'

On his shouted order, the eight Koreans split into pairs and headed for the first four vehicles. One of each pair was equipped with a black case, which they snapped open to reveal an array of tools and equipment, recessed into foam plastic in the body and lid. Brady studied the contents with interest: mirrors, torches, pliers, nylon fishing-line, illuminated probes. It was all there: right down to the hand-held explosive sniffer.

Captain Park, whose Americanised English was better than Kim's, was delegated to provide a commentary.

'As you see, we operate on the two-man principle: any more and they could become careless; any less might be too risky. Our men are completely familiar with these Presidential vehicles; they would spot added parts or wiring immediately.'

The searchers were down on their knees now, with torches, playing their beams along the ground beside the wheels.

'Before approaching a vehicle we search the area immediately surrounding it. There is always a chance some inexperienced assassin may have left evidence of their work: footprints, snips of wire, or even scraps of paper torn from sticks of explosive. Next we conduct a visual check on the external surfaces. It's a rule that drivers must clean each vehicle thoroughly last thing at night before locking it away. That makes it easier to spot tampering from telltale fingerprints and smears, particularly around the door handles, the hood or the boot.

'Next, you will see that a clean sheet is laid out on each side, and a visual check of the underneath made with high-powered torches. They're looking for any obvious colour difference between the blackened underside and a suspect device. Fortunately this vehicle has a high profile, otherwise we would have to slip trolley mirrors underneath to take a proper look.

'Then comes the first contact with the vehicle. The torch is carefully played inside the wheel arch, followed by a hand to probe behind the wheel for anything unfamiliar.'

The Irishman tensed, remembering the time eight years ago when he had seen off a part-time UDR man with two sticks of gelignite placed inside the wheel arch, under the prop shaft. That had been easy: the old Ford Anglia was parked on an unlit patch of waste ground. His first kill.

Unerringly the Koreans explored the entire wheel arch, including the prop shaft. Not bad.

'Before proceeding, my men will use a hardened nylon spike to remove the hub caps. Nylon produces no sparks and does not conduct a current – either of which could initiate an explosion. Behind the hub cap is an excellent hiding place for a tilt-switch booby-trap which will initiate the instant the wheel turns. But, of course, *your* people would know all about that. It's one of their signatures, yes?'

Brady folded his arms. 'We have used it in the past, but not any more. Good ideas have a limited lifespan. That one's well known to British Security, and was discarded years ago. We always have to keep one jump ahead.'

355

Park's face became animated and he nodded vigorously. 'Perhaps later a discussion of your new techniques. I have some ginseng brandy in my quarter, but do not tell the Libyans. I wish to hear more sometime.'

'I'll bet you do,' murmured Brady under his breath so that neither Park nor Kim could catch the remark.

'Please?'

'That will have to be cleared with Colonel Azziz's office. It's up to him what intelligence he passes on.' The silent reproof was clear. A quick jerk of the head from Kim meant that Park was not to pursue the matter. The limits of their cooperation were now obvious.

'Please continue, Captain,' said Brady.

For a moment Park said nothing, then he muttered a casual phrase whose vehemence caught those searching the wheel arches by surprise. Park rarely resorted to such Seoul gutter-speak.

'Remember your manners,' Kim steadied him in Korean. 'you have nothing to fear and little to learn from this foreign devil.'

There was less deference in Park's delivery now, and Kim knew this was his subtle way of dishonouring the ungracious barbarian. Several times he turned his back on Brady, a contemptuous act which no Korean would have brooked.

'The next movement is dangerous – second only to the crucial act of turning the key in the ignition. The man by the passenger door, man B, looks inside the vehicle for any wiring attached to the driver's door. He must look very diligently, because both lives depend on it. The man at the driver's door, man A, then inserts the key – after checking the lock has not been forced or picked – and operates the lock. He then operates the handle and allows the first two centimetres of pressure to be released. B is looking for the wires which spring out once the door opens, and he then gestures for A to proceed – opening the door by two centimetre increments on each signal.' The clicks echoed in the silence of the hangar.

In each case man A slipped a slim perspex ruler between door and pillar, drawing it around the edges of the door with a delicate touch: feeling, probing, testing for the telltale tug of the wire that would draw a peg from a spring-clothespin whose teeth had been fitted with drawing-pins – the terminals of a collapsing circuit. Booby traps are designed to be operated by the intended victim: a bastardised form of suicide – totally without honour.

Four doors opened in a slow, tortured ritual, the movements of the first two men mirrored exactly by the others. Perfect drill. Each man A then took a hand-held sniffer from his case and checked the air inside the vehicle for traces of explosive chemicals – the breath of death.

The same ritual then with the passenger door.

'Does it bore you, Brady?' Kim had found himself a stool on which to perch, and was eyeing him curiously.

'A little – but I'm getting the general idea.' There was grudging admiration in the response.

'Boring leads to careless. Careless leads to dead.' A soft-spoken smack on the cheek.

Brady said nothing. Folding his arms once more, he was aware of the wet patches at his armpits, the stink of engine oil and petrol in the warm still air of the hangar.

'Carefully man A searches for hidden pressure pads under the rubber mat by the pedals, and under the seats, front and back. If there was a device attached to the courtesy light, both men are already dead . . .'

The B men were now standing directly in front of their respective vehicles, hands pressing down upon the bonnet to prevent the kick that would come when the release catch was operated. Prior to this, the perspex strip had been inserted around the edges of the bonnet, and they raised it by painfully tiny increments, ever-watchful. When the bonnet had been safely raised,

357

his slim attaché case and placing it upon the table. The task-force controller had worked late to produce it in time for this meeting. 'Here are the latest developments for you to read. They confirm our fears and underline your need to cancel all public engagements, including the visit to Marsa el Brega. However, that is not what really troubles me.'

'Indeed not? Then may God give you strength to enlighten me.' The President's brows knit together, his mouth was tight and defiant.

Azziz swallowed hard, aware of the gamble he was about to take.

'I am troubled because once I was trusted and now, it seems, I am not.'

'What foolishness is this!' thundered Qadaffi. 'Have you not scattered my enemies? Have I not given you power over all foreign operations? What is that if not trust?'

'And the Houn project, what of this?'

For a while Qadaffi said nothing, recovering from the blow, for that was what it was: a blow to the cheek. There was no way of knowing just how much Azziz had discovered, but he could ill afford to make an enemy of his Intelligence chief at this crucial point in time.

He sighed a long deep sigh, experiencing some measure of relief from the pressure which had been building steadily since his decision was taken. A brief smile replaced the care-worn look which had twisted the President's face.

'What do you know of Houn?'

'I know of the submarine, and of its target. But we both know there is more than that. For some time I have been aware that brother Jalloud has been working upon something linked closely to the atomic programme – a project so secret and so important that, although I have worked tirelessly against this coalition of the NSFL, you saw fit to exclude me from it.' Azziz's fingers were pressed upon the desk, and Qadaffi could some fishing line was looped around the battery terminals, and yanked from a distance to disconnect the battery.

'Normally the disconnection is done from a distance of fifty metres, the vehicles being treated one at a time before driving them clear of the transport compound. These were cleared this morning. The battery is frequently used to supply power to the electrical detonators in the explosive device, and so must be cut out. On the other hand, the very act of yanking the battery may collapse an electro-magnetic circuit and sky the vehicle anyway. Either way, fifty metres is a pretty safe distance. We lost three Range Rovers this way eight months back, so you'll understand our caution.

'The engine compartment is a bomber's delight. You could hide a device almost anywhere. That's why my men are all auto-mechanics to a degree. No hard and fast rules about searching here: just be damned sure you get it right! No clean new wires, plenty of torch and illuminated probe work. And particular care in examining the firewall; the force of an explosion here would be directed towards the driver and front passenger. Result – no legs.'

'We generally allocate two hours in the morning to completing the vehicle checks,' interrupted Kim. 'That's surrounding area, under the vehicle, external surfaces, doors, passenger areas, engine compartment, boot, and finally a test of the electrics.'

'Even after all that, are you sure?' said Brady.

'After all that, the Libyans are sure,' answered Kim, with a touch of amusement.

'Huh?'

'As a final precaution we have the Libyan drivers take the vehicles round the block.'

'Yes,' said Park enjoying the joke. 'If they come back, and they're happy, then we're happy.'

Later that afternoon, Brady asked to see the convoy procedures used when escorting Qadaffi around the city, and Kim arranged for three of the big four-wheel drives to do a circuit of the fifteen-mile barracks perimeter.

The barracks described a six-mile-long teardrop, with wall and electrified fence forming a continuous barrier against intruders. Passage in and out of the *cordon sanitaire* was through one of several gatehouses guarded by members of the Islamic Legion.

'You don't care much for these Libyan's, do you?' observed Brady from the rear bench-seat of the second vehicle.

'Do you?'

'Maybe not. This isn't my kind of place. The little grass there is isn't green enough. We all want something from them, though.'

The change was, for Kim, quite insidious: an attempt to involve him in personal secrets – a test of his own true loyalties. The Irishman was making sufficient effort to convince him that his brief went further than just techniques and equipment. Clearly Azziz wanted to know which way Kim would jump when the fire-fight started.

'Give me your weapon, Major Brady. You will not need it.'

'You sound surer than I am.'

'Believe me, it would be unforgivable if I allowed anything to happen to a guest of Colonel Azziz.'

Still unsure, despite the logic, Brady reached under the left armpit of his summer jacket and offered the automatic on his open palm.

'Come now, Major Brady. Surely you don't expect me to accept an unproved weapon. Part of your review?'

The Irishman felt a flashback: MacStifoin outside that farmhouse on a rainy night in Armagh. He shivered at the imagery. There would be other MacStifoins waiting on his return, he knew. Eddie Kelly would have burned a trail home with news of the stunt he had pulled in Valetta – the General Staff would be after his head. He was playing for high stakes all right, gambling for control of the whole terror apparatus – with his own life as the ante. But success was all he could consider. They would change their bloody tune when he returned with a pledge of six million over two years, and with information about Lochinvar, the SIS mole on the staff.

Strange to think of Lochinvar sitting there with the others in the farmhouse kitchen that night in Armagh, like a wolf come to tea amongst sheep. What balls! How long had it taken that mouthpiece to get so high? he wondered.

The sound of a car horn close by.

Suddenly a squeal of brakes. A blinding flash stung his eyes, followed by a blanket of scudding smoke.

The attack came near the north-west extremity of the perimeter, where the road passed between two long Nissen huts. At that place the vehicles were forced to slow down to negotiate a hairpin bend, and the sun, low now in the sky, was blinding the men in the front seats.

Park's idea.

More thunderflashes. Total confusion. Brady struggled upright in the seat, catching the silhouette of a large truck which had slammed across the path of the lead vehicle. From behind came the roar of a second truck pulling across the road, sealing the trap. Barely a second later, the doors and windows of a hut to the right swung open, and the stutter of automatic gunfire rattled out.

Moving with speed and agility, Kim cleared the back of his seat and fell headlong on to Brady, forcing him to the floor where the Korean could cover him with his own body against the murderous fire being laid into the flank of the stricken convoy.

Barely five seconds elapsed before a third vehicle cut in to the right of the centre vehicle, acting as shield whilst the Koreans in the rear ripped away the velcro fasteners on the fabric covering the machine-gun housing in the recesses of the front two seats, then returned fire into the Nissen hut. Already the Koreans in the lead vehicle had scrambled out of it and made their way, under covering fire from their handguns, to the left rear door of the centre vehicle. Whilst one of them wrenched the door open, and continued laying down covering fire into the hut, two more muscular bodyguards hauled Brady out from under Kim. Kim followed quickly, barking off orders in Korean above the bedlam of gunfire. Brady felt disorientated, his head pounding, ears burning. He let himself be hustled into a laundry building to the rear of a Nissen hut. There he fell to the stone floor, nose and eyes streaming with the sting of CS smoke. Powdery particles were dissolving into the sweaty creases in his armpits and groin – acidic burns. He was hyperventilating and his eyes were unfocused.

Then came a whistle, and the shouting and shooting stopped.

The men who had rescued him were joined moments later by others dressed in blue tracksuits – they being the attackers. Like spacemen, they stood looking down at him, with guns and respirators.

One of the spacemen pulled off his respirator. It was Kim. He smiled disarmingly, smoothing down his hair where the rubber straps had ruffled it. It was a gesture as precise and measured as the man himself.

When Brady's breath returned and his lungs had ceased to ache, Kim ordered his men outside, knowing it was now between the two of them.

Brady coughed. 'Some kind of joke?'

'No joke.' Kim's stony features confirmed it. 'You asked to see everything, and so you shall. We do not play children's game: bang bang, you're dead. Vehicle ambush very frightening. Very real. We use blank ammunition, tear smoke, thunderflashes. You think you come here to civilise the natives?'

'Next time you pull something like that, make sure I get earplugs and a respirator, too. Or, so help me God, I'll put holes in you, you slant-eyed bastard.'

'With this?' The Korean pulled the Colt from his waistband, mocking Brady's helplessness. The Irishman's anger climaxed and he punched the wall, putting a hole in the plasterboard with his fist. But there was nothing more he could do for the moment. Slowly, his anger subsided.

'I can wait.' He smiled. 'And I have important friends.'

'Be sure you can rely on them, Irishman. Azziz will change with the wind; he's a clever man and these are dangerous times. There are things going on that . . . but that is not your concern. They say we must cooperate fully. To me that means giving face.'

'A deal? Is that what you're suggesting?'

'A truce, for now, with mutual respect and good manners on both sides. No more rudeness, Brady. I despise nothing so much as bad manners.'

'You're saying you'll cooperate if I stay off your case? You'll help me find this Nimrod and take him?'

'I am. It's very simple: I give you face, you give me face.'

Brady would have like nothing more than to carve that face he valued so highly with a straight-edged razor, but in the circumstances a temporary alliance had much to offer. Kim knew his way around, and he clearly had little time for his paymasters. Perhaps he had the President's ear, and that might be useful if Colonel Azziz proved to have a short memory for promises.

'I get your help on condition that my report to Azziz is favourable?'

'As for myself, your opinion is meaningless. But this is a valuable contract we would not wish to lose. Some of my countrymen have heavy gambling debts to meet back in Seoul. Wives and children to support. We can keep the President alive – be sure of that – just don't break anyone's rice bowl.'

Brady allowed himself a moment's consideration, but his answer was not in any doubt. A shrug and a quick nod was all it took, and a grudging alliance was struck.

TWENTY-FIVE

THEY ROSE AT first light and ate a breakfast of yogurt and dates. Once again al Tayyih offered two of his sons as escort, and when Tyler refused he shook his head in disappointment and warned them to watch the horizon carefully at all times.

As they left the camp, the Sulubbi family stood before their tents to see the Cruiser bounce away across the plain in the cool, blue-tinted first light of day. They continued watching until the red speck disappeared into the southern horizon, heading for the place of the Stone Curtain.

'OK, now some answers, Sara,' Tyler demanded almost immediately. 'All this may be cosy as hell for you but it was my understanding that the Sulubbi would be completely in the dark about our operation. I want to know where he fits in, and I'm tired of being treated like a tourist who doesn't know the time of day.'

'Rababah al Tayyih's family are friends of Israel. That's all you need to know. He may be trusted.'

'Oh no, you'll have to do a little better than that. I want the full version this time – none of this "I think I know a place and some one who will help us".'

Extracting information from this girl was like asking for her soul.

She heaved a deep sigh as if she was complying against her better judgement. Or was such a disclosure merely against all that her training had taught her.

'All right, I'll tell you, but remember one thing: when you and I are gone from here al Tayyih and his family remain, and their lives depend upon your silence.' Tyler said nothing. 'For many years Libya was controlled by the powerful Sanussi family. The old King, Idris, was Caliph of the Sanussi even before the British liberated the country from the Italians and the Nazis, and placed him on a newly created throne. Because Sulubbi families are at the bottom of the social ladder, they often attach themselves to a Bedu tribe and act as their retainers. Tayyih's family was with the Sanussi in Benghazi for years, performing many vital military services for them. Their loyalty and bravery were legend. Then, when the Qadaffi revolution came, anyone associated with the royals was hunted down and put on trial for treason. Many were executed. So al Tayyih took his family away where Qadaffi's agents could not reach them.'

'And where was that?'

'East, through Egypt, across the Sinai and into the Negev desert.'

'He went to Israel? An Arab went to Israel?'

'You know so little about the Middle East, Tyler.'

'Maybe. It's just a little hard to believe.'

'What's so hard to believe? There are many Bedu in Israel who go about unmolested. We welcome all peace-loving people, and we have no wish to destroy all Arabs the way some of them want to destroy us.'

'Fine, so it's open-house in Israel. But go on.'

'Our people found out about al Tayyih and persuaded him to work for us against the Qadaffi government.'

'Just like that?'

'No, not just like that. We're professionals. We built a relationship first. We began by debriefing him on his knowledge of the resistance movement. In return we sent his children to school and then on to our universities; the Bedu know the value of education. He gave us information which enabled us to infiltrate Libya; he gave us contacts amongst the nomads who still retained their tribal loyalty towards the Caliph. After six years, we persuaded him to return here himself as part of a communications network, and that's his role today. There is an old Arab saying: "Whoever is the enemy of my friend is my enemy; whoever is the enemy of my enemy is my friend". He works for us content in the knowledge that he works against his Caliph's enemies.'

'You must have paid him a hell of a lot.'

'Don't judge everyone by your own standards, Tyler. For a number of years he made a very respectable living in the Western Desert, salvaging scrap metal from the tank graveyards; blowing them apart with explosives and hauling the pieces into the towns for a few cents a kilo. He's not a greedy man, and the things he values cannot be bought with money.'

She was right; his careless remark had been inappropriate. He thought of the old days in Northern Ireland when he, too, had been driven by a sense of duty and by his belief in certain basic ideals. What did he believe in now? Was it only in himself? If that was true, would a million in sterling really be proof against such poverty of the spirit? He tried to apologise.

'Hey, look, I'm not much good at ... well, I'm sorry. That's all I wanted to say.'

'That's OK,' she responded. 'I understand. No one should trust his life to strangers if he can avoid doing so. But don't forget we're all taking risks here – the Sulubbi more than most.'

'So we are,' said Tyler distantly. 'But some have more to protect them than others.'

They saw the bluffs long before they reached them. A dried-up wadi snaked forlornly into the far distance between limestone outcrops left by countless years of erosion. Sara indicated a series of smooth round white stones, the size of kneeling camels, which lay dotted across the landscape like giant ostrich eggs. Beyond these stones, rock façades rose almost three hundred feet, forming a stone curtain that enclosed a half-kilometre-wide open space on three sides. It was a dazzling sight. The rock, which had been a pale purple in the dawn, was now reddish-orange as the fierce late-morning sun struck its surfaces, casting rugged shadows into nooks and crevices. It was the only natural landmark in an undulating yellow blanket as far as the eye could see.

'This is the place,' she said, gulping a drink from the aluminium water-bottle. Then, as she swallowed, something dark and man-made caught her eye. 'What's that up ahead? Below the rock face at ten o'clock.'

Tyler's eyes squinted through the polarised lenses, and he made out the shape of a vehicle lying on its side.

'Looks like a jeep. Do they use this place as a vehicle dump?'

'People dump vehicles everywhere. If something breaks down here, it's hard to find a truck to haul it in for repairs.'

He remembered the broken-down Volkswagen buses they had passed, just sitting out in the middle of nowhere, abandoned by tour groups who had tried to cross the Sirtica; their windscreens opaque from the friction of flying sand.

'Better not take any chances,' said Tyler reaching under his seat and passing her the Uzi, just in case. She took hold of the weapon and automatically cocked it, slipping the change lever on to FIRE without lowering her gaze.

Cautiously they drove on, Sara keeping the

muzzle of the weapon trained through the window on the jeep while Tyler scanned the lower rock formations for sudden movement. He stopped twenty metres short and, drawing the Browning from his belt, stepped out on to the hot sand and crunched his way over to the upturned hulk. Sara swung her door open and stood behind it with the weapon poking through the rolled-down window port. Already he had come to rely upon her combat instincts and he knew, without looking, that she was covering him and would not flinch from opening fire, if necessary.

He checked the jeep thoroughly.

'It's OK. No passengers, no petrol, no water in the radiator. Looks abandoned.'

Sara smiled her relief and flicked the change lever back into the SAFE position. 'Actually, this little baby might prove very useful. An ideal target.'

Laying the Uzi back on the passenger seat, she looked up and found him staring back at her. For a moment she was confused by the sunglasses and unable to discern whether the expression on his fine mouth was a smile or a grimace at the bright sunlight. He seemed to sense her dilemma, and when he casually removed the glasses, she saw that his whole face was smiling. The instinctive smile she returned was a confession of something she thought maybe should have stayed hidden. She was glad that Yariv was not with them.

'It's pretty out here,' he said, still smiling warmly. 'Let's take a look around.'

They walked about for a while under the shade of that majestic rock. In a cool spot covered with wild grasses, Sara knelt to touch the crimson petals of the wild poppies, finding pleasure in their determination to bloom in soil so arid. It was peaceful here, and after the constant whine of the engine the quiet was balm to the ear. The soft twitter of sparrows in the thorn bushes made them smile again. And while she studied the flowering plants, Tyler studied her. He awoke to the delicacy of her dark features, the fine black hair growing coyly at the nape of her neck, the healthy tan of her smooth skin. She was beautiful.

When he turned to look at the Land Cruiser, she said, 'Don't worry. It's safe here. We have all the time we need.'

Something in her voice went deep inside him then, and he caught hold of her hand, pulling her nearer. It was an awkward, self-conscious gesture. Her eyes checked his fearfully. Yet he knew it was right, and felt sure that she wanted him just as he wanted her. She stood close, unable to speak, waiting for the strength of his arms to pull her towards him. Her breathing became rapid, and just when she felt those black eyes might be mocking her after all, he drew her closer. Reaching behind her head, he drew out the pin restraining her hair and let it fall in a dark cascade upon her shoulders. She looked once more into his eyes, unsure of what she was searching for there – she an adult who ought to know better – then to her relief his mouth closed upon hers. He pulled her to him fiercely, exploring the softness of her body. His eager fingers peeled back the cotton blouse, freeing her breasts and releasing her own trembling passion. They sank into the wild grass, lost in a hungry kiss, and before she realised it she was pulling at the buttons of his shirt, uttering requests only half-remembered.

Their lovemaking was fierce at first, laced with heat and sweat, and seized with the hunger of a last request. But later they were gentle with one another, almost like children exploring the unknown. And it was sweet.

It was over far too quickly, as stolen moments often are, but when it was over they clung to one another like drowning souls, each trying to understand what had happened and fearful of what it might mean.

He heaved the long crate from the LandCruiser and laid it on the ground. The missiles inside their protective tubes had been packed tight with ballast, and strapped down tight for protection in transit; thick plastic sheets shielded them from the dust. He had brought along only two of the missiles; that would be enough for testing and practice. The detachable aiming unit was packed separately, and jammed behind the driving seat.

Of course it was incriminating cargo; Sara had said as much back in Tripoli. 'If we're stopped for any reason – and make no mistake the security forces find many reasons to stop foreigners – the end will not be pretty. Were you briefed on the methods of Libyan Intelligence? They are truly animals.'

Yes, it was a risk. But once clear of Tripoli not so much of a risk. Now all he needed was one test to be sure, then they would be clear to go.

Sara leaned back against the Cruiser, her arm spread along the side wall, watching him strip the first missile from its case. She had heard of the Javelin, but never before had she seen one. The dark green tube came sealed, about a metre and a half in length, like a piece of drainpipe, but in a matter of seconds the aiming unit containing the guidance system and monocular eyepiece was clipped to it, and it was ready to use. Tyler struggled for a moment to make the connection, before the soft click told him he was in business.

'It's an ugly brute,' said Sara. She was more familiar with the Russian-made missiles used by the Arab armies, like the slim-line SAM-7.

'No, I guess it won't win any beauty contests, but they say this baby can really move.'

He looked around and fixed his eyes upon a rocky promontory some half-mile distant and two hundred feet up the rock face. At one point a chimney of red rock grew out of the face, no more than six feet in height, forming the most obvious visual target in an otherwise barren expanse. It was important that the aiming point be above eye-level, in order to test the

369

climbing power of the rocket. He had heard reports of the flying speed it developed, but he needed to observe it for himself.

Tyler dropped to one knee and heaved the assembled unit onto his right shoulder, placing his left hand on the broad, frontal barrel which contained the cruciform tailfins of the missile. These would flip out and backwards into position as the missile left the launch tube. His right hand held the pistol grip that steadied the aiming unit and contained the ignition trigger. Immediately above the pistol grip was an optically enhanced viewer which magnified the target area. He scanned the rock face until the red chimney was in view.

'Don't move,' he called to Sara without shifting. 'Cover your eyes, the flash may damage them.'

But she was not to be so easily cheated, and took a pair of sunglasses from her pocket. 'If you think I'm going to miss this . . .'

'Suit yourself, but just stay clear.' He flexed his shoulders to obtain a more comfortable position. 'This sucker goes off with a bang.'

Then he pressed the ignition trigger. Immediately there was a searing yellow flash that seemed to erupt from both the front and rear of the tube, making a dark silhouette of the operator. Then came the whoosh and thud of the shockwave as the first-stage rocket blew the missile clear of the tube, The next thing Sara saw was the explosion and disintegration of what had been the red chimney, and the shattered rock fragments dropping to the ground below. It all happened so fast that she did not see the missile in flight at all.

'Quite a mover, I would say,' she murmured, staring up at the blackened surface of the rock.

'Fearsome! About mach one, I'd say. It needs more ground to develop full velocity. The important thing is that it climbs well, and it hits whatever you're looking at.'

'What sort of distance are we talking?' She remembered that the SAM-7 was good for up to ten kilometres.

'The makers claim an effective range of four thousand metres.'

'Pah!' Clearly unimpressed. 'A fraction of what the Grail is capable of!' Sara was using the NATO nickname for the Russian rocket system.

'Come with me, my dear,' said Tyler as if to a disbelieving child. 'You are about to receive a lesson in British ingenuity.'

They took the Cruiser half a mile beyond where the abandoned jeep lay, and climbed to a low-lying ledge where Tyler could obtain a good view of the target.

'From here we should see this thing really move. I need a longer run to test the guidance unit. It's a system called SACLOS – stands for semi-automatic command line of sight, which is another way of saying "what you see is what you hit".'

'But the Grail does that anyway, by infra-red homing.'

'True, but modern defence systems are more sophisticated than they were in the Seventies when that missile was popular. Grail is ineffective against the kind of heat decoys used today. Javelin, on the other hand, can be monitored and corrected all the way to the target, because the aiming unit talks to the missile in flight. Like I said, the missile hits whatever you're looking at. It's beautiful, and it's British.'

Sara grinned at his smugness. 'So, you're proud of your country after all. It's a pity we have no moving target.'

'Oh, I wouldn't say that,' he answered thinly, looking over her shoulder. 'Take a look behind you.'

'You're pulling my leg . . .'

But it was not a joke. Sara put on her sunglasses to check what her eyes could not believe. In the bright mid-distance, between the horizon and the ostrich-egg stones, a fast-moving cloud of dust was burning its way towards them. The dust rose so high that until it came closer it was impossible to discern what lay behind it. But without doubt it was heading their way.

Tyler glared at her accusingly. 'You expecting someone – like a Sulubbi escort or anything?'

'No, this can only mean danger. Let's get back to the LandCruiser.'

'Not yet, best not show ourselves until we see what we're up against.'

For interminable seconds the moving dust cloud was lost in an undulation, and the mounting roar of its engine muffled, then it sprang into view once more, louder now and suddenly recognisable as an army jeep manned by a driver and three bearded and ragtag-looking uniformed soldiers. Mounted on the back of the jeep was a murderous-looking heavy machine-gun fed by a belt.

'Deserters,' whispered Sara, her voice choked. 'Just as al Tayyih said. They must have heard the explosion. Better run for the truck while we still have a start on them. We might outpace them; their vehicle is overloaded.'

'Jesus Christ,' spat Tyler touching the bulge of the Browning once more. Then with dawning horror. 'Where's the Uzi?' Her face was a mask.

'Inside the Cruiser.'

It was more than two hundred yards to the Toyota. Two hundred yards of open ground, giving the deserters ample time to zero in on them with the belt-fed monster they were toting. Suddenly they heard a whoop and a shot from the charging vehicle, and the gun began to bark lead in their direction. Four hundred metres. A metallic smack as a lucky round struck the door of the Cruiser, holing it.

'I guess those bastards are trying for the sneak attack.'

'You must do *something* now, if you want us to live. They'll take everything and kill us. Hurry, they must spot us soon.'

Cursing, Tyler clipped the aiming unit to the other missile tube, aware of the rising rate of his own breathing. He would have to step clear of the rocks that had covered them to get a line of sight. The jeep was closing at three hundred. Tyler fell to one knee again, flinging the forty-five pounds of Javelin onto his right shoulder and momentarily losing his balance on the smooth rock surface. That movement got them spotted, and a hail of bullets was directed at the rocky ledge.

'Get down. Take cover,' Tyler snapped.

'No, give me the Browning! I'll cover you while you aim.'

'No time for that.' Rock fragments were drilled from the cliff face around them. 'Don't get us both killed – do as I say. If I get hit, you can take over.'

Her operational brain knew he was right, and she flattened herself against the rock floor screaming 'Do it, for God's sake, do it!'

Tyler's body was braced against the weight of the launcher now, his mind made clearer by the risk of being riddled with machine-gun fire. His cheek fitted close to the aimer and his eye into the monocular sight-cup. The sight picture scanned the churning dust and zeroed upon the flamming muzzle of the gun; above it the screaming face of the soldier was topped by the green bandana of Islam. Suddenly there was an eruption of glass as a bullet destroyed the Toyota's rear window.

'Lord, make this son-of-a-bitch fly true,' prayed Tyler and squeezed the trigger. The blast happened all around him, as the rocket shot forward towards his prey, ringed in the viewer by a fine black circle. It seemed to hang in the air – then a quick correction and the roaring bird struck the front of the moving jeep, penetrating the radiator grille and detonating in the engine block. Three human torches were flung skyward as the vehicle erupted in a ball of flame and somersaulted, rolling end-over-end and landing upside-down. The driver, impaled upon the gearshift, was incinerated instantly.

Minutes later the pall of oily smoke had decreased to a thin grey plume, and they sat still on the rock ledge in silence.

Sara was the first to speak. 'There, you have the proof you need now.' Her jaw was trembling with involuntary contractions. It was all madness. Barely a half-hour ago they had made love – was that a dream? Now they were back to killing again. When would it end? she asked herself. Make it soon. Please make it soon.

Tyler looked at her and read her thoughts instantly. But the harsh intensity in his face did not soften, nor did the hard edge to his voice. He stood up and took her hand firmly, drawing her to her feet.

'Come on. It's time to go.'

Azziz came out into the hard, bright sunlight of the barracks complex more troubled than ever. He had tried to gain audience with the President and had been refused. For the first time ever. Damn them all! he cursed softly, as he stood on the steps of the administration block. Why go to the trouble of bringing Brady to Tripoli only to have him languish in his hotel room? The mere cancelling of the Brega trip did not negate the threat against Qadaffi's life, for God's sake!

Judicious interrogation of his source, Zadmeh, had revealed that it was Jalloud who was monopolising Qadaffi's time; and that there were helicopters standing by to fly up the coast, but the destination was a secret which even Zadmeh could not discover. There was one further piece of information which he did supply, however: the latest rumour from Internal Security was that the Education Secretary was believed to be the new leader of the opposition. That rumour was being investigated vigorously; such knowledge could be useful.

As Azziz came out of his reverie, suddenly the full extent of the new, higher level of civil alert became suddenly apparent, like a smack in the face. It was visible confirmation of Qadaffi's resolve to take on his opponents – both inside and outside the country. For a long while Azziz stood rooted to the spot, watching. At the main gate the battle tanks were fully manned – a quite extraordinary sight – and the banks of truck-mounted Crotale missiles were being rotated into various skyward angles by their whirring motor drives. He swallowed hard. All across the great parade squares soldiers waited, ramrod straight. They were massed in their hundreds: serried ranks of scarlet berets and fixed bayonets; port arms and shoulder arms. The war fever was everywhere, like a whispered cry that is taken up first by one, then another, and yet another, until every voice is screaming and chanting.

The soldiers were being primed and aimed.

'*Long live the revolution! Long live Qadaffi!*
'*Long live the revolution! Long live Qadaffi!*'

They split up into platoons, doubling into armoured personnel carriers, intent on the drills they would use to close off the city, if necessary – to lock it up with cordon and curfew until all the traitors were captured or killed.

Azziz listened to the rapid thrumming of their powerful engines, but in his head it sounded like a warning signal. Finally, he understood! He understood the reason for all this. Provocation and retaliation. The prelude to decisive and violent action. Yes, Qadaffi was fearful enough of the NSFL traitors; they were a potent political force which had gradually penetrated the lower officer cadre in the People's army, just as Qadaffi had done himself those many years ago. Jalloud was his watchdog, but even he was losing his grip on events and had resorted to the summary imprisonment of intellectuals and civil servants who fell under suspicion. But, more than that; Quadaffi was a man desperate to win back favour at street level, a man for whom personal adulation was as vital to his life as desert rain was to the winter wheat. To secure his role as Messiah to all Islam, he was now willing to precipitate a deadly confrontation with the Zionists – one which would cause all Arabdom to rally behind him, inspired by his outrageous example.

By Great God, Azziz was sure of it now.

Qadaffi was a shrewd leader, and he still had the majority of the army's support, but he needed also the hearts and minds of the ordinary people: the Moslem clergy and the working classes. They were the ones whose voices had fed the fire of the revolution. Now it was they who were turning away from him. The alarm bells were already sounding: in the sports stadiums of Benghazi the common people, bedouin and Berber, were now openly discussing the aims of the NSFL. Azziz had seen the reports on this himself. They increasingly chanted anti-Qadaffi slogans in spite of the infiltration of the Revolutionary Committees. It was a dangerous time, indeed, for the tide of popular opinion was veering in unpredictable directions.

What better time to cloud the waters of internal politics than now! What better devil to have them hate than the Zionists! It was perfect, mused Azziz coldly, as he watched the soldiers drilling. Perfect madness!

He turned on his heel and marched away across the asphalt to the BMW waiting in one of the bays assigned to senior Government personnel. At his approach the driver leaped from the front seat and held open a door, closing it respectfully once Azziz was inside.

'Important call from Operations Control, Colonel, barely a moment ago. You are requested to respond urgently.'

Azziz pulled the slim black car-phone from its mounting and contacted the Operations Controller. He was able to speak freely, for this phone operated on the Bureau's secure channel – not even Jalloud's Internal Security dogs could penetrate its scrambler.

It was the call he had hoped for. Operations reported that Nimrod had broken cover; only this time he had left a trail.

As Azziz hurried into the control room he was intercepted by the man he had delegated to collate intelligence on Nimrod. Major Hameidi was a tall, pallid man with large cow-like eyes and many years of intelligence duties to his credit. He steered his Colonel to the computer console, always proud of the technology at his fingertips.

'A gift from God, Colonel. Look at the screen. This is the log of the People's Militia.' He found the correct page, and his finger indicated the second entry on the screen. 'A report of two deaths yesterday at a warehouse out by Tripoli International. Two warehousemen, killed quickly and quietly.'

'How?'

'One with his head beaten in, the other with a stiletto driven into his brain.'

'What else?'

'No one heard any disturbance but the duty customs inspector states that the last people to enter the warehouse were two infidels, a male and a female.'

'This happened yesterday?' queried Azziz, noting the date and time on the incident log.

The Major was forced to defend his position. 'I was passed the information just two hours ago by an intelligence monitoring officer. Immediately I sent over two investigators, Unit Five, to interview the Customs man. He recognised Nimrod from the photograph, but says the man has considerably darkened his appearance.'

'A gift indeed!' enthused Azziz, his mind assessing the new pieces of the puzzle. 'Any information on the goods they collected?'

'Two small wooden crates documented as personal effects. Probably weapons or explosives – could be anything.'

Azziz again checked the screen information.

'Something which kills,' he mused. 'Shipped by air via Rome. I don't recognise the air-freight company.'

'I do,' said Hameidi, with pride in his memory for detail. 'A small outfit based in Rome. They fly mostly old Dakotas and other junk for short haul. Larger companies undercut them, but they make out by flying cargo no one else wants to shift. We've used them ourselves before now. Last year they received hefty fines here for smuggling alcohol and pornographic videos.'

'Well, follow it up, and find out who arranged the shipment and who connived to receive it here. We should arrange suitable punishment. But tell me first of this trail left by Nimrod.'

The Major turned to pick up the draft report he had been working on, and handed it over deferentially.

'Best news of all, Colonel, a fork-lift driver witnessed the two suspects drive away. He was admiring the vehicle, and says it was a red Toyota LandCruiser with a double zero in the registration plate.'

'Lucky number plate. Good. Run that through the transport computer.'

'Already done, Colonel. We've checked for zeros and letter 'O's and for combinations. Only one vehicle fits, and that's registered to an Italian company, a petrochemical engineering consultancy. Their head office is in Bab Benghashir.' He consulted the gold Omega on his wrist. 'Unit Five should be there within fifteen minutes.'

Azziz clapped him on the shoulder and his neat black moustache stretched into a short-lived smile.

'Major, I want to know the instant you get a name and address. We must assume that Nimrod now has everything he needs to carry out his plan. But if we can locate the assassin and his Zionist accomplices we can spring a trap that will crush them all.'

Cigarettes were lit as they waited nervously, watching the silent radios and willing them to speak. At times the whole operations room seemed to hold its breath, listening to the rapid click of worry-beads. Azziz had much on which to ponder, perched on the corner of Hameidi's desk with one foot on the floor and the other swinging busily. He examined the enlarged street map of Tripoli on the wall, the coloured magnetic markers indicating areas already covered by search teams. The circle was tightening. The searching had been thorough, and had brought a flood of expatriate complaints, as their ambassadors registered protests against intrusion and rough treatment by his men. That proved his men's diligence. Still, searching every one of the hundreds of foreign residences could take them weeks – assuming it was foreigners and not the NSFL traitors who were hiding Nimrod. But no, Brady's tapes had confirmed they were Zionist agents. He prayed desperately that this lead would prove reliable; and lead them straight to Nimrod.

It was mid-afternoon as Qadaffi's security party left Azizyah airfield in two Soviet Mil 24 helicopters, flying west for eight miles across the edge of the Jefara plain, until the vast grey-blueness of the Mediterranean loomed before the aircraft, and below them the orderly steel and concrete of the Jamahiriyah's only submarine base was visible. The second helicopter, equipped with standard cannon and rocket pods and carrying an elite eight-man detachment of the Presidential Guard, maintained a stand-off escort position, and it did not land until the President's party had safely disembarked and been escorted to the waiting vehicles.

Captain Kim checked the faces and noted that this time it was top brass only. But where, he wondered, was Colonel Azziz?

Jalloud was there, of course, and a tight pack of naval and army officers, who were being marshalled at the entrance by Rear-Admiral Omar al Mukhtar, clearly the man behind this gathering. On that day Captain Kim was the only Korean allowed to board the aircraft, and he stayed close to the President, knowing how such large groups made Qadaffi nervous. But Qadaffi himself seemed relaxed and smiling as the party moved into the lecture theatre, where a mobile broadcast unit was already installed and a large matrix-board television screen had been erected before lines of well-upholstered chairs. Qadaffi and Jalloud took the central positions just before the screen, and Kim took a chair immediately behind the President's head, to cover him.

They had been seated only seconds when the Korean sprang to his feet, hand in jacket. One of the technicians, wearing pilot's headset, had darted forward to place a microphone stand before the President. Seeing his mistake, the technician cowered back and offered a gesture of meek apology. Unruffled, Kim took his seat once more.

'Today's party would be about the correct size,' said Qadaffi leaning close to Jalloud so that only he could hear. 'I do not wish to be choked by a crowd of sycophants when I am at Houn.'

Jalloud pursed his lips and nodded his agreement. 'It shall be so. With good communications, a handful of your best men is all that will be required. I suggest we use the Russian helicopters; in the open desert they are a formidable weapon, and two of them may hold off an army yet escape at high speed if necessary.'

Suddenly the giant screen burst into life, and the President saw his own live image flash onto the screen. It was the test broadcast.

'Thirty seconds to live transmission, brother Colonel,' warned al Mukhtar, seated on the President's left.

'Excellent,' crooned Qadaffi with pleasure as he tilted left and right, examining the splendour of his own profile on the screen. 'Begin when ready.'

His pleasure intensified as two bright lamps were

brought to bear on him, and the camera crew zoomed in for a tight head-shot.

The room fell silent.

A flickering green light on the engineer's console switched to steady red. He issued the call. 'Microwave link established. Live and running!'

Somewhere in the cloudy skies three miles north of the coastal port of Zuwarah, a Libyan Airforce communications plane caught the signal and projected it out into the open Mediterranean, where it was received and flashed to a television monitor in the control room of a the People's submarine *First of September*. Immediately there was a spontaneous cheer from those assembled, and the loyal officers applauded. Morale was excellent.

The *First of September* had been cruising, fully submerged, at a speed of twelve knots just off the island of Gozo in the Malta Channel, and had only now come to periscope depth to enable its aerial and dish to receive the transmission. The captain, a shrewd and somewhat pragmatic officer, apprenticed in the cat-and-mouse game of submarine warfare in a Soviet naval academy, had misgivings about breaking cover in this way, but the honour of this personal message both touched and excited him.

They had been vigilant in their task, tracking the target eastward from the moment it first nosed through the Straits of Gibraltar, and listening to radio reports from agents based on the ground in Tangiers, Cartagena and Algiers. Like an angel of death they had waited, hovering off Sardinia, the whole submarine holding its breath, listening to the routine noise of a hundred cargo vessels and tramp steamers until finally the radar signature of the giant liner fell within the pulsing sweep of the illuminated screen, and the hydrophones caught the thrashing thunder of her propellors. Deadly silent, they had followed, matching speed and remaining within two sea miles. Only once, at night, had the captain dared to stray closer and raise periscope to observe the target. He was immediately struck by the majestic beauty of the ship: broad passenger decks flooded with neon strip; elegant ballrooms hung with coloured lights and thronged with the dancing shadows of revellers. As a naval man he could appreciate the magnificence of the vessel, but as an Arab and as a warrior he could not forget that those on board were his sworn enemies.

Now in daylight, with a clear spring sky overhead, and the green and orange shoreline of Gozo just visible through the sea haze, the sub broke surface two miles due east of the ship's position and turned to face west and into the path of the pride of Cunard.

'Camera team to conning tower,' ordered the first mate. 'Standby, weapons officer.'

In the lecture theatre the communications engineer made small, final adjustments, then announced to the Presidential party: 'Switching to submarine transmission.'

The picture on the screen changed suddenly from the seated members of the Presidential party to the view from the conning tower of the *First of September*. Someone whistled tunelessly. A second later the camera operator zoomed close to catch the white bow-wave being churned in the path of the ship, then its dark blue hull loomed large upon the screen.

Qadaffi stroked his neck in concentration. 'Do they see the submarine yet?' he asked.

'Unlikely.' Omar al Mukhtar shook his head. 'At such a range, and so close to the water . . . But they will see the missile – of that I am sure.'

The President took metal-framed sunglasses from his breast pocket and opened them slowly.

'Good, Mukhtar. I have waited more than fifteen years for this moment,' he said, his lower lip quivering. 'Now, in the name of Allah the Merciful, whose blessings are without end, tell the Captain to proceed.'

On the bridge of the *QE2*, second officer Bill Hammond was receiving a ship-to-shore weather forecast from the authorities in the port of Valetta when a flash in the water ahead caught his eye. At first he thought he was seeing a dolphin leap, but when the blue shape kept rising and he realised that its tail seemed on fire disbelief changed to mounting dread.

'Jesus Christ!' What the hell is that?'

The harpoon missile had been launched in a sealed canister from the submarine's torpedo tube, and on ignition it climbed clear of the water and achieved its high sub-sonic speed within a matter of seconds. Coming at a height of twenty feet, a dark slender body with three groups of cruciform fins and a yellow nose, it closed with deadly sureness upon the civilian ship, leaving a trail of pale grey smoke hanging in the air to trace the course of its flight. As it struck, a dull metallic clang rang through the bow – an unearthly noise. It punched through the steel of the great ship, detonating its high-explosive warhead on impact and tearing wide the lady's hull.

The secondary explosions continued for many minutes, as combustible materials flared under the intense heat generated by the blast. Dazed crew members staggered, scorched and bleeding, in quest of escape routes, not sure which way to turn and relying on instinct to pull themselves and their colleagues through.

It was the fires which did the real damage. They raged below decks all through the forward areas, accompanied by thick choking smoke. Suddenly the carpets in the passenger corridors were alight. Blind panic took over in a mad scramble for the stairways leading to the boat deck. Even as the first of the lifeboats were being lowered through the dense smoke, it was obvious that the liner was listing badly. No one knew how much water she was shipping. The wound was very close to the water line, and she might even go down!

The screams were pitiful.

It was almost an hour before the first air-sea rescue helicopters arrived from Valetta: four Sikorsky S-61Ns. By that time the Libyan submarine had already concluded its broadcast, and had melted into the black depths of the Mediterranean.

At the radio console one young, moustached officer adjusted the squelch key and jerked upright. He clutched his headphones and turned excitedly to the Operations Controller of the Bureau for External Security.

'Unit Five reporting. They have a name and address for the red Toyota.'

Azziz sprang forward, reaching the console before Hameidi. He grabbed the auxiliary handset microphone, and switched from headset to room broadcast.

'Azziz speaking. Go ahead.' He released the transmit button and waited the few seconds it took the field agent to recover from the shock of talking directly to such an exalted figure.

'*Salaam alaikum*, Colonel. We have interviewed the personnel director of the company, who says the Land Cruiser is a pool vehicle and is currently assigned to one of their consultants: an Italian. The director claims not to know the man's current whereabouts, but says he covers hundreds of miles when visiting prospecting sites all over the coastal region. They don't expect him back in the office for three days, yet.'

'The name and address, man!' snarled the Colonel in frustration.

The nervous agent read quickly from his notebook: 'Tintorini, Mario Antonio. Apartment 11, block B, 117 Sharia al Fatah, Bab Benghasir. Unit Five awaiting instruction to proceed and arrest.'

Azziz pressed the transmit button once more.

'Unit Five, there's to be no arrest. Proceed to location and confirm information. Record visible movements of occupants, and any contact with others. Is that understood?'

A crackle on the line.

'No arrest – confirmed.'

'Await instructions and prepare to receive reinforcing units. Out.'

The handset clicked back into its housing, and the Colonel turned to face the Ops Controller. He counted off instructions on the gold-ringed fingers of his left hand as the Controller reached for his pad and made hurried notes.

'Throw a covert observation cordon around that location and get a technical operations team there fast. But nothing too visible. It will be dark soon, and there are plenty of apartment blocks in Bab Benghasir from which to aim their cameras without being seen. I want infra-red link back here where I can control things. See what you can do about directional microphones and phone taps, and when you've done all this, mobilise the special weapons team, placing them on immediate one-hour state of readiness. Is all that clear?'

'At once, Colonel. And I'll send a driver to Public Works Administration, where they'll have building plans left over from installation of utilities. Room layout will be important. By Great God, I should like to be there when our Assault Team goes amongst the infidel with automatic weapons!'

Suddenly Azziz froze, struck by what the Controller had just said. He too would love to see his Islamic warriors take the infidel to their graves, but now a more appealing idea was ringing in his head – one which was beautiful in its ruthless economy. He was thinking of the coded telex message from the import warehouse in Dublin, and the cold and final words upon the sheet.

The Ops Controller was already punching out numbers on his phone, when Azziz seized his wrist.

'No wait. I have a better idea.' The venomous green tattoos pulsed at his temples. 'Send a car to the Libya Palace Hotel on al Mukhtar, and bring the Irishman to me. Those who eat at the table must also pay for the privilege.'

385

Major Hameidi stepped forward. 'Excuse any impertinence, Colonel, but can we trust him?'

Azziz looked at him sideways and considered.

'He has fire, and he longs to bathe in the blood of the assassin. Is that not enough?'

'Passion is one thing, but we have seen the handiwork of this Nimrod. A single error could be fatal – for all of us.'

Azziz took in the implication and nodded. 'You're right to be concerned, Major. But fear not, he will receive assistance. Yes, the best – we'll give him the Korean. Tell your driver to go first to the barracks. Captain Kim will be waiting at the Guard Room.'

The Ops Controller acknowledged these orders, and began the first of many calls he would make that night.

'One more thing,' interrupted Azziz as he headed for the door. 'The Militia and Internal Security are to receive no information about this. And Jalloud must not hear anything of it.'

When Azziz returned to his own desk, he immediately called the Education Secretary and requested a meeting at the earliest opportunity. Only after much reassurance would the man agree to see him. The two would meet alone at his house, and without any witnesses.

It was already dusk when Unit Five reached Sharia al Fatah in the well-to-do district of Bab Benghasir on the eastern outskirts of Tripoli. Apartment blocks and pale stucco houses stood pink and slab-like in the glow of the setting sun, interspersed with the dark green of palms and wild succulents by the roadside. An army of gardeners and construction workers were wandering back from building sites to their own homes or on their way the mosques, their long jellabas swaying slowly.

The men parked on the far side of the public garden, a tree-lined space near the entrance to 117 Sharia al Fatah. Osman, the senior agent, climbed out and headed across the playground, where a handful of barefooted children were kicking a soccer ball across an asphalt pitch. Walking quickly into the courtyard, he approached the elderly superintendent and confirmed the floor level of the target apartment. Setting down his bowl of couscous, the old man was eager to assist, for like all such caretakers there was little to occupy him but the business of others.

When he saw the photograph, he held it close to his failing eyes and nodded vigorously. Yes, that was the house-guest in apartment 11, and he had been staying there several days. There was no one in at the moment: Tintorini was out for the day, and his wife had gone off with the other man on Tuesday. The old man considered the Italian a fool to leave his wife alone with another man. What had the foreigner in the photograph done, he inquired, but Osman told him this was Militia business and to keep his mouth shut and stay out of the way. He nodded vigorously and returned to his meal.

The back-up vehicles arrived thirty minutes later, and deployed under the sparse street lighting according to Osman's directions. Three units: two in the road to the rear of the block, on either side of the junction with Sharia Khaled Ibn Walid; the remaining unit parked in the road on al Fatah, outside number 96 facing the courtyard gate.

Osman knew the area well, having attended nearby Al Fatah University in his student days, and he knew that between them the units could not fail to spot anyone entering or leaving the block from whatever direction. There were eight field agents on the ground, all young and tough men; he had worked with most of them before. From his position in the darkened square, he watched a yellow VW bus pull into the car-park of the fifteen-storey block opposite the target, and he recognised three men from Technical Surveillance carrying their metal cases into the building to set up their o.p. in a commandeered apartment on the eight floor.

It was quiet now in the square, and Osman turned down the volume of the secure radio to further conceal their presence. He pulled the heavy automatic from his belt and cocked it in the silence, chambering a round. He smiled to himself – Oh God, he loved that sound! Then, purposefully, he engaged the safety catch and laid the weapon carefully in the open glove compartment. Ready.

In the early evening Yariv returned home with some information that disturbed him. So great was his hurry to reach the communications equipment that he failed to notice that some of the cars in the square were occupied.

Two hours he had waited in the camel market, choking on the stink of fetid hides, before his man had shown. Sweat and camel shit all around – but in the end worth it for such information: a warning which might save all their necks from Jalloud's torture squad and a Libyan rope. The agent was a good operative and perfectly positioned: a captain in the People's Militia, he was a tough intelligence man responsible for liaison with Internal Security. But what was most remarkable about this man was that he was actually an Israeli citizen in deep cover. And had been so for six dangerous years.

When Yariv flung open the door and found the apartment empty he cursed out loud, knowing in his heart he could not leave without alerting his colleagues to the danger – no matter how much his head told him to get out fast. Damn Tyler for the stupidity of those airport killings! After learning of the visit by Government heavies asking about the LandCruiser, he knew that time was short: a matter of hours now, depending on the bureaucratic-sloth factor built into the Libyan civil service. Another day at most. Damn Tyler for blowing their whole set-up!

Yariv had spent a feverish two days trying desperately to find out what was going on, and the results were frightening. From his people at Azizyah he had heard of the build-up of forces there. After communicating with his source in Cabinet, he further learned of imminent military action that would set the Moslem world ablaze. Now he had also learned that External Security were asking questions about him specifically. He could feel the noose begin to tighten at his throat. They were very close.

They might even be watching him at this very moment, monitoring the phone. But he would have to pass a warning to Tel Aviv, whatever the risk.

Yariv went quickly to the desk in the small third bedroom and fired up the personal computer. Taking a book from the shelf, he opened to a page and read off a word from it according to date sequence. This would be the kernel word for the encryption algorithm. Rome would use their copy of the book to effect decrypt.

The cypher and communications software were carefully masked on the computer's hard disk so that the directories held no record of them. Yariv typed in the password and accessed a blank white screen which was the cypher pad area, where he tapped in the terse message. He felt the sweat break on his shoulderblades and threw off his jacket, revealing the beretta pistol in its leather shoulder rig. It was only April, so why was he so damn hot?

When the message was complete he read it over:

BEGINS: FLASH FROM MARCUS. 20.42 HRS. TRIPOLI 08/04.

POLIT. SIT. UNSTABLE. HIGH-PROB COUP D'ETAT. ARAB AMBASSADORS WARNED OF IMMINENT PRECIPITATIVE ACTION. INFO SUGGESTS INT-SEC MOBILISATION. LIBYAN MILITARY UNITS ACTIVE IN MEDITERRANEAN. MARITIME TARGET UNSPECIFIED. HIGH-PROB ISRAELI NAVAL (UNCON). SCHEDULED TOMORROW (FRIDAY, 09/04). FURTHER AGGRESSIVE ACTION ANTICIPATED FOR LAND TARGETS. NIMROD OUT OF CONTACT. BLOWN AND UNLIKELY TO COMPLETE. WILL ACTIVATE FALLBACK AND ABORT.

ENDS:

Sombrely, he stabbed the function key, entered the encryption kernel, and engaged the algorithm that would code the message. The disk whirred briefly and stopped, indicating the action was complete. Then Yariv checked the connection from the telephone socket to the internal modem that would fire the message down the international phone-line. Correct. His fingers began to shake as he entered the Rome telephone number of the cut-out exports office used by Israel Military Intelligence and waited for the flashing sign that would mean the number had been reached. What was wrong with him, he wondered, as the hot flushes came in waves. He fought back his nausea. Then came the contact, and he punched the 'enter' key, squirting the message at high speed to a similar terminal in the Rome office, where it would be stored, decoded, then passed to the Military Attaché at the Embassy for onward transmission to Tel Aviv.

Yariv was gratified to think that any Libyans monitoring the line with headsets would be deafened by the high-pitched squawk of binary transmission. The volume had been amplified to ensure data integrity of the message. Had they been clever enough to catch the signal with their own modem, and then fed it into their own computers, they would be no wiser, for the encryption was extremely sophisticated and even added nonsense words to the message to confound decryption.

When the communications software registered that the message had been received by Rome, he deactivated the machine and went to the bathroom to wash his face and hands.

He did not feel good. Already he was suffering the first griping pains in his stomach, and when he looked in the mirror the dilation of his pupils indicated that he was really strung out. He took two blue tablets from the mirror cabinet, knocking them back without water, and knowing that they were pain-killers and therefore no help at all for his real problem. What he really needed, what he had always needed, was amphetamine – speed. They had weaned him off it once while they treated him for combat depression syndrome. But he knew he could not work fully effectively without it; his nerves were just too shot.

It had started in the Paras, where most men used amphetamine to combat fatigue when under fire in the battle zone for protracted periods. The habit had grown, imperceptibly, into a need to be satisfied from whatever source available. Here in Tripoli his source had been Nineveh. Now Nineveh was gone – and he was really hurting for those regular yellow pills.

Nervously, he went out onto the darkened balcony, knocking over some empty plant pots with his feet. For God's sake, why didn't they come: Tyler and the girl? The street below was silent save for the distant hum of traffic on the main road into Tripoli. The kids playing soccer had gone inside, and the square was empty of people. His eyes tried to focus on the parked vehicles, the bent and rusting wrecks the locals never thought to repair until they were totally clapped out and ready to be dumped, but from where he stood he could not tell whether any were occupied.

Nimrod blown, he repeated to himself. And Nineveh missing. God, what a mess!

A sudden stab in his stomach made him groan and he doubled up, choking with pain. The nausea was returning. He staggered inside and fell on the sofa, the beretta bouncing from its holster and clattering on the wooden floor. He stared at the weapon but could not focus upon it, so in the end he left it where it lay.

Just after midnight, Brady climbed the wall and dropped silently onto the balcony. He waited a while, green eyes peering into the lighted room where the man lay sleeping. He was checking the angles, feeling the silence. The balcony door was still open. Brady made a signal over his shoulder and Captain Kim sprang nimbly in behind him, hugging the shadow of the balcony wall. Both men wore black combat suits and hoods, and their silenced Heckler-Koch machine-guns were clipped across their chests to leave their hands free for the climb. Brady stepped forward in a crouch and unclipped his weapon. Suddenly there was a loud crack – something beneath his foot. Broken terracotta – plant pots.

Jesus Christ!

The Israeli jerked awake in an instant, panicked by the sound. As he scrambled wildly for the beretta, his eyes attempted to focus on the figures launching from the balcony into the room. Too late, he sprang onto the floor, a sitting target in the full glare of the room. His fingers closed around the weapon, and he came up on one knee, levelling and firing on instinct before he had fully fixed on his target. Before he could squeeze off a second shot, three rounds of nine-millimetre, full load, caught him square in the chest, flinging his body backwards and overturning the glass coffee table.

Brady stepped over to where the Israeli lay on his back, limbs twisted and chest heaving in diminishing breaths. Yariv's eyes were staring at the ceiling as if in disbelief. Brady kicked the beretta from his fingers and it skittered across the polished floor to smack against the table leg.

'It's not him!' Brady's voice was muffled by the black hood. 'Fuck! It's not him!'

Kim's eyes blazed through the slits of his mask. 'Better for you, too, Brady, you fool. Alive – we want Nimrod alive! We could have had this one alive, also.'

'Back off! I had no choice. He was drawing down on me.'

'Shit! Your feet cost us surprise!'

Brady fingered the trigger of his weapon, angered by the Korean's reprimand, and he turned back to the bleeding body of the Israeli.

'You could live, Jew,' he whispered from behind the black hood. 'So tell us where they are, or shall I let you bleed to death?'

The Israeli's face was immobile as he stared up, only half-conscious, at the black figure leaning over him. It was strange: he could actually feel himself dying now, and he was not afraid. Only grateful for the release it would bring.

'Quickly, you haven't much time,' Brady snarled, but the dying man only smiled a last mocking smile, and was gone.

TWENTY-SIX

THE RED LANDCRUISER ploughed on across the rough desert piste of the Sirtica, a full-throated roar in its large diesel-powered engine, negotiating with ease the hardened undulations which would have shattered a lesser machine, and coming finally to the long black ribbon of asphalt that wound back into the capital. Tyler's hands gripped the wheel confidently. He was sure now of what to do and how it would go. The only questions now were: when would Qadaffi run for his desert base; and would he need some incentive to get him moving? A culvert mine on the road out of Azizyah Barracks might do the trick. He could make it look as if the timing device had exploded prematurely, but it would make his target think twice about travelling by road again. Tyler wanted him up in the air, where he was most vulnerable – where the missile would take him cleanly.

Conversation had been nearly impossible since they started the drive back. Too much had happened, and there was a kind of safety in silence.

Eighteen kilometres outside the city Sara clicked on the set and tuned to Tripoli Radio to catch the sabbath broadcast by the Secretary for Information. It was the most important broadcast of the week for, behind the howling rhetoric, astute Libya-watchers could read the mood of the Revolutionary Government: its attitudes, priorities and targets.

The Secretary spoke faster than usual, betraying a feverish excitement as he offered first a prayer of thanks, before stunning the listening population from Benghazi to Sebha with news of a victory.

'My God!' Sara's hand touched her throat in shock.

Tyler shot a sideways glance, unwilling to take his eyes from the road, which was strewn with stones from a recent sandstorm. 'What is it? What's happened?'

'Quiet a minute,' she hissed, her ear cocked against the roar of the engine. She turned the volume high. 'He's saying a Zionist maritime target has been destroyed at sea by missile attack. There's a roadhouse up ahead, with a phone and a television. Stop there.'

Incredulous, they jumped from the vehicle and entered the small restaurant, ordering coffee. There were just twelve tables, each with a red and white checked cloth, but most were empty. A handful of locals were sitting around listlessly, but in one corner a group of young men wearing Western jeans were arguing over the news bulletin relayed on the monochrome set perched high up behind the counter. Feelings were running high, Tyler noticed.

'Death to all Zionists!' spat one youth aggressively.

The monochrome set was tuned to an Italian TV channel's coverage of the missile attack on a Cunard liner. Between flickers and tracking lines of interference which provoked angry jeers, they were showing live pictures of the rescue operation proceeding off the Maltese coast. There were clouds of black smoke billowing hundreds of feet into the air from the badly listing superstructure, as helicopters circled overhead, trailing rescue winches.

'God, Tyler – it's the *QE2*. Fires are raging below decks. Passengers are trapped. God knows how many are dead. They say she's going down!' Sara translated the bulletin in a monotone of disbelief. The passengers were all Jews, and the ship's ultimate destination Haifa. Dear God, here was history repeating itself.

'This explains the signals Yariv has been picking up. But how could Qadaffi dare such an attack?' she stammered in disbelief. 'Doesn't he know Israel will retaliate?'

'Keep cool, Sara.' He held her hands tight between his own, lending her his strength. 'Tell me again what the radio said earlier.' He kept his voice low.

'The Information Secretary holds a strictly controlled post – he would have to be one of Qadaffi's trusted men. He announced that there had already been accusations levelled from Tel Aviv and Washington, and that there was no alternative but to mobilise the armed forces, as a precautionary measure in self-defence. They deny everything, whilst voicing support for this blow struck by the United Arab Armies. Martial Law is not far off – and once that happens, there'll be roadblocks and curfews to contend with.'

'Also confusion in the streets – that will be useful. Do you think Israel will retaliate?'

'Tyler, we have whole sections of Military Intelligence responsible for dreaming up Arab strike scenarios. They spend many hours planning measured responses to each such possibility. In this case there will have to be a spectacular strike against an appropriate economic target – one closely linked with Libyan national prestige. *Of course* there'll be retaliation. The political right-wingers will demand it.'

'Where does that leave Qadaffi?' Tyler was thinking out loud.

'Long gone from Tripoli, and well hidden. My guess is he'll make straight for the desert base outside Houn, and will stay there until the heat's off.'

'Good. That's what I figure, too. I've been looking for some opportunity, and now he creates one for me. It's a cold-blooded political move, this, giving him ample reason to mobilise his forces against internal opposition, while also providing a uniting effect through telling the Libyans they're under attack by the enemies of Islam.'

He studied the screen, where casualties were being hauled aloft in a strong wind. Forlorn figures swathed in blankets, microscopic against the vastness of the listing vessel – a vessel which had served its country well throughout the war in the South Atlantic and had come home unscathed, only to be destroyed in peacetime.

'More victims of power politics,' he murmured. Haven't we had enough of these madmen?'

Listening to his voice, Sara sensed Nimrod's new resolve. In her sorrow she wished for his arms around her, to feed her own spirit just for a moment.

'We'd better leave,' he said, suddenly aware that the eyes of the young men in the corner were fixed on them. 'Qadaffi has now made a scapegoat of every foreigner in this country.'

Sara pushed her coffee aside and stood up. 'Fine. We must go straight to Bab Benghasir. Yariv will know what's happening behind the mobilisation.'

'Phone first?'

'Later. It would be better if we left now.'

A further look at the stony faces ranged around them was enough to convince him. He paid for the coffee they had hardly touched, and they went quickly outside.

It was like witnessing the panic caused by a bush fire. All the way into Tripoli they passed troop transports on the move, and bedouin fleeing the city in trucks filled with camels; fleeing for fear of their livestock being impounded. Tyler guessed that the soldiers were now deploying to cover civil-defence keypoints against internal violence. They would guard the public utilities – power and water sources; and the communications centres – telephone, radio and television. So long as Qadaffi kept those secure, he would remain in control.

Overhead, MiG vapour trails criss-crossed a pale blue sky, as fighters flew sorties against the anticipated approach of unspecified enemies. This display of force was calculated to impress Libyans below of the imminent danger, and in response the chants of Arab Nationalist fervour began to ring through the crowded streets. It was carefully orchestrated confusion.

Sara fought her way to a public phone-booth off a crowded boulevard in Bab Benghasir, and listened to the phone ring unanswered in her apartment. Ten feet away, at the roadside, Tyler shaded his face and watched the jeeps buzzing back and forth, scattering slow-moving pedestrians. The soldiers were at large in the streets now, watching nervously as the groups of Revolutionary Committees formed up with their green banners and old Soviet rifles. The military perhaps even cursed Qadaffi for having armed the masses so readily during his Cultural Revolution in the Seventies. Clearly, neither group trusted the other, and each kept its distance from the other.

'Jesus, just look at this,' said Tyler as Sara climbed back inside. 'Got to get clear now. It's only a matter of time before they attack this vehicle with sticks and bloody stones. How about Yariv?'

'Not there. I couldn't get an answer.'

'What does that mean? He was told to wait.'

'I don't know!' she snapped. 'Maybe he got caught up in this lot. Come on, let's get out of here.'

He swung a wide arc in the road and raced the engine threateningly, clearing a path until they came back onto an arterial route, and made for Sharia al Fatah. By the University they came across several gangs of armed students. Most were just chanting slogans, but some smaller, more determined groups were firing off rifles into the air and attempting to block the roads. One group pressed menacingly close, and as the screaming hoard threatened to engulf the vehicle, Tyler slipped into low gear, jammed his foot down hard and drove straight ahead, scattering any human obstacles. Suddenly there was a deafening eruption of automatic weapon fire, which shattered the left rear window and showered glass fragments inside the vehicle. Tyler threw the LandCruiser into a random weaving motion, flinging it left and right, rocking madly on its suspension, and trying desperately to avoid the gunfire from the rear. But there was a plus to it: the reckless shooting had the effect of clearing the way ahead of them, and he slammed into the first intersecting avenue, thanking his stars for the welcome cover of roadside trees.

'Just pray that we don't stall now!' she said through clenched teeth.

'You pray – I'm driving! All we need now is a bloody roadblock!' Tyler smacked the big gear-lever into third for the extra power it afforded, and let the engine scream through two sets of traffic-lights.

The avenue was increasingly clear. Street demonstrations were confined to the main thorough-fares, thank God!

'That was close,' breathed Sara, when he had put two miles behind them. 'They want blood!'

'You said it, love. What's wrong with these kids? Why aren't they out screwing or something, like real students?' He was mechanically checking the rear mirror, relieved to find they were not being pursued.

'Stay on this road. There's a friendly nearby: a garage we use. Very discreet, very reliable. I can get us a change of wheels.'

'Fine by me. Time's about up on this one. It must be on the Militia's Ten Most Wanted list by now.'

The repair shop was impossibly small, and cluttered with the remains of dead Land-Rovers, but the skinny wire-haired kid in charge hid their vehicle without asking questions, and provided another LandCruiser with silver and black markings and a new plate. Tyler breathed easy again; they could now move freely once more, without fear of the Militia. He was pleased he had decided to hide the two remaining missiles; they were safely wrapped and buried in an orchard twenty klicks east of Suq al Jumah.

Against a blood-red sunset they took a good look around Bab Benghasir, finally closing in on al Fatah just as darkness fell. There were none of the telltale signs of saturation surveillance, but that did not stop either of them worrying. They knew it was the right amount of concern that would keep them alive. Sara called the apartment one last time from a public phone-booth. When no answer came, reluctantly they decided to go in anyway.

Parking the Cruiser in the square, where it would not be barred from a quick escape, they walked under the shadows of the trees and slipped quietly across al Fatah into the courtyard. There was no one around – not even the old superintendent. The balconies were quiet, though room lights were burning as usual. Tyler listened intently to the silence, punctuated by the regular chirp of cicadas and the distant hum of milling crowds. Damn it! If only he had more than a gut-sense to act on!

The elevator arrived and the door opened with its usual rattle. They rode to the sixth floor without speaking. Tyler's gun was clasped in his right hand, pressed discreetly against his right leg. There was at least some comfort in the smell of cleaning oil, and in the feel of the metal tight in his fist. But there was ice in his belly.

When the door slid open, they exchanged glances and moved cautiously out on to the landing, ears straining for some clue they could not pinpoint.

Sara fumbled in her pocket and produced the door-key, holding it poised like an archaeologist about to enter some cursed pyramid. The landing was only dimly lit, and Tyler could see that the apartment was in darkness from the absence of light spilling under the door. He took the key from her hand, operating the lock gently to kill any sound. There was a soft click as the deadbolt turned. He rotated the handle, opening the door just a foot and a half, took a deep breath and went blindly in. Sara followed quickly, closing the door behind her.

Inside, the curtains were pulled almost together, leaving a bare slash of light across the ceiling from the street-lamps below. Tyler stood still, just a few paces from the door, his eyes probing the grey shapes in the darkness. Slowly, inexplicably, the hairs on his neck began to rise. A strange, unquiet atmosphere; a new smell that was almost there. The girl moved close, alerted by his uneasiness; he placed a firm hand against her shoulder, cautioning her to remain still. His eyes glazed over, giving way to the superiority of his ears in the darkness. Somewhere in the room, as faint as imagination, he could hear the sound of someone breathing. Not just one – two! God above, he thought, they're here!

As if in a nightmare, there came the unmistakable grating sound of a cocking mechanism, close behind him in the darkness. Not just any old sound, its spring-coiled voice described the nature of the beast: automatic and powerful, with a good rate of firing.

'Move at all, Tyler, and you're dogmeat.' It was like some final judgement handed down from on high in a hellish Armagh accent. The nightmare made flesh. There were thirteen rounds in his Browning – no match for the weapon now trained upon him – but he knew this was their only chance. In the space of a second he pushed Sara to the floor, turned hard to rear and levelled the pistol towards the source of the sound he had heard. A glint of dull metal caught his eye, and he squeezed off a double tap before he had properly acquired the target. In the confinement of the room the explosion was jarring to the brain. The two bullets ploughed harmlessly into the plaster of the wall.

The two shots were all he managed before the second breathing someone, a noiseless and rapid silhouette, stole in beside him, gripped his wrist with fingers of steel, and smashed the ball of a boney wrist-joint against his left temple. Suddenly the room exploded into yellow flashes, and Tyler fell to the floor, concussed. As he fell, confident hands stripped the pistol smoothly from his hand and met his body at the floor, pinning it expertly with one hand and a knee.

Unable to see their attackers, Sara took his lead and was back on her knees in an instant, with dagger at the ready. It came like an electric shock: she felt the kiss of the barrel on her neck, and heard the murmured ultimatum. There was nowhere to go, and a million ways to die. The dagger clattered to the floor.

After long seconds someone slapped the light-switch. Tyler's throbbing eyes refocused painfully under a ceiling light, and he found himself pinned by the short square frame of his assailant. With the cold, slant eyes of an oriental, the man looked down at him without blinking, his face close enough for Tyler to catch the whiff of garlic on his breath. Korean and a martial artist, for sure. The oriental's speed had been frightening, almost inhuman. So why wasn't Tyler dead already?

Both the men were dressed in black from toe to chin. They had removed their hoods now, and with an electric shiver Tyler recognised the rough looks of the Armagh gunman he knew was bound to cross his path, sooner or later.

Nailed-down certainty had decreed their meeting.

'Hello there, Tyler.' A weird, unsettling, high-pitched voice emerged from the husky frame.

Tyler checked the blunt features once more – to be sure. 'That you Brady?' he responded.

Brady laughed. 'You know bloody well it is, my dear. How's it feel, eh? Glad it's over, I'll bet. Didn't we both know it would end like this with me laying out your corpse.'

The weapon Tyler recognised now, an H and K. He ought to be used to having machine-guns pointed his way, but you did not ever get used to that. Brady's voice pulled at his guts. What must it have done to poor, soft George Stephenson? Christ he hated that blunt, savage face; the whine of his nasal threats.

'Your fun's over, Tyler. We have the whole team. It's good-night for you.'

Vainly, Tyler tried to move, but the Korean had him incapicated as if a rugby scrum was holding him down.

Brady laughed quietly. 'Don't wast your energy, man. Save it to pray for yourself and this Jew lady.' He waved his weapon towards Sara, who was sitting awkwardly on the floor. Her eyes went to Tyler's, but there was more than casual concern in that look, and Brady was too shrewd to miss it.

'What's this, then? She your woman, Tyler, is that it? Brady grabbed the girl by her shirt collar, hauling her up roughly onto the sofa.

'You sit there, bitch. I want a word with your boy-friend – this fuckin' murdering Brit.' He swaggered forward again, with the machine-gun at his waist, until he was standing just three feet from where Tyler's left ear was pinned to the floor.

Tyler gazed back unflinching. 'That's great from a cold blooded shit like you, Brady.'

Before Kim saw what would happen, Brady swung his boot squarely into the Englishman's face, sending out a spurt of blood from his nose to paint the shiny, wooden floor. Sara gave a shriek like some small animal, as Tyler's body recoiled in agony. Immediately Kim loosened his grip and leapt up, eyes burning with something more than mere rage.

'That is all! No more!' he thundered.

Brady blinked back his surprise and retreated a pace, the memory of their last clash still fresh in his mind. His sneer was instantly replaced by anger. The Chink was pushing it again, only this time Brady had a gun in his hand. And if he had to use it, then to hell with Colonel Azziz!

Rage took over, his voice building to a harsh crescendo. 'Let him up, Kim. Come on, just let the bastard up. I've come a long way for his hide. This bastard's mine!' he raised the barrel of the weapon – almost screaming now. 'Come on, let him up. I'll do it here! Come on!'

Kim stared silently back at him, square as a barn and just as unrelenting. Disgust was evident in the slight downward turn of his mouth; disgust at the barbarian's lack of equilibrium. This was what Azziz had warned him of: the unreliable element in the man's nature, which made him a liability as well as an asset.

It was a moment Tyler saw and seized, lacing his words with sarcasm. 'Look, Kim. The poor boy wants to kill so bad he'd kill you, too, just to get to me.'

'Shut him up, Kim,' warned Brady, but the Korean just went on staring silently.

'Get it through your thick skull, Mick,' Tyler taunted. 'The Libyans want me alive, and there's nothing *you* can do about that. Course, you want your revenge for Terence Lynch. Tough luck, mate. Take it from me, he wasn't worth it. Just before I gave it to him, he cried like a baby and peed in his pants.'

Brady flipped the machine-gun safety off, his voice now a hoarse scream. 'Stand away from him! I'm doing it! I'm doing it!'

Kim did not move except to raise his own weapon and aim it squarely at Brady's head. 'Put it down, Irishman,' he warned, tiring of the outrage.

'You wouldn't dare,' said Brady, unsure.

'There's one way to find out.'

Once again Brady found himself backing off, lowering his attack. It hurt, as Tyler hoped it would.

Tyler laughed out loud over Brady's climb-down, and more blood shot across the floor.

'You shut your face, Brit!' The machine-gun stared into Tyler's eyes. Brady's fingers itched like hell.

Tyler knew that he would be dead already if not for the Korean. He also knew there was no way he could take both of them unarmed. If he could keep needling Brady, perhaps the Irishman would try to put away the Korean for a chance to get to him. At least then Tyler would have chance. Otherwise he was dead, anyway.

As Kim looked into the blazing green eyes of the Irishman, he realised why it was he hated this coarse barbarian.

'No. It is not worthy,' he began. 'It is not worthy that he should die here, like this. Not if you have a personal quarrel. That would be without honour, and I will not allow it.'

'Fuck honour!' Brady's words sounded like a whipcrack, and for once Kim's placid face broke into a sneer of revulsion.

'Do not fuck honour,' he warned quietly, now almost shaking with suppressed emotion. 'Do not fuck what you cannot understand. Now, go make the phone-call.'

The stand-off lasted barely a second, before Brady broke eye-contact and turned with a curse to the telephone. Tyler was allowed to stand and move to the sofa, where he sat without bothering to wipe the blood from his face. His fevered brain could not guess how long they might live, but he felt a small sense of rapport of some kind growing between himself and the Korean. What it was and how far it extended, he had no idea, but it was welcome. Perhaps, it was nothing more than the fact that Kim clearly cared so little for the Irishman. 'Whoever is the enemy of my friend is also my enemy; whoever is the enemy of my enemy is my friend.'

She had been quiet for some time, but now Sara felt compelled to speak. 'I am an Italian national, where is my husband Mario, who lives here?'

Kim turned to her and spoke with some regret. 'There was a struggle and he was shot resisting arrest. I wish it could have been avoided.'

For some mad reason she looked at Tyler, perhaps hoping he might reassure her that the Korean was lying. Lacking any words, he turned his face away. She stared at the wedding ring upon her left hand: a part of their cover, but somehow more real today than ever before.

'You bastards!' she murmured bitterly, holding back the tears.

Brady had by now contacted the Operational Control room. Immediately Azziz demanded to speak with Captain Kim.

'You have them?'

'We have them both – alive.'

'Good. Keep it that way. I am standing down the other units now. Do what you have to do, then bring Nimrod to me.'

'And the other matter ...?' The Korean said, carefully watching the Irishman, who was guarding the handcuffed prisoners.

There was a pause on the line.

'Yes. Finish the other matter, too. I'll be waiting here when you arrive.'

That was good enough for Kim.

An official car and driver were waiting in the square below when they emerged from the apartment block in a tight group. Kim looked around cautiously, just in case Azziz had deceived him and despatched some senior officer to supervise the arrest. Seeing there was just one standby unit, he ignored the official Mercedes – in defiance of Azziz's instructions – and steered the group towards a green Range Rover parked on the opposite side of the road. Immediately two young Arabs jumped from a red Fiat, one of the mobile intelligence vehicles, demanding to know what was going on.

Captain Park was out of the Range Rover in a second, his machine-gun swinging easily into his hands, cradled by a concealed harness under his jacket. He gestured the young Arabs to stand clear. Official orders, he explained, from highest authority. They were the only unit still on the scene, and both lean, moustached figures moved away, unsure of their authority and unwilling to argue with the Koreans.

Powerless, Tyler was shoved into the Range Rover beside Sara. The steel hand cuffs bit savagely into his wrists, but at least they were both still alive. Brady was ordered into the front passenger seat, with Park at the wheel and Kim sitting immediately behind his fellow countryman, cradling the machine-gun in the crook of his elbow.

'What's going on here?' Brady demanded, unsettled by this sudden side-step away from the supposedly friendly unit back in the square. 'Are we taking these prisoners to Azziz, or have you got something else in mind?'

The Korean's manner changed completely. 'Shut your mouth, Brady. There is still unfinished business.' There was a quick interchange between the two Koreans in their native tongue, then an emphatic nod of acknowledgement from Park.

Somehow the rules of the game had changed, and Tyler guessed that Brady was now no happier than himself about the situation. He could feel the growing tension in that naked silence.

The vehicle sped along al Fatah, turned left and then out on to an unlit dirt track that bounced roughly out of Bab Benghasir. In the light of the headlights sweeping the ground ahead, Tyler saw the vegetation die away and he realised they were heading for the scrub. Whatever was on Kim's mind, he clearly wanted no witnesses.

Tyler had heard the Korean talking to Azziz on the radio. These must be Azziz's own orders – but something was not right. Was Kim going his own way instead?

Fifteen minutes later the Range Rover lurched to a halt, kicking up a cloud of dust as the rear wheel came to a standstill. It was a deserted stretch of open ground, except where ancient ruins stood tall and black against the moon. The remains of a line of half-columns stood glowing pale on the perimeter, like so many broken teeth.

Kim knew this place well. He knew it to be the remains of a Roman amphi-theatre, where slaves and gladiators had once fought to the death with wild animals, or with each other, for the entertainment of their masters. It was one of many lesser archaeological sites largely ignored by the Libyans, who tended to deny their much-conquered past. Now it was left to herdsmen to make what use of it they could. A range of mud huts and livestock pens was scattered on the broken ground of the old arena. Some weekly market must have occurred only a day or two previously for a strong smell of dung came through the open windows, lying heavily on the night air.

Sara also knew this place: it was the main holding area used by the bedouin herdsmen coming out of the Sirtica with their herds and flocks on the way to be sold.

'Everybody out,' ordered Kim, as he threw wide the door and stepped into the dust.

In the distance glimmered the orange lights of the University district, and the vague outline of the Jebel was just discernible as the pale grey ghost of a silhouette against the dim horizon to the west.

All the while Brady had sat still and held his tongue, but he was nervous.

'What the fuck are you playing at, Kim? Where do you call this?' When no answer came he swallowed hard. 'Azziz will have your arse if you screw this up. Or have you come here to kill the Brit?' Nerves were making him sound so excited that Park moved in and had the Heckler-Koch out of his hand before Brady even noticed him at his side.

'What the hell . . .'

'Shut up, Brady. There will now be a small change of plan,' said Kim, levelling his own weapon. 'Please everybody do exactly as you are told. Follow Captain Park, and don't do anything stupid.'

In the darkness the various faces were all unknown quantities. How was a man supposed to judge? Tyler, who had been waiting for a chance to jump either of the Koreans the instant the Rover stopped, decided to let it go a while: there would be many chances to make his move in the darkness of the arena.

The headlights were still burning, their beams washing over the first and largest of the stock pens. With a slam Park closed the driver's door, and moved forward in the light to where it caught the metal bars of a tall gate. They all followed, as ordered. Park lifted the wire loop, and heaved the gate open with some effort. Its hinges moaned. The sides of the pen were over five feet high.

Kim turned first to Tyler.

'I have heard much about you. They say you're a soldier?'

What the hell's going on now? Tyler asked himself, but replied, 'I was once, yes, that's true. What of it?'

'That is good. So at least *you* understand what is meant by honour.'

Now Tyler was sensing the message, the significance of this place. The Korean was setting it up between them.

Before he could deliberate further, Kim took out a set of keys and unlocked the handcuffs. 'Go inside,' he said gently, though one look at the menacing weapon convinced Tyler this was no mild request.

Tyler stepped gingerly inside the pen, testing the ground beneath his feet like the first moon-walker. The compounded dirt was softened by a layer of dust. Already he was searching the littered ground for potential weapons, and his eyes fell upon a scattered heap of wooden posts. This God-forsaken square of earth would be where it all happened.

The Korean pointed his machine-pistol toward Brady. 'What are you waiting for? Get in there with him.'

Brady's face showed he had not foreseen that one coming.

'What do you mean? You going to shoot me, too, you crazy Chink?'

'Do as I say! Go in now or I'll shoot you where you stand.' Slowly but furiously, Brady stepped inside, watching Tyler change position and keeping clear, his eyes flicking between him and the Korean. Finally, Brady too understood.

'Oh, I get it,' he nodded. 'It's a show you're after? You want to see me kill this Brit with my two bare hands. That's bloody fine by me!'

Tyler spread his feet and lowered his stance, in expectation of sudden attack. Glancing towards the mouth of the pen he saw Sara silhouetted against the lights of the vehicle, closely covered by the other Korean. He wondered which way she would run if he made a break.

'Kill him if you can, Brady. That should be a small matter for a man who talks as loud as you do.'

'Too right!' Brady countered, quickly reaching down to the thigh pocket of his black combat suit and tearing open the velcro fastener. As his hand emerged, the car headlights glinted on the blade of a combat dagger – Sara's dagger. 'You'd better have the stomach to watch this, you bloody Chink!'

Kim laughed bitterly. 'Always weapons and bombs, you people. Killing by remote control from a safe distance – and without honour. Always without honour. But there is your enemy.' His short finger indicated Tyler standing in the gloom, powerful, angular and ready. 'So redeem yourself, purge your soul. Kill your enemy with honour – looking into his eyes as he looks back into yours.'

Tyler watched the glint of the knife as Brady turned and moved towards him. They changed ground, circling and jinking left and right, avoiding the face-on glare of the headlights, neither man allowing the other to attack with the light to his back so that it would kill his own night-vision. Tyler knew the odds were against him if Brady knew how to handle that blade properly. He watched the Irishman take up a battle crouch, well balanced with his weight evenly divided between both feet. The blade was gripped in his right hand, not as for slashing downwards like an amateur, but held point-upwards and close to his body, while his left hand was stretched out in front to ward off any attempt to seize the knife. He knew what he was doing, all right. The bastard!

Even now Brady's feet were edging closer, cutting down the space inside the pen, like a boxer. Tyler did not fancy his own chances bare-handed – too much could go wrong in the dark, and one arterial wound would be enough to finish it. God knows how much blood he had lost already from that kick in the nose. He needed a weapon badly, but the damn wood-pile was behind and to the right of the oncoming knifeman. Well, he would have to go through him. So Tyler moved in, swinging a kick to Brady's middle, following up with a punch that struck him high on the side of the head as the Irishman lurched backward. He had not expected Tyler to take the fight to him, and he thrust the knife forward wildly

411

to protect himself as he stumbled back. The blade touched only air.

Now Brady had recovered his balance, and he launched forward with a slice at Tyler's throat, forcing him to raise his arms in defence – just as he had hoped. At the last moment Brady changed his attack, and cut across the soft edge of Tyler's hand, dragging the blade up his forearm and causing him to scream out in pain. It was a disabling cut; he was going for attrition. Tyler jumped backwards, clear of the blade, but realising he was now further away from the wood pile than before.

Suddenly his left forearm felt cold, and there was a loss of feeling in the blood-soaked fingers. Damn them for giving up on him now! Seeing a chance, he moved in towards Brady's legs with both feet, placing one behind the Irishman's leading leg, and kicking with the other against the knee. This painful lever action threw Brady backwards with a thump, jarring the breath from him as he hit the ground. Tyler turned to spring on to the fallen body, but Brady's flailing legs caught him in the chest and pushed him away, giving the Irishman time to flip back on to his feet and begin his slow stalking again. There was no vocal sound between them – no change in facial expression save when one or the other struck a painful blow. Tyler knew they were well matched – but for the knife. The savage cuts were adding up quickly. He had to do something about that knife . . . or die.

Then the swaying motion of the knifeman's arm reminded him of something: a compound movement from a Chinese combat form he had picked up in Bangkok. The rhythm was a perfect match; the culmination totally appropriate. Once more Tyler took the initiative, leading with his left arm, pushing Brady backward with a crunch from his elbow, oblivious now to the pain of his wounds.

Brady grabbed for his neck and slashed at Tyler's left shoulder, the blade cutting deep into

412

the flesh. Another wound, much deeper and more dangerous than the others. Brady mouthed a savage grunt of exultation. But this was a gamble on Tyler's part: he had to get close enough, and to do that he had needed to make a sacrifice.

Now it paid off: he had drawn his man into the trap.

Brady had turned just enough for Tyler to swing a punch into his unguarded throat and knock him sideways, choking as the muscles of his larynx automatically contracted. As Brady came up coughing and clawing at his neck, Tyler faked left and lunged right, grabbing at the pile of wood, now well within reach, before Brady could cut him off from it again. As he stopped, his fingers skipped desperately across the various widths until he found one rounded and narrow enough to close his fist around. But when he snatched it up, it was over eight feet long. Shit! A bloody liability. Then his eyes lit upon the metal bars of the enclosure, and he smashed the wood down against the top with all his strength. It broke cleanly, leaving a four-foot length which sat squat in his hand like a baseball bat. Just right!

When he saw this, Brady took a couple of steps backward, his eyes reassessing. A widening dark patch meant Tyler's arm was losing blood fast, but now he had the advantage of reach. Brady began to close again, and it was not until he started swinging, and the pain shot through his shoulder muscles, that Tyler realised just how much damage he had sustained.

'You'll bleed to death now, Tyler,' grinned Brady, noticing his opponent wince. 'I'm going to take you, boy!'

Tyler could already feel the first waves of dizziness, and he knew there was no time for caution. The cut was deep, and he was hyperventilating. Brady was jabbing forward with the knife, aiming toward the fingers gripping the bat. Tyler waited his moment, then thrust the bat towards Brady, knowing the Irishman would try to parry it. That happened just as he wanted, and with a slight deviation he brought the wood down hard upon the gunman's elbow. There were two loud cracks, one of splitting wood, the other of bone. A second blow to the knee-joint broke the bat clean in two, and sent Brady hurtling into the dust.

Instantly Tyler fell across the fallen figure and grappled for the dagger. It came into his hand easily – almost too easily. Brady was lying on his back as the blade went into his left side, between the third and fourth ribs. Tyler held firm to the convulsing figure, his forearm crushing against the man's rough, unshaven throat. His senses felt his enemy's breathing diminish, heard the first faint gurgle as blood ran into Brady's airways, and Tyler held on all the tighter, flushed with a primitive urge to complete the kill. A flailing hand grabbed Tyler's hair, trying to drag his head to one side, but in the end the hand relaxed and fell away. There was a final curse of rage, then Brady was still.

Long moments after, Tyler kept staring into Brady's face, knowing he was once again free of a nightmare. Liam Brady would kill no more.

'Sleep tight now, George,' he whispered into the night. The cold made him shiver.

Somewhere behind him there was the groan of metal gate hinges. Captain Kim appeared and stood behind him.

'The pig is dead. Congratulations. Now it is time for you to leave this place.'

Tyler climbed weakly to his feet and almost fell forward. Sara ran over and caught his good arm, supporting him till he recovered his balance. The blood had soaked his whole left side, and he was shaking all over. It took all his strength to stand and face Captain Kim.

'Yes, he's dead. So what happens now?'

'What do you think, Tyler? Am I to shoot you, do you think?'

'I've given up thinking. I leave that to others. You could easily turn me over the Libyans – but somehow I don't think you have that in mind?'

'Save your breath for Qadaffi. You will need it.'

'What does that mean?'

'It means that you have just escaped from my custody – and killed the Irishman in the process.'

Tyler's weak laugh was laced with sarcasm.

'Just like that, eh? I don't buy that and Azziz won't buy it, either. If you go back without us, and without Brady, you're as good as dead. So what's your game?'

'Don't worry about him.' Kim nodded towards the corpse. 'You see, Brady was not expected to survive this operation. Explicit orders. His power-seeking has made him very unpopular with his own people in Ireland, and yesterday Colonel Azziz received a telex requesting his deletion. Azziz was very pleased to grant this request. He would never antagonise such a close ally as the IRA for the sake of a man so head-strong and unreliable as Brady. I was ordered to killed him myself – and you were to be blamed. But it was my personal pleasure that Brady should meet you on equal terms. I have no particular liking for terrorists; and this man Brady seemed to me a coward in many ways – a man filled with hate. And hated by even his own people. I needed to know what kind of a man you are, Tyler. I don't risk my own life for just anyone.'

'Are you saying you mean to help me kill Qadaffi?'

Tyler winced as Sara began to peel off his blood-soaked jacket and shirt, staunching the wound with a field dressing.

Kim paused for a deep breath before speaking. 'I have my own reasons for hating this country, though they are not your business. But this morning I watched while this President ordered a submarine to shoot its missiles into a defenceless passenger liner, and from what I hear that won't be the last such dishonourable attack. He has cruise-type missiles, and plans to use them soon against Israel. That is all I know. I cannot go back to the barracks after this. By tomorrow morning I'll be across the border into Egypt. But if you still mean to kill him, then I can tell you where to find him. There is a purpose-built camp in the Sirtica, and the missiles are there, too.'

'Yes I know of it. That's where I plan to take him.'

'Not there, Tyler. Believe me, there will be too many soldiers. There's another way. It's a place he always visits whenever he returns to the land of his family – a sacred duty, he believes. I have been there, and it will be perfect. Now I will tell you.'

An hour later, with Tyler sufficiently bandaged up to hold him together, they were back on the road, heading in darkness for the great desert of the Sirtica and the camp of the Sulubbi.

Driving through the night, Sara sobbed out of sheer relief that they were both still alive. On the bench seat behind her, Tyler lay exhausted and sleeping, his nose dark and swollen.

Later, in the quiet of the desert, she stopped the vehicle to rest a while and prayed for the soul of Yariv, her dead comrade, and gave thanks for the life of Richard Tyler. How she wished they could both just disappear together and live their lives in peace. The Sulubbi could so easily guide them undetected into the safety of the Sudan. But there was more than their own lives to consider: her paramount concern must be for the lives of her people in Israel, threatened now by Qadaffi's cruise missiles. If he was capable of attacking a harmless passenger ship, what else was he capable of? As there was no way to contact Tel Aviv, their only chance now was to cut down the very source of the threat: Qadaffi himself.

Somewhere in the night a clock was ticking its way to a nuclear nightmare.

TWENTY–SEVEN

THE SILENCE WAS deafening. There was no word of Captain Kim or of Brady – nothing but static on the Bureau net. With mounting horror Colonel Azziz pulled back the operational units. Furious, he demanded to see all concerned.

'By Great God! Why didn't you stop them?'

No answer. The group of men in tropical suits was silent as the grave. The Colonel's hawklike gaze fell upon Osman, who had commanded the last unit to leave the scene, forcing an explanation.

The answer was faltering. 'Please, it was ... difficult.'

'Difficult! How?'

'The Korean refused escort. They threatened us with their machine-pistols. By the beard of the Prophet, I swear I thought he was acting under your direct order. Let us go back now. They cannot get far. We will run them down like stray dogs!'

The man with the green tattoos was unimpressed, and he had no clues to go on. There was no way to tell whether Brady or Kim had turned traitor, or whether Nimrod had somehow managed to kill both of them and escape. Who now was alive and who was dead? Damn all infidels! They must be found and dealt with; the details could be sorted out later.

'Like dogs, you say. It is you who are the dogs! You are imbeciles! Alert all immigration points and get back out there. Don't return without them. All of them!'

There was a scramble for the door, then he found himself alone once more in his office. He lit a cigarette, but it tasted bitter. Azziz's problems were multiplying. All night he had monitored reports of unrest on the city streets: clashes between the Revolutionary Committees and groups of dissenters. The Committees had even clashed with the police and the army when they attempted to intervene, causing casualties on all sides.

Government shops were under siege by ordinary people trying to buy up flour and rice in preparation for what was to come. There were rumours of an imminent coup.

In spite of reams of intelligence reports, no one knew for sure how many military units had been covertly recruited to the NSFL cause, nor would they find out until it was too late. Qadaffi was vulnerable, and Azziz could feel it in the air: like the pressure change before a rainstorm. His enemies were waiting for his next departure from Tripoli – then they would strike.

If they did overthrow Qadaffi, Azziz pondered, inevitably anyone linked with him would also be targeted. Must they all suffer for one man's excesses?

He sucked deeply on the cigarette and reached for his gold worry-beads. Nimrod was out there somewhere, poised to strike – perhaps aided by one of Qadaffi's own bodyguards. Perhaps all the better if he did succeed. Azziz knew that the morning would bring a summons from Azizyah Barracks and there would be questions, difficult questions. Qadaffi would demand to know what had become of his Korean bodyguard, the one seconded to Azziz for a sensitive operation. Jalloud would be there, too, twisting the knife.

And how much did Kim know of the Houn Project? The name burned in Azziz's brain as he thought of the file in his safe outlining the destruction of Israel's nuclear facility. It would mean knee-jerk retaliation: Libya's population centres reduced to smoking waste. The madness of it. The risk.

But what if Nimrod should succeed? Would that not be altogether better for Libya? What if now was the time to make his peace with the opposition he had persecuted so ruthlessly in the past at Qadaffi's behest. He took a small, silver-plated pistol from the top draw of his desk and placed it in his jacket pocket

A safe and secure future could be there for the taking. If he went straight away to the Education Secretary and offered his services to the NFSL cause, they were bound to see the value of recruiting a strong intelligence service. And he would gladly testify against Jalloud if called upon. He would condemn him with pleasure.

Quickly he opened the safe and withdrew two files: that relating to the Houn Project and one other. It was the one not even Qadaffi knew about – his guarantee of immunity.

Shortly after midnight he took the coast road westwards and drove out to Janzur and the villa of the Education Secretary. Lights were still burning inside, and he counted no less than five security men, armed with automatic rifles, attentively guarding the plush twenty-roomed house. It seemed that Azziz was not the only one to sense a change in the political weather.

The Education Secretary himself came out to greet him.

'I didn't think you would dare come. Let me compliment you upon your courage.' At a wave of his hand, the guards lowered their weapons. Quickly he ushered the visitor inside, ever unsure of where Jalloud's spies might be.

The atmosphere was cagey at first. The Secretary had agreed to this meeting without any prior admission of his own complicity with the NSFL.

'We must speak in private – just the two of us.' Azziz fished in the pocket of his impeccably cut jacket and handed his silver pistol to one of the guards as a sign of good faith.

'All right. My study. Please follow me.'

They sat down in two wing-backed armchairs of burgundy leather.

At first the Secretary was clearly sceptical, for Azziz over the years had arranged the liquidation of many good NSFL people in Europe and the Middle East.

'Our organisation bears you much ill-will. Even if we two reached some personal agreement, I might not be able to protect you when the trials begin.'

'Mr Secretary you are too modest. Everyone with an ear to the ground knows yours is now the most significant voice. If you will speak for me, I am content.'

The Secretary nodded thoughtfully.

'What is it you offer?'

'There are other factors to consider. A new government needs the skills of loyal civil servants. But loyalty is no substitute for experience: an incompetent zealot is worse than useless, particularly in a role such as mine. Furthermore, I have very detailed knowledge of Qadaffi's myriad foreign relations: his secret alliances, his unpublished agreements. A pity to waste all that?'

'A pity indeed. But what if we decide to renounce all previous affiliations and begin afresh?' The Secretary steepled his fingers, enjoying the other man's discomfiture.

But Azziz turned confidently to the documents he had brought.

'I have here two secret files which you should read. When you have read them, I am sure you will appreciate the value of my assistance.

The Secretary put on heavy reading glasses and accepted the folders. The first contained the Houn papers which had been smuggled out of Azizyah. Whatever self-satisfaction the Secretary had felt evaporated quickly as he read. He stared in horror at the words, extending the document to arm's length as if that might alter the dreadful meaning.

'By great God, he must be stopped. I must contact our interception units tonight and direct them to converge upon this base at Houn. For your sake, Azziz, this had better not be some fabrication.'

'On my life.'

'So be it. He has forced our hand, and we must bring forward our initiative. Now we'll see who the army will choose to follow.'

But it was the second file which strengthened Azziz's personal case, and the Secretary's jaw fell open as he read it. Five pages of closely printed handwriting contained full details of the interrogation of a male prostitute and drug-trafficker: an agent of the Israeli Government codenamed Nineveh. In his confession this agent gave details of his previous sexual liaisons with top Government men.

Suddenly the Secretary was confronted by his own name.

'I feel sure,' said Azziz, 'that we can now come to some arrangement.'

'Yes, Colonel,' the other man replied. 'Perhaps we can . . . for the good of our country.'

On the morning of the Jewish sabbath, whilst the world was still reacting to the news of the destruction of the *QE2*, three governments prepared to face their people. In London the British Cabinet met in emergency session to discuss its options, both diplomatic and economic, for the stricken ship had been sailing under a British flag. In Washington, the President would remain closeted the whole day with his Secretary of State, National Security Adviser and the Secretary for Defense. Intervention in the Middle East was always the difficult one; the last thing they wanted was another round of US hostage-taking. Yet over half the casualties flown off the ship in body-bags had been US citizens. But in Tel Aviv talk was more decisive. It was enough that Jews had been cold-bloodedly murdered, and the State of Israel now girded its loins – as in the days of Abraham – to meet its enemy head on.

As the sun rose over the Gulf of Sirte, a hundred and twenty miles out to sea, its rays fell upon the sleek backs of four pairs of Fighting Falcons travelling due west: ground-attack F–16s of the Israeli Air Force flying sub-sonic and at almost wave-top height to conserve fuel. Against the clear blue sky the sharp, clean lines of the Falcons made an impressive sight, a gold sheen on their upper surfaces and pregnant with maximum bomb load. Their camouflage pattern was the familiar green and *café au lait* much-favoured by the Israelis in desert conditions; and, as always, the blue star of David was mounted above each wing. Taking off in darkness from a forward airstrip near Gaza, they had flown through the night on a long dog-leg route to avoid coastal radar until the last possible moment, and refuelling far out at sea. Now, with the sun behind them, each plane dropped its left wing and turned inexorably for land.

'Ghostriders at point one-five. Check.' The radio crackled: electronic voices from another world.

'Roger that. This is Almighty. Clear and begin.'

'Seraphim, Seraphim, Attack Group One. I have the lead! Eleven minutes to contact!'

Right then the big radar-jamming plane loitering to the rear began to put down maximum interference. The Hawkeye was a sophisticated early-warning aircraft which the pilots jokingly described as resembling a troop transport being molested by a flying saucer. Seraphim attack group leader stared past the head-up display on his canopy and noted the distant cloud bank which indicated the Libyan coastline ahead. He breathed a prayer into his microphone for all to hear: 'Put your trust in E–2Cs and pray for God.'

At Marsa el Brega, 810 kilometres east of Tripoli, the pride of the Libyan oil and gas industry lay basking in the morning sun, unaware of the advancing threat to the north. As far as the eye could see was a massive humming jungle of pipes surmounted by shining steel spires spewing black smoke and yellow flame from vented gases. On a coastline otherwise unbroken along its extent of sand and scrub, this was the ultimate destination of millions of gallons of crude oil pumped from the Zelten and Raguba fields to the south. Two miles out to sea a tanker of the Libyan fleet lay tied to the giant 3000-ton mooring platform and rode easily under the swell of the ebb tide, supported by a 140-foot boom and a 500-foot arm connecting it to the shore. It was a brilliant feat of engineering, allowing the big tankers to safely load up to ninety thousand tons of the black stuff from a 41-inch submarine pipe without fear of the high winds which often prevailed in the gulf. Moored to the stationary structure by a single line from the bow, the tanker could swing through 360 degrees, at the dictates of wind and tide, without interrupting loading.

It was here that the Libyans had first taken control of the oil they produced by building their own refineries instead of selling crude at a cut rate to be refined and exploited by western moguls. Now they were producing all manner of derivatives in their own specialised laboratories at Brega and at Zawia: gasoline, kerosene and liquified natural gas. And it was around this jealously guarded jewel that Qadaffi had built his air defences, challenging even the US Sixth Fleet not to cross the Line of Death and enter the gulf.

Out of the dawn sky came a howling roar of retribution that electrified the air, as eight jet engines switched to after-burn and scorched in from off the sea. Tucked in close together, they split into two attack groups at five miles out, Seraphim leader taking his team in first while Ghostrider hung back to act as second-strike insurance. Under the wing pylons, their 750-pound high-explosive bombs strained in their mountings under the severe five-g turns being pulled.

Suddenly coastal radar command went wild – their red screens were a mess of bright pink interference. No one doubted it was a real attack, and in this coastal quadrant the target was obvious. Grabbing the microphone, the air-quadrant commander ordered immediate scramble for all standby fighters. Missile command was cursing, knowing its SAM–6 radar-seekers were blind until they could burn through the jamming signal. Individual caterpillar-mounted batteries stationed along the coast were ordered to shoot on sight.

Against the flatness of its surroundings the Brega installation presented an easy target for acquisition. Seraphim leader checked the head-up display on his windshield and pared the attack angle in response to the computer's illuminated instructions. The first attack group had popped up high in readiness for a dive-toss manouevre, and now their leader was aware of the riot of orange and steel rushing hard below and towards him at just under mach one. Inside his helmet he heard a rapid bleep and, without looking, he knew the computer had locked and confirmed trajectory. He hit the arming switch and throttled back, concentrating on keeping the Falcon to its computed course, confident that the electronic brain on board would drop the bombs at the exact point when all its ballistic geometry said 'go'.

Suddenly he felt the plane buck and surge with new strength as the bomb load fell away. They were retarded bombs that would allow them to get clear. Then he pulled hard on the stick and twisted out into a high Immelman turn that would take him clear of the blast area. Behind him the other Falcons were already scorching in, fanning out to engage designated targets. The shrill whistle of falling ordnance gave way to the murderous roar and flash of sundering metal. The main laboratory block took a direct hit, erupting into blue flame and initiating a series of secondary explosions in nearby storage vessels. The foul stink of oil distillates clogged the air – even the Israeli pilots could taste it.

They were in and out in under a minute.

Barely twenty seconds later, Ghostrider made his approach to the mooring platform. A difficult strike, but back on the base in Gaza they had been planning that particular move for the past two years, as they did with all potential Arab targets. Without this plant Libya's capacity to produce refined products would be severely diminished, but the loading platform was of greater significance – without that their bulk crude shipping programme would be devastated. Facilities at other terminals could not cope with the traffic.

But pickings were not to be so easy for the second strike. On their pass, Ghostrider heard the sharp report of the onboard radar, and his eyes narrowed on the fast-moving white specks on the display, coming in fast from the south-west. It was just as he had expected, nevertheless the sight sent an electric shock through his nervous system. Sixteen Libyan interceptors were bearing down. They were MiG 25s, known outside the Soviet Union by their NATO designation Foxbat. Not yet visible, but the radar knew they were arriving fast.

Ghostrider called the alert, keeping the hysteria out of his voice and hoping the Foxbats were piloted by Libyans and not their Soviet advisers. Then he saw the smaller blips part company with the aircraft at a range of eight miles. They were under missile attack. Immediately both attack groups dropped to ground contour flight and came wide of the target, drawing the speeding missiles to a course of due east. A brilliant tactic. Too late, the Libyan pilots realised their mistake, as the infra-red homing in each of the missiles locked on the low, burning orb of the morning sun and pursued it to the horizon. A cheer went up on the Israeli radio net!

Ghostrider moved back into position and released his bombs, too quickly. The explosions erupted all around the platform, causing giant waves of white water to rock the boom and to lash the giant tanker moored there. He pulled clear and climbed upwards, watching the approach of the Foxbats on his radar. Now he had visual contact on the attacking planes, and he saw that there were MiG–23s in the party.

'Oh shit!'

The Foxbat had never been meant to engage in dog-fighting; it was first and foremost a long-range killer, and for this reason had not been fitted with cannon. The MiG–23 was another story: it had the means and the motion – a sky predator. Ghostrider held his breath and waited for them to close.

Behind him there was another explosion at sea-level as his number-two man scored a direct hit on the platform. Ghostrider had never seen anything like it before. The massive platform tore free of its boom as if it was a child's toy, twisting over onto its back and catapulting a water-spout two hundred feet into the air. The fuel was the next thing to go, blasting the superstructure, and the tanker with it, and sending fragments skipping along the water's surface.

One quick glance at the array of approaching fighters was enough to tell Ghostrider it was time to get out of there. In the last thirty seconds his radar had become a mass of activity: there were fighter missiles in the air. It was like watching microbes through a microscope – all of them hostile.

'Seraphim, Seraphim, this is Ghostrider. Bogeys everywhere. Run like hell! Anytime now, Almighty!'

The MiGs came in far too high and much too visible, gaining height and sacrificing surprise for a good look-down position on the enemy. The Foxbats, in pure white livery and bright Islamic-green roundels, stood out clearly against both land and sky. But disguise was not everything, and Ghostrider had no illusions about the Foxbat: it was one of the fastest planes in the skies, and its heat-seeking Acrid air-to-air missile system was still deadly at ranges up to ten miles. Even Libyan pilots could make kills with those.

As the Israelis ran and the Foxbats strove unsuccessfully to lock onto their elongated tail pipes, the MiG–23s closed the gap and brought air cannon to bear, stripping the wings from one Falcon and downing a second in a ball of flame. There were shouts of glee on the Libyan radio net. *Insh Allah!* God willing, it was going to be like shooting fish in a barrel!

Then, five miles clear of the coastline, with death on the tails of the Falcons, the clouds parted and the Eagles fell out of the sky from their station at twelve thousand feet: a dozen Israeli air-superiority-enhanced F–15s armed to the teeth and piloted by veterans – aces of aerial combat with over a hundred kills between them.

'This is Almighty. Contact, contact. We must go amongst them!'

They came down like the wrath of God from on high and completed the trap, Vulcan cannons crackling as they danced around the 23s. Scattering them like sparrows. The Eagle had been conceived as the fastest, most agile fighter ever to fly, but in the hands of men who understood the soul of the machine – really understood – it moved with awesome and deadly grace. Impossibly tight turns followed by sudden flip-overs, evasive steep dives that ended as tail chasers, and then the inevitable radar lock-on followed by the flash and white-light whoosh of Sidewinders striking home. The Eagles made four rapid kills and eight partial disablements before the MiGs cut their losses and disengaged, cursing the disappearing bombers that had raped their land.

As the Israeli attack force left the smoking wreckage of the oil-terminal and returned to the sea and their second rendezvous with a refuelling tanker, suddenly the heavens were quiet again. Almost peaceful.

But Marsa el Brega was belching flame and black smoke into the morning sky, and bleeding its black life-blood into the sea. It had taken less than twelve minutes to destroy the pride of the Libyan oil industry – a dream which had taken years in the making.

Tel Aviv issued its statement to the world's press only minutes after the bombers had landed and their pilots had been born at shoulder height into the cheering pilots' mess. The message said simply that the Israeli defence forces had conducted a punitive raid on a major Libyan economic target, destroying it completely and defeating the Libyan Air Force in the process. At the press conference an army of reporters fired off cameras and questions in rapid sequence, but all the Government spokesman would add was that their Military Intelligence had received incontrovertible evidence of the Libyans' role in the sinking of the *QE2*.

The Arab world responded immediately, and with universal condemnation of the raid. Just as Qadaffi had planned, there was a subtle but definite drawing together amongst the Arab peoples. Meetings between diplomats were arranged at short notice, and even Libya's estranged neighbour, Egypt, lent its voice to the appeals for a UN vote of censure on Israel.

But such calls were routine, and behind the blare of official denunciations there was widespread confusion. Flash-coded diplomatic communications buzzed between Arab heads of state in an attempt to establish who, if anyone, was backing Qadaffi in his latest adventures. What further madness was he planning? And what crisis might those further actions precipitate?

In Tripoli and Benghazi the clamour erupted within an hour of the raid. Months of preparation and propaganda by the National Front were coming to a head, and here at last was an unexpected catalyst to abet the political and emotional backlash.

In a rising hubbub of discontent, memories of a previous humiliating air-raid came into sharp focus. In coffee shops groups of men huddled around radio sets and listened with tears of anger to the reports of death and destruction; it was a body blow to national pride. Shopkeepers, factory workers and civil servants milled about in the streets, not quite sure which way to turn or who to blame. Weapons were openly toted, and rumours spread of impending invasion by the Zionist forces. As the men ranted and speculated, their women besieged the food stores with huge baskets, adding further to the rising tide of hysteria.

In the Green Square the hard-line cadres of the Revolutionary Committees attempted to control public emotions by starting to chant in support of Muammar Qadaffi; but with increasing clarity it seemed these men were becoming the focus of the mob's frustrations. Whose fault would it be if Libya reaped the whirlwind? Suddenly a young woman raised her fist and gave voice to the mood of the crowd: 'No more dictators! I say no more Green Revolution!' The response was immediate as the heaving mass of bodies took up the cry and shook their fists in unison. Members of the Revolutionary Committees were forced to fight their way out of the square with whatever came to hand, overturning chairs and hurling bottles grabbed from tables in street cafés.

'Down with the traitor!'

'Death to the Revolutionary Committees!'

The crowd had found it's voice, and all it wanted now was targets for its resentment. Suddenly a young army conscript – perhaps a victim of one of Qadaffi's press-gang recruitments staged outside some football stadium after a big match – snatched off his uniform tunic and tried unsuccessfully to rip it apart. Several men nearby took hold and tore the garment to shreds. Suddenly conscripts all over the square were shedding their uniforms in similar fashion.

As the mob spilled out of the square and along Omar al Mukhtar, one thing seemed certain: the Libyan people would be ridden no more.

A ripple of fear spread quickly through the fashionable diplomatic quarter, where the initial reaction was for staffers at foreign embassies to abandon their homes and gather in the safety of their chancery buildings behind locked doors. There was an anguished flood of cypher traffic requesting advice and instruction. And it was safe now for members of the National Front to slip out of the shadows and steer the wave of disaffection in the direction of Government offices all over the city.

Only a handful of the most loyal Cabinet members attended the President's emergency meeting that morning. When news of the raid had first reached Azizyah, Qadaffi flew into an immediate rage, haranguing his Air Force commanders and threatening charges of treasonable dereliction of duty. But later, when he had dismissed them, Jalloud was on hand to calm him down and remind him of his grand design: the completeness of the victory yet to come.

430

'Peace, brother Colonel, you will be avenged. The Arab peoples are behind us.'

'Yes, Jalloud, everything is happening the way I had planned.' Qadaffi's eyes changed to a hard glitter. 'You are right. God sends many challenges to test our resolve. Soon the forces of Islam will have their day, and the bedouin will return to Palestine as masters. What news from the base at Houn?'

'Nothing but good – a blessing to the ear. The technicians finished programming the guidance system two days ago. Weather conditions in the Negev will be perfect over the next few days. Good northerly winds will mean excellent dispersal of fall-out. There will be massive contamination of crops and water supplies. Livestock will perish and population centres will die slowly.'

'Excellent. It's a small price to pay. The Arabs have learned to be patient, and they will readily wait a few more years before reclaiming a land that has been purged.'

He had taken the news of defections hard, and Azziz was only one of the many members of Government who had gone into hiding overnight. Jalloud's men had been watching their homes – he trusted no one. Now it was his duty to lend succour to his leader.

'Forget the traitors and enemies, and think only of your destiny. Who could now lay blame if you unsheath the flaming sword of Islam?'

'Yes, *Insh Allah*,' said the President with tears in his eyes. Slowly he turned to the eastern wall of his bunker and fell to his knees, touching his forehead to the floor. When at last he stood up, his eyes were staring far away, past the walls of the stronghold to some distant point of contact with the desert he loved so fiercely. His voice was tight with emotion: 'Go prepare the helicopters. It is time.'

Qadaffi stepped briskly down the steps to the waiting Range Rover, his white bedouin robes

431

billowing slightly in the breeze he generated. He was flanked by two uniformed officers of the Presidential Guard who wore their weapons conspicuously. All available troops were now manning key-point defence positions at the walls. Qadaffi smiled as he looked around, and was reassured by what he saw. Jalloud was already inside the vehicle, clutching a metal briefcase which was also chained to his left wrist. When the President reached the open door he stopped and looked around.

'Where are my Koreans? Why aren't they here?' he asked of the tall officer holding the door.

'They left in the night, brother Colonel. Their quarters are empty.'

'Deserters.' The President curled his upper lip.

Beyond the walls the sound of distant artillary came as muffled thunder. Qadaffi turned to his deputy in surprise.

'In God's name, Jalloud, what was that?'

Jalloud's manner was sombre, and he avoided his President's eyes.

'It is the army, firing its guns on the head-quarters of the Revolutionary Committees.'

'They have turned?'

'Some of them, yes.'

'How many? A few hundred? A few thousand?'

'Enough. We have sufficient forces to safeguard the barracks . . .'

'What is happening? Tell me, Jalloud.'

'The Opposition has learned of the Houn Pro-ject. You can blame Azziz for that. Now the Front is spreading its poison within the army. This morning they made a broadcast from a secret radio transmitter.'

'Why was I not told!' Qadaffi interrupted furi-ously.

'After the news of the Brega terminal I thought to spare you further distractions. But since you demand to know, they are feeding the people's fear with threats of Zionist reprisals, and are holding up the

432

Egyptians as an example to be followed. They blame you for everything.'

It was impossible to gauge the sympathies behind Jalloud's words. Suddenly Qadaffi feared to be alone.

'And you?'

Jalloud would not be drawn. It was as if even he was now reserving his judgement against the possible failure of their desperate plan.

'There's not much time if we are to succeed. It is only a matter of time before they move against the base outside Houn. We need this victory, brother, now more than ever. Let's go quickly.'

Qadaffi's eyes flicked back and forth as he grasped the realisation that the very project conceived of as his legacy to the Libyan people might now be the very cause of his political demise. Heaven grant strength to a poor goatherd! Another ringing crump of artillery shells shook him from his reverie.

'You are right, Jalloud. We must go swiftly, and succeed, *Insh Allah!*'

Quickly the line of vehicles, headed by the President's own Range Rover, set off towards the helipad.

They couched the camels in a tight group beneath the shade of a clutch of acacia palms which bordered the watering hole, then settled themselves to the inevitable wait. They were the only people within five miles of the well, and around them the bleached earth of the Sirtica rose in ripples and undulations, with a gentle rise to the north-west – the direction from which the helicopters would come.

There were four of them, each dressed in pale bedouin riding habit, with blue cloaks and cowls shielding their noses and mouths against the drifting sand. Tyler, Sara, al Tayyih and his eldest son – they had ridden hard on al Tayyih's swiftest camels to reach this place, with two pack animals to carry the Javelin

433

and other vital stores and munitions. These, the old Sulubbi had said, were the lands of the Qadadfa bedouin, as far as the eye could see. Now, in the still of the mid-afternoon, with the sun at its fiercest, they rested their animals and drew water from the Qadadfa well.

Tyler moved as little as possible, so as to conserve his energy and to avoid the pain that any sudden movement brought to his left shoulder. He sat quite still, listening closely to Sara's translations of the hourly news bulletins issuing from the newly liberated Radio Tripoli. The National Front was making its move. Inexplicably, Tyler found himself remembering the creased but comfortable features of George Stephenson and that time back in London when they had sat together in a car outside the Savoy Hotel, watching the unrelenting rain wash the windscreen.

Years ago.

'The open-air mosque you seek,' said al Tayyih when he had drunk his fill, 'is over that rise. It has been there for more than one hundred years – perhaps two. It is the Qadadfa mosque. It has neither roof nor proper walls, just a series of small boulders, as big as your head, which trace its perimeter; and a raised stone platform at its eastern wall to help the faithful find Mecca.'

'A strange place for worship,' commented Tyler, absently.

'Not so!' the Sulubbi countered. 'There are hundreds of these places all over the Sirtica, and in the Great Sand Seas also. You must remember that Islam demands strict observance of the five periods of prayer each day, and not everyone lives near a fine mosque. These places may be rude and primitively constructed, but for the peoples who live out here with their herds and flocks they offer great comfort. To them they are as grand a place of worship as any city mosque. You must remember that God is everywhere, and He will meet the faithful under a tree if necessary.'

The Sulubbi knew much about the Qadadfa tribe, and he made it clear to Tyler just how significant this place must have been to the young Muammar al Qadaffi. As a boy he would have brought his father's goats to this well many times. He would have climbed the nearby rise and paused to look across the bare landscape, noting the subtle patches of colour where coarse grasses grew, ever watchful for the distant curling spout of an approaching sandstorm. Many times he would have walked down to the mosque alone, put off his leather sandals and given thanks for water and good grazing.

Tyler listened with interest, hooked by the ghost of a boy in sandals. Sure now that he would return to haunt this place.

He turned to look at Sara, who had been silent a long time, but she flushed and avoided his eye.

'What is it?' he asked, sensing some inner darkness troubling her.

She did not answer but got up and walked away from where they had been sitting, her footsteps sighing across the sand.

Responding to an unspoken request, Tyler stood and followed her. 'Hey, what is it?'

The bedouin riding habit left only the upper part of her face visible, and the soft brown eyes might easily have belonged to an Arab.

'Now we are here I want to say something.' Her eyes flashed at him a sudden searching glance, then she looked away again. 'We came through something last night that . . . something that can turn things around, change all those answers we thought we were sure of. Like why we're here, doing this. Last night I expected to die,' she confessed, her eyes still staring blankly out across a shimmering plain where nothing lived or moved. 'Last night I truly felt what that means: the debilitating terror. I never felt that before, and I have you to thank for it.'

'Me?'

'Yes. You've made me into something selfish – someone no longer willing to die for a cause. When you find someone you love after so long alone, you fear anything that might come between you and that someone. Now I love you, and I'm scared to death. I don't want to lose that love. Right now I just want us to walk away from here.'

'You know I can't do that.'

'Can't?' Sara turned to face him abruptly, challenging his answer. 'What vanity. What monumental stupidity.' Tyler frowned back at her and, realising he was not a man to be influenced by belligerence, she softened her tone. 'Forget him. It's all changed now. Remember the radio. This morning saw the start of a chain-reaction that even he cannot stop. The Libyans know why we bombed their oil installation, and they know who to blame for that. I tell you, Qadaffi's support is crumbling away; he won't last the week. It's not worth the risk. He doesn't matter any more!'

'Are you crazy? Have you forgotten what the Korean told us about that bloody missile base of his? What about that, then? We have to stop him contriving the deaths of countless innocent people.'

'Innocent? Who is innocent these days? Particularly in Israel. What if there is no missile base? We've only the word of a damned Korean who almost got us both killed.'

'No, you're wrong!' Tyler turned upon her. 'It's because of that damned Korean that we're alive at all. Don't you see? Our lives were a gift.'

For a moment she stood trembling, her chest heaving with emotion. She knew he had trapped himself with his own rhetoric, but she waited until her voice was calm before she answered him.

'Then do not abuse that gift, Tyler. Take it and live.'

This time it was he who looked away, squeezing his fist in frustration.

Again she pursued him. 'What is it with you, the money? Is it the money?'

'No!' he blurted out. 'Not any more.'

'What then – revenge?'

'I don't know ... Maybe we've just come too far and lost too much already not to finish it. Otherwise what has it all been for?'

'Over forty years of war with five Arabs armies – what has any of it been for? All my life I had to learn to let go. One by one I have lost everyone I ever loved, everyone I ever felt close to. My family, my husband, my baby. Now even Yariv has gone. What's it all been for?'

Tyler said nothing, he just listened from within his own cocoon, feeling the depth of her sadness.

'When you lose that much you tell yourself you'll never care again – until the next time. This time I tried like hell not to care. I tried to make it just another mission. But the truth is, Tyler, I fell in love with you. I'm in love with you now. That's why I'm scared: because I'm foolish enough to hope somehow you'll feel the same, and that we'll come through this, and I'll have a life to go back to when it's all over. For God's sake, say something! Even if it's only to tell me I'm asking for too much. Perhaps it *is* too much to ask that we could leave the killing behind us, and somehow get back the . . .' she struggled for a word and a tear spilled onto her cheek '. . . get back the humanity in our souls – whatever it is that war takes from us.'

He did not know how to begin to explain his feelings.

'Sara, try to understand, a man like me doesn't have that much to give at the best of times. And yes, you're right, many of the things I've done haven't had much to do with humanity. I really don't know whether we can save each other from ourselves.'

'And you're not willing to try?'

'No, you've got it all wrong. I just can't worry too much about you and me, when we both know there are bigger matters at stake here. There's still Qadaffi. There's still his missile threat against Israel. When it's all over, then we'll think about ourselves and where we go from here.'

'And will our lives be built on his death.'

Her bleak words cut him more than she knew. But the sad eyes were now hardened, and he felt her retreating like a ghost into the shadows. He was fighting against the urge to promise her the world. Suddenly he pulled her to him and her arms went immediately around his waist, her head burrowing into his shoulder, forgetting his wound and causing him to wince in pain.

'Oh! I'm sorry!' she cried.

'It's OK, Sara. Believe me, it's OK. We always hurt the one's we love.' He laughed awkwardly.

'You're making fun of me.'

'No, Sara. I'm trying to say that I love you. I love everything about you, all that you've given me and everything we've shared. I'm just sorry if what I am only hurts you.'

'If we can't run away together, then I'll stay and take my chances with you. Together, win or lose.'

He saw the pain of compromise in her brief, crushed smile, then he kissed her hard.

'Take care,' she crooned thoughtfully, tugging back his headcloth and stroking his face. 'How does the shoulder feel?'

'Numb. God only knows what was in that poultice of al Tayyih's. It smells like camel dung. Come on.'

They turned and walked over to the pack animals, where Tyler unfastened the leather straps which held the Javelin tubes. He carried the tubes and the aiming unit back to the shade of the trees.

The Sulubbi's eldest son was the first to hear them. He snatched up the binoculars and scanned the sky, eyes striving against the heat haze.

'There, there,' he cried in Arabic. 'The devil's chariots approach!'

Now they all heard them. Tyler took the binoculars and made out the silhouettes of two Mil 24 Hind helicopters coming hard towards the water-hole at about three thousand feet. He passed the glasses to Sara.

'That must be the President's aircraft out in front. The escort is standing off the starboard side, acting as cover. Tell the others to get ready.'

Sara passed on the word and both Sulubbi primed their assault rifles, taking cover behind the nearest available stonework. From their position they could see the flat plain where the aircraft would land – the only ground firm enough to take their weight without bogging down.

'How many soldiers in that second helicopter?' asked Sara, catching up the Uzi and shoving the spare clips into her belt.

Tyler snapped the first missile tube into the grip of the aiming mechanism.

'According to Kim there should be eight. But they're the least of our worries. Don't forget those machines have some fearsome ordnance on board. I can only take them one at a time. And if these babies miss, they can run us down at leisure. There's no cover here. We'd be torn apart by their rocket fire before we knew it.'

'Then don't miss,' she urged.

'I won't. If they don't explode in the air, just be ready when they come down. We'll have to finish it quickly.'

The helicopters came lumbering in like galleons at five hundred feet, wheeling above the rise and turning to approach the landing area. The incessant chopping of their blades struck deep into Tyler's combat memories. Even without the binoculars he was able to make out the armaments: squat rocket pods and Swatter missiles below the short, grotesque wings. But it was the nose-gunner he feared most, seated in his bubble of bullet-proof glass ahead of and below that of the pilot; armed and trained to cut down ground troops with a murderous four-barrelled rotary cannon mounted on the floor of the cockpit at his feet.

There was only one way to win this. Get both of the monsters – fast.

Tyler saw the escort plane turn in the air to approach the landing area, exposing its rear, but he waited until both planes were lined up with their gunners facing away from his position. He raised the Javelin to his right shoulder – the good shoulder – and placed his eye against the cup. There was no time for prayers or doubts. The escort plane turned broadside and he squeezed the launch trigger.

There was a burning flash all around him as the missile cleared the tube, climbing like a bat out of hell. It flew as if along a kite string, straight to the machine, and struck the Hind just behind the port wing, exploding as the proximity fuse sensed its target, less than four feet away, and tearing a gaping hole in the fuselage. All at once the plane's spine seemed to shatter, as grey smoke belched out from the hole and the tail section broke and swung downwards. A dragonfly with a broken back. The Hind rocked under the force of the impact and a moment later the fuel system exploded and the burning carcase fell the last four hundred feet to earth. There would be no survivors.

The shock-wave smacked the Presidential plane into a drunken gait. Desperately the pilot fought with the controls, unaware of the cause of explosion, but fearing a potentially deadly autorotation if his own engines failed. The aircraft turned and stabilised, and the pilot saw with sudden horror the grey smoke-trail of the missile hanging in the air: the kite string leading back to earth.

'Missiles,' he screamed into the rubber radio cup. In another second the nose-gunner had picked out the group of trees and the figures hiding there. The escort was gone, crashed and burning, with the reek of aviation fuel already stinging his nostrils. He grabbed the aiming stick of the rotary cannon, fingers fighting with the reluctant mechanism, forcing it to point in the direction of attack whilst the aircraft rolled into position. The pilot signalled his intention to run for it, and hit a switch which released a hail of burning magnesium to distract a second missile.

'No! by Great God!' cursed the nose-gunner. 'I have them now.'

Tyler saw the hesitation and discarded the spent tube, thanking his stars for more luck than he had any right to expect.

Sara was watching the gunner, too. 'Quickly,' she called urgently. 'They see us now!'

As she spoke, a hail of cannon fire and flashing tracer rounds began to pour from the nose of the aircraft, tearing up the ground twenty-five metres away – but closing.

When he had fitted the second missile tube and turned back to sight, Tyler saw the pilot's plan. He was swinging away towards the rise in the hope of dipping behind it out of line of sight. He was hovering low above it – just a hundred feet now.

'Get down!' screamed Sara. The cannon rounds were very close now, tearing chunks from the stonework – suddenly a tree to his left was sliced in two.

'Jesus Christ!' Tyler ducked, almost losing his grip on the missile. It was only a matter of time before the pilot and gunner got it together and finished them off. Striving to buy time, Sara and the two Sulubbi fired off their weapons against the helicopter, with no appreciable effect. Tyler knew that taking cover was no use; he would never be able to sight the missile. The only way was to stand in the clear.

'This is it, man,' he told himself. 'Do it right!'

Forsaking cover he stepped into the open and raised the missile. The target was close now, big within the monocular sight, and bathed in the glow of the falling flares, facing him head-on in its most threatening aspect. A flying fortress with Qadaffi inside it. The ground boiled with gunfire around his feet. He squeezed the trigger once more, holding his aim as the Javelin climbed higher. Suddenly a searing pain shot through his left thigh as a deflected round hit home. The pain made him flinch, deviating the missile by just a few degrees. Important degrees. Shit!

The missile did not strike cleanly, and when detonation came the Hind was holed in the tail section but still in one piece and autorotating out of control to earth. In moving closer to the ground, the pilot had secured at least a chance of survival.

The machine fell onto the brow of the rise, embedding its undercarriage in the soft sand of the dune. There was a groan and the snapping of metal as the rotors touched the ground, catapulting the machine onto its side and slewing further into the sand. Tyler and Sara waited braced, but the fuel tank did not explode. The engine merely died and the bird lay crippled and still.

Tyler dropped the aiming unit and snatched up his Browning pistol. The machine had landed hard but its passengers might still be alive. His drilled leg hurt like hell, but the bullet had not severed anything significant. Suddenly there was a cheer from the old Sulubbi and his son, and they were all running up the rise towards the wreckage. Sara reached it first, and peered carefully inside the cockpit area. There was blood on the glass; pilot and gunner were both dead – necks broken. The young Sulubbi heaved open the port boarding-hatch, which now faced skyward, and gazed inside at the tangle of limbs.

'That one's still alive,' said Sara behind him. 'Tyler, come quick – it's Jalloud.' But she had spoken too soon, for by the time Tyler limped up to the door Jalloud had ceased to move. Tyler looked from one body to the next, examining the faces.

'For God's sake where is he? Where's Qadaffi?'

They looked at one another in disbelief, then back at the bloody heap of Government men. Sara turned around to look at the second burning hulk, half a mile distant.

'I don't know. Maybe he was in the other one. Maybe he changed aircraft. Anything's possible.'

Then Tyler noticed the thin trail of blood leading away from a hole in the fuselage – a tear in the metal just big enough for a body to squeeze through. He walked around the wreckage clutching his leg with one hand and the Browning in the other. There were tracks in the sand: long, deep tracks laced with blood, ascending the rise and down the other side. Someone had escaped from the aircraft. It had to be him.

Suddenly Sara was behind him. 'What did you find?' Then she saw the tracks.

'He's on his own now, Sara. Heading for that open-air mosque. You stay here. I'll be back in a moment.'

'For God's sake, be careful.'

Nimrod, the hunter, turned without another word, and followed the traces in the sand that would bring him finally to Qadaffi.

They led him straight to a small square of level ground bordered by rocks, just as al Tayyih had described. As Tyler came closer he could see the raised stone of the east wall – and, kneeling there, a solitary figure dressed in the pure white robes of a bedouin prince. Nimrod approached the mosque to stand by the outer wall.

At first the figure did not move, apppearing to be at prayer. As Nimrod's foot caught on a large stone, the white-cowled head turned, unconcerned. The head of Muammar al Qadaffi.

He shifted slowly and without fear, squaring his shoulders under the folds of the robe. Blood covered his left side, staining the pristine cotton, but it was impossible to judge if he himself was wounded or

443

if this was the blood of one of his aides. A gust of wind from the nearby hills tugged at the Libyan's headcloth. The cloth billowed slightly under the cowl. Nimrod did not move. At length the Libyan turned his back once more to face the east, prostrating himself before the God of Islam. His ringing voice the only sound in that wilderness.

'*Allah U akhbar* – God is great! I testify that there is no god but Allah and that Mohammed is his beloved prophet!'

Nimrod examined the stony ground surrounding the supplicant, noticing immediately the huge Magnum revolver discarded carelessly just out of arm's reach. He shifted his feet uneasily. There was a powerful one-ness between this Libyan, the ancient splendour of this wilderness, and the God who had made them both. It was a vibration so powerful that he felt their strength uniting against his own determination to take that life. Here, in his own element, amongst the rocks which had witnessed his birth, Qadaffi seemed truly a powerful force.

'Do you yet have time for prayer?'

There was no direct response from the bowed figure, his forehead touching the ground, as an almost musical chant emanated from his lips, to be lost in the warm breeze.

'Muammar al Qadaffi, do you still have time?'

Unhearing, the Libyan ran on to the conclusion of his prayer. He bowed once more and stood up, turning at last to face Nimrod. There was anger upon his brow.

'There is always time for prayer. And who are you, a paid assassin, to question that?'

Nimrod held his gaze, matching wills. He adjusted his grip on the Browning. Impelled by the purest strain of hatred, he raised his right hand carefully, deliberately, making sure his target was aware of the pistol's small, obscene mouth.

Qadaffi took a step backward, not a large one, but telling enough. His fingers fidgeted and he swallowed.

444

'You know who I am. You've been expecting me – someone like me – for a long time.'

Qadaffi managed a faint, taut smile, and nodded his agreement.

'You are the one called Nimrod, a British assassin. But you are not the first. Tell me, was it Azziz who brought you here?'

'No, it was the Korean who told me where to find you. But it was you yourself who brought me here. Each death you planned, every dollar you spent on arms for terrorists, they brought me one step closer.' There was a dull ache now in his thigh where the hot metal had cut into him.

'You speak of matters you could never understand. You don't know what it is to be an Arab. You cannot judge me – nor will that weapon pointed at my head.'

Stung with sudden rage, Nimrod punched back the slide of the Browning, cocking the hammer noisily in one quick, fluid movement. The trigger moved to its furthest travel, placing Qadaffi a mere finger stroke away from death. His eyes were closed, hands springing up instinctively to protect his face. Anticipating the buck of the weapon.

Waiting to die.

Nimrod flexed his fingers on the pistol grip. A single, shining bead of sweat ran back along his forearm. This was the moment he had planned for: the whole reason for his activation. The reason why George Stephenson had died. But it was not Nimrod's moment, of that he was sure. He was only the medium which expressed the will of his political masters. Under a blistering sun, this one charged fragment of time was a moment bought with dirty money by men such as Halliday. Men who would meet later over a sherry and clink glasses after its successful conclusion, with no thought of the true cost of the operation in terms of human life. And in many ways the actions they prescribed made them no better than the malignancy they sought to end.

445

He knew then that Sara had been right – about everything. That it wasn't worth the risk – or the money – to be the instrument of those men's will. That it was impossible for them to stack up a life together, however thinly diluted with moments of happiness, against this sad and savage game demanded by a misguided sense of duty.

Perhaps the Korean had shown himself to be the only true man of honour.

There was nowhere for Qadaffi to run to. Nimrod knew it would take no effort at all to pull the trigger and empty the ammunition clip into his body, but that wouldn't change a single thing. It was too late for that. The National Front had already taken control of the public buildings in Tripoli, amid a growing surge of popular support for their cause. The Green Revolution was over: it's death had been signalled by the crash of the second helicopter, in which Qadaffi's closest and most powerful allies had died.

Tyler's hand began to ache under the weight of the weapon. Still he watched his target.

Inexplicably he thought of Sara, and of the tenderness with which he had touched her. And he found it impossible to reconcile that newly awakened side of himself with this act of pulling the tiny, tiny trigger. All at once, with startling clarity, he knew what he wanted – and the cold blue fire that had burned within him for as long as he could remember was gone. And in its place was calm.

His thumb gripped the hammer of the pistol, drew it carefully back, and eased it forward to the safe position.

All the time Qadaffi had stood there, braced against the shot; perhaps, in his final defeat, even welcoming the solace of the bullet. But when he heard the soft clink, he lowered his hands and opened his eyes. The pistol was now pointed towards the ground. The assassin's expression had changed, devoid of motive. The Libyan breathed deeply, unsure of his fate even now.

446

'Why don't you shoot? This home of my childhood is as good a place as any for me to die.'

Tyler walked over to the flat grey stone of the mosque's low wall and picked up Qadaffi's discarded Magnum. There was a full load of hollow-point ammunition in the cylinder. He emptied the bullets into his hand as a precaution, then tossed them away into the sand before laying the weapon down again.

'I chose not to shoot, because I have chosen life.'

The Libyan wiped his hands upon his robe, distractedly, aware now that his fingers were trembling. Confusion was written deep into his tanned features.

'I leave you your life, and this weapon to protect yourself from wild animals. You will find the bullets if you look carefully.'

'You intend to leave me here alone?'

'You will not be alone for long. A camel train or else some herdsman is bound to come along to use the well.'

'That could be days.'

Tyler could not resist one final word.

'Provided you don't use the pistol to blow your brains out, you should make it out of here. After that it's up to you. If the Green Revolution has been a blessing to the Libyan people, as you claim, then surely you have nothing to fear. I have given you the same chance I myself was given. New life. A close-up view of your own mortality may help you re-evaluate.'

'Save your teachings for another mosque, infidel!' said Qadaffi bitterly.

Tyler shrugged, amused by this almost expected response. Perhaps he was wasting his breath.

'Fine. Make your own way, then. Whether or not you have a role to play in your country's future is now in your own hands.'

At last Tyler turned to walk back up the hill to where the crippled helicopter lay. There was much pain in his leg now and fresh bleeding from his shoulder caused by sudden movements. Awkwardly, he tore a strip from the sleeve of the riding habit and tried to bandage the wound with the gun still clutched in his right hand. But when he saw he could not manage both, he threw the Browning into the sand. It seemed a fitting end for it.

He would not be needing the weapon again, he mused as he tied the strip of cloth across his shoulder and started back up the rise, cheered now by the sight of the two Arabs brandishing their rifles aloft, a desolate trail of black smoke weaving up into the open blue of the sky behind them. And there, at the brow of the hill, with her headcloth pulled off and one hand holding back the raven-black hair from her face, was Sara.

Waiting.